About the Authors

Author of the acclaimed Discworld series, **Terry Pratchett** is one of the UK's most popular – and bestselling – writers. His books have sold over 75 million copies worldwide and been translated into nearly forty languages. He is the winner of multiple prizes, including the Carnegie Medal, as well as being awarded a knighthood for services to literature. He lives in Wiltshire.

Visit www.terrypratchett.co.uk to discover everything you need to know about Terry Pratchett and his writing, plus all manner of other things you may find interesting, such as videos, competitions, character profiles and games.

Stephen Baxter is one of the UK's most acclaimed writers of science fiction and a multi-award winner. His many books include the classic *Xeelee* sequence, the *A Time Odyssey* novels (written with Arthur C. Clarke) and *The Time Ships*, a sequel to H. G. Wells's *The Time Machine*. He lives in Northumberland.

More details of Stephen Baxter's works can be found on www.stephen-baxter.com

DECLASSIFIED

Initial concept drawings for the prototype military-specification airship upon which the USS *Benjamin Franklin* was based, reproduced courtesy of the TDD (Twain Design Division) of the United Technologies, General Electric, Long Earth Trading Company and Black Corporation military-supply consortium.

THE LONG WAR

Terry Pratchett and Stephen Baxter

CORGI BOOKS

TRANSWORLD PUBLISHERS
61–63 Uxbridge Road, London W5 5SA
A Random House Group Company
www.transworldbooks.co.uk

THE LONG WAR
A CORGI BOOK: 9780552167758 (B format)
9780552165092 (A format)

First published in Great Britain
in 2013 by Doubleday
an imprint of Transworld Publishers
Corgi edition published 2014

Addresses for Random House Group Ltd companies outside the UK
can be found at: www.randomhouse.co.uk
The Random House Group Ltd Reg. No. 954009

The Random House Group Limited supports the Forest Stewardship Council®
(FSC®), the leading international forest-certification organisation. Our books
carrying the FSC label are printed on FSC®-certified paper. FSC is the only
forest-certification scheme supported by the leading environmental organisations,
including Greenpeace. Our paper procurement policy can be found at
www.randomhouse.co.uk/environment

Typeset in 11.5/14pt Minion by Falcon Oast Graphic Art Ltd.
Printed and bound by CPI Group (UK) Ltd, Croydon, CR0 4YY.

2 4 6 8 10 9 7 5 3 1

For Lyn and Rhianna, as always
T.P.

For Sandra
S.B.

1

ON AN ALTERNATE WORLD, two million steps from Earth:
The troll female was called Mary by her handlers,
Monica Jansson read on the rolling caption on the video
clip. No one knew what the troll called herself. Now two
of those handlers, both men, one in a kind of spacesuit,
faced Mary as she cowered in a corner of what looked like
a high-tech laboratory – if a beast built like a brick wall
covered in black fur could be said to cower at all – and she
held her cub to her powerful chest. The cub, itself a slab of
muscle, was similarly dressed up in its own silvery spacesuit, with wires dangling from sensors attached to its flat
skull.

'Give him back, Mary,' one of the men could be heard
to say. 'Come on now. We've been planning this test for a
long time. George here will haul him over into the Gap in
his spacesuit, he'll float around in vacuum for an hour or
so, and then he'll be right back here safe and sound. He'll
even have fun.'

The other man stayed ominously silent.

The first approached Mary, a step at a time. 'No ice
cream if you keep this up.'

Mary's big, very human hands made gestures, signs, a
blur. Rapid, hard to follow, but decisive.

As the incident had been replayed over and over there had been a lot of online speculation about why Mary hadn't just stepped away at this point. Probably it was simply that she was being held underground: you couldn't step into or out of a cellar, into the solid rock you'd find stepwise. Besides, Jansson, a retired lieutenant formerly of Madison Police Department, knew there were plenty of ways to stop a troll stepping, if you could get your hands on the animal.

The theory of what these men were trying to do was much discussed too. They were in a world next door to the Gap – a step away from vacuum, from space, from a hole where an Earth ought to be. They were building a space programme out there, and wanted to see if troll labour, highly useful across the Long Earth, could be exploited in the Gap. Not surprisingly adult trolls were very reluctant to step over into that drifting emptiness, so the GapSpace researchers were trying to habituate the young. Like this cub.

'We haven't got time for this,' said the second man. He produced a metal rod, a stunner. He walked forward, holding the rod out towards Mary's chest. 'Time for Mommy to say goodnight for a while—'

The adult troll grabbed the rod, snapped it in two, and jammed the sharp, broken end into the second man's right eye.

Every time you saw it, it was shocking.

The man fell back screaming, blood spilling, very bright red. The first guy pulled him back, out of shot. 'Oh my God! Oh my God!'

Mary, holding her cub, her fur splashed with human blood, repeated the gestures she had made, over and over.

Things happened quickly after that. These space cadets had tried to put down this troll, this mother, immediately. They even pulled a gun on her. But they'd been stopped by an older guy, more dignified, who looked to Jansson like a retired astronaut.

And now retribution was on hold, because of the attention focused on the case.

Since this lab recording had been leaked it had become an outernet sensation in itself, and had led to a flood of similar reports. There was cruelty to beasts, and especially the trolls, it seemed, all over the Long Earth. Internet and outernet were alight with flame wars between those who believed in mankind's right to do as it wished with the denizens of the Long Earth, all the way to putting them down when it suited – some referring back to the Biblical dominion given to humans over fish, fowl, cattle, and creeping things – and others who wished that mankind didn't have to take *all* its flaws out into the new worlds. This incident at the Gap, precisely because it had taken place at the heart of a nascent space programme, an expression of mankind's highest aspirations – and even though it betrayed a kind of insensitivity, Jansson thought, rather than downright cruelty – had become a poster case. A vociferous minority called for the federal government on Datum Earth to do something about it.

And others wondered what the trolls thought about it all. Because trolls had ways of communicating too.

Monica Jansson, watching the clip in her apartment in Madison West 5, tried to read Mary's hand signs. She knew the language trolls were taught in experimental establishments like this one was based on a human language, American Sign Language. Jansson had had a little familiarization with signing in the course of her police career; she was no expert, but she could read what the troll was saying. And so, she imagined, could millions of others across the Long Earth, wherever this clip was being accessed:

I will not.

I will not.

I will not.

This was no dumb animal. This was a mother trying to protect a child.

Don't get involved, Jansson told herself. You're retired, and you're sick. Your crusading days are over.

There was, of course, no choice. She turned off the monitor, popped another pill, and started making calls.

And on a world almost as far away as the Gap:

A creature that was not quite a human faced a creature that was not quite a dog.

People called the humanoid's kind *kobolds*, more or less inaccurately. 'Kobold' was an old German name for a mine-spirit. This particular kobold, peculiarly addicted to human music – in particular 1960s rock music – had never been near a mine.

And people called these dog-like creatures *beagles*, equally inaccurately. They were not beagles, and they were like nothing Darwin had seen from the most famous *Beagle* of all.

Neither kobold nor beagle cared about names humans gave them. But they cared about humans. Or rather, despised them. Even though, in the kobold's case, he was also helplessly fascinated by humans and their culture.

'Trollen unhap-ppy, everywhere,' hissed the kobold.

'Good,' the beagle growled. She was a bitch. She wore a gold finger-ring set with sapphires on a thong around her neck. 'Good. Smell of c-hrr-imes of stink-crotches stains world.'

The kobold's speech was almost like a human's. The beagle's was a matter of growls, gestures, postures, pawing at the ground. Yet they understood each other, using a quasi-human language as a common patois.

And they had a common cause.

'Drive stink-crotches back to their-hrr den.' The beagle lifted her body and stood upright, raised her wolf-like head, and howled. Soon responses came from all across the humid landscape.

The kobold exulted at the chance of acquisition as a result of all this trouble, acquisition of the goods he treasured himself, and of others he could trade. But he strove to hide his fear of the beagle princess, his unlikely customer and ally.

And at a military base on Datum Hawaii, US Navy Commander Maggie Kauffman gazed up in wonder at the USS *Benjamin Franklin*, an airship the size of the *Hindenburg*, the brand new vessel that was hers to command . . .

And in a sleepy English village the Reverend Nelson Azikiwe pondered his little parish church in the context of the Long Earth, a treasured scrap of antiquity amid unmapped immensity, and considered his own future . . .

And in a bustling city more than a million steps from the Datum, a one-time stepwise pioneer called Jack Green carefully phrased an appeal for liberty and dignity in the Long Earth . . .

And at Yellowstone Park, Datum Earth:

It was only Ranger Herb Lewis's second day on the job. He sure as hell didn't know how to deal with this angry in-your-face complaint from Mr and Mrs Virgil Davies of Los Angeles about how upset their nine-year-old, Virgilia, had become, and how Daddy had been made to look a *liar*, on her *birthday*. It wasn't Herb's fault if Old Faithful had failed to blow. It was no consolation at all when, later that day, the family found their faces all over the news channels and websites as the geyser's misbehaviour hit the headlines . . .

And in a Black Corporation medical facility on a Low Earth:

'Sister Agnes? I have to wake you again for a little while, just for calibration . . .'

Agnes thought she heard music. 'I am awake. I think.'

'Welcome back.'

'Back from where? Who are you? And what's that chanting?'

'Hundreds of Tibetan monks. For forty-nine days you have been—'

'And that dreary music?'

'Oh. You can blame John Lennon for *that*. The lyrics are quotes from the Book of the Dead.'

'What a racket.'

'Agnes, your physical orientation will take some time yet. But I think it should be possible for you to see yourself in the mirror. This won't take long . . .'

She could not tell *how* long, but eventually there was light, very soft but growing steadily.

'You will feel some pressure as you are lifted to a standing position. It should not be unpleasant. We cannot work on your ambulant abilities until you are stronger, but you will meld into your new body with minimal pain. Trust me, I have been through this myself many times before. You will be able to see yourself about . . . now.'

And Sister Agnes looked down at herself. At her body: pink, naked, raw, and *very* female. Without feeling her lips move – and indeed without actually feeling her lips at all – Agnes demanded, 'Who ordered *those*?'

2

SALLY LINSAY ARRIVED at Hell-Knows-Where fast and furious. But when had *that* ever been unusual?

Joshua Valienté heard her voice coming from the house, as he was heading back from an afternoon's work in his forge. On this world, as on all the worlds of the Long Earth, it was late March, and the light was already fading. Since she'd shown up on the day of his wedding nine years ago a visit from this particular old friend had been rare, and generally meant that something was amiss – amiss in spades. As Helen, his wife, would also know all too well. His stomach knotting, Joshua hurried his step.

He found Sally sitting at the kitchen table, nursing coffee in a local-pottery mug. She was looking away from him, she hadn't noticed him yet, and he paused at the door to study her, taking in the scene, getting his bearings.

Helen was in the dry store, and Joshua saw she was digging out salt, pepper, matches. On the table, meanwhile, Sally had dumped enough butchered meat to last for weeks. This was pioneer protocol. The Valientés didn't need the meat, of course, but that was no matter. The deal was that the visiting traveller brought the meat, and the householder repaid the gift not only with a meal, the catch properly dressed and cooked, but also with some of those little comforts that were hard to find in the wilderness, such as salt, pepper, a good night's sleep in a proper bed. Joshua smiled. Sally prided herself on being somewhat more self-sufficient than Daniel Boone and Captain Nemo put together, but surely even Daniel Boone must've craved pepper – just like Sally.

She was forty-three years old now, a few years older than Joshua – and sixteen years older than Helen, which didn't help their various interrelationships. Her greying hair was tied neatly back, and she wore her usual garb of heavy-duty jeans and sleeveless, multi-pocketed jacket. Just as she'd always been, she was lean, wiry, eerily still – and watchful.

Right now she was watching an object on the wall: a gold ring set with sapphires, hanging on a loop of string from a stubby local-forge iron nail. It was one of the few trophies Joshua had kept of the journey of discovery across the Long Earth that the two of them had made with Lobsang. Or, *The Journey*, as the world knew it ten years later. It was a gaudy thing, and too large for a human finger. But then, humans hadn't made it, as Sally would remember. Just below the ring hung another bit of jewellery, a monkey bracelet, plastic and paste: a thing for a kid, gaudy, silly. Joshua was pretty sure Sally would remember the significance of that too.

He walked forward, deliberately pushing the door to make it creak. She turned and surveyed him, critical, unsmiling.

He said, 'Heard you arrive.'

'You've put on weight.'

'Nice to see you too, Sally. I take it you've a reason for coming here. You always have a reason.'

'Oh, yes.'

I wonder if Calamity Jane was like this, Joshua thought as he reluctantly sat down. Like a gunpowder explosion going off periodically in the middle of your life. Maybe, though Sally had marginally better access to toiletries.

Helen was now in the kitchen, and Joshua smelled meat on the griddle. When he caught Helen's eye she waved away his silent offer of help. He recognized tact when he saw it. Helen was trying to give them some space. Tact, yes, but he also feared this was the beginning of one of Helen's icy silences. Sally after all was a woman who'd had a long, complicated and *famous* relationship with her husband before he'd even known Helen. Sally had been at his side, in fact, when he first met Helen, then a seventeen-year-old pioneer in a brand new Long Earth colony town. His young wife was never going to jump for joy when Sally showed up again.

Sally was waiting for him to respond, ignorant of such subtleties, or uncaring.

He sighed. 'So tell me. What brings you here this time?'

'Another slimeball killed another troll.'

He grunted. There had been a blizzard of such incidents in the news brought by the outernet – incidents occurring across the Long Earth, from the Datum to Valhalla and beyond, evidently all the way up to the Gap, judging from recent sensational reports of a lurid case involving a cub in a 1950s-type spacesuit.

'Butchered it, in this case,' Sally said. 'I mean, literally. Reported at an Aegis administration office at Plumbline, just inside the Meggers—'

'I know it.'

'It was a young one this time. Body parts taken for

some kind of folk medicine. For once the guy's actually been arrested on a cruelty charge. But his family are kicking up because, what the hell, it was just an animal, wasn't it?'

Joshua shook his head. 'We're all under the US Aegis. What's the argument? Aren't Datum animal cruelty laws supposed to apply?'

'*That's* all a mess, Joshua, with different rulings at federal and state level, and arguments about how such rulings extend to the Long Earth anyhow. Not to mention the lack of resources to police them.'

'I don't follow Datum politics too closely. You know, here we protect trolls under an extension of our citizenship rights.'

'Really?'

He smiled. 'You sound surprised. You're not the only one with a conscience, you know. Anyhow trolls are too damn useful to have them bothered, or driven away.'

'Well, not everywhere is as civilized, evidently. You must remember, Joshua, that the Aegis is presided over by Datum politicians, which is to say, buttholes. And they really don't get it! They are *not* the kind of people to get mud on their shiny shoes anywhere much beyond a park in Earth West 3. They have no idea of how important it is that humanity stays friendly with the trolls. The long call is full of it.'

Meaning every troll everywhere would soon know all about this.

Sally said now, 'You know, the problem is that before Step Day most of what trolls knew and understood about humanity came from their experiences in places like

19

Happy Landings, where they lived closely with humans. Peacefully, constructively . . .'

'If a little creepily.'

'Well, yes. What is happening now is that trolls are encountering ordinary folk. That is, idiots.'

With a sense of dread he asked, 'Sally – why have you come here? What do you want me to do about this?'

'Your duty, Joshua.'

She meant, Joshua knew, that he was to go with her, off into the Long Earth. Saving the worlds once again.

The hell with that, he thought. Times had changed. He'd changed. His duty was *here*: to his family, his home, this township which had, foolishly enough, elected him mayor.

Joshua had fallen in love with the place even before he had seen it, reckoning that the first-footers who had given their home a name like Hell-Knows-Where were very likely to be decent people with a sense of humour, as indeed they'd turned out to be. As for Helen, who had trekked out with her family to found a brand new township, this way of living was what she had grown up with. And this place they had come to, in a million-step-remote footprint of the Mississippi valley, had turned out to have air that was clean, a river lively with fish, a land rich with game and replete with other resources such as lead and iron ore seams. Thanks to a twain mass-spectrometry scan of nearby formations that Joshua had called in as a favour, they even had the makings of a copper mine. As a bonus, the climate here happened to be just a little cooler than on the Datum, and in the winter the local copy of the Mississippi regularly froze over – a thrilling spectacle, even if it did threaten a couple of careless lives every year.

When they'd arrived, Joshua, even compared with his new young wife, had been a novice settler, for all his trekking experience in the Long Earth. But now he was recognized as a skilled hunter, butcher, general artificer – and pretty nearly, these days, blacksmith and smelter. Not to mention mayor until the next poll. Helen, meanwhile, was a senior midwife and a top herbalist.

Of course it was hard work. A pioneer family lived beyond the reach of shopping malls, and bread always needed baking, hams needed curing, tallow had to be made, and beer had to be brewed. Out here, in fact, you worked all the time. But the work was pleasing. And the work was Joshua's life now . . .

Sometimes he missed isolation. His sabbaticals, as he called them. The sense of emptiness when he was entirely alone on a world. The absence of the pressure of other minds, a pressure he felt even here, though it was a ghost compared with what he felt on the Datum. And the eerie sense of the *other* that he'd always called the Silence, like a hint of vast minds, or assemblages of minds, somewhere far off. He'd once met one of those mighty remote minds in the extraordinary First Person Singular. But there were more out there, he knew. He could hear them, like gongs sounding in distant mountains . . . Well, he'd had all that. But *this*, he'd belatedly discovered, was far more precious: his wife, their son, perhaps a second child some day.

Nowadays he tried to ignore what was going on beyond the town limits. After all, it wasn't as though he owed the Long Earth anything. He'd saved lives on stepwise worlds on Step Day itself, and later had opened up half of them with Lobsang. He'd done his duty in this new age, hadn't he?

But here was Sally, an incarnation of his past, sitting at his kitchen table, waiting for an answer. Well, he wasn't going to rush to reply. Generally speaking Joshua wasn't a trigger-fast speaker at the best of times. He took refuge in the concept that sometimes slowest is the fastest in the end.

They stared it out.

To his relief, Helen walked in at last, and set out beer and burgers: home-brewed beer, home-raised beef, home-baked bread. She sat with them and began a pleasant enough conversation, asking Sally about her recent ports of call. When they'd eaten, Helen bustled about once more, clearing the plates, again refusing Joshua's offer of help.

All the time there was another dialogue going on under the surface. Every marriage had its own private language. Helen knew very well why Sally was here, and after nine years of marriage Joshua could hear the feeling of imminent loss as if it were being broadcast on the radio.

If Sally heard it, she didn't care. Once Helen had left them alone at the table once more, she started in again. 'As you say, it's not the only case.'

'What isn't?'

'The Plumbline slaughter.'

'So much for the chit-chat, eh, Sally?'

'It's not even the most notorious, right now. You want an itemized list?'

'No.'

'You see what's happening here, Joshua. Humanity has been given a chance, with the Long Earth. A new start, an escape from the Datum, a whole world we already screwed up—'

'I know what you're going to say.' Because she'd said it a million times before, in his hearing. 'We're going to bollocks up our second chance at Eden, even before the paint has dried.'

Helen deposited a large bowl of ice cream in the middle of the table with a definite *thud*.

Sally stared at it like a dog confronted by a brontosaurus bone. 'You make *ice cream*? Here?'

Helen sat down. 'Last year Joshua put in the hours on an ice house. It wasn't a difficult project once we got round to it. The trolls like the ice cream. And we do get hot weather here; it's wonderful to have something like this when you're bartering with the neighbours.'

Joshua could hear the subtext, even if Sally couldn't. *This isn't about ice cream. This is about our life. What we're building here. Which you, Sally, have no part of.*

'Go on, help yourself, we have plenty more. It's getting late – of course you're welcome to stay the night. Would you like to come see Dan's school play?'

Joshua saw the look of sheer terror on Sally's face. As an act of mercy he said, 'Don't worry. It won't be as bad as you think. We have smart kids, and decent and helpful parents, good teachers – I should know, I'm one of them, and so is Helen.'

'Community schooling?'

'Yes. We concentrate on survival skills, metallurgy, medical botany, Long Earth animal biology, the whole spectrum of practical skills from flint-working to glass-making . . .'

Helen said, 'But it's not all pioneer stuff. We have a high scholastic standard. They even learn Greek.'

'Mr Johansen,' said Joshua. 'Peripatetic. Commutes

twice a month from Valhalla.' He smiled and pointed to the ice cream. 'Get it while it's cold.'

Sally took one large scoop, demolished it. 'Wow. Pioneers with ice cream.'

Joshua felt motivated to defend his home. 'Well, it doesn't *have* to be like the Donner Party, Sally—'

'You're also pioneers with cellphones, aren't you?'

It was true that life was a tad easier here than for pioneers on the Long Earth elsewhere. On this Earth, West 1,397,426, they even had sat-nav – and only Joshua, Helen and a few others knew why the Black Corporation had decided to use *this* particular world to try out their prototype technology, orbiting twenty-four nanosats from a small portable launcher. Call it a favour from an old friend . . .

Among those few others in the know was Sally, of course.

Joshua faced her. 'Lay off, Sally. The sat-nav and the rest are here because of me. I know it. My friends know it.'

Helen grinned. 'One of the engineers who called to fix up that stuff once told Joshua that the Black Corporation sees him as a "valuable long-term investment". Worth cultivating, I suppose. Worth keeping sweet with little gifts.'

Sally snorted. 'Meaning that's how Lobsang sees you. How demeaning.'

Joshua ignored that, as he generally ignored any mention of that particular name. 'And besides, I know that some people are drawn here *because* of me.'

'The famous Joshua Valienté.'

'Why not? It's good not to have to advertise for good people. And if they don't fit, they leave anyhow.'

Sally opened her mouth, ready for a few more jabs.

But Helen had evidently had enough. She stood up. 'Sally, if you want to freshen up we've got a guest room down the passage there. Curtain up is in an hour. Dan – that's our son, maybe you remember him – is already down at the town hall helping out, which is to say bossing the other kids about. Take some of the ice cream when we go over if you like. It's only a short walk.'

Joshua forced a smile. 'Everywhere's a short walk here.'

Helen glanced out through the crude glass of the window. 'And it looks like another perfect evening . . .'

3

I<small>T WAS INDEED</small> a perfect early spring evening.

Of course this world was no longer pristine, Joshua thought, as the three of them walked to the town hall for the school show. You could see the clearances nibbling into the forest by the river banks, and the smoke from the forges and workshops, and the tracks cutting through the forest straight and sharp. But still, what caught your eye was the essentials of the landscape, the bend of this stepwise copy of the Mississippi, and the bridges and the wooded expanses beyond the banks. Hell-Knows-Where looked the way its parent town back on the Datum – Hannibal, Missouri – had back in the nineteenth century, maybe, Mark Twain's day. That was perfection, for his money.

But right now that perfect sky was marred by a twain hanging in the air.

The airship was being unloaded by rope chains, trunk by trunk, bale by bale. In the gathering twilight, its hull shining like bronze, it looked like a ship from another world, which in a sense it was. And though the town hall show was about to start, there were a few students outside watching the sky, the boys in particular looking hungry – boys who would give anything in the world to be twain drivers some day.

The twain was a symbol of many things, Joshua thought. Of the reality of the Long Earth itself, for a start.

The Long Earth: suddenly, on Step Day, twenty-five years before, mankind had found itself with the ability to step sideways, simply to walk into an infinite corridor of planet Earths, one after the next and the next. No space-ships required: each Earth was just a walk away. And every Earth was like the original, more or less, save for a striking lack of humanity and all its works. There was a world for everybody who wanted one, uncounted billions of worlds, if the leading theories were right.

There were some people who, faced with such a land-scape, bolted the door and hid away. Some people did the same thing inside their heads. But others flourished. And for such people in their scattered settlements across the new worlds, a quarter-century on, the twains were becoming an essential presence.

After the pioneering exploratory journey ten years back by Joshua and Lobsang in the *Mark Twain* – that ship had been a prototype, the first cargo- and passenger-carrying craft capable of stepwise motion – Douglas Black, of the Black Corporation who'd built the *Twain*, and the majority owner of the subsidiary that supported Lobsang and his various activities, had announced that the technology was to be a gift to the world. It had been a typical gesture by Black, greeted with loud cynicism about his motives, welcomed with open arms by all. Now, a decade later, the twains were doing for the colonization of the Long Earth what the Conestoga wagon and Pony Express had once done for the Old West. The twains flew and flew, knitting together the burgeoning stepwise worlds . . . They had even stimulated the growth of new industries themselves. Helium for their lift sacs, scarce on Datum Earth, was now being extracted from stepwise copies of Texas, Kansas and Oklahoma.

Nowadays even the news was dispersed across the Long Earth by the airship fleets. A kind of multi-world internet was growing up, known as the 'outernet'. On each world they passed through the airships would download rapid update packets to local nodes to be spread laterally across that world, and would upload any ongoing messages and mail. And when airships met, away from the big Datum–Valhalla spine route, they would hold a 'gam' – a word resurrected from the days of the old whaling fleets – where they would swap news and correspondence. It was all kind of informal, but then so had been the structure of the pre-Step Day internet on the Datum. And being informal it was robust; as long as your message had the right address, it would find its way home.

Of course there were some in places like Hell-Knows-Where who resented the presence of these interlopers, because the twains, one way or another, represented the reach of the Datum government: a reach that wasn't always welcome. The administration's policy towards its Long Earth colonies had swung back and forth with the years, from hostility and even exclusion, to cooperation and legislation. Nowadays the rule was that once a colony had more than one hundred people, it was supposed to report itself back to the federal government on Datum Earth as an 'official' presence. Soon you would be on the map, and the twains would come, floating down from the sky to deliver people and livestock, raw materials and medical care, and carry away any produce you wanted to export via local links to the great stepwise transport hubs like Valhalla.

As they travelled between the old United States and the worlds of its Aegis – all the way out to Valhalla, the best part of a million and a half steps from the Datum – the twains connected the many Americas, comfortably suggesting that they were all marching to the same drum. This despite the fact that many people in the stepwise worlds didn't know which drum you were talking about or what the hell beat it was playing, *their* priority being themselves and their neighbours. The Datum and its regulations, politics and taxes seemed an increasingly remote abstraction, twains or not . . .

And right now two people looked up at this latest twain with suspicious eyes.

Sally said, 'Do you think *he* is up there?'

Joshua said, 'An iteration at least. The twains can't step without some artificial intelligence on board. You know him; he is all iteration. He likes to be where the action is, and right now *everywhere* is where the action is.'

They were talking about Lobsang, of course. Even now Joshua would have difficulty in explaining who exactly Lobsang was. Or what. *Imagine God inside your computer, your phone, everyone else's computer. Imagine someone who almost is the Black Corporation, with all its power and riches and reach. And who, despite all this, seems pretty sane and beneficent by the standards of most gods. Oh, and who sometimes swears in Tibetan . . .*

Joshua said, 'Incidentally I heard a rumour that he has an iteration headed out of the solar system altogether, on some kind of spaceprobe. You know him, he always takes the long view. And there's no such thing as too much backup.'

'So now he could survive the sun exploding,' Sally said

dryly. 'That's good to know. You have much contact with him?'

'No. Not now. Not for ten years. Not since he, or whichever version of *him* resides on the Datum, let Madison be flattened by a backpack nuke. That was my home town, Sally. What use is a presence like Lobsang if he couldn't stop that? And if he *could* have stopped it, why didn't he?'

Sally shrugged. Back then, she'd stepped into the ruins of Madison at his side. Evidently she had no answer.

He became aware of Helen walking ahead of the two of them, talking to a gaggle of neighbours, wearing what Joshua, a veteran of nine years of marriage, called her 'polite' expression. Suitably alarmed, he hurried to catch her up.

He thought they were all relieved when they got to the town hall. Sally read the title of the show from a hand-painted poster tacked to the wall: '"The Revenge of Moby Dick". You have got to be kidding me.'

Joshua couldn't suppress a grin. 'It's good stuff. Wait for the bit where the illegal whaling fleet gets its come-uppance. The kids learned some Japanese just for that scene. Come on, we've got seats up front . . .'

It was indeed a remarkable show, from the opening scene in which a narrator in a salt-stained oilskin jacket walked to the front of the stage: 'Call me Ishmael.'

'Hi, Ishmael!'

'Hi, boys and girls! . . .'

By the time the singing squid got three encores after the big closing number, 'Harpoon of Love', even Sally was laughing out loud.

In the after-show party, children and parents mingled in the hall. Sally stayed on, clutching a drink. But her expression, Joshua thought, as she looked around at the chattering adults, the children's bright faces, gradually soured.

Joshua risked asking, 'What's on your mind now?'

'It's all so damn *nice*.'

Helen said, 'You never did trust *nice*, did you, Sally?'

'I can't help thinking you're wide open.'

'Wide open to what?'

'If I was a cynic I would be wondering if sooner or later some charismatic douche-bag might stomp all over this *Little House on the Prairie* dream of yours.' She glanced at Helen. 'Sorry for saying "douche-bag" in front of your kids.'

To Joshua's amazement, and apparently Sally's, Helen burst out laughing. 'You don't change, do you, Sally? Well, that's not going to happen. The stomping thing. Look – I think we're pretty robust here. Physically and intellectually robust, I mean. For a start we don't do God here. Most of the parents at Hell-Knows-Where are atheist unbelievers, or agnostics at best – simply people who get on with their lives without requiring help from above. We do teach our kids the golden rule—'

'Do as you would be done by.'

'That's one version. And similar basic life lessons. We get along fine. We work together. And I think we do pretty well for the kids. They learn because we make it fun. See young Michael, the boy in the wheelchair over there? He wrote the script for the play, and Ahab's song was entirely his own work.'

'Which one? "I'd Swap My Other Leg For Your Heart"?'

'That's the one. He's only seventeen, and if he never gets a chance at developing his music there is no justice.'

Sally looked uncharacteristically thoughtful. 'Well, with people like you two around, he'll get his chance.'

Helen's expression flickered. 'Are you mocking us?'

Joshua tensed for the fireworks.

But Sally merely said, 'Don't tell anybody I said so. But I envy you, Helen Valienté née Green. A little bit anyhow. Although *not* over Joshua. This drink's terrific, by the way, what is it?'

'There is a tree in these parts, a maple of sorts . . . I'll show you if you like.' She held up her glass in a toast. 'Here's to you, Sally.'

'What for?'

'Well, for keeping Joshua alive long enough to meet me.'

'That's true enough.'

'And you're our guest here for as long as you wish. But – tell me the truth. You're here to take Joshua away again, aren't you?'

Sally looked into her glass and said calmly, 'Yes. I'm sorry.'

Joshua asked, 'It's the trolls, right? Sally, what exactly is it you want me to do about that?'

'Follow up the arguments about animal protection laws. Raise the current cases, at Plumbline and the Gap, and elsewhere. Try to get some kind of troll protection order properly drawn up and enforced—'

'You mean, go back to the Datum.'

She smiled. 'Do a Davy Crockett, Joshua. Come in from the backwoods and go to Congress. You're one of the few

Long Earth pioneers who have any kind of profile on the Datum. You, and a few axe murderers.'

'Thanks.'

'So will you come?'

Joshua glanced at Helen. 'I'll think about it.'

Helen looked away. 'Come on, let's find Dan. Enough excitement for one night, it will be a trial getting him to sleep . . .'

Helen had to get up twice that night before she got Dan settled.

When she returned the second time she nudged Joshua. 'You awake?'

'I am now.'

'I've been thinking. If you do go, Dan and I are coming with you. At least as far as Valhalla. And he ought to see the Datum once in his life.'

'He'd love that,' Joshua murmured sleepily.

'Not when he finds out we're planning to send him to school at Valhalla . . .' For all she'd bigged up the town's school to Sally Linsay, Helen still wanted to send Dan to the city for a while, so he could broaden his contacts, get an experience wide enough for him to make his own informed choices about his future. 'Sally's really not so bad when she isn't channelling Annie Oakley.'

'Mostly she means well,' murmured Joshua. 'And if she *doesn't* mean well the recipient of her wrath generally deserves it.'

'You seem . . . preoccupied.'

He rolled over to face her. 'I looked up the outernet updates from the twain. Sally wasn't exaggerating, about the troll incidents.'

Helen felt for his hand. 'It's all been set up. It's not just Sally turning up like this. I get the impression that your chauffeur is sitting waiting for you in the sky.'

'It *is* a coincidence that a twain should show up just now, isn't it?'

'Can't you leave it to Lobsang?'

'It doesn't work like that, honey. *Lobsang* doesn't work like that.' Joshua yawned, leaned over, kissed her cheek, and rolled away. 'Grand show, wasn't it?'

Helen lay, still sleepless. After a while she asked, 'Do you have to go?'

But Joshua was already snoring.

4

JOSHUA WASN'T SURPRISED when Sally didn't turn up for breakfast.

Nor to find she'd gone altogether. That was Sally. By now, he thought, she was probably far away, off in the reaches of the Long Earth. He looked around the house, searching for signs of her presence. She travelled light, and was fastidious about not leaving behind a mess. She'd come, she'd gone, and turned his life upside down. Again.

She had left a note saying simply, 'Thanks.'

After breakfast he went down to his office in the town hall, to put in a few hours' mayoring. But the shadow of that twain in the sky fell across his office's single window, a looming distraction that made it impossible to concentrate on the routine stuff.

He found himself staring at the single large poster on the wall, the so-called 'Samaritan Declaration', drafted in irritation by some hard-pressed pioneer somewhere, and since spread in a viral fashion across the outernet and adopted by thousands of nascent colonies:

Dear Newbie:
The GOOD SAMARITAN by definition is kind and

forbearing. However, in the context of the Long Earth land rush, the GOOD SAMARITAN demands of you:

ONE. Before you leave home find out something about the environment into which you are heading.

TWO. When you get there, listen to what the guys already there tell you.

THREE. Don't be fooled by maps. Even the Low Earths haven't been properly explored. We don't know what's out there. And if we don't, you certainly don't.

FOUR. Use your noggin. Travel with at least one buddy. Carry a radio where feasible. Tell somebody where you're going. That kind of thing.

FIVE. Take every precaution, if not for your own sake, then for the sake of the poor saps who have to bring what's left of your sorry ass back home in a body bag.

HARSH language, but necessary. The Long Earth is bountiful but not forgiving.

THANK you for reading.

The GOOD SAMARITAN

Joshua liked the Declaration. He thought it reflected the robust, good-humoured common sense that characterized the new nations emerging in the reaches of the Long Earth. New nations, yes . . .

The town hall: a grand name for a solidly built wooden building that housed everything the settlement needed in the way of paperwork, and looked kind of battered this morning, in the aftermath of the kids' show. Well, it was fit for purpose; marble could wait.

And of course it had no statues outside, unlike similar buildings in towns back in Datum America. No Civil War cannons, no bronze plaques with the names of the fallen.

When the growing town had registered for the twain service the federal government had offered a kind of home-improvement monument kit, to cement this community of the future to America's past. But the residents of Hell-Knows-Where rejected that, for a wide number of reasons, many of them going all the way back to great-grandpa's experiences at Woodstock or Penn State. Nobody had shed blood for *this* land yet, apart from when Hamish fell off the town clock, and of course the predations of the mosquitoes. So why a monument?

Joshua had been startled at the vehemence of his fellow citizens on the issue, and he'd since given it some thought, in his patient way. He'd come to the conclusion that it was all to do with identity. Look at history. The founding fathers of the United States for the most part were Englishmen, right up until the moment when they realized that they needn't be. The folk of Hell-Knows-Where by default still thought of themselves as American. But they were starting to feel closer to their neighbours on *this* world, a handful of communities in stepwise copies of Europe and Africa and even China with which they communicated by shortwave radio, than to the Datum folks back home. Joshua found it interesting to watch that sense of identity shifting.

And meanwhile the relationship with Datum America itself was becoming increasingly uncomfortable. The wrangling had been going on for years. Legally speaking, a few years back President Cowley's administration had worked out – Cowley having previously argued successfully to have all the colonists' rights and benefits removed – that in practice it was losing out on significant tax revenues, from the trade that was blossoming both between the various Long Earth communities, and between the remote worlds on the one hand and the Low Earths and Datum on the other. And so Cowley had declared that, if you were under the 'Aegis' of the United States – that is, if you lived in the footprint of the nation, projected across the stepwise worlds out to infinity, East and West – you were de facto a United States citizen, living under United States laws, and liable to pay United States taxes.

And there was the rub. Taxes? Taxes on what? Taxes to be paid how? A lot of local trade was conducted by barter, or using local scrip, or even with intangibles: a service for a service. It was only when you traded with the Low Earths that dollars and cents came into play. It was a burden on many tax-payers, in fact, to assemble enough currency to satisfy said tax demands.

Even if you did pay, the taxes bought you what? The colonists were rich in food, fresh water and unspoiled air, and land: lots and lots of land. As for advanced products, even ten years ago you had had to run home to Uncle Sam for anything high-tech or complicated, from dentistry to veterinarian services, and you needed US dollars to purchase such things. But now, why, there was a spanking new clinic in Hell-Knows-Where itself, and a veterinarian downriver in Twisted Peak, and he had a fast horse and a partner *and* an apprentice. If you needed a city, well, Valhalla was an authentic campus city growing up in the High Meggers, with everything cultural and all the tech you could want.

The colonists found it increasingly hard to understand what they needed the Datum government *for* – and, therefore, what they were buying with their taxes, principally sliced off the profits on the shipments of raw materials the twain caravans hauled endlessly back to the Datum. Even in this neat and civilized town, far from the think-tanks of Valhalla inhabited by the likes of Helen's father Jack, there were some who called for cutting ties with the old US altogether.

And meanwhile, in turn, after years of relative appeasement, in recent dealings with the Datum Joshua had detected an increasing unpleasantness about the federal government's regard for its new young colonies. There were even mutterings back in Datum USA that the colonists were in some way parasitical, even though all their residual holdings back home had long since been liquidated. All this was no doubt linked to Cowley's push for re-election this year; having tacked to the centre during his first run for the White House – a necessity in the aftermath of the Madison incident, when much of the population had been saved from a nuclear attack by stepping away from ground zero – some commentators suggested he was now veering back to his original support base, the virulently anti-stepper Humanity First movement. The United States had long been used to being suspicious of every other country on the planet, and was now becoming suspicious of itself.

Joshua, looking at the sunlit sky through his window, sighed. How far could this go? It was well known that Cowley was putting together some kind of twain-based military arm to go out into the Long Earth. Seeping through the outernet there had been darker rumours, or maybe disinformation, of sterner actions to come.

Could there even be war? Most wars of the past had been over land and wealth, one way or another. Given the

39

literally endless riches of the Long Earth, surely there was no longer any reason for war. Was there? But there were precedents, when the repressive taxation and other policies of a central government had led to its colonies agitating for independence . . .

A Long War?

Joshua gazed at the twain still mysteriously hanging over the town. Waiting to take him away, to participate in the affairs of the wider world once more.

He wandered out to look for Bill Chambers, the town's secretary, accountant, best hunter, excellent cook, and amazingly good liar, although this latter skill threw minor suspicions on his claim to be a distant heir to the Blarney estate in Ireland.

Bill was about Joshua's age, and had once been a buddy at the Home, as much as a recluse like Joshua had had any buddies at all. A few years back Joshua had welcomed Bill, when he'd shown up at Hell-Knows-Where, with open arms. When Joshua had returned from his journey with Lobsang and discovered his unwelcome celebrity – not helped by the fact that Lobsang himself, along with Sally, had retreated to the shadows, leaving Joshua exposed – he'd found himself turning increasingly to people he'd known *before* he was 'famous', and who therefore were discreet and tended not to demand anything of him.

In some ways Bill hadn't changed. He had an Irish background, and he liked to play that up when he got the chance. Also he drank a lot more than he had as a teenager. Or rather, *even* more.

Right now, Bill was ambling to the lumber yard when he spotted Joshua. 'Top, Mister Mayor.'

'Yeah, top to you too. Listen . . .' Joshua told Bill about his need to go to the Datum. 'Helen's insisting on coming, with Dan. Well, it's not a bad idea. But I could do with some backup.'

'The Datum, is it? Full of hoodlums and thugs and other bad lads. Ah, sure, I'm your man.'

'Will Morningtide let you go?'

'She's busy making tallow in the yard right now. I'll ask her later.' He coughed, his best attempt at delicacy. 'There is the question of the fare.'

Joshua looked up at the waiting twain. 'I have a feeling none of us will be paying for this trip, buddy.'

Bill whooped. 'Fair play to you. In that case I'll book us the finest ride I can find. And you've got your own release forms signed by Helen, have ye?'

Joshua sighed. Another hard scene waiting in his future. 'I will do, Bill. I will do.'

They walked together.

'How was your lad's show, by the way?'

'Jumped the shark.'

'Oh, was it that bad?'

'No, Captain Ahab really did jump the shark. Big set piece of the second act. Pretty impressive on one water-ski . . .'

5

HELEN VALIENTÉ, NÉE Green, remembered very well the moment when relations between the Datum and its far-flung children across the Long Earth had first soured.

She'd been a young teenager, still living at Reboot, on Earth West 101,754. She'd kept a journal throughout those years, all the way from her childhood in Datum Madison, their move to Madison West 5, and then her family's trek across a hundred thousand worlds to found a new town in an empty world, a town they had hammered together themselves, starting with nothing but their own hands and minds and hearts. And their reward from Datum America – and they *had* still thought of themselves as Americans – had been rejection. That had been the moment, in retrospect, even more than her mother's illness, when Helen's mild-mannered father Jack Green had completed his own inner journey from Datum-raised software engineer, to sturdy colonist, to firebrand radical thinker.

Twelve years ago. She had been fifteen years old . . .

Crisis. The still-young town of Reboot had split apart.

Some people had walked out, to start up again on their own. Others had gone back to the Hundred K station to

42

wait for a Company to form up for a trek back to Datum Earth.

Worst of all for Helen, Dad wasn't speaking to Mom, despite her illness.

It was all the government's fault. They all got The Letter, every household, delivered by shamefaced mailman Bill Lovell. Bill himself had already been fired by the US Mail, but he said he was going to keep making his rounds even so until his boots wore out, and the people promised to feed him, in return.

The Letter was from the federal government. Everybody with a permanent residence beyond Earth 20, West or East, with assets back on Datum Earth, was having those assets frozen, and ultimately impounded.

With Mom ill in bed, Dad had to explain all this to Helen – words like 'assets' and 'impounded'. Basically it meant that all the money Dad and Mom had earned before upping sticks for their trek into the Long Earth, and had left in bank accounts and other funds back on Earth to pay for stuff like Mom's cancer medicines and for stay-at-home brother Rod's care and for a college education for Helen and sister Katie if they ever wanted it, had been stolen by the government. *Stolen.* That was Dad's word. It didn't seem too harsh to Helen.

Dad said the economy on Earth had taken a knock from stepping. That was obvious even before the Greens had left. All those people who disappeared into the Long Earth had been a big drain from the labour pool, and only a trickle of goods came back the other way; those left behind were furious at having to subsidize work-shy hoboes, as they saw the departed. Meanwhile some people couldn't step at all, and had started to resent those who could. People like Rod, of course, Helen's own home-alone non-stepper brother. She often wondered what he was feeling.

Dad said, 'I'm guessing the government is appeasing the anti-stepper lobby by perpetrating this *theft*. I blame that loudmouth Cowley.'

'So what are we going to do about it?'

'We'll hold a meeting in city hall, that's what.'

Well, they didn't have a city hall, at that time. They did have a communal field cleared of forest and rocks that they *called* city hall, so that was where they gathered. Just as well it wasn't raining, Helen thought.

Reese Henry, the former used-car salesman who was the nearest they had to a mayor, chaired the meeting, in his usual bullying way. He held up The Letter. 'What are we going to do about this?'

They weren't going to put up with it, that was what. There was a lot of talk about forming up a mass hike and marching on Datum Washington. But who was going to feed the chickens?

They resolved to make inventories of all the stuff they still imported from Datum Earth. Medicines, for one. Books, paper, pens, electronic gadgets, even luxuries like perfumes. By sharing and swapping and mending, maybe they could manage with what they had until things settled down. The idea was floated of getting together with the neighbours. There was a bunch of nearby settlements spread over a few dozen worlds that some were starting to call 'New Scarsdale County'. They could help each other out in case of scarcities and emergencies.

Some spoke of going back. A mother with a diabetic kid. Folk who found that advancing age wasn't mixing well with the hard work of farming. A few who just seemed to feel scared without the backing of the government, however remote it was. But others, like Helen's dad, urged nobody to leave. They all relied on each other. They had put together a spectrum of complementary skills that enabled them to survive if they worked together. They couldn't let the community they'd built be pulled apart. And so on.

Reese Henry let it all ramble on, and run down. They broke up without resolution.

The next morning, however, the sun rose on schedule, the chickens needed feeding and the water needed toting from the well, and somehow life went on.

Three months later.

Helen's sister Katie had quietly brought forward her wedding. She and Harry Bergreen had been planning to wait until the following year, when they were hoping for a proper house-raising. Everybody knew that they were getting married now while Mom was still around to see it.

Helen was enough of a girly girl that she had grown up dreaming of fairytale-princess weddings. Well, this day turned out to be a pioneers' wedding. Kind of different, but still fun.

The guests had started arriving early, but Katie and Harry and their families were ready to meet them. Bride and groom were dressed in informal clothes, no white gowns or morning suits here, but Katie was wearing a small, pretty veil made by sister Helen from the lining of an old hiking jumpsuit.

As time wore on people showed up from outside Reboot itself, friends and acquaintances from communities like New Scarsdale and even further afield. The guests brought gifts: flowers and food for the day, and practical stuff – cutlery, pots, plates, coffee pots, kettles, frying pans, a hearth set, a boot scraper. Some of this stuff had been made locally, pottery cast on Reboot wheels, or iron gadgets hammered out in Reboot forges. It didn't look much, piled up before the Greens' big hearth, but Helen realized it soon amounted to pretty much all a young couple would need to equip their first home.

Around noon Reese Henry arrived. Wearing a reasonably smart jacket, clean jeans and boots, and a string tie, he scrubbed up well. Helen knew that nobody in Reboot took 'Mayor Henry' as seriously as he took himself. But still, you needed one individual in a community with the authority to formalize a marriage – an authority backed by some remote government, or not – and he played the part well. Plus his hair was magnificent.

And when Harry Bergreen kissed his bride a little after midday and everybody applauded, and the bride's mother held on to her husband's arm to make sure she stayed standing for the pictures, even Bill the mailman had tears welling in his eyes.

That one was a *good* day, Helen recorded in her journal.

And three months later:

'2nd baby for Betty Doak Hansen. Hlthy B, 7lb. Mthr ill, ndd stches & bld . . .'

Helen had been tired. Too tired to write in this damn code in her journal, even if they did have to conserve paper now.

This latest delivery hadn't been a bad birth, as they went. Belle Doak and her little team of midwives and helpers, including Helen, were pretty competent at it by now. Although, this morning, it had been a close-run thing. Helen had to run around town asking for blood donors. They were all walking blood banks, for the benefit of their neighbours. But it wasn't always fast enough. Memo to self, she thought: set up some kind of list of blood types and willing donors.

Dad had left early this morning, not long after Helen got in. Down at Mom's grave probably, the stone by the river. Mom had always loved that spot. It was already a month since she'd died of her tumour, and Dad was still racked by guilt over it, as if it were somehow his fault, somehow caused by his bringing her here. It made no sense, especially since as far as Helen remembered her mother had always been the driving force behind their leaving the Datum in the first place.

A month, though, which made it more than six months since they had all been fired en masse by the federal government. Gosh, Helen thought now, we're still here, who'd have thought it?

They had had to learn fast. They had relied more than they'd realized on various props from the old country. Now they made *everything*! They knitted, brewed beer, dipped candles, made soap. You could make a good vinegar from pumpkin rind. Toothpaste! – from ground-up charcoal. It helped a lot when Bill Lovell came round selling his new product: miniaturized sets of encyclopaedias, and copies of *Scientific American* from pre-1950, full of exploded diagrams of steam engines and practical advice on a whole slew of stuff. They were even rethinking the crops they were growing in the farms and gardens, after the vitamin pill supply dried up and they'd even had a couple of cases of scurvy. Scurvy!

And they helped each other out: I fetch water for you while your little one's ill, you feed my chickens when I'm away up country. There was a kind of unwritten price for everything, recorded as 'favours', a loosely defined currency based on service and barter and promissory notes. Mom would probably have loved the theory of it all, an emerging, self-organizing local economy.

Despite dire warnings from some about what would happen when the theoretical protection of the Datum government had been lifted, they *hadn't* suddenly been overwhelmed by armies of bandits. Oh, there had been problems, for instance the waves of 'new' colonists who sporadically walked out from the Datum or the Low Earths and tried to settle in Reboot's country. Legally it was a tricky situation, since such claims as the Reboot colonists did have were lodged with a Datum federal government which showed no interest in them any more. But the mayor in New Scarsdale was usually able to buy the newcomers off by signing bits of paper granting them land fifty or a hundred worlds further up West, a deal lubricated with fistfuls of vouchers for drinks in the tavern. There was always *room*, so much room up here that almost any problem like that could be resolved.

Of course there was a steady drizzle of thefts, of food, from the fields – even, in this age of stepping, from within houses. Mostly you turned a blind eye. Things got more serious when a boy called Doug Collinson was caught red-handed taking beta blockers from Melissa Harris's medicine chest, prescribed for her mild heart condition. Doug didn't need them himself; he was just going to sell them someplace else. Decent drugs were among the most precious commodities they had. Well, Melissa caught him, and she had the presence of mind to swing her stick and smash his Stepper so he couldn't get away before the neighbours came running in. Right now Doug was in confinement in somebody's cellar, while the adults debated what to do about it. Slowly, out of the need to react to such incidents, a framework for maintaining law and order was emerging, maybe ultimately based on some kind of court shared with communities like New Scarsdale in the neighbouring worlds.

The framework of Helen's own life was slowly emerging too. Dad constantly pointed out that Helen was sixteen years old now and needed to choose a path in life. Well, fine. There was her midwifery. And she was thinking of specializing in medicines: herbs and stuff. A lot of the plants and fungi they found on Earth West 101,754 weren't familiar from Datum Earth. She could become an itinerant seller, or maybe a tutor, a guru, taking her arts and wares and unique flora across the worlds. Or not. She thought she'd find her way.

They weren't in paradise. The Long Earth was a big arena, where you could feel lost, and you could lose yourself. But maybe all this room was going to be the ultimate gift of the Long Earth to mankind. Room that gave everyone the chance to live as they liked. Helen had decided she liked the happy compromise they were figuring out in Reboot.

Well, not long after that, along had come Joshua Valienté, returning from the far stepwise West, towing a defunct airship and trailing the romance of the High Meggers – and, yes, with Sally Linsay at his side. Helen, then seventeen years old, had had her world turned upside down. Soon she'd moved away with Joshua, and married him, and now here they were building another fine young community.

The Datum government, meanwhile, had reached out to its scattered colonies once more, and gathered them into the embrace of its 'Aegis'. Suddenly everybody had to pay taxes. Jack Green, who had been enraged by The Letter and the cut-off, was if anything even more enraged by the imposition of the Aegis . . . Without her mother, Helen believed, he was filling an empty life with politics.

And then Sally showed up again, and once more Joshua was distracted.

The night before they were due to leave on the twain for Valhalla, with their bags all packed, Helen couldn't sleep. She went out on to their veranda, into air that was warm for March on this chilly Earth. She looked at the twain still waiting at anchor in the sky over the town, its running lights like a model galaxy. She murmured, '*We were young, we were merry, we were very very wise . . .*'

Joshua came out to find her. He folded his strong arms around her waist, and nuzzled her neck. 'What's that, honey?'

'Oh, an old poem. By a Victorian poet called Mary Elizabeth Coleridge. I helped Bob Johansen teach it to the eighth-graders the other day. *We were young, we were merry, we were very very wise, / And the door stood open at our feast, / When there passed us a woman with the West in her eyes, / And a man with his back to the East.* Isn't that haunting?'

'You won't lose me, to West or East. I promise.'

She found she couldn't reply.

6

NELSON AZIKIWE – or the Reverend Nelson as his congregation called him in church, or Rev as they called
him down the pub – watched as Ken the shepherd
grabbed a pregnant ewe and slung it over his shoulder. To
Nelson this was an astounding display of strength: Ken's
ewes were no lightweights. Then Ken walked forward
towards a hedgerow.

And took another step and completely vanished.

And reappeared a few seconds later, wiped his hands
with a none too clean towel, and said, 'That will do for
now. There's still a few wolves that haven't got the message
yet. I suppose I'd better get Ted to draw me another
thousand yards of electric fence. Don't you want to come
and see, Rev? You'll be surprised at how much we've done.
Just a step away, you know.'

Nelson hesitated. He hated the nausea that came with
stepping; they said that after a while you hardly noticed,
and maybe so, at least for some, but for Nelson every step
was a penance. But it paid to be neighbourly. After all it
had been a long time since breakfast, and with luck he
might get away with a few dry heaves. So he fingered the
Stepper switch in his pocket, clapped his handkerchief
over his mouth . . .

When he'd recovered somewhat, the first thing he noticed, in this England one step away from home, was not the painstakingly cleared field of grass at his feet but the trees of the remnant forest beyond Ken's dry stone wall. Big trees, old trees, giants. Some were fallen, their trunks bright with moulds and fungi, and to a clergyman that could have been the spark for a nice little inspirational sermon on the mighty and the futility of their ambitions. But Nelson, in his late forties now, wasn't planning to be a clergyman for much longer.

The light seemed to be a little more golden than it was pre-step, and he glanced up at the sun, which seemed to be in the right place this March day ... more or less. Though time on the various Earths seemed to flow at the same rate, and the events that defined the calendar – sunrise and sunset, the seasons – seemed synchronized from world to world, according to last week's *Nature* some of the new Earths did not appear to tick *exactly* to the same clock, sometimes leading or following their immediate neighbours by a fraction of a second, as you could prove by such means as very precise astronomical observations, like the occultation of stars by the moon. The discrepancies were minute but real. Nelson could think of no plausible explanation for this. Nobody knew how or why this phenomenon happened, but as yet nobody was researching it because it was just one of a multitude of puzzles generated by the multiple worlds. How strange, how eerie ...

Of course he had stopped thinking like a priest, having, perhaps shamefully, reverted to his ground state of being: a scientist. But still, people all over the world – including some of his own flock – had for a quarter of a century now been abandoning their homes and packing up their kids and buggering off into this great hall of worlds called the Long Earth, and yet nobody knew how it worked, even on the most basic level of how time flowed, or how all those worlds had *got* there . . . and still less what they were *for*. How was a priest supposed to react to that?

Which was, indirectly anyhow, the reason for Nelson's current inner turmoil.

Fortunately for the goats and the gravid sheep around him, and for Joy, the young sheepdog Ken was training, *they* did not have to lie awake at night wondering about this sort of thing. Having given him their usual slotted glances the animals ambled away, the sheep eating the grass, the goats devouring just about everything else.

Shepherd Ken had told him how the whole Long Earth deal worked for the likes of him. In England West and East 1 and 2, the farmers had been clearing forested land on a scale not seen since the Stone Age – and they had had to relearn how to do it. First you cut down a *lot* of trees, being careful to put the timber to good use, and then you set loose the animals, either bred here or carried over as young from the Datum one by one. Any hopeful saplings would succumb to the onslaught of the sheep and goats, forestalling the return of the forest. And in time the grass would come. Clever stuff, grass, Ken liked to say, a plant that actually thrived on being eaten down to the ground.

Nelson had rather misjudged Ken when he had first met this suntanned, rugged, rather taciturn man, a local whose ancestors had lived on these hills since there were such things as ancestors. It was only by chance that he found out that Ken had been a lecturer at the University of Bath until, like many others, shortly after Step Day he re-evaluated his lifestyle and his future – which turned out, in his case, to be this farm just one step away from the Datum.

In that, Ken was typical of his nation, in a way. The British experience of the Long Earth had been in the beginning mostly a painful one. Such had been the early exodus from these crowded islands, particularly from the battered industrial cities of the north, Wales and Scotland, regions isolated from the increasingly complacent city-state that was London, that a rapid population loss had led to an economic crash – even a collapse of the currency, briefly. They had called it the Great Bog Off.

But then the stepwise Britains had begun their own economic growth. And there had been a second wave of emigration, more cautious, hard-headed and industrious. By now there were whole new Industrial Revolutions going on in the Low Earths; the British seemed to have the building of steam engines and railways in their genes. Some of that hard-acquired wealth had already started to flow back into the Datum.

In the long run, in their exploration and colonization of the Long Earth, the British had proved to be thorough, patient, careful, and ultimately pretty successful. Just like Ken.

But now Nelson had his own journey to make.

They spent some time discussing the vigour and health of Ken's flock. Then Nelson cleared his throat and said, 'You know, Ken, I've loved my time here in the parish. There's been a kind of peacefulness. A sense that although the surface of things changes, the soul of them does not. Do you know what I mean?'

'Umm,' said Ken.

'When I first came here I walked the hills. There are signs of people having lived here for ever – since before England was England. In the graveyard and on the war memorial I found family names repeated across hundreds of years. Sometimes a man went away to fight for a king he didn't know, in a place he'd never heard of. Sometimes he didn't come back at all. And yet the land endured, you know? Even as this countryside, remote from the urban centres, has survived more or less intact through the great convulsions since Step Day. It must have been very hard for such men to leave such a place. Just as it will be for me.'

'You, Rev?'

'You are the first to know. I have had a word with the Bishop, and he has agreed that I can move out just as soon as my successor is in place.' He looked out over the flocks. 'Look at them. They graze as if they will graze for eternity, and are content with that.'

'But you're no sheep, Rev.'

'Quite so. The fact is I've spent a lot of my life being a scientist, and am obligated to a different covenant than the one I bow to at the moment – although I must say that in my head the two have rather melded together. In short I need to find a new purpose, one more suited to my talents and my background. If you'll pardon my immodesty.'

'You've pardoned me for worse, Rev.'

'Perhaps, perhaps not. Now if you're done here let me stand you a pint down the pub. And then I have some calls to make.'

Ken said, 'Well, that's nice. About the pint, I mean.' He whistled. 'Joy! Here, girl.'

The dog came bounding up, tail wagging, and leapt into Ken's strong arms, just as she'd been trained, so she could be carried back to the Datum. She was a dog whose supper bowl was currently lodged in a different corner of the multiverse entirely, but who had no concern about that as long as her master whistled for her.

7

TELLING KEN A bit of news like that was as good as hiring a sky-writer, Nelson knew. Well, what was done was done.

Once back at the rectory Nelson made a few follow-up calls, disclosing, apologizing, accepting congratulations.

Then, with relief, he told his computer to boot up, leaned back in his office chair, and watched the multiple screens light up. 'Search terms. One: the return of the airship the *Mark Twain*. Two: the Lobsang Project. Supplementary: soc-media streams for last twenty-four hours, slanting towards current concerns, depth three Occam's razor . . .'

Bandwidth here was generally dreadful, but not for Nelson. A man with a past like his – he'd once worked for the Black Corporation itself, if only indirectly – had a great many contacts in many useful places: favour speaks unto favour. Only last year a black helicopter had landed just short of the graveyard and the team of technicians that stepped out on to the glebe had left him with access to as much satellite traffic as he wanted – including some channels known to very few people indeed – and moreover the means to decipher those channels.

When he'd done with the latest soc-media chit-chat, he

left his study for the kitchen. A search like the one he'd just initiated was never going to be quick, and, while his software agents were scuttling across the web, he warmed up a microwave curry.

And he reflected, as he often did, about the previous inhabitants of this parsonage. The equipment in his study – his phone, laptop, tablets – was all state of the art, more or less, though it would mostly have been familiar to a user of ten or twenty years ago. This was an argument seized on by some critics of the Long Earth migration. Need exerted a necessary pressure on humanity: you had to be hungry to innovate, and you needed to be surrounded by competitors to be driven to achieve. And in the Long Earth, with bellies filled too easily and plenty of space to spread out into, invention had stalled. Still, none of Nelson's predecessors here, not even the most recent, had had access to anything like the technology at his fingertips now, retro or not.

And every single one of them had been unable, just like Nelson, to make the antique toilet work properly. He liked that reflection; it helped keep him down to earth.

The cooking done, he returned to his study – the Lobsang search was still in progress – and as he ate he logged into the Quizmasters.

This was a little-known chat room, access to which would only be vouchsafed to you by invitation – and the invitation was a series of tests. Nelson, intrigued by a quiz he'd been sent without explanation, had completed it after evensong one day a few weeks ago. It took him twenty-seven minutes. His reward was to be sent another quiz, of similarly fiendish intricacy. Over the following days more quizzes turned up randomly. Nelson had been impressed by the questions, which demanded not only knowledge in a vast number of fields but also the ability to make use of that knowledge against the clock, while drawing on a multiplicity of disciplines, including *un*-disciplines . . . In the nerdosphere, in pursuit of the elusive and the strange, the strongest intellect, Nelson knew, was good for nothing without a propensity for pack-rat fact accumulation, an appreciation of serendipity, and an endless interest in the incongruous, the out of place. And that was what the Quizmasters' tests seemed to select for.

The room had opened for him on the seventh day. That was the first time he'd learned the group's name for itself. Initially the Quizmasters seemed like any other chat room, except that everybody in it knew that in some way they had been *chosen*, which gave a frisson to the proceedings. A self-selecting elite of the nerdosphere – and very useful, he'd found, if directed to a task.

But time and again conversations in that room came round to the monopoly known as the Black Corporation, which was for the most part detested by the circle members. That itself being a puzzle, of course.

When Nelson went online, or, more accurately, on*lines*, he mixed in cyberspace with a lot of people who had a marked dislike of black helicopters, governments, washing more than once a week, and above all, *secrets* – and, just to top it off, particularly didn't like the Black Corporation. Which was kind of strange if you thought about it, since the infrastructure of the nerdosphere itself nowadays was more or less supported by Black products. Certainly the nerdosphere was always full of speculation, scuttlebutt and downright lies about what was happening in the most ultra-secret laboratories of the organization.

Yes, everybody knew Black's story, the elements of which had become as familiar, it sometimes seemed to Nelson, as the Nativity. It was a classic American narrative of its kind. It had all started when Douglas Black and his associates had set up 'just another computer company', with the help of Black's late grandfather's oil-money bequest. This was the early 1990s; Black had only been in his mid-twenties. From the beginning Black's lines had included such much-longed-for-by-customers products as computers with long battery power and fault-free software, machines that were your partners, not just a gadget for extracting money from you, not just an ad for some superior future version of themselves. Machines that seemed mature. And from the beginning Black had begun to make philanthropic donations of various kinds around the world, including a scholarship pro-gramme in South Africa that Nelson himself had benefited from.

With time the Black product line went from strength to strength, and began to innovate significantly. Black was entitled to rewards aplenty for his intellectual courage, as far as Nelson was concerned. He was after all the founder of the first 'serendipital laboratory'. The logic was that since so many important new discoveries in science were made by accident, then the process would be speeded up if you set up a situation in which a very *large* number of accidents happened, and watched the results carefully. According to legend Black had even deliberately employed people who didn't *quite* know what they were doing, or had a bad memory, or who were known to be congenitally unlucky and careless. It was, of course, a lunatic idea. Black did take some precautions, such as building his laboratory to the same safety standards as were employed by explosives manufacturers . . .

Black's innovations had won him huge sales, public praise, and a concerted attack by instant enemies. The established companies he was wrong-footing, and whose profits he was trashing, accused him of everything from monopolistic practices to a lack of patriotism. The public didn't buy any of these lies, it seemed, but it did keep on buying Black's neat stuff. And indeed the public bought into Black himself, who became a hero, a cheerful rogue thumbing his nose at older, lumbering companies, investing in spectacular super-rich indulgences like homes under the sea and jaunts into orbit, while sprinkling charities and good causes with staggering amounts of money.

Then the gods truly smiled on Black's project when an experiment to find a new type of surgical plaster was left too long in the sunshine and turned into 'gel', as it became known, a curious quasi-organic matter embedded with self-designing, self-repairing bio-neural circuitry, smart enough to morph itself physically to fit the circumstances it found itself in. The newspapers called it the *intelligent bandage*, after its first applications, but it had soon proved to be much more than that – and much smarter. As a self-correcting, self-repairing, physically malleable data and processing store, gel in all its forms had become the mainstay of the Black Corporation's output. There was a wave of new products, and indeed new types of product. This time many of Black's competitors were wiped out completely.

Now it was the turn of governments to become suspicious. Black was simply too rich, too powerful – not to mention too generous and too popular – to be borne. The US administration made attempts to take control of Black's operations under various national-interest fig-leaves, or at least to break up his empire. Eminent domain was quoted; militarization of Black's enterprises was attempted.

But Black hastily diversified into obviously non-security, non-military applications, such as medicine. Suddenly the corporation turned its attention to the disadvantaged: to letting the dumb speak and the lame walk. Nowadays there were people seeing, hearing, walking, running, swimming, even juggling, thanks to the prosthetic aids, implants, and other products developed by the Black Corporation and its subsidiaries. With such a portfolio behind him Black was able to argue that there was no national interest served in the government's pursuit of him; its actions were anti-capitalist – whisper it quietly, *socialist*.

Since then Black had made an even grander gesture when, nearly a decade ago, he had more or less gifted twain technology, through an international consortium of manufacturers, to the UN, governments worldwide, and the peoples of the new Earths. Nowadays the twains that plied the US Aegis – even the few police and military craft as well as the commercial fleets – were all Black Corporation products, built at cost. Not only that, the conglomerate disbursed even vaster funds to good causes, and Black became even more of a hero.

Despite all this, however, the name of Douglas Black was anathema to many in the chat rooms.

Nelson had searched in vain for plausible reasons, and found none. It wasn't as if many of those who poured out their bile could have any personal grudge: none of them, for example, had been executives of the moribund companies whose careers might have been ruined by Black's rise. It seemed the worst you could say about Douglas Black as a human being was that he was a workaholic, who worked hard and expected people to work hard for him. Maybe this had cost him, even significantly. There had been an online legend that Black's serendipity lab was even behind the Stepper box that had opened up the Long Earth. Somehow Black had pissed off the inventor, and in the end the box design had been dumped into the public domain, galvanizing all mankind, but earning not a penny for anybody, not directly at any rate.

That was all behind the scenes. And yet Black was hated, by some.

The minds hiding behind the various pseudonyms Nelson found himself staring at among the Quizmasters were not stupid. They could not be, given the high bar set for entrance in the first place; indeed it sometimes felt as if a membership of Mensa might just about qualify you to make the coffee for this particular metaphorical kaffee-klatch. Not stupid, no. But . . .

Nelson had met many people in different walks of life, and he thought he could read at least some of them. These men and women were bright, truly bright. But in some, even through the impersonal medium of the chat rooms, he sensed something dark and hidden, sometimes betrayed by the occasional comment, or curious turn of phrase. Envy, to start with. Paranoid suspicion, for another. A kind of seam of malevolence – a capacity for cold hatred – a capacity that needed an outlet, *any* outlet. A man like Black, who presented a public face, who could seem either an object of envy, or too good to be true and therefore deserving of suspicion, was an ideal target. This didn't show itself often, no, but it was apparent to those who really *watched* other people.

And especially to a man who had grown up a black kid in South Africa, and had not forgotten the experience.

Anyhow, whatever you thought about Black, Nelson *did* like the Black Corporation, in all its wonderful and manifold manifestations. And in particular he liked the mysteries their various activities threw up for him to ponder over.

For example, as he had drifted somewhat aimlessly through the periphery of the information cloud that surrounded Black, he had started to notice how often the 'Lobsang Project' was mentioned. But it was always a dead end in any search, a link to nowhere. *Lobsang*: of course the name meant 'big brain' in Tibetan, which showed that somebody in the Black Corporation had not only a sense of humour but also some skills when it came to languages. But Lobsang was a personal name too, and, slowly, Nelson had come to envisage Lobsang as a person. A person to be tracked down. Him *and* his 'Project'.

And now Nelson, all alone in this rather chilly rectory, with all eight screens windows to the world, smiled. For suddenly his search had borne fruit.

One of his screens filled up with an image of the airship *Mark Twain*, rather battle-worn after its now famous journey, being towed into what remained of Madison, Wisconsin after the nuke attack ten years back: towed by Joshua Valienté and a young woman whom no one to

Nelson's knowledge had subsequently been able to identify.

Nelson was pretty sure that he'd seen just about everything that Joshua Valienté had brought back from the extraordinary voyage of the *Mark Twain*. The Black Corporation – in a gesture typical of Douglas Black – had dumped Godzillabytes of data from the voyage into the archive of any university that wanted it, for open public access and study. (*Godzillabytes*: Nelson had an irrational dislike of 'petabytes', the recognized term for a particular, and particularly large, wodge of data. Anything that sounded like a kitten's gentle nip just didn't have the moxie to do the job asked of it. 'Godzillabytes', on the other hand, shouted to the world that it was dealing with something very, very big . . . and possibly dangerous.)

Nelson had seen this particular clip, or variants of it from other camera angles, many times before, and he wondered why his search engines had thrown it up now. Watching, he saw that this bit of hasty amateur footage showed a scene where Valienté, in a radiation-exposure processing camp in West 1, seemed to be carrying a cat under one arm. Some bystander off-screen burst out laughing and called, 'What's that, the ship's cat?' And somebody else, almost certainly Valienté's unknown companion though she was out of shot, called back, 'Yeah, wiseass, and it can speak Tibetan.'

You had to listen very carefully to make out this piece of nonsense. But that word was evidently what the search had picked on: 'Tibetan', a subsidiary search tag from 'Lobsang', had brought this fragment of the complicated saga of the *Mark Twain* drifting to the surface for his attention.

What had the woman meant? Why use such a word, 'Tibetan', if it wasn't somehow relevant? He had no idea yet where this was leading. But now he had a link between one of Black's more high-profile projects, the *Twain* and its journey, and one of the most low-profile, Lobsang, embodied in that single word.

Of course the complete absence of any *other* link was itself suspicious.

For now the search was going no further; he was covering what he already knew. Nelson yawned, blinked and shut down the screens. There was a mystery here, he was sure, and he felt a tingle of anticipation at the prospect of following this trail further. And this was precisely why he was shedding his parochial duties: to have the time, while he had the resources and the strength, to follow such trails wherever they led him.

But of course the overarching mystery that obsessed him in a background kind of way was the conundrum of stepping itself: of the sudden discovery of the Long Earth, into which Joshua Valienté and his airship and his loud-mouthed partner and, apparently, his Tibetan-speaking cat had wandered so famously – of the utter realignment of the cosmos, in Nelson's own lifetime. How could he not be intrigued? What could it all mean for mankind, the future – indeed, for God? How could he *not* pursue such questions?

Well, the best strategy was usually to tackle smaller mysteries first. And right now, in that spirit, before getting ready for bed, he put on an apron, grabbed one of his toolboxes and walked to the stone-floored toilet. This throne was a massive edifice that even included straining bars, and would have been a wonderful asset if anybody over the years could have made it work properly, whereas now it worked in various forms of *im*properly. He had vowed to get the thing functioning before his tenure was over, taking especial care to find out why it always backed up during an east wind.

On the whole, he thought, as he knelt before the cracked china sculpture, as if before a pagan idol, it was amazing what the English put up with.

8

So the Valienté family travelled to the High Meggers city of Valhalla, to catch a long-haul twain to Datum Earth. The twain journey, across less than three thousand Earths, took only a few hours.

At Valhalla, Thomas Kyangu was waiting to greet them with a big handwritten sign: VALIENTÉ. Another old buddy of Joshua's, Thomas was around fifty, with long black hair pinned back in a ponytail, and a wide grin splitting a dark, reasonably handsome face. His accent was thick Australian. 'Greetings, clan Valienté! Welcome to Earth West One Million, Four Hundred Thousand. Well, officially it's one point four million plus thirteen, since our founding fathers were stoned when they first got here and lost count, but we like to round it down for the TV ads . . . Good to see you again, Joshua.'

Joshua grinned and shook his hand. Thomas dived in to help with their bags.

Getting their bearings, some of them a little woozy from the step-nausea medication, they stood on a concrete apron under the swollen hull of the airship: Joshua, Helen, Dan and Bill Chambers, with their baggage accumulating at their feet. They and the other disembarking passengers were lost in the expanse of this apron, Joshua thought.

And beyond sprawled the city of Valhalla itself, clusters of heavy buildings under a blue sky faintly tinged with smog, with a din of traffic, and construction engines clanking and roaring. The air was warm, warmer than at Hell-Knows-Where. But still, behind the hot tar and oil aroma of this brand new city, Joshua could smell the salt of the nearby inland American Sea, just as he remembered from his first visit to these worlds ten years ago.

A huge form swept over their heads, with a drone of engines and a wash of displaced air: a twain, a big one, a freight vessel heading for the transit routes to the Low Earths and the Datum. Valhalla's principal function was as a transport nexus, one terminus of the river of airship traffic that flowed endlessly across more than a million Earths to the Datum and back again, carrying freight and passengers. And it was no coincidence that Valhalla had grown up on a location that in most stepwise Americas lay close to what in Datum terms was the Mississippi: the twains took you across the worlds, while the river could carry your goods across *a* world.

Daniel Rodney Valienté, eight years old, had never seen ships of such a size, and he jumped up and down, thrilled. 'Are we going to ride in one of those things, Dad?'

'In a little while, son . . .'

'And here comes Sally Linsay,' Helen said. 'Surprise, surprise.'

'Give her a break,' Joshua murmured to Helen. 'I did arrange to meet her here.'

Sally was wearing her usual pioneer-type gear, her signature fisherman's jacket with the thousand pockets, and she carried a light leather pack. 'What a racket,' she said as she walked up, theatrically clamping her hands over her ears. 'Noise, everywhere you go. We ought to call ourselves *Homo clamorans*. Noisemaking Man.'

Helen just looked at her, unsmiling. 'Travelling with us, are you? The great wanderer hitching a ride on a commercial twain?'

'Well, we're all going the same way. Why not get reacquainted? We can swap recipes for ice cream.'

Joshua grabbed his wife's arm in case she felt like throwing a punch. It wouldn't have been the first time.

As he watched this byplay Thomas's grin was becoming a little more fixed. 'Ri-ight. I'm sensing a little tension here.'

Bill murmured, 'It's complicated. Don't ask.'

Sally snapped, 'Who's this character?'

'He's called Thomas Kyangu,' Joshua said. 'An old friend of mine.'

'You don't know me, Ms Linsay, but I know of you, through Joshua.'

'Oh, God, a fan-boy.'

Helen stepped forward. 'And we still haven't been properly introduced, Mr Kyangu. My name's Helen Valienté, née Green—'

'The wife. Of course.' Thomas shook her hand.

' "The wife"?' Sally laughed.

'You have all your bags? I have a buggy just over there. Joshua sent a message ahead; I booked you all a hotel in Downtown Four . . .' As they walked over the apron, through a dispersing crowd of passengers, Thomas said, 'You can't blame a Valhallan for following Joshua's exploits, Ms Linsay.'

'He's a married man,' Helen said sternly. 'There'll be no more "exploits" if I have anything to do with it.'

'Yes, but he did *discover* this Valhallan Belt itself, during The Journey. A band of North Americas with generous inland oceans, ripe for colonization.'

'"Discover"?' Sally snapped back. '*I* was there already, as I recall.'

They reached Thomas's buggy, a low, open electric-engine vehicle with eight plastic seats. 'Please, jump in . . .' The cart pulled away, heading south.

'Thomas and I are old buddies,' Joshua said to Sally, by way of explanation, or peacekeeping.

'You mean, he's a long-term stalker,' Sally said.

'We met up out in the High Meggers, years ago . . . We were both on sabbatical, though Thomas calls it going walkabout. We're like minds, kind of. Knowing he was here in Valhalla I asked him to help us out.'

Helen said, 'Well, thank you, Mr Kyangu. But what do you do the rest of the time?'

'Look at him,' Sally said. 'Can't you tell? Look at the way he's dressed. He's a comber. A professional drifter.'

'More or less,' Thomas called over his shoulder as he drove. 'I grew up in Australia, and I've always been fascinated by combers. Many of my family's people went off to become combers themselves, you know, in stepwise versions of Oz. And I'm intrigued by natural steppers – like you, like Joshua, the whole phenomenon. Though I'm not one myself. I'm also interested in the whole question of how human civilization is going to be shaped by the Long Earth. I mean, it's still only a single generation since Step Day; we're only at the beginning. I had a hand in the concept design of Valhalla, of the city itself.'

Sally snorted. ' "Concept design!" '

Thomas was unperturbed. 'The purest way of life in the Long Earth is the comber – the solitary individual, or maybe a family, a small cohesive group, just wandering, picking the lowest-hanging fruit. The Long Earth is so rich there's no *need* to do anything else. But the point of Valhalla is that it's a city, a genuine city with all the essential attributes of a Datum community, but *sustained by combers . . .*'

They were entering a more built-up area now, Joshua saw. He glimpsed a sign: DOWNTOWN FOUR. The buildings, of brick, concrete or timber, were low, squat, massively constructed, and set out in sprawling, empty plots: typical colony-world architecture. If this was a downtown it was definitely a High-Meggers downtown, full of room, with more of the feel of a suburban mall back on the Datum. There were few vehicles on the wide roads, most of them horse-drawn, and few pedestrians to be seen, with most of *them* wearing Steppers. This wasn't a place you stayed put in for long.

But it was evidently a city in political ferment. Some of those big blank walls were adorned with posters and graffiti:

SUPPORT THE FOOTPRINT CONGRESS
NO TO DATUM TAXES!

And:

DOWN WITH COWLEY THE GENOCIDE

Thomas was still talking about combers and cities. 'I've written a book on the subject,' he said now. 'Combers, and a new theory of civilization.'

Helen frowned. 'A book? Nobody reads books now. Or at least, not new books.'

Thomas, steering one-handed, tapped his forehead. 'All in here. I travel the worlds and give readings.'

'A regular Johnny Shakespeare,' Sally said dismissively.

The cart pulled up outside a four-storey building with an expansive street-level frontage. Thomas said, 'Here you go. The Healed Drum, the best hotel in Valhalla. You're in there for three weeks if you need it.'

Sally scowled. 'How long? Why? We've only come here to catch a twain down to the Datum.'

Joshua said gently, 'Sally, Helen and I are here to look at a school for Dan.'

Dan's little jaw dropped. 'You're sending me here? To school?'

Helen glared at Joshua. 'Great way to break the news.'

'Sorry.'

She patted Dan's arm. 'Valhalla's schools have got a reputation as the best in the High Meggers, Dan. It would be fun, and you'd learn so much new stuff. Things you could never learn at Hell-Knows-Where. But if you don't want to be away from home—'

Dan scowled. 'I'm not a little kid, Mom. Can I learn to be a twain driver here?'

Joshua laughed and tousled his hair. 'You can be anything you want, kiddo. That's the point.'

Helen said to Sally, 'Also I need to see my father.'

Thomas nodded. 'Jack Green! Fast becoming another hero. A founder of the Children of Freedom movement, now an organizer of the Footprint Congress which has attracted delegates from thousands of inhabited Americas—'

73

'He's fast becoming a major embarrassment, is what he is,' Helen said sternly.

'This hanging around wasn't part of the deal,' Sally snapped at Joshua. 'Why didn't you tell me?'

Joshua shrugged. 'Well, you didn't wait to be consulted. Besides, how would you have reacted? Just like this, right?'

Sally picked up her pack. 'I'm out of here.' She disappeared with a pop of displaced air.

Thomas sighed. 'What a woman. I hope I have a chance to get her autograph. Come on, let's get you checked in.'

9

IN THE MORNING, Bill went off for 'a bit of an old explore on me own', as he put it. Joshua made sure he had a cell-phone so he could call for a ride back, if he got 'incapable'.

Bill had gone by the time Thomas showed up to give Joshua, Helen and Dan a lift to Dan's prospective school. This was in a different urban 'hub' called Downtown Seven, on the other side of this intricately designed city. So they climbed into Thomas's buggy once more, and set off across town.

The city had grown hugely since the last time Joshua had seen it. Valhalla, starting from a clean slate, was always intended to be more than just another city. It looked attractively different even in its basic layout, built on hexagonal plots that were spreading around the southern shore of the American Sea of this world, and cutting into the native forest. Many of the houses glittered with solar paint, but others had grass and other plants growing thick on their roofs, a natural thatch.

And wherever the view opened up to the north, Joshua glimpsed the sea, a flat, silver horizon. The coastline lay at about the same latitude as Datum Chicago. At the shore the city took on an older feel to Joshua's eyes, an echo of an antique America, a maritime past. There was a respectable port now, mostly wooden buildings, warehouses and boat yards, even what looked like a fishermen's chapel – he supposed the chapel would already have its memorial stones to those lost in this version of the American Sea, stones without graves, stones with no bones beneath. Further out there were wharves and jetties and moles. On the sea itself there were ships, grey shadows, some mechanically driven, mostly coal-burning probably, but many were sailing ships, like reconstructions, museum pieces.

Sailors were working this new ocean, fishing, trapping. They hunted tremendous reptilian swimmers, something like plesiosaurs, and adorned their boats with their giant jaws and vertebrae. Like the whalers of the eighteenth and nineteenth centuries back on the Datum, these seafarers were studying their worlds with an intensity that outshone the more scientific explorers, and were linking together the scattered, growing communities around the shores of these stepwise American oceans. They weren't whalers, for there were no whales here, but Joshua thought he would try to make time to explore all this with Dan, and they could talk about *Moby Dick*.

And whenever they glimpsed the city's landward edge the party saw something much stranger, in its mundane way. The outer suburbs, thick with factories and forges, just ended, terminating in cut-back forest, or partially drained swamp and marsh. There wasn't a field anywhere, no cattle grazing, not a blade of cultivated grass outside the city boundary. This was a city without a hinterland of farmers.

Joshua knew the theory of Valhalla. It was part of this generation's response to the challenge of the endless spaces of the Long Earth. On Step Day, mankind (or most of it, those unlike Sally and her family who had known it all already) had begun to spread out across an extended Earth that had a diameter of eight thousand miles and a surface area that made a Dyson sphere look like a ping-pong ball. *How* they lived out there depended on preference, education and instinct. Some dashed back and forth between the Datum and the Low Earths, looking for a little more room, a way to make a little more money. Some, like Helen's family the Greens, had gone trekking out into the stepwise wilderness and had begun to build new communities: the story of colonial-era America, rerun across an infinite frontier. And some just wandered off, helping themselves to the inexhaustible riches of the Long Earth: Thomas's combers.

All of which was fine, until the day you needed root-canal dentistry. Or your e-book reader broke down. Or you worried whether your kids were ever going to learn anything more than how to plough a field or trap a rabbit. Or you got sick of the mosquitoes. Or, damn it, you just wanted to go *shopping*. Some people drifted back to the Datum, or the crowded Low Earths.

Valhalla was another response: a brand new city growing out in the High Meggers, the remote Long Earth, but deriving from Long Earth lifestyles: that is, supported by combers, not farmers. There had been precursors in human history, across Datum Earth. Given time and a rich environment, hunter-gatherer populations could achieve huge feats, and develop complex societies. At Watson Brake, Louisiana, five thousand years in the past, nomadic Native American hunter-gatherers had constructed major earthwork complexes. Valhalla had just taken this to a new, modern, more consciously designed level.

As it happened, the theory of the city was the first topic Jacques Montecute, the school's headmaster, chose to talk about when he brought Dan and his family into his office for an introductory chat.

'The central ethos of Valhalla is balance,' Montecute said.

Aged about thirty, slender, slightly severe, he had an accent that Joshua might have pegged as French, but with a naggingly familiar overlay. His name rang a bell too. *Montecute . . .*

There was one other child here, aside from Dan, a dark, unsmiling girl of about fifteen, called Roberta Golding.

'Most of our adult citizens *chose* to leave the old world, to leave the old ways behind. They want some of what a city can give, but they didn't come out into the Long Earth to break their backs farming, or to live in some slum suburb, in order to serve that city's needs. But here we are, maintaining city life without all that.' He smiled encouragingly at Dan. 'Can you see how we make a living, without farmers to grow our food for us?'

Dan shrugged his slim shoulders. 'Maybe you're all robbers.'

Helen sighed.

Roberta Golding spoke for the first time since being introduced. 'Valhalla is a city supported by combers. Hunter-gatherers. The logic is elementary. Intensive farming can support orders of magnitude more people per acre than hunting and gathering. On a single world a comber community, even if natural resources are rich, would necessarily be spread out, diffuse; the concentration of population needed to sustain a city would be impossible. Here, it is sufficient for the combers to be spread out, not geographically, but over many stepwise Earths – over a hundred parallel Valhallas, left wild for the hunting.' She made a sandwich of her hands, pressing. 'The city is the product of a layer of worlds, each lightly harvested, rather than the product of a single intensively farmed world. This is *intensive gathering*: a uniquely post-stepping urban solution.'

Joshua thought the kid spoke like a textbook.

'You've been reading up,' said Helen, as if accusing her of cheating.

'Very good, Roberta,' said Montecute. 'I mean, it also helps that we live in such a rich location, geographically, by the shore of a fecund sea . . .'

Joshua snapped his fingers. 'Happy Landings. That's it. You're from Happy Landings. Both of you, right? You, Mr Montecute, I recognize your accent – and your name. I may have met your grandmother once.'

He looked a little uncomfortable, but he smiled. 'Kitty? Actually my great-grandmother. She always remembered running into you, Mr Valienté, all those years ago. Yes, I'm from Happy Landings, as it's become known. As is Roberta.'

'Happy Landings,' Helen murmured to Joshua. 'Sally Linsay's name for it, right? Seems to have stuck. Happy Landings, where all the kids are super-smart. That's what they say.' She glanced uneasily at Dan, who seemed to be trying to tie his legs in a knot.

'It's good for you to have met a schoolmate already, Dan,' Joshua said.

'Actually I will not be here long,' Roberta said, politely

79

enough, but rather blankly. 'I've been invited to join the East Twenty Million mission.'

Joshua goggled. 'With the Chinese?'

Montecute smiled. 'And me,' he admitted. 'Though I'll be there more in a supervisory capacity. Roberta has won a sort of scholarship, a gesture of good faith between the Datum US government and the new regime in China . . . All of which is by the by. Well.' He stood up. 'Why don't I show you around the school, Dan? While Mom and Dad grab a coffee, perhaps – our canteen is just down the corridor.' Dan followed him, willingly enough. 'So what do you like at school? Logic, mathematics, debating, technical drawing?'

'Softball,' said Dan.

'Softball? Anything else?'

'Wood-chopping.'

'Really?'

'I've got a badge.'

Joshua and Helen glanced at each other, and at the silent, serious Roberta. Then: 'Coffee,' they said together, and followed Montecute and Dan out of the room.

10

To get to see her father Helen actually had to make an appointment, which infuriated her.

Jack Green, sixty years old, had an office in the modest building which served as Valhalla's city hall, courtroom, police headquarters and mayor's residence. He was working when Helen was shown into the room, sitting behind a desk laden with a laptop, a couple of cellphones, a stack of grainy-looking writing paper. A big TV screen was fixed to the wall. He barely glanced up at the daughter he hadn't seen since – when? The Christmas before last? Now he held up one finger, eyes fixed on the laptop, while she stood there, waiting.

At last he tapped a key with finality and sat back. 'There. Sent. Sorry about that, honey.' He got up, kissed her cheek, sat down again. 'Just a few last tweaks to the speech we've been writing for Ben.' Ben being Ben Keyes, she knew, mayor of Valhalla, for whom her father worked. 'Oh, which reminds me—' He picked up a remote and pressed it; the big wall screen lit up with an image of a podium, a couple of aides in suits, the Stars and Stripes and the ocean-blue flag of Valhalla hanging from poles side by side in the background. 'Ben's delivering the speech any moment now. Talk about last minute, right?

But as soon as he's done his words will be all over this world, of course, and will go all the way down to the Datum as fast as the outernet can carry them. Impressive, huh?'

Evidently Helen had picked a bad moment to call. 'Can I sit down, Dad?'

'Of course, of course.' He got up again, a little stiffly, and pushed over a chair for her. Like many of his generation, who had built Long Earth towns like Reboot from scratch, in his late middle age he was plagued by arthritis. 'How's Dan?'

'You got his age wrong on the last birthday card you sent.'

'Umm. Sorry about that. I hope he wasn't upset.'

She shrugged. 'He's used to it.'

He smiled, but he kept glancing at the screen.

She pushed down her irritation. 'I'm just dropping in, Dad. You know we're going on to the Datum. We're here to show Dan around the Free School. We're hoping to get him a place, if it suits him.'

'Good idea,' Jack said firmly. 'That's one point of Valhalla, of cities like this, to found good schools and incubate free, open and educated minds. Essential in any democracy.'

'Dad! Less of the lectures.'

'Sorry, sorry. It's just my way, honey. And I'm sorry to be distracted. But the situation is urgent. It's not just the increasingly repressive taxation. There's a vicious undercurrent that seeps out of the Humanity First douche-bags who are paying for Cowley's re-election campaign, no matter how inclusive he pretends to be. It's worse than racism. In their language we steppers are a lesser *species*, we're malevolent, moral-free mutants ... We have to stand up for ourselves. And now we're doing it. Some of the commentators are already saying that Keyes's speech today will be our Declaration of Independence moment, before they've even heard the text. Think of that!'

'And you just have to be involved, don't you?'

'Well, what else should I be doing?'

'You were just the same at Reboot. Distracting yourself from your own life by ordering other people around, right?'

'What's this, are you channelling your sister?'

Katie, a few years older than Helen, married, had stayed in Reboot, and generally disapproved of the rest of the family moving out. 'No, Dad. Look, I know you're not *old*.'

'I'm not about to become a minuteman, honey.'

'I know, I know ... I just think you need to stop running away.'

'Running from what?'

'It wasn't your fault Mom got ill.'

'Go on,' he said. 'What else wasn't my fault?'

'It also wasn't your fault Rod did what he did.'

'Your brother planted a nuke under Datum Madison, for God's sake.'

'No, he didn't. He was part of a dumb plot by resentful homealones, which— I'm sorry, Dad. It's just that I think you're working on all this stuff to, to—'

'To assuage some kind of Freudian guilt? My daughter the psychologist.' His tone turned harder now. 'Look, it's not about blame, or guilt. People do what they do. But that doesn't mean that, whatever your deeper hidden personal motives, you can't try to do something *good*.'

She pointed at the screen. 'Like your Mayor Keyes right now?'

He turned that way.

Ben Keyes walked up to the podium, a sheaf of pulpy locally manufactured paper in his hands. Aged maybe forty, he had media-star good looks, but he'd let his hair grow long, pioneer style, and he wore, not a suit, but a practical worker's coverall in a drab olive. When he began to speak Helen could barely make out his words over the clapping and hollering from an off-stage audience: 'People of Valhalla! This is an historic day in this world, in all the worlds of the Long Earth. Today, we have it in our power to begin the world over again . . .'

Her father grinned. 'Tom Paine! That was one of my lines.'

'. . . *certain unalienable Rights, that among these are Life, Liberty and the pursuit of Happiness . . . That whenever any form of government becomes destructive of these ends, it is the right of the people to alter or to abolish it . . .*'

'Ha!' Jack Green clapped his hands. 'And *that* is straight out of the Declaration of Independence. What a moment for an American government, to have its own founding principles thrown right back at it!'

Now the screen showed images of the crowd before Keyes, who were making sign-language gestures, just like the troll at the Gap, and chanting, '*I will not! I will not!*'

Helen had lost her father to the screen, to the speech, to the commentaries that would follow. Quietly she stood and crept out of the room. He didn't look round.

Helen knew nothing about revolutions. She couldn't imagine what might flow from this moment. She did wonder, however, about where the 'rights' of the trolls and other creatures who had to share the Long Earth with mankind might fit into all this.

Thomas Kyangu was waiting for her in the lobby, with sympathetic eyes. She guessed he knew enough about her complicated family now to understand how she was feeling.

'Come on,' he said. 'I'll stand you a Valhallan coffee.'

And, in a cosy coffee shop a couple of blocks away, Thomas told her something of his own story.

11

THOMAS KYANGU COULD remember precisely the day his life had turned. The day he had left the conventional world and become a professional comber – if that wasn't a contradiction in terms. It had been twenty years ago, just five years after Step Day itself, when the whole phenomenon was still startling and new. Thomas had been thirty years old.

He had borrowed his father's car, had driven out of Jigalong to a weathered wooden marker, and climbed out into the midday heat, Stepper box at his side. Apart from the dirt road back to Jigalong, and a fenced-off scrap of bloodstained land that marked the portal to stepwise roo farms, there was nothing here, even in the Datum. Nothing but the expanse of the Western Desert, vast, crushing, its flatness broken by a single, heavily eroded bluff of rock. Nothing anyhow in the eyes of the first Europeans to come here, who had barely been able even to see the people who already lived here. To them it was a *terra nullius*, an empty land, and that had become a legal principle which justified their land-grab.

But Thomas was a half-blood Martu. He had always been welcomed by his mother's people, even though her marriage, to a white man for love, had broken the Martu's strict marriage rules. And to Thomas's eyes, educated in the ways of his ancestors at least to a theoretical level, this land was rich. Complex. Ancient: you could feel the weight of deep time here. He knew how this at first glance barren land worked, how it supported its freight of life. He even knew how to survive, how to feed himself out here, if he had to.

And he knew of a secret out here, that was his alone.

He bent to look into a cave, cut into the side of the bluff by millennia of wind. It was hardly a cave at all, just a hollow half choked by dry drifting sand. But it was a site he had discovered for himself as a boy, visiting his grandparents at Jigalong, exploring alone in the bush: even then he'd been a solitary kid. And, so deep inside the cave you had to crouch to see, there was the Hunting Man, as he called it, a stick figure with some kind of spear chasing a huge, ill-defined creature, while spirals and starbursts spun around him. It was thousands of years old, he'd figured out, as you could tell by the patina over it.

And, as far as he knew, it had been discovered by nobody before his own boyish eyes had settled on it. Nobody found it later, either. He'd kept the secret of it ever since.

He'd always thought of the Hunting Man as a kind of friend. An invisible companion. A stable point in a life of whirling change.

Thomas had been a bright kid. Picked out of the local school and groomed for better things, he'd gone to college at Perth and even spent some time in America, before returning to Melbourne to become a whizz-kid games designer. He'd been black enough to serve as a poster boy for liberals, white enough that those around him had been able to treat him as one of their own.

87

Then he'd had his crisis of conscience, and he started to find out about the plight of the people he'd left behind, his mother's family. How a culture a staggering sixty thousand years old, a people free and self-sufficient a mere three centuries ago, had become the most dependent on the planet: marginalized, removed from their lands, shattered by unemployment and drug abuse, their culture broken up by forced evictions and 'white' education. How in his own grandmother's time her clan had been moved from their country to avoid the British Blue Streak missiles test-launched from Woomera.

Granted, all this hand-wringing had been brought on by Thomas's own beating-up by a bunch of thugs in Sydney who didn't like his kind in their city, even one in a suit and tie. But it was a real eye-opener even so.

Then he'd got married. Hannah was a trainee lawyer, another bright young thing, white, from a well-connected New South Wales family. They'd been hoping for a kid.

But then the cancer had taken her, and that had been that. She had been just twenty-three. Helen could sympathize with that part of his story, remembering the suddenness of the loss of her own mother.

After that Thomas's work seemed pointless. He'd gone back to Perth and worked for a progressive association there, promoting Aboriginal rights. And he'd taken the chance to study his mother's culture. He'd even become a 'native guide' for parties of earnest white tourists. His mother's family had sneered at that, but he'd learned a lot.

And then had come the Stepper box, and the opening up of the Long Earth. Another huge jolt to Thomas's personal universe, as to everybody else's. Many Aborigines, especially young men, had immediately grasped the potential of the technology, and stepped away in search of a better world than the Datum, and its bloody history.

Thomas himself had rarely stepped, in those early days, save for a couple of experiments. Why should he? After all the turnarounds in his life, Thomas no longer felt he knew who he was. He was a contradiction, neither white nor black, married but alone. What was he going to discover about himself out in all those other worlds that he couldn't find right here? Rather than travel forward, he kept on being drawn back, in fact, to the same point, the Hunting Man in the cave, the one stable locus in his life, like a nail hammered through his psyche.

But this time he had come back here with his Stepper. He had an experiment in mind.

He picked a direction at random, and turned the switch.

Australia West 1.

They were farming kangaroos here, as indeed they were in East 1: he saw heaps of carcasses, tethered horses, a stack of bronze-based rifles heaped up like a tepee. A couple of ranchers sat on a log. When they saw Thomas they raised plastic bottles of beer to him. He waved back.

Roo farming was becoming commonplace, even in the Datum. Kangaroos were efficient as food animals. Pound for pound a roo needed a third the plant material a sheep did, a sixth the water, and produced almost no methane; roo farts were parsimonious. Thomas didn't object for any rational reasons. It just didn't *feel* right. Anyhow this new world was an annexe to the old, and nothing to do with him.

He stepped away, to West 2. And 3. And 4. Each step was a wrench to the stomach, and he needed time to recover.

It took him two hours to get to West 10, where he stopped. He sat on an eroded shelf at the edge of the rocky outcrop, which appeared unchanged from the 'original' in the Datum. He looked around, taking his time, absorbing the new world.

And off in the distance he saw movement. A herd of some huge, slow-moving, rather lumbering creatures, seen in silhouette against a pale blue sky. Walking on all fours, they looked like rhinos to his untutored eye. Presumably they were some marsupial equivalent, perhaps hunted by a local version of a lion. There were kangaroos here too, standing up, plucking at the lowest leaves of some tree, but these were big animals, bigger than any roo in the Datum, big and muscular. And there, scampering in the distance, a thing like a dinosaur, a raptor, that was probably a flightless bird. The world was intensely silent, save for the distant bellow of one giant herbivore or another.

He drank water from a plastic bottle. Some of the nearer worlds had been visited by hunters unable to resist the lure of going after the native megafauna, but here, ten steps out, there was no sign of humanity, not so much as a footprint.

And it was a different sort of world, without humans. Naively you'd think that one copy of the Western Desert was going to be much the same as any other. Not so. This country was always going to be arid, but Thomas could see at a glance that it was greener than he was used to, with patches of tough-looking grass, scrubby trees. On the Datum his mother's people had shaped the land with fire for sixty thousand years; this was a land without Europeans, but without the Martu and their ancestors too.

Thomas wasn't here for the flora and fauna, however.

When he felt well enough to stand he walked around the bluff to the cave – it was here just as in the Datum – and knelt down, the Stepper box awkward at his waist. He had to shield his eyes against the light of a descending sun to see inside.

And there it was, in the cave. Somehow he had known it would be. Not *his* Hunting Man, not exactly. Another human figure chasing another crudely sketched animal. Around it, a different array of spirals and starbursts and hatchings and zigzags. And when he touched the drawing, cautiously, he could feel the patina that covered it. It was every bit as ancient as the one in the Datum. Put there by some scrawny guy who had figured out how to step, all by himself, millennia ago.

He sat with his back to the rock. He would have laughed, save he didn't want to disrespect the silence, or indeed draw the attention of any nearby marsupial lions. Of course there must have been Aboriginal steppers. Where would an ability to step have been of more use than in the arid heart of Australia? If his ancestors *had* been able to exploit a sheaf of worlds, even just in emergencies, the resources available to them would have been multiplied hugely. And they had had sixty thousand years to discover how.

But even so, surely not in such numbers as today. Maybe this was a new Dreamtime, he thought, a replay of the age when the Ancestors had moved across an empty landscape, and in doing so had brought the land itself into being. It was the turn of his generation to become the new Ancestors, to begin a new Dreamtime that might encompass all of the Long Earth.

And this time they would shape a landscape no white colonist could ever appropriate.

So here was Thomas, with a cellphone in his pocket, sitting by a rock, alone in this world.

He could go back and report his bit of archaeology, at last.

Or maybe it was his own time to go walkabout. He could strip down to his boxers, just dump everything, and wander off . . .

Living off the endlessly generous land, he became a comber – this was before the word itself, derived from 'beachcomber', had become common currency. In due course he would start to hear legends of Joshua Valienté and other super-steppers, legends that were spreading across the Long Earth, and he would begin to take a more academic view of those who shared his new lifestyle . . . And then he met Joshua himself, in the silence of a very distant America.

'But all that lay in the future,' he told Helen now. 'As I remember it, I just patted the Hunting Man – Hunting Man West 10 – and straightened up, and touched my Stepper, and I was gone for good.'

She smiled. 'The Long Earth has given us all stories, I guess.'

'Too right. So what about yours? Tell me about this place Reboot. Another coffee?'

12

THEY SPENT THREE more weeks in Valhalla, trying to get Dan used to the place, and to the idea of coming here to school – even though headmaster Jacques Montecute and the taciturn Roberta had in the meantime left for the Datum, to join the Chinese expedition. Helen had plenty of time to sample the local cuisine, including lots more coffee – enough to establish that, whatever Valhalla was good at, coffee wasn't it.

But that was remedied once they boarded the *Gold Dust*. In the first twenty-four hours Helen spent most of her time relaxing, sitting in the family's saloon, sipping the finest coffee she'd drunk since – well, since the last time her father had taken her to a Datum Madison mom-and-pop local coffee shop aged about twelve, before they left the old world behind for good.

That was the *Gold Dust* for you. It was like the best hotel in all the worlds, she thought, uprooted and drifting in the sky, an eight-hundred-foot-long envelope from which hung a gondola of polished High-Megger hardwood, like one vast piece of furniture. Helen had felt embarrassed just to climb aboard. Even the gangplank was carpeted, and you could have lost their whole Hell-Knows-Where house in the reception hall.

Of course they were honoured guests, Joshua, Dan, Helen, even Bill Chambers – and Sally Linsay, who Helen noticed wasn't too high-minded to hitch a ride aboard this flying palace. Honoured because of Joshua, of course, the hero explorer. If he wished, *the* Joshua Valienté could dine out on his legend, but he hardly ever did. Full of contradictions, her Joshua. But when he got offered such treats as this ride in the *Gold Dust*, he'd learned not to turn them away – that was how Helen had trained him anyhow.

Dan was in his element, of course. He'd wanted to be a twain driver since he could walk, and would run after even the scrubby little local ships that drifted over Hell-Knows-Where. Helen had thought his eyes would pop out when they walked aboard the *Gold Dust*.

But there was some concern for him, at the beginning. This was Dan's first long-distance haul. Helen was not a natural stepper, while Joshua was the world's *model* natural stepper. Just as his colouring was mixed – Dan had his father's dark hair but his mother's paler complexion – as a stepper Dan was somewhere in between his parents. And in his genetic background he did have a phobic uncle, Helen's brother Rod, who couldn't step at all. The medicinal treatments for controlling the symptoms of stepping nausea were advanced now, so that almost everybody could withstand even a high-speed journey like this – almost all, but not quite all. If Dan had shown any distress, it would have been the end of the journey for his parents (well, for Helen anyhow; she had no doubt Joshua would have gone on with Sally) – and the end of a dream for Dan. Joshua and Helen were both privately relieved when the ship's surgeon, who had been hovering over the passengers as the twain set off, gave them a discreet thumbs-up.

After that the crew made a huge fuss of Dan. At Helen's insistence he was to be accompanied at all times by either one of his parents or a junior crewman, appointed by the Captain. The crewman told Dan his name was Bosun Higgs, and Helen didn't believe that for a *second*. But apart from that the crew gave Dan the run of the ship, from the ladders and gantries inside the envelope itself with its huge sacs of helium, to the gondola's cargo hold and engine room, and the staterooms and restaurant cum ballroom – even the wheelhouse, a huge transparent-walled blister at the prow, where you could watch the great ships rising from world after world to join the fleet as it ploughed East towards the Datum, with views of the American Sea and its forest-coated fringe shivering by, a new world with every heartbeat. An incredible, thrilling sight, even to a sedentary type like Helen.

On the second evening of the voyage the grown-ups had a treat, when they dined at the Captain's table. What else would you expect, for the Valienté family? The restaurant was at the prow, just beneath the wheelhouse itself. Helen couldn't believe how ornate the place was, with white wooden filigree work everywhere, and gilt mammoth tusks and oversized acorns hanging in the corners, and what looked like original oil paintings of various Long Earth scenes hanging on the walls, and arm-chairs and carpets soft as puppy fur – even a chandelier hanging over the table. All of which was a pleasant dis-traction from their fellow diners, who were generally the obnoxiously rich: Long Earth traders splashing the profits, or tourists from the Datum on the 'cruise of a

95

lifetime', who mistook Helen and Joshua for staff more than once.

The view outside was the main attraction. From the Captain's table right up by the forward window you could see the worlds flash by below, and the gleaming hulls of the companion ships of the fleet, dozens of them hanging like Chinese lanterns under the changing sky. They had already travelled a long way – at its top speed of a step a second, the twain could cover the best part of ninety thousand worlds a day – but they would be slower than that on average, and it would take some weeks to reach the Datum. As the evening gathered in, most of the landscapes that washed beneath the ship's prow were dark, largely uninhabited – though one sparkled with town lights, and the Captain told them that this was Amerika, the new Dutch nation, one whole copy of the footprint of the United States given by the federal government. The Long Earth hadn't been much use to the Dutch at first, since on all the stepwise worlds the landscapes they had spent centuries carefully preserving from the sea were still drowned . . .

The climax of the show – the Captain had timed the meal so they could witness the specific moment, just as the dessert trolley reached their table, and just as the setting sun touched the horizon – came when the great American Sea, the inland ocean whose footprint had been their constant companion since they left Valhalla, melted away, first crumbling into scattered lakes, then submitting to a forest cover that stretched as far as the eye could see, dark green-black in the light of the setting sun. Helen's heart ached a bit when they lost contact with their sea, or at least its footprint.

But as the light faded further they began to see what had taken its place, below the prow: a river, wide and placid, a shining ribbon cutting across the land. It was the Mississippi, or a remote cousin of that great river on the Datum, a constant in most Americas – indeed Hell-Knows-Where stood on the banks of one stepwise copy. The river would be an unfailing companion for the rest of the trip.

They had a hell of a time getting Dan to sleep after that. Helen blamed the dessert: too much chocolate. Joshua, meanwhile, went off to find Bill, who'd spent his own raucous night with the crew.

13

THE GOOD PEOPLE of Four Waters City, deep in a step-wise Idaho, seemed happy to see the USS *Benjamin Franklin* appear in the skies above their town. They quickly threw a kind of mass lunch for the dirigible's entire fifty-person crew; the beef was so flavoursome and so relished that the ghost of the steer was probably look-ing down approvingly, Maggie thought.

But afterwards the conversation soon grew tricky, to say the least.

Captain Maggie Kauffman strolled along the main, indeed the only, drag of Four Waters City. Somewhere in the region of a hundred and fifty thousand steps from the Datum, set in a typical Corn Belt farming world, the place was neatly laid out and was bustling with people. It looked at first glance like Dodge City without the gunplay, but with, of course, the inevitable mobile communications tower courtesy of the Black Corporation. Maggie's local guide, Mayor Jacqueline Robinson, pointed out with some pride various other civic improvements, including a reasonable hospital which the town shared with similar cities in neighbouring stepwise worlds.

But the mayor, a tough-looking woman of about fifty, was oddly tense, nervous. Maggie wondered if that was because of the small stands of cannabis she saw flourishing in one or two gardens, along with a few other exotic blooms, out in open view, by the street.

When Mayor Robinson finally noticed Maggie looking, she said, 'Actually, that's mostly just hemp. Blameless. Gives a good fabric for working clothes. My maternal family were originally Czech. My grandfather told me that one day the cops raided what was eventually to have been his new shirt . . .'

Maggie let that stand. She knew when to let silence do the questioning. Then she said, '*Mostly*?'

Robinson admitted, 'Look, as for the other usage – the kids don't seem interested, and the opinion of the town meeting, in *this* town, is that for mature people it's OK, but keep the kids off it. Also, I have to tell you, there's some local stuff – an exotic flower in the woods to the west, native to this world apparently. Wow, *that* blows your head off. Even a walk in the woods – well.' She was talking too quickly; eventually she ran down, and shrugged. 'No offence to you, Captain, seeing as you are, in theory at least, a representative of the government. We have our own set of values here. I mean, we regard ourselves as American, bound by the Constitution. But we don't believe in any remote authority telling us what we should or should not be doing, or thinking for that matter.'

Maggie said, 'I'm a serving Navy officer. I'm not a cop; in fact, traditionally the Navy has specific directives against carrying out internal policing functions. Mayor Robinson, I'm not here to criticize or judge. On the other hand, we in the dirigible fleet are here to offer help. As Captain, I do have a lot of discretion in how I interpret my orders.' She wasn't sure how convincing that was. The mayor still betrayed that odd nervousness. 'Look – is there something else you want to tell me?'

Suddenly the mayor looked as if she'd been caught out doing something bad. 'What would you do? I mean, about something serious.'

Maggie repeated deliberately, 'I'm not a cop. Maybe we can help.'

Robinson still looked uncertain. But with a nervous defiance she said at last, 'There has been . . . a crime. In fact *two* crimes. We're not sure how to handle the situation.'

'Yes?'

'A child was harmed. Drugs. OK – it was drugs. And a murder.'

Maggie felt her stomach turn. But she had thought that garbled defence of the local drug culture had been a little forced.

'Look,' Robinson said, 'I don't want to talk any more out here. We'd better go into my office.'

14

THE CREW OF the USS *Benjamin Franklin* did not have a specifically military mission, even though the dirigible was a Navy vessel.

The *Franklin*'s voyage, a long jaunt across the Long Earth, was strictly speaking an exercise in maintaining the integrity of the United States Aegis, the concept of which was still prized in Datum Washington, DC, if nowhere else. Oh, the voyage did have scientific purposes. Every stepwise world was to be logged, every Joker recorded. The crew was to sample novel life forms, geological formations and climatic conditions – and was specifically tasked to search for sapience wherever it could be found. So, a ship fit for such a mission, the *Benjamin Franklin* was no cargo scow: it was an extremely modern aircraft, bristling with scientific sensors – as well as weapons.

But the true reason for the voyage of the *Benjamin Franklin* was to travel the stepwise Earths within the footprint of the United States of America and to show the flag to as many of the new colonies out there as it could locate – or indeed discover; many of them had not registered their existence with any Datum authority. It was the job of the *Franklin* to find, and count, Americans, and to remind them that they *were* Americans.

The operation had been launched three weeks before, on an April day in Richmond, Virginia, Datum Earth. Maggie Kauffman had stood there in the open, in a downtown park, with her officers and crew, Executive Officer Nathan Boss and ship's chief surgeon Joe Mackenzie at her side, before an empty stage with an unoccupied podium, a big Stars and Stripes dangling limply to either side, and a huge banner draped above: UNITY IS STRENGTH. This downtown park wasn't far from the north bank of the James, and, this being Datum Earth, high-rise buildings had loomed out of the smog, some obviously abandoned, their windows boarded up like poked-in eyes.

The hundreds of Navy personnel drawn up here were separated by a barrier from members of the public, lured in from across the Datum city and even neighbouring worlds for the show. And it was quite a show, even if you weren't too impressed by rows of Navy grunts standing on their hind legs. The twains themselves were a staggering sight, you had to admit that, six brand new state-of-the-art military-specification airships hanging in the sky, proudly constructed by a consortium of United Technologies, General Electric, the Long Earth Trading Company and the Black Corporation: *Shenandoah. Los Angeles. Akron. Macon. Abraham Lincoln.* And *Benjamin Franklin*, thirty-eight-year-old Maggie's own command. Proud old names on proud new vessels, and the mightiest in the fleet save only for the experimental USS *Neil Armstrong*, already dispatched on its own exploratory mission into the very remote stepwise West.

At last there had been a stir by the podium, and here came President Cowley, a heavy-set man visibly sweating in his dark suit, and with lustrous hair sprayed so thick it was like a plastic sculpture sitting on his head. He was flanked by security guys in regulation black suits and glasses.

On stage he was greeted by Admiral Hiram Davidson, USN. Based in Camp Smith, Hawaii, Davidson controlled the newly formulated Long Earth military command, USLONGCOM. He in turn was shadowed by an aide, Captain Edward Cutler, a straight-as-a-die bureaucrat if ever Maggie had met one, and he was welcome to the desk he commanded as far as she was concerned.

The famous, or notorious, Douglas Black was present in person too, one of a group of pols and other dignitaries already lined up on the stage to shake Cowley's hand. Black was surprisingly short in person, Maggie thought, staring curiously. In his seventies, kind of wizened, bald, wrinkled, he looked like Gollum in sunglasses. Of course it was Black who had donated the basic technology behind these military twains, the same technology that under-pinned all stepping twains; he had a right to be here if anybody had. And whether or not he was handing over money to Cowley's re-election campaign (he was prob-ably funding *both* sides and a gaggle of independent candidates, Maggie's cynical side suspected), his presence was going to make this telegenic event even more so for Cowley.

As the handshakes and backslaps proceeded on the stage, a chopper clattered overhead, a Little Bird, a sign of protection and menace. This mission and the launch event had been planned for some time, but in response to the Valhalla Declaration the military symbolism had been beefed up.

But as Cowley approached the podium, despite all the hoop-la and the obvious politicking, Maggie Kauffman felt a visceral thrill to be standing here in front of the President himself.

Cowley started to speak, his voice amplified, his face projected on a screen behind him. After some good-old-boy introductory stuff, he cut to the chase. 'On Step Day it was as if a tremendous door opened in the wall of the world, to reveal a beguiling new landscape. And what were people going to do with that? Why, some of them were just going to walk away – those who believed that a better life waited for them out there, rather than on this fine green world God gave to us, which we must now call the Datum.

'And off they went! Every family that ever felt dis-possessed, every gang or cult or faction that felt it could do better someplace else – the restless, the antisocial, the just plain curious – all of them went stepping off down the trek trails into the blue yonder. I can't deny the appeal of it. It was a door that couldn't be locked, not ever again. History will show that we lost fully a fifth of mankind from the Datum Earth, the true Earth, in the first few years after Step Day.

'And we all know the consequences of *that*.' He waved a hand at the mute buildings around the park, the boarded-up high-rises, and there was a growl of agreement from sections of the crowd. 'We are poorer, we who remained in our homes to care for our families, to do our duty. We are poorer, we who were left behind. Not only that, suddenly our secure world was opened up to threats – new kinds of threats, pan-dimensional threats we never faced the like of before.'

The screen behind him filled up with images, a

kaleidoscope of horrors, from notorious would-be assassins, terrorists, rapists, child abductors and murderers who'd quickly learned to exploit the destructive potential of stepping, to a gaggle of grubby High Meggers bandits who looked as though they'd stepped out of a spaghetti western, to some of the existential weirdness that had come down the turnpike from the strange new worlds: distorted-looking humanoids wearing mockeries of human clothing – and Mary, the gentle-eyed yet murderous troll, a picture that brought boos from the crowd.

'That is why I, as your commander in chief, have assembled a new force from across our fine armed services to deal with these new situations. It is called USLONGCOM, as an analogy with our nation's other geographical commands. Many of its members are gathered here today, in the historic heart of Richmond, Virginia. And many thousands more are in training at sites around the world, and indeed in the nearby stepwise neighbourhood. Let's show them our appreciation.'

He led applause, which rippled around the watching crowd.

'And today,' Cowley boomed on, 'I announce their first significant mission: Operation Prodigal Son.' More scattered applause, a little puzzled. 'I'm sure the name I chose is self-explanatory. This is a mission, not to oppose any foe, but to reach out to our own lost children. A demonstration not of military power but of the firm hand of strong parenting. In these six fine new aircraft, companies of our young warriors will set out across the worlds, heading West – and showing their strength to the "colonies",' and he emphasized the quotes with crooks of his fingers.

There were a few whoops at that, and cries of 'Kick butt!' and 'Turn Valhalla into a twain park!'

Cowley held up his hands. 'Let me emphasize again. This is *not* a punitive mission. Indeed, my administration has nothing but support for those entrepreneurs who are busily developing the economies of the so-called Low Earths, as contributions to the overall national good. Our argument is not with them. Our argument is with those who live further out, some living entirely unproductive and feckless lives – who are prepared to accept the protection of life in the American Aegis, and yet contribute nothing to its upkeep.' More applause and whoops.

Now Cowley held up a bit of paper. 'I have here their so-called "Declaration of Independence". Nothing but a mockery of this nation's finest hour.' Theatrically he ripped up the paper, to more cheers. 'This operation will reach a climax when its overall commander, Admiral Davidson here, stands on the steps of the city hall at the rebel enclave of Valhalla, and welcomes those particular prodigals back into the bosom of the national family. America has scattered across the worlds. Now is the time to gather those lost flocks back together again. Time to pick up the pieces, and grow strong again, in unity,' and he gestured up at the slogan over his head.

Now he turned to the troops ranked before him. 'And to fulfil this holy mission, I turn to these fine young people. Isaiah six, verse eight: *Also I heard the voice of the Lord, saying, Whom shall I send, and who will go for us? Then said I, Here am I; send me.* Who shall I send on Operation Prodigal Son? Who will go for us?'

They had been coached to respond: 'I'll go. Send me! Send me!' The discipline of the ranks softened a little, as the sailors and marines whooped and yelled.

Beside Maggie, Joe Mackenzie grunted in grudging appreciation. 'Cowley may be a slimeball, but he is still the President.'

'And he's supple, Doc,' Maggie murmured. 'Here he is pleasing one constituency by appearing to take on the colonists, while appeasing the colonists by presenting our mission as a kind of embrace.'

Mac glanced up at the heavily armed twains. 'Some embrace. That isn't Santa's sleigh up there. We'll be lucky if we don't provoke some kind of shooting war.'

'It won't come to that.'

'Well, however it turns out you can't beat being given a mission to fulfil.'

'Ain't that the truth,' said Maggie.

Of course, once they were actually out in the Long Earth, they had encountered much wariness about their mission.

Many Long Earth pioneers, at least the first generation, had left the Datum precisely *because* they had been intensely suspicious of central government, deriving from a country in which from its founding that sentiment had always run deep. What could the Datum government offer a far-stepwise colony now? It could threaten to tax, but provided damn few services – and over the years had withdrawn what little it had once offered. Protection? The major problem with that argument was that there was no detectable adversary, no bad guys to spy on or shadow, no bogeymen to point to as hostiles. China was still reeling from its own post-Step Day revolution. The parallel Europes were filling up with peaceful farmers. A new generation of Africans were reclaiming their ravaged continent, or stepwise copies of it. And so on. There was no threat to counter.

However weak the case, Maggie Kauffman knew she was expected to diplomatically remind these estranged colonial sheep that they were part of a bigger flock, because back in DC there was a profound sense that, under the American Aegis, this newly extended country was fragmenting – and *that*, it was instinctively felt, couldn't be allowed. That had been true even before the provocative 'Declaration of Independence' that had come out of Valhalla.

All that was for the future. Right now Maggie found the present hard enough to manage: a horrible ethical and legal knot for her raw crew to untangle, in a ship still being shaken down, that they'd encountered just weeks after Cowley's send-off.

15

THE OFFICE OF the mayor of Four Waters City was pre-dictable pioneering architecture, though a veritable mansion compared with anything that Daniel Boone would have known, Maggie thought. However, he *would* have recognized and approved of the drying pelts, the jars of pickles in the corner, the miscellaneous shovels and other gardening implements – all the detritus of a pioneering life busily being lived. And there was a base-ment, which suggested that the mayor and her family were thoughtful people, and perhaps mildly paranoid (or sensibly cautious): it was impossible for an intruder to step into an underground room—

'The child,' Robinson blurted. 'Let's get to it, Captain.'

'Fine.' Maggie sat down.

'Her name is Angela Hartmann. It happened a week ago. She was found by her family, stoned out of her mind . . . Sorry. She wouldn't wake up, she was in a kind of coma, took days to come out of it. We know who did it, who gave her the drugs and got high with her. And we know who committed the murder.'

What murder? 'Where are these people now?'

The mayor shrugged. 'It never dawned on us before to build a jail. We were building a stone ice house for the winter. We used that. It's pretty well made. I don't think anyone could possibly get out of it, it's real big and heavy.'

'And this is where you put the guy who gave the kid the drugs?'

Robinson glanced at her. 'I'm sorry. You've misunderstood, I've not been clear, I kind of gabble stuff out when I'm nervous. *That* bastard isn't in the ice house. That bastard's in the mortuary. Such as it is. The guy we're keeping in the ice house – he was the father of the little girl.'

'Ah. So the father found the pusher—'

'And killed him.'

'OK.' Maggie began to see it. 'Two crimes: the drugs, the murder.'

'Nobody's denying any of this. But as a result of all this, we are – riven. About how to handle this. What to do with the father.'

Why me? Maggie thought to herself. She was supposed to be cheerfully showing the flag, and maintaining goodwill. Right now Nathan Boss, her XO, was out bartering for fresh vegetables. And now this. *Well, why not me? This is what I came out here for.* 'I take it you haven't tried to contact the Datum authorities.'

Robinson flushed. 'To tell you the truth, we were scared. We never even told the Datum that we were here. We thought it wasn't their business, after all.'

'And there's no local justice system, in the stepwise neighbourhood?'

She shook her head.

Maggie sat in silence, letting the moment extend. 'Very well. Here's what you're going to do. First of all, you are going to get your act together and make it clear to the

Datum government that you *are* here. We'll help you with that, and such details as ratifying property claims. Then you have a man in custody without trial, or any due process, and we need to sort that out. Look, to repeat: I'm not here with any mandate to police you. But we can help. And before all that, you're going to let my ship's doctor have a good look at the girl.'

A few hours later Joe Mackenzie came out of the Hartmann house. Mac was in his fifties, grizzled, beaten up by a long career in emergency and battlefield medicine. He was old for a field posting, in fact; Maggie had helped him bend the regulations to have him at her side on this mission. This bright afternoon, the doctor's expression was as dark as twilight.

'You know, Maggie, sometimes there are no words . . . If I were to say that it could have been worse, you need to understand that even so I would like to spend some time alone in a room with the gentleman concerned and a baseball bat, knowing with surgical precision the right spots to hit—'

It was at times like this that Maggie was glad she'd stuck to her career, never married, never had kids of her own, left the glorious burden of caring for children to her siblings, cousins, friends; she was happy to be an aunt, honorary or otherwise. 'It's OK, Mac.'

'Well, no, it isn't OK, not for that little girl, and may never be again. I'd prefer her to be sent to a Datum hospital for a full examination. At the least I want to take her up on to the ship for observation for a while.'

Maggie nodded. 'Let's go meet the leaders of this joint.'

They met in the mayor's office. At Maggie's side were

111

Mac and Nathan Boss. Maggie had invited Robinson herself, and a few chosen citizens from the town meeting whom the mayor reckoned to be well-balanced and sensible, at least by the standards of this community, to consider the verdict.

As they sat down, everybody looked to the Captain – looked to her as a saviour, she realized. Maggie cleared her throat. Time to step up to the plate, she thought.

'For the record – and we are being recorded – this session is nothing more than a panel of inquiry. Judicial processes can follow as necessary. I have no policing role here. But I have taken it upon myself, at the request of the mayor of the town, to ascertain fairly all the facts of the matter.

'I'll summarize what I've been told; the facts are apparently not being denied. A week ago Roderick Bacon plied with drugs Angela Hartmann, a girl of nine years old, the daughter of Raymond Hartmann and Daphne Hartmann. Hearing the girl cry out her father, Ray Hartmann, rushed to her room and saw Bacon with her. The girl was vomiting, fitting. Hartmann pulled the man away, handed the girl to her mother, and then beat Bacon, dragged him out of the house, and set about him again, causing, after a minute or two, his death. The neighbours, alerted by the screams, told us that Bacon was pleading for his life, saying that "a lurid angel" made him do it, made him want to give this "pure child" the gift of his own "inner light" . . . You get the picture.

'In the absence of a lawyer I've had my XO, Commander Nathan Boss, take a personal statement from Hartmann about the events of that night, and also a statement by Bacon's wife. And according to the wife, before the crime Bacon had been out processing a harvest of the apparently psychoactive flowers endemic in the woods hereabouts. He ran a side business, of dubious legality, selling the stuff in stepwise worlds . . .'

Maggie stopped there. She wished she'd had better training for something like this. She looked around at the others in the room. 'For the record the child will be cared for overnight on the *Benjamin Franklin*, under the care of Dr Mackenzie. I'll invite the girl's mother to spend the night with her daughter; I'll send a crewman down to escort her up to the ship. Meanwhile – well, Bacon is dead, and Ray Hartmann is in custody.

'I think I understand the feelings of all involved in this. I'm no lawyer, I'm no judge, but I can give you my personal assessment. I have to say that Bacon was guilty, in any reasonable sense of the word. He knowingly exposed himself to narcotics, these flowers from the woods; my view is he's responsible for his behaviour thereafter. As for Hartmann, murder is murder. Yet I find myself loath to condemn the actions of an overwrought husband and father.

'So, what next? We'll file a report, and in the end the Datum cops will come out here, go through this fully, refer it to the judicial system – but that could take years; the Aegis is a big place, and tough to police. In the meantime you have Ray Hartmann stuck in that ice house. What to do with him? Well, frankly, you – *all of you* – must be judge and jury, prosecution and defence. We can leave you advice on due process. But it's up to you to run your own affairs, and I urge you to work out how to deal with this yourselves, within US law as best you understand it.' She eyed them one by one. 'This kind of autonomy was, after all, presumably what you wanted when you came out here.

'In the longer term, get together with your stepwise neighbours. I'm sure that together you could support the equivalent of a county court. I'm told that's becoming common in the colony worlds. Hire a lawyer or two – even a visiting circuit judge.' She ran out of steam. She stood up. 'That's all from me. The rest is up to you as a community. But for God's sake – Nathan, make sure the science boys take samples first, and make sure they do this when the wind isn't blowing into the town – *burn those flowers.* That's all, people, at least for today. I'll have the minutes of this session ready for all of you tomorrow.'

That evening, Maggie met Joe Mackenzie coming out of the ship's small medical bay.

'How is she?' she asked.

'Thank goodness I spent a semester in a children's hospital before I signed up.'

'Would coffee help?'

In Maggie's sea cabin, Mackenzie accepted the mug with gratitude, and after two blessed swigs, said, 'You know, the bastard got what was coming to him, in my personal view. But we are officers of the United States Navy. Even Wyatt Earp had to *look* as if he respected the law.'

'I'm hoping they'll work that out for themselves. Plenty of other communities out here have done.'

'But other communities don't have those damn flowers. And, to me, there was a definite feel of *hippie* about the place – you know what I mean? – the feeling that people aren't taking care of business. The counter-culture gone

114

bad scenario, too many people frazzled out of their brains.'

Maggie stared at the medic. 'Where did all that come from, Mac?'

'My grandfather left me a complete collection of the Whole Earth Catalog, a load of sixties and seventies counter-culture stuff ... I got quite interested in it, you know. Some of their values were laudable. But when it comes to the meat and potatoes – the secret to building a home in a place like this isn't about ideals and theory, and not about getting high. It's about hard work, alongside a sense of humour, and the goodwill of your neighbours, and putting your back into the future. But what you've got down there, I think, is the seed of tragedy. Along with Margarita Jha from biology, I analysed that lovely little flower that grows everywhere in their woods. Addictive and hallucinogenic like there's no tomorrow. Growing like a weed.'

'But, Mac – ye gods! Are we going to have to send a Drug Enforcement Agency unit to every settlement? They have to work it out for themselves.'

'That's how it got resolved on the Datum, in the end. After Step Day there was an explosion in the drug trade – with stepping pushers, there was no way to police it. In the inner cities, the cops pulled back and ... Well, let's say they let natural selection take its course.'

She looked at him as he said these words, his tone neutral. In the course of his career Mac had evidently seen a lot of stuff even she, in the military, had been shielded from. She said, 'Well, we're done with this particular can of worms. I think they'll let this guy Hartmann out. But it's been a salutary shock; they'll figure out ways to order their affairs better.'

'Sure. A neat wrap-up,' said Mac sourly. 'But the frightening part of it is that we've barely started this mission. What's waiting for us in the world next door?'

16

SIX DAYS OUT of Valhalla, somewhere around the Earth million mark, the *Gold Dust* made a stop at a clearing cut into yet another raw world's continent-sized forest. From the air the Valientés saw it as a neat little rectangular patch etched out of the green, an oddly touching island of humanity all but lost in this global forest.

But when you looked more closely you could see that it wasn't humans who'd created the clearing but a party of trolls, under the direction of a human, labouring even as the passengers looked down on them, those massive muscles working under their black pelts.

Bosun Higgs had proved to be a bright kid and surprisingly knowledgeable about the Long Earth – and the importance of the trolls. The big humanoids were ubiquitous, though not necessarily in large numbers. And they shaped the country they moved through, just on account of what they ate, pushed through, moved aside. In their ecological role they were like the big animals of Africa, maybe, like elephants or wildebeest. As a result, Helen learned now, the landscapes of the stepwise worlds, while quite unlike the Datum, were not quite *like* the Datum as it had once been before humanity either, not for a long time – because as mankind had risen up, the trolls had fled.

Well, the working trolls below looked content enough. But their overseer carried a whip, as Sally quickly pointed out. Joshua suggested he only used it to make a noise, to attract the trolls' attention.

'Yeah, right,' said Sally.

Helen knew it was hard to tell how happy a troll was. You did hear of distressing incidents, such as the notorious case of the troll called Mary at the Gap, the case everyone was talking about, even the snobs aboard the *Gold Dust*. But you saw trolls wherever people were, working like this. They seemed to enjoy it. Of course if you pushed them too hard they could simply step away.

Maybe they were just too useful to have a conscience about. Disturbing thought. And, as Sally said to Joshua, you wondered what *they* thought about humans.

The party dropped off supplies for the logging team, and brought up samples of exotic lichen in little plastic packs, lichen taken from very *old* trees. Old trees were rare on Datum Earth and were becoming so even on the heavily logged Low Earths. That was the nature of the trade across the 'Long Mississippi', as Helen had learned the pilots called this stepwise route. Raw materials flowed in towards the Datum – timber, foodstuffs, minerals – but bulk goods mostly came from the Corn Belt worlds further in, and only rare or precious items were worth bringing in from beyond the half-million-step mark, such as unique old-tree lichens and other exotic flora and fauna. Indeed, Joshua suggested as they watched this trade proceed, their own community ought to think about exporting Hell-Knows-Where maple liquor. In exchange the Datum shipped out low-mass but high-tech goods, from medical kit to electrical generators, to coils of fibre-optic cable so the colonists could establish decent communication networks in their new worlds. It was the kind of trade that had always characterized the settlement of new territories, such as between Britain and its American colonies before the Revolution, with high-quality manufactured products being sent out from the homeland in return for raw materials. Helen's father and his Footprint Congress buddies would probably claim it was exploitative. Maybe, but it seemed to Helen to work.

And besides, whoever was ripping off whom, it had to be a good thing for this great river of airships to be linking all the worlds of mankind together. So Helen thought, anyhow.

Twelve days out from Valhalla and they crossed a diffuse boundary into the Corn Belt, the great band of farming worlds a third of a million steps thick, stretching in towards the Datum from about four hundred and sixty thousand worlds out. The skies were a lot busier now, with twains like their own heading towards the Datum passing those heading back out, 'upstream', so to speak.

The *Gold Dust* had made pretty fast progress to this point, but from now on the stops would be more frequent. There were waystations spread out stepwise all along the Long Mississippi, and further down the river geographically too, in many of these worlds. Helen was told that as they approached the Datum these stations would show up more often. At the waystations the twains stopped to take on cargo loads gathered here from the nearby worlds for collection. Sacks of corn were the staple export from these particular Earths, and the crews, with plenty of troll labour, worked in chains to get the twains'

119

gaping holds loaded up. The stations had inns and the like for rest and recreation. These weren't polite places, Helen observed. Many of them had a calaboose, a little jailhouse.

One waystation they stopped at, however, was in a world that happened to be a little warmer than the rest, and the owners had taken the opportunity to establish sprawling sugar plantations and orange groves and palmettos, rare this far north in any America. The sugar-house where they processed their cane was a huge clanking factory. The owners' house was like a colonial mansion constructed of the local timber, with verandas and carved pillars draped with magnolias, and the Captain, the Valienté family, and a few other guests were invited down to drink orange liqueur. In the fields you could see the bent backs of the troll workers, and their song floated on the hot breeze.

The real tourist spectacle in the Corn Belt was the timber trade. Rafts of the stuff from the forests to the north were floated downstream on one Mississippi or another. At a waystation the rafts would be lifted out of the water by a twain or two, and then ganged together by trolls and human workers. The end result was one tremendous platform that might be an acre in size, suspended in the air, constructed of long straight trunks stripped and roped together, each held up by a squadron of airships. And off the twains would go, stepping across the worlds with their vast dangling freight, with parties of trolls and their human supervisors riding in huts and tents on the timber platforms. Just an astounding sight.

What was even more remarkable was what they saw going the other way. One of the principal exports of the Low Earths to the outer worlds was horses. So you'd see a twain descend, and the great ramps from the hold fold down, and out would trot a herd of young horses, supervised by cowboys on horseback.

Occasionally they passed over relics of what used to be an old trekking trail, like the one Helen's family followed to get out to Reboot, on Earth West 101,754: information flags or warning posts, abandoned halfway houses. Thanks to the twains the days of pioneer trekking, of foot-slogging across a hundred thousand worlds, were gone, a phase of history that had only lasted a few years but was already passing into legend. Helen wondered what the likes of Captain Batson, who had led her particular trek, were doing now. Yet the trails were still in use, by gangs of humans driving troll bands one direction or the other across the Long Earth. Helen could never tell if the trolls were singing, or not.

These sights were mostly just glimpses, gone in a second or two as they travelled on.

17

TEN YEARS AFTER the epic journey of Joshua Valienté and Lobsang, twain technology, offered as open source by the Black Corporation, had become the standard way of moving groups of people and large cargoes around the Long Earth. But, Jacques Montecute reflected gleefully as he prepared for his mission into deep stepwise China, some twain journeys were more spectacular than others.

This particular journey, with Roberta Golding, was to begin from Datum China. Once the rather lengthy preliminaries were complete, the sister ships *Zheng He* and *Liu Yang* lifted into the dome of smog that hung over Xiangcheng, Henan province. Standing in the *Zheng He* gondola's main observation lounge, Jacques was able to look up through the window to see the ship's great silvery hull overhead, the skin flexing like the hide of some muscular animal, as the twain began, literally, to swim through the air. The ship's mobile hull would have been a remarkable sight even if it hadn't been adorned with the clasped-hands symbol of the eight-year-old Federated Republic of China.

They soon left the airfield behind, and drifted over the factories and car parks and rubbish tips of a grimy industrial zone. Roberta Golding, Jacques's charge, fifteen years old, stood by the big floor-to-ceiling windows, impassively inspecting the landscape drifting below.

And a dozen trolls, here in the observation lounge, began to sing 'Slow Boat To China', the song strung out into a round and layered with harmony like honey piled on a piece of toast, in the trolls' usual fashion.

Around Jacques a scattered handful of crew, along with a few more informally dressed types who looked like scientists, glanced out of the windows and laughed at jokes Jacques couldn't catch, and couldn't have translated if he had. Jacques and Roberta, from Happy Landings, were used to having trolls around. But some of the crew stared at the trolls, as if they were an utterly unfamiliar sight. Jacques noticed one crewman close to the big animals wearing a conspicuous weapon of some kind at his hip, as if they might be about to go on the rampage.

A uniformed young Chinese, a woman, evidently a crew member, offered Jacques and Roberta drinks: fruit juice, water. Jacques took a water and sipped it. 'Thanks.'

'It is my pleasure.'

'Nice choice of song.'

'We thought it was an amusing choice to welcome you,' she said brightly. 'We being the crew. For this is a *fast* boat *from* China, you see.' She proffered a hand for a strong shake. Dark-haired, sensible-looking rather than attractive, she might have been twenty-five years old. 'I am Lieutenant Wu Yue-Sai. A Federal Army officer, but attached to the China National Space Administration.'

'Ah. Which is running this East Twenty Million project.'

'Exactly. You can see the logic. Our space engineers are trained to handle advanced technology in unfamiliar and extreme environments. Who better to confront the mysteries of the far East worlds? I however trained as a pilot. I have ambitions to become an astronaut, some day. For now I have been assigned an informal role as companion to your protégée, Ms Roberta Golding. If that is acceptable to you, and indeed to Ms Golding. You will call me Yue-Sai, I hope.'

'And she'll want you to call her Roberta, I'm sure.'

'Perhaps she has informal names. Robbie, Bobbie . . .'

Jacques glanced at Roberta, who was solemnly sipping her orange juice. 'Roberta,' he said firmly. 'What do you mean – what kind of companion?'

'I am relatively close to her in age. Of course I am the same sex. I have enjoyed a broad education, in philosophy and the humanities as well as science and engineering, just as Ms— as Roberta has.'

'Well, Roberta's basically self-taught.'

'My primary duty is to ensure her safety, whenever we leave the ship. During ground excursions and so forth. No doubt we will encounter many hazardous incidents.'

'That's a thoughtful gesture.'

'It is my honour. I have been studying English especially. As have many of the crew, including the Captain.'

'I can tell. Thank you. We'll make a good team.'

'I'm sure you will.' Captain Chen Zhong approached now, bustling across the carpeted floor of the deck. As he passed, his crew subtly straightened up, and their faces became more solemn. Chen shook the hands of Jacques and Roberta. He brandished some kind of control box in his left hand. 'In a moment we'll be off! Of course we are already in the air, but soon we will be swimming stepwise too . . .'

His accent was stronger than Wu's, but more complex, some of his phrasing almost British. Aged around fifty he was short, a little stout for a military man, Jacques thought, but sleek, supremely confident. Jacques would have been prepared to bet he was a survivor of the fallen Communist regime.

'So glad you could come with us, that all the various formalities were overcome. A tricky process given the newness of our nation. Of course the welfare of Ms Golding is a top priority.' Now he faced Roberta. 'I hope you'll have time to enjoy the experience. Such a pretty thing! Forgive me for saying it. Yet you are so serious.'

Roberta, taller than he was, just looked back at him.

Chen winked at Jacques. 'Quiet one, is she? But observant. No doubt you're drinking in the details of the airships even as they are launched. The unusual mode of propulsion, for instance.'

To Jacques's relief, Roberta deigned to reply to this. 'The flexible hull, you mean. Strung with some kind of artificial muscle, contracting when electrical impulses are applied?'

'Very good, very good. With the electricity provided by solar power. You can see why such a system is appropriate? When we observe the worlds we explore, why not do it with as little noise and other disturbance as possible? We hope to reach Earth East 20,000,000, our nominal target – nearly ten times further than any human has ventured into the Long Earth before! – in a mere few weeks. We estimate we will also need to maintain a velocity, that is a lateral velocity, of over a hundred miles per hour in the process. I'm sure you can see why.'

Roberta shrugged. 'That's trivial.'

Jacques exchanged a glance with Yue-Sai. That was one of Roberta's more annoying verbal tics; the need for a sideways speed might be obvious to her, but wasn't at all obvious to Jacques, or, it seemed, to Yue-Sai. The point went unexplained.

Chen said, 'You know your engineering, then. But what of your wider education? Are you aware of the provenance of the names of our pioneering ships?'

'Liu Yang was the first Chinese woman in space. And Zheng He was the eunuch admiral who—'

'Yes, yes. I can see we have little to teach you.' He smiled. 'Then let us explore together.' He held up the gadget in his left hand; it was like a television remote, Jacques thought, and on it was a familiar corporate logo: a Black Corporation marque. Chen said, 'I hope you have all been following your nausea inoculation regimes? Now – are you ready? – every journey must begin with a single step.' He pressed a button.

Jacques felt a familiar jolt to the gut, but faint, a ghost sensation.

The crowded landscape of Datum Henan was whisked away. Suddenly rain clattered on the windows and bounced off the great hull overhead. The trolls, apparently unperturbed, sang on.

Chen led the party to the big downward-looking windows at the gondola's prow, so they could see better. At first glance Jacques could see little difference in the landscape below, Henan East 1, compared with the original: more, cruder factories and coal-burning power stations belching smoke, roads like muddy tracks, a smoggy tinge to the air. Yet in the distance there were patches of green, of forest, and that *wasn't* like the original.

Chen said, 'Henan! Long ago the cradle of Han civilization, you know. But in more recent times something of a hellhole, exploited, over-industrialized. A hundred million people crammed into an area the size of the state of Massachusetts.' That was a Datum Earth reference that meant little to Jacques, but he got the idea. 'Datum Henan was once a prime source of migrants to cities like Shanghai, who became the cleaners and the clerks and the barkeeps and the prostitutes. You can imagine that on Step Day a rather large proportion of the population of such places as this wandered over into the new worlds with alacrity. It took the authorities some time to restore order. You should not underestimate the impact that stepping had on the Chinese people as a whole in those early days – and not just the economic or other practical effects. I mean rather the psychological, as you will see. Of course you know that the disruptions after Step Day eventually led to the, ah, *retirement* of the last Communist regime.' He studied Roberta, evidently curious about her reaction. 'So we begin our exploration, Ms Golding. Here we are on Earth East 1, of twenty million. What do you understand the purposes of this expedition to be?'

She thought before answering. 'To see what's out there.'

He seemed pleased by the simplicity of the reply. 'Yes! We will count the worlds, and we will catalogue them, number them. We will establish the longitude of the Long Earth East, so to speak. I have seen your academic record: your intellect is evidently remarkable. You don't think a mere voyage of exploration, of fact-gathering, is *trivial*? We are like butterfly collectors, are we not?'

She shrugged. 'If you want to understand butterflies, you first have to collect butterflies. Or finches.'

Chen seemed to puzzle over that word. 'Ah! Like Darwin on Galapagos. A neat reference. Well, I can't promise you finches, but butterflies . . .' He let that tail off mysteriously.

'Why did you bring the trolls?'

He glanced at her sharply. 'Good question. I should have known you would ask it. In the planning, most people dismissed our trolls as – what, as a cabaret, an animal show? Not you! The trolls, in a sense, *are* the Long Earth, are they not? Their long call stitches it together – and, I believe, appeals to the musical sensibilities of all Chinese people. Now we may be venturing further than *even any troll* has travelled before. Think of that! And we want whatever we discover in those remote footprints of China to become part of the troll song.'

Jacques said, 'Of course you know that trolls are an integral part of our lives, in the community we come from.'

'Ah, yes. So I hear. Although you keep its location secret, don't you?'

'We treasure our privacy.'

'Of course you do.' Chen pressed his button, and they stepped once again. Jacques noticed a counter on the wall: flickering digits that would count the worlds.

In East 2 the sky was bright, the sun high, and the land was carpeted with green, with forest. The contrast with the Datum, and even East 1 – the sudden flood of colour, the light illuminating the observation deck – was breathtaking.

Chen said, 'You can see why a sudden access to all this

so *startled* people. Our nation is older than yours, older than Europe. China has been cultivated, built on, fought over, mined, for five thousand years. It was a shock for us to walk into this primordial green. There were immediate cultural responses. An upsurge in support for environmental protection. Songs, poems, paintings, most of them bad. Ha! Well, there was nothing much we could do about East 1, or West 1. Quickly ruined by the first flood of travellers, the first helpless and hapless migrants. Each footprint became one big shanty town. But the government organized quickly, and we kept East 2 as a kind of national park, a memorial of Step Day, of our sudden access to our country's own past – as best we could, anyhow; even here we are harmed by pollution from the heavy industrialization of this Low Earth in such places as the United States footprint, and there are ongoing negotiations in the United Nations about that. We also store some of our treasures here – the heritage of our deep culture. Even a few buildings, temples dismantled and rebuilt. Just as humanity is preserved from extinction by the existence of the Long Earth, should any calamity befall our home world, so now is our cultural past.'

Roberta pressed her forehead against the window, gawping, briefly looking like any curious teenager. 'I see animals, moving through the forest. Elephants? Heading towards that river over there, to the north.'

Chen smiled. 'Elephants, which roam as far north as Beijing in some worlds. And camels, bears, lions, tigers, black swans, even river dolphins. Tapirs! Deer! Pangolins! On Step Day, our children choked in the smog-free air, were frightened by the brightness of the sun, and goggled at the animals.'

The Captain pressed his control button again.

In East 3 the forest had been cleared, and the river dammed to flood the ground. In the resulting paddy fields, people laboured, bent over, not looking up as the shadows of the airships passed. It was the same in East 4, 5, 6 and beyond, though the methods of farming differed. In some worlds there was industrialization, with smoke rising from distant power stations and foundries, and crude-looking machines rolling across vast fields; in others, just the people and their animals.

'Very organized,' Jacques said.

'Oh, yes,' Yue-Sai said brightly. 'We Chinese were able to move out into the stepwise worlds in a disciplined and industrious way, matched, I would suggest, nowhere else in the world. Under the Communists we were a one-party state equipped with the tools of late capitalism – capable of very large-scale feats. In recent decades we had already had experience of massive projects on the Datum: infrastructure like dams and bridges and rail lines, even a space programme. Now the Long Earth offered a blank canvas. Since the regime change, despite a revision of ideology, we have lost none of those skills. That's China for you!'

Roberta said, 'Could we pause here?'

'Of course.' Chen pressed his buttons.

Jacques looked down. The airship was hovering over a waterlogged field, where a peasant stood patiently, holding a piece of rope tied around the neck of what looked like a buffalo. 'That's a scene that could be two thousand years old,' he said.

Roberta said, 'Captain Chen, in some of these

agricultural worlds there are factories. Producing artificial nutrients?'

'Also genetically engineered crops. Modern farming machinery—'

'Yet here, you are evidently manuring the soil. It seems a contradiction.'

Yue-Sai said, 'We use both ways. This is an expression of an old tension in Chinese philosophy.'

'The Dao versus Confucianism,' Roberta said.

Chen looked impressed.

Yue-Sai nodded. 'Essentially correct. The Dao is the way – to follow the way means a harmonization with nature. The Confucians by contrast argue that man must master nature, for the betterment of nature as well as the benefit of mankind. Wars have been fought over these ideas. The Confucians won in the second century BC. But now we have room to spread out, to explore other ways.'

'*Dao zai shiniao*,' Roberta said.

Chen laughed out loud. 'The way is in the piss and the shit! Very good, very good.'

Roberta seemed neither pleased nor offended by his praise.

The airship moved on. Around East 20, a belt of more industrialized worlds began. Jacques looked down on factories, power stations, mine heads, industrial parks cut into the green. Lines of workers moved between work-shops and shabby-looking dormitory, refectory and shower blocks. Cargo airships hovered, or were tethered to masts. On many of these worlds, smoke and soot and smog hung thick in the air.

Chen was observing their reactions. 'Few westerners have seen this. Save for those who have put money into these Third Front developments. Douglas Black for one.'

Jacques asked, 'Why "Third Front"?'

'Ah, that's a reference to Mao,' Chen said, and winked again. 'In response to aggression from the Soviets in the 1960s Mao scattered industrial production facilities across China – into the remote west, for example. So that it became more difficult to cripple us with nuclear bombs, you see. He encouraged workers to go out there. "The Further from Father and Mother, the Nearer to Chairman Mao's Heart" – that was the slogan. As then, so now. One can despise Mao's crimes while admiring his ambition.'

Jacques wondered if you could have one without the other. He said, 'You can't seriously be suggesting there's a risk of some kind of shooting war with the west.'

'There are other threats. Stepping itself has destabilized nations – including China of course. And climate collapse on the Datum, with all that would follow, could yet be a serious issue.'

They came to a world – East 38, according to the wall counter – where a thunderstorm was raging. The two airships drifted in a sky populated by huge, lumpy, rushing grey clouds, and rain lashed down on the forest below. Jacques observed what looked like the scars of lightning strikes, blackened craters in the forest cover.

Chen watched them expectantly.

'I don't understand,' Jacques said. 'What is it we are meant to see here?'

'You could only perceive it properly from orbit, perhaps,' Chen said. 'Here, soldier-engineers are using atomic weapons to blast paths and tunnels through the Himalayas, thus removing an accident of geology that disrupted the flow of air and moisture across Eurasia. In this world, the interior of Asia will be green.'

Jacques was astonished. 'You're reshaping a whole mountain range?'

'Why not? And in another neighbouring world, we are diverting all the rivers arising in the Himalayas, save for the Yangtze, again to bring moisture to the heart of the continent.'

Roberta said, 'More dreams of the Maoists.'

'Yes! You know your history. Schemes that were too expensive, or too risky, to be tried out when the Datum was all we had. Now we can experiment with no harm done. What dreams we have, what ambition! Aren't we Chinese great?'

Maybe. But Jacques wondered what the experience of these new worlds, these diverse environments, was doing to the souls of the colonists here. In the West worlds, different Americas were evolving, sharing their parent's values maybe but subtly diverging. Here too that must be true, with new kinds of China developing, still rooted in the same deep history – surely the Chinese would always stay Chinese – but each acquiring a whole new character. And he wondered how soon it would be before those new Chinas became restless in search of freedom from their gigantic parent, like the Valhallan Belt Americas.

As the lightning cracked in the sky, the trolls were growing anxious, their song fragmented.

Chen lifted his remote control, apparently with regret. 'I would love to show you our new mountains. But we cannot linger; it is unsafe here.'

Jacques asked, 'Why, the lightning?'

'No, no. The fallout from the atomic mining. On we go

. . . Now we will speed up. You understand these ships are an experimental sort, developed by our own engineering companies in conjunction with the Black Corporation. One purpose of this exploration is to test the new technologies.'

The passing of the worlds accelerated until, as Jacques could tell from his own pulse, the realities were washing past at the rate of roughly one a second, blink, blink, blink, then faster still. Most of the worlds were unremarkable, blankets of green under sunshine or cloud. But in some glaciated worlds the sunlight glared from ice sheets, safely far beneath the prows of the twains.

They were shown to a kind of lounge area. A steward circulated with food, soft drinks, China tea, and they sat, chatting while whole worlds flapped by, unremarked. Jacques suspected Roberta would rather have been alone, studying, reading, making her own observations. But she sat politely enough, if mostly silently.

After an hour or so the airship paused, the light subtly different. When Jacques looked up he saw butterflies, a tremendous swarm of them, all around the ship, battering silently at the windows of the observation deck. Most were small, plain, but some were more colourful, and some had wings the size of saucers. The sunlight shone bright through their pale substance.

Chen laughed at their reaction. 'Butterfly world. What the westerners call a Joker. Of course an ecology needs more components than just butterflies. Nevertheless, here in this part of China, butterflies are all that come to greet us. We have no idea how this has come about, what is different here. Yet here we are. You see, Roberta Golding, I told you we would be counting butterflies! What do you think?'

At length Lieutenant Wu Yue-Sai said, 'It would certainly be hard to demonstrate chaos theory here.'

They were all silent as they worked that out. Then Jacques was the first to laugh.

Roberta, however, merely looked puzzled.

18

THE CREW OF the *Benjamin Franklin* did take seriously their mandate to project the authority of the US Datum government across the Long Earth. It wasn't *all* about saving kittens stuck up trees, as Maggie told her crew.

Which was why the twain made an unannounced stop at a town called Reboot, Earth West 101,754, in a stepwise New York State.

A small group led by Executive Officer Nathan Boss – a rare jaunt for him away from his desk – were landed from the twain in a kind of clearing of trampled-down mud, beside a spidery trail that ran up from the coast of the local copy of the Atlantic. Nathan had seen the layout for himself clearly from the air, aboard the *Franklin*. The town itself was out of sight but a short walk away, cut into the green of the crowding forest: neat little fields and houses with smoke rising up, all connected by wide dirt tracks.

This was one of the first of what Captain Kauffman was calling their 'hearts and minds' assignments. They would turn up unannounced at a community on some world like this, in order to make themselves and their mission known, and, well, to gently remind these colonial

Americans that they were still Americans . . . This early in the mission they were still finding their way. So was Nathan Boss, his first time in charge of a ground team.

And in this case the logistics were surprisingly complicated. This town and its stepwise neighbours were linked in a kind of extended Long Earth 'county'. So the *Franklin* was hopping between the worlds, visiting one community after another, dropping equipment and setting down groups of sailors and marines at each of those neighbours.

There were lots of ways such an operation could go wrong, as Nathan was all too well aware.

Add to that the fact that the worlds of the Long Earth were themselves somewhat bewildering, for the twain's mostly Datum-born crew. As the Navy guys waited for the marines to follow them off the *Franklin*, reflexively they spread out to form a perimeter, though there was no visible threat here in Earth West 101,754. They looked around, evidently kind of baffled. Most of them were from urban backgrounds. Well, there was no urban background *here*. Nothing but the muddy clearing. Nobody around but a deer (well, Nathan *thought* it was a deer) that peered at them from out of a clump of forest. Nothing to read but a sign, home-made, hand-lettered:

WELCOME TO REBOOT
FOUNDED 2026, A.D.
POP. 1465

Ensign Toby Fox, the IT nerd type from engineering who had been tasked with making a census of the Long Earth, dutifully wrote down the population number.

There was no sign of sun under a clouded-over sky, but

the warmth was intense for an early May day, and Nathan was immediately sweating in his combat fatigues, with his pack on his back.

It was when Lieutenant Sam Allen came down from the twain, the last to land, and the *Benjamin Franklin* popped away stepwise with a soft implosion of air, that the real trouble started.

Allen was in charge of the small chalk of marines attached to this expedition. As his own guys stood around, evidently feeling a little lost in this latest new world just like the sailors, Allen started badgering Specialist Jennifer Wang. 'So where's our equipment?'

Wang already had her own pack off her back and was working her radio and locator gear. 'Lieutenant, our gear was supposed to be landed within a half-mile, not on top of us—'

'I know that. Which way, Specialist?'

Nathan knew that the equipment drop, a bunch of trunks in rope nets, had radio beacons to alert the arriving troops of its location. But Wang looked confused. She worked touchscreens, and even twisted dials on a very old-fashioned-looking radio receiver. All she picked up was squawking music, a clatter of guitars.

Midshipman Jason Santorini, listening in, grinned. 'Chuck Berry. My dad's favourite. Mint stuff, even if it is like a hundred years old, or something.'

'That's just some dumb local station,' growled Allen. 'Some kid in his barn . . . Turn it off.'

Wang complied.

Ensign Toby Fox was a small guy, and more nervous than the rest. Now, before Nathan had a chance to get hold of the situation, Fox was the one who was unwise enough to ask Allen, 'So, Lieutenant, where *is* our stuff?'

Allen turned on him. 'In the wrong fucking place. Isn't it obvious?'

'Actually it's probably in the wrong, umm, fucking world, Lieutenant,' Wang put in. 'Or I'd be picking up its bleep by now.'

By checking rosters, they soon figured it out. The drop had been made at another town, New Scarsdale, the 'county' seat.

Wang said, 'There's your error, sir. Scarsdale is over on 101,752.'

Allen said, 'Whereas this dump—'

Fox checked his milspec Earth counter. 'Right now we're on 101,754, sir. Where we were supposed to be.'

Somebody had miscounted the stepwise worlds. Nathan suspected miscommunication between the two command lines, the Navy crew and the marines, Datum-born, Datum-trained crew who weren't used to thinking in terms of planning for operating across different stepwise worlds in the first place. It happened.

'What a screw-up,' Allen raged. 'And those damn Navy boys stepped on without checking they got the rendezvous right.'

Everybody else just stood around, too nervous to be the one to reply. Somewhere something growled, a huge bear maybe, a deep rumble like an earth tremor, and they gathered closer together.

'OK, OK,' Allen said. 'We need to send a runner. Get that ship back here, and bring us to the gear, or the gear to us.' He poked a finger at random. 'You, McKibben. Get your Stepper out and get moving—'

'Sorry, Lieutenant,' said the man, 'no can do. I left behind my Stepper.'

'You did what? . . . OK, who the hell else is here in Earth One Hundred Thousand and Shit without the most elementary and obvious piece of kit of all, a Stepper to get him home again?'

They all looked at each other.

It was an obvious omission, Nathan thought. They were putting on a show of force here; they had come down lightly armed but wearing flak-vests, load-bearing harnesses, and packs with general gear and ammo, and whatever specialist stuff they had to carry. Anyone with any experience knew the score. From the K-pot on your head to the combat boots on your feet, it was a heavy load, and you left behind whatever you didn't specifically need for the mission. They were only supposed to have been down here, in this small town in this one peaceful world, for a couple of hours. Why carry a Stepper box? Which, built to military specification, was a heavy, robust piece of kit.

Turned out *none* of them had a Stepper. Not Nathan, not even the Lieutenant, and nobody dared grin at that. Nathan hadn't the nerve to meet Allen's eyes.

Then one of the guys asked his buddy if he had some water to spare because he was getting thirsty in the heat, but the other guy didn't. Turned out none of them had brought water either, because that was all supposed to be in the drop. Not even Nathan, not even the Lieutenant. There was a stream not far away, you could hear it running. But these were all Datum-born types who had had drummed into them from childhood that you didn't drink the local water, not without an iodine tablet in it at least, and none of them had even that.

Not even Nathan, not even the Lieutenant.

Allen prowled around, his fists clenched, looking as if he needed somebody to punch. 'All right, then. All right. So we go to this dump Reboot, and start from there. Agreed, Commander Boss?'

Nathan nodded.

'Which way, Wang?'

But there was no GPS on this world, no airship hovering to give them orientation, and even their paper maps were, predictably, in the air drop. Surrounded by trees like cathedral spires they couldn't see the rising smoke from the township; they couldn't even get a direction from the sun, given the cloudy sky. The fuck-up just got fucked-upper with every second.

Then a man came strolling into the clearing, whistling, rods in his hand, and some kind of big fish on a line he had thrown over his shoulder. He might have been fifty, Nathan thought, with a deep-tanned face, and a lithe toughness about him when he walked. When he found a dozen armed warriors glaring at him he briefly froze, but then his face broke into a broad grin. 'Hey, soldiers,' he said. 'Did I break an ordinance? I'll throw it back, I promise . . .'

Lieutenant Allen glared at the civilian. Then he turned to Wang. 'Ask him if he knows the way to this Reboot place.'

'Sir, do you know the way to Reboot?'

'My name's Bill Lovell, by the way,' he said heavily. He looked around at them; Nathan felt profoundly embarrassed, and somewhat overdressed. 'Don't tell me you're lost.'

Allen didn't respond.

Nathan tried to explain.

Lovell shook his head as he listened. 'How the hell did your pilots manage to make a drop in the wrong world?'

Nathan said ruefully, 'We're kind of learning our way around here, sir.'

Lovell was still grinning. 'I can see that. You folks just don't get the Long Earth way of thinking, do you? Here you are, lost as babies. And you're really planning to go all the way up to Valhalla?'

Wang asked, 'You know about our mission?'

'Oh, news travels fast out here. That might surprise you, not me. I used to be a postman. I mean, for the US postal service, before they cut out the service to the far stepwise worlds. Yeah, we heard about you.'

Allen looked as if he longed to pistol-whip this guy. 'You going to show us to Reboot, or not?'

Lovell mock-bowed. 'Follow me.'

Nathan wasn't sure what he'd been expecting of Reboot. A Dodge City movie set? Some kind of cluttered steampunk nirvana? A few primitive farms hacked out of the wilderness? Banjo players? In fact, as you could clearly see as you walked down the main drag from the river, it was a town. An American town, judging by the big Stars and Stripes hanging over the schoolhouse.

Bill Lovell pointed out the sights. 'That's the old Wells place. One of the original plots.' A woman worked a garden behind a neat whitewashed fence, a real Acacia Avenue kind of scene. She looked up, smiled. 'Not that it looked like *that* when the first trekkers got here in '26 . . .'

Toby Fox asked, 'As recently as that? Just fourteen years ago?'

'There's Arthurson's general store. The only store in town right now, though a few of the farmhouses will sell you beer or liquor, or make you a meal, or hire you a room.'

Santorini asked, 'Will they accept dollars?'

Lovell just laughed.

There were horses, and *camels*, tied up at the rail outside the store. Laughter sounded from within.

Then a bunch of children burst out of one of the houses and ran across the street. They might have been Native American kids to Nathan's urban eye, with hand-sewn leather trousers and jackets, and some kind of moccasins on their feet.

'School's out,' Bill said. He cupped a hand behind a fat ear. 'And can you hear that?'

When the kids had dispersed and their chatter subsided, Nathan heard a distant clank-clank-clank . . .

'The new sawmill. Or rather the old sawmill with its new steam engine. Everything made locally, or at least every iron part. They've promised themselves a water-turbine power supply soon. They're even trialling a telegraph system, to keep in touch with some of the outlying farms, which are pretty remote. Geographically, I mean.'

He sounded as if he was proud of the citizens of Reboot, Nathan thought. Fatherly.

'Lots of little kids,' Wang observed.

'Well, you have population booms going on across many of the settled Earths. In a few centuries you might have hundreds of Earths teeming with billion-fold

143

populations. Think of it. All those little tax-payers!'

Wang's eyes widened. Her mind was being opened up almost visibly, Nathan thought.

'But probably nobody's ever going to count them,' Wang said.

'Actually that's my job,' said Toby Fox, with a touch of pride.

'Hey, there she is. Katie! Katie Bergreen!'

A woman, strawberry-blonde, aged maybe thirty, was crossing the road with a determined stride. She glanced over in surprise at Bill Lovell, and with evident caution at Nathan and his buddies in their bristling combat gear. 'What's this? An invasion?'

Lovell shrugged. 'I think they're here to count us. Or something. Right now these guys have lost their way. You think your father would give the US Navy some water?'

She grinned, almost cheekily. 'Well, they could ask. This way,' she said to Nathan. 'But you'll need to leave your weapons at the door . . .'

19

JACK GREEN, AGED about sixty, was a bookish firebrand kind of a guy, it seemed to Nathan Boss. He stared down Lieutenant Allen on his doorstep – actually stared down this huge, armed marine – before allowing him and his troopers into his house. Even then they did indeed have to leave their weapons at the door, and take their combat boots off at the porch.

So they were all in their socks when they walked into the house's big living room, with its unlit hearth and a few hunting trophies, and heaps of books and papers. It was very neat, Nathan thought, almost military neat. He already knew this man had a daughter, the woman called Katie; Nathan immediately guessed this was the home of a widower, with too much time on his hands.

Jack Green glared at them all, as though they were naughty children. 'OK. I'll let you in, out of the heat. Common humanity demands that. I'll give you water. There's a pump out back.'

With a nod, Allen deputized a couple of the guys to go fetch a few jugs. They dumped their kit by the door and moved. Soon the guys were all drinking from pottery mugs. 'Glugging it faster than Boston natives on St Patrick's Day,' observed Wang.

Jack faced Lieutenant Allen. 'I can loan you a Stepper. Then you can send one of these warrior children of yours to track down your airship, can't you?' He laughed. 'What a comical mess.'

'Thank you, sir—'

'Don't thank me, because it's all I'm going to do for you.' He waved a hand. 'Oh, you may as well sit. Just don't break anything, or play with anything, or mess up my papers.'

The marines began to dump more kit, unhook their body armour, take off their camouflage jackets. They sat in little huddles, talking quietly, and Nathan saw that within minutes one of them had his Travel Scrabble set out and had started a three-hand game with a couple of the guys.

Allen looked on with disgust. 'You don't bring your Stepper, McKibben. You don't bring any goddamn drinking water. But you bring your Scrabble.'

'Got to get your priorities right, Lieutenant.'

Jack sat down at his paper-laden desk. All the furniture looked hand-made, Nathan saw, kind of rough but sturdy. Jack said, 'Well, I can't say I'm surprised to see you. The news of your triumphant progress across the worlds precedes you. But, Bill, why the hell did you bring these people to me?'

The former postman looked mischievous. 'Why, who better in our little community to welcome our, umm, liberators?'

That little exchange put Lieutenant Allen on alert. Without being asked, he sat opposite Jack, and pulled a printed list of names out of his jacket pocket. 'John Rodney Green, called Jack. That's you, right?'

'What have you got there, your Christmas card list?'

'A list of signatories of your so-called Valhalla "Declaration of Independence", sir, and their advisers.'

Jack just grinned. 'So what are you going to do now, shoot me? Arrest me and bundle me aboard your airship?'

'We're here to protect you, sir. Not to create trouble.'

'Thanks!'

'In fact we're grateful to you for your assistance so far, Mr Green,' Allen said, precisely. 'And you can help us out further. Now, Ensign Fox here—' he snapped his fingers to summon Fox '– is working on a census.'

'Is he? Good for you, sonny.'

'Now we're here I can see it's going to take some time, what with you having this mish-mash you call a "county" spread over several worlds, and so on. So if you have a spare room where Fox can bunk down—'

'I'm not having Datum troops under my roof.'

'We're prepared to compensate you.'

Jack looked amused. 'With what?'

'Well . . . Monetarily, obviously. I'm authorized to sign cheques, up to a limit. We carry cash.'

'What cash? Dollars, right?'

Allen said sternly, 'The legal tender of this community, being in the US Aegis as it is, sir.'

Jack sighed. 'But what am I going to do with dollars? You imagine I can pay Bill here in dollars for a catch of fish? What the hell is *he* going to do with them? You'd end up with bits of paper circling around and around this community like flies over a cowpat . . .'

Allen was going to snap back some angry response.

But Fox leaned forward, interested. 'Then how *would* you want paying, sir? How does that work around here?'

'We call it favours,' Jack said.

'Favours?'

'I give you a room for a few nights. That's a favour. Now you owe me a favour. We agree what that is before you move in, right? If it was Bill it would be so many pounds of fish. He does the favour for me, and we're square. Or – if I don't need any fish, then Bill can go to old Mike Doak down the street, who can shoe horses like he was raised to it, and give him the fish, thus transferring the favour he owes me to Mike, and then when my horse throws a shoe—'

'I get it.' Allen raised his hands.

Fox said, 'So you don't use paper money. But you must get outside workers coming through. Doctors, dentists—'

'We support them with favours, one way or another.'

'Specialists, like engineers to build you a dam. Something like that. There must be occasions when there's *nothing* you can do for someone like that. You can only eat one meal at a time, wear one pair of trousers—'

Jack winked at Fox. 'Good question. OK, we do have stashes. Gold, silver, jewellery. Even a little paper money, if you must know – we accept all this if there's no other way for a person to pay, who's desperate enough. We're not monks here, enslaved to a rule book. We cheat a little. Whatever works. But basically we're self-sufficient, locally; almost all of it is favours.'

Allen eyed him. 'So you do take dollars. But you won't take dollars from *us*. From members of the US armed forces.'

Jack laughed in his face. 'Listen, you and your paymasters in Washington forfeited any right to help from me and my community when you cut us off a dozen years ago. When you trashed Pioneer Support, and impounded my life savings. You even fired poor old Bill, here.'

Lovell grinned. 'Don't bring me into it. I'm doing fine.'

'And none of the "Aegis rights and responsibilities" crap spouted by President Cowley cuts any ice with *me*,' Jack said. 'Yes, Lieutenant, I'll give you water to relieve the discomfort of these children you're leading astray. Other than that – I could take your dollars, but I won't, because I don't like you, or the Datum government you represent, and I want to see the back of you.'

Nathan could see Lieutenant Allen's temperature rising, like a volcano on slow heat. 'This is all bullshit!'

Fox said earnestly, 'With respect, sir, it's not. This kind of meeting of minds is precisely why—'

'Shut your cakehole, sailor.'

'Yes, sir.' Fox shrank back immediately.

Allen produced a fold of currency from an inside pocket, hundred-dollar bills. He set this on Jack's homemade desk. 'I'm asking you to take this, sir. Or face the consequences.'

Jack, totally at ease, just faced him. 'What is it that poor troll said, when the likes of you tried to take her cub away?'

'That was nothing to do with the US military—'

'*I will not.*' He repeated the phrase, backing it up with troll sign language. '*I will not*, sir. *I will not.*'

Allen glowered. 'Ensign Fox, cuff this man.'

Jack just laughed. Fox sat frozen, indecisive.

There was a flurry in the corner where the guys were playing Scrabble. 'McKibben, you butthole, there is no way under the sun that DUCTTAPE is a single word . . .'

'I don't think cuffing is an appropriate response, Lieutenant Allen,' Nathan said calmly.

Allen stalked out of the house, furious.

Nathan wondered how the hell he was going to explain all this to Captain Kauffman.

When he did try, the first thing she did was to put Lieutenant Sam Allen off her ship, the first opportunity she got.

The second thing she did was to ask to meet this character Jack Green, so she could learn all about this business of the favours for herself.

20

IN THE MINE Belt, the Valientés aboard *Gold Dust* witnessed a crisis.

The airship fleet had stopped a couple of times over the arid worlds of this band, to take on board ore of various kinds – not just bulky stuff like bauxite, or even obviously precious metals like silver and gold, but a slew of minerals that were scarce now on the Datum, or at any rate hugely valuable: germanium, cobalt, gallium.

But it wasn't a colonized world where the incident happened.

The family happened to be making one of their visits to the wheelhouse at the time, and Helen and Dan saw it all. The twain had slowed because they were approaching a notorious Joker, some eighty thousand steps from the Datum, and the pilot knew to take care, driving them forward at only a couple of steps a minute. When they finally stepped into the Joker, the landscape of the neighbouring world – a sparse green with forest clumps and prairie – vanished to reveal bare, brick-red, dust-strewn rock. Even the local Mississippi was reduced to a rusty trickle, striped down the centre of a valley that looked much too wide for it. From unknown causes, this Joker happened to be suffering from some kind of global desertification. It was like a landscape on Mars.

And here was the downed ship.

She was called the *Pennsylvania*. She had been caught in a dust storm when she tried, cautiously, to cross the Joker, and then one of her helium sacs, maybe already carrying a fault, split open at the sudden expansion caused by the heat of the Joker's dry air. The leak had been quick but the crash slow, relentless; it must have been a terrifying experience. The *Gold Dust* passengers saw the wreck now through a veil of windblown dust that hissed against the windows, the remnants of the storm that had killed the ship. From the air it was a six-hundred-foot reef already half covered by drifting red sand.

The *Gold Dust* was the first of the following fleet to come upon the wreck, and the largest. As Dan and Helen hung back, trying to keep out of the way, there was a hasty conference call with the Captain in his cabin, and the commanders of the other craft as they arrived in this world. A strategy was soon cooked up, and the crew swung into action with an efficiency and dedication that warmed Helen's soul. They dropped anchor, and soon had a kind of improvised elevator working, taking crew to and from the ground on an open platform. Helen saw Dan's buddy Bosun Higgs go down, joining working parties assembled from all the crews of the fleet.

Then, as the crew worked, the Captain used the ship's intercom to ask for volunteers from among the passengers to go down to help. *Volunteers from among the passengers.* Helen's heart sank when she heard that phrase.

Of course she couldn't stop him.

* * *

It all went well enough, for three, four hours, as the sun slowly went down, and the sandstorm finally petered out. From Helen's godlike point of view high in the sky, she watched what looked like very organized ants working on the carcass of the fallen ship. They cut channels through the wreckage, led out walking wounded, and carried out the worst afflicted, and the dead. A field medical post was set up under a tent, and soon the first of the most seriously injured were being brought up to the *Gold Dust* on the elevator. The *Gold Dust* was the best placed of the fleet to take the injured on board, with a well-equipped medical bay that could be quickly expanded into a hospital. Other parties worked at salvaging what they could of the *Pennsylvania*'s cargo, mostly Corn Belt wheat. Still others performed the sad duty of digging out graves around the crash site.

Then there was an alarm in the wheelhouse. One of the *Gold Dust* contingent had got himself trapped, deep in the interior of the *Pennsylvania*'s envelope, when a bit more of the structure had collapsed around him as he was trying, heroically, to reach one last group of stranded passengers. He was stuck in the collapsed framework, too high off the ground to be able to step out safely. A rescue attempt was quickly improvised.

'Wow,' Dan said, listening to the crackly radio messages. 'Who do you think it is, Mom?'

Not your father, Helen pleaded silently. Not Joshua. Just this once, not Joshua.

A new line was let down from the nose of the *Gold Dust*, with two individuals clinging to it: Bosun Higgs and Sally Linsay. Helen's hopes sank faster than the platform. With great caution they were lowered through a rip in the twain's collapsed envelope, and disappeared into darkness. Helen heard muttered reports on the radio link, saw the spark of cutting torches deep in the *Pennsylvania*'s carcass. Then a period of silence.

At last Sally called: 'Take her up!'

Slowly, cautiously, the winch turned. The platform came up first, with Sally and the crewman, trailing a length of cable. Then the line shuddered, and Sally waved a halt. Helen heard: 'He's OK. Not very dignified, but OK. Keep lifting.'

Up came the cable, rising out of the wreck. And at last, lifted into the low sunlight, dangling upside down with the cable wrapped around one ankle, was Joshua.

Dan rolled his eyes. 'Oh, *Dad!*'

Helen thought that summed it up.

Eventually, to Helen's chagrin, the whole incident made it on to the outernet, and the news channels. Sometimes it was hard being Lois Lane.

And – as Joshua had to point out later, for Helen hadn't been looking at *her* – as soon as Joshua was clear of the wreck, Sally had grinned up at the watching crew of the *Gold Dust*, and disappeared.

21

As it happened the *Benjamin Franklin* passed through the Mine Belt only a few days after the wreck. Via an outernet communiqué, the *Franklin* had been ordered to backtrack from Reboot to a Mine Belt world around seventy thousand steps from home, where some idiot had shot a couple of trolls.

As the *Franklin* ploughed through the worlds, Maggie Kauffman wondered – not for the first time since the start of this mission – whether the whole Long Earth was a test which humanity was singularly failing. On the one hand there were still Datum-Earthers who led lives that had nothing to do with the landscape outside their heads, the immensity beyond their garden walls; and on the other hand, even now, twenty-five years after Step Day, there were still people stepping East and West, even to the High Meggers and beyond, without so much as looking up which mushrooms were safe to pick. One of the unstated duties of this voyage, as it had emerged, was to give a ride to a place of safety to the wounded, or even just the severely embarrassed, who had given up after their first winter without electricity, or a visit by an unexpected bear or pack of wolves – or maybe the odd dinosaur-descendant if you went far enough. Smart people, while they might at first have everything to learn, soon developed effective ways of making things work out here, but Maggie was seeing very little of *them*. Dumb people kept doing dumb things – such as shoot trolls, despite the intense political atmosphere after the Gap incident. And it was to the fallout from such dumbness that the *Franklin*, Maggie was finding, was repeatedly summoned.

So the dirigible drifted across arid versions of Texas, listening out on shortwave, looking for a party whose location stepwise and geographically was only roughly known. The crew was intrigued by accounts of the disaster that had befallen the *Pennsylvania*; Maggie ascertained that no assistance was needed from her in the aftermath.

At last, not far from the footprint of Houston, the ship flew over a rough campsite, with a small, solitary figure looking up from below. Nathan Boss pointed out a clump of woods near by which showed a lot of disturbance, the result of some kind of fight maybe.

And Mac gently drew her attention to an infrared image of slumped, cooling forms, deep inside the forest clump. Where the bodies had been dumped, evidently.

Maggie, Nathan and Joe Mackenzie descended. The lone figure at the campsite, a woman, waiting for them by a smoking fire, was a tough-looking forty-something – a few years older than Maggie – evidently a pioneer type. She gave her name simply as 'Sally'. Among the weaponry lashed to her back was a ceramic composite rifle, and she had a face full of unfinished business.

Maggie knew her officers well enough to be sure they would step lightly. And she also knew, she thought, from her pre-mission briefings on the Long Earth, who this woman was.

Sally offered them coffee, rolls of bedding to sit on. After that she didn't waste any time. 'I don't want you here. I believe in handling this kind of stuff myself. *I* didn't call you.'

Nathan asked, 'Then who did?'

'*He's* long gone – lit out of here. However, you're here. So here's the set-up. I've secured near by several so-called scientists who have killed at least three trolls.'

Nathan asked, 'Scientists?'

'Biologists. Actually up here to study the trolls, so they say. One of them was the one who called for help; I let him go. The rest—'

'And "secured"?' Maggie asked sharply. 'What do you mean by that?'

Sally grinned evilly. 'The trolls were captured here for some kind of "experiment" in cross-breeding with other humanoids. Unsurprisingly they resisted and stepped away, heading due West, which led to a chase, and a male and two females being shot dead – at least that number, I didn't see it all. Left behind one orphaned cub. I'm sure you're aware of the furore around our treatment of the trolls just now—'

'That doesn't sanction some kind of vigilante action by you, whoever you are,' Mac said thickly.

Sally just smiled. 'Oh, nobody's dead. They're not exactly comfortable, but nobody's *dead*. Unlike those trolls. And by the way if your crew try to apprehend me I'll step out of here faster than you can say "beam me up".'

Maggie was all too aware that for all Sally's self-confidence the slightest evidence of a threat from her would bring down the lightning from the *Franklin*. On the other hand Maggie needed to get a hold of this situation – and, as she thought she recognized this woman, she saw a way.

'OK,' she said now. 'I've no intention of trying to apprehend you – umm, *Sally*. We're not out here to be a police force. For all I know, these characters deserved whatever you dished out. However I would advise you at the least to put aside those weapons on your back. Let's just calm tensions here. And then I suggest that you and I stroll over to that clump of woods, where the bodies are, and have a little parley. Get this situation resolved.'

Sally hesitated. Then she nodded, dumped her weapons, and the two walked towards the woods, leaving Mac and Nathan to sample a little more much-brewed coffee.

'Of course, I know who you are,' Maggie said quickly, seeking to put Sally off her stride.

'You do?'

'Sure. You're the woman who stepped out of the *Mark Twain* with Joshua Valienté. News gets around.' More specifically, she had cropped up in Maggie's briefings as a well-known rogue element – and, yes, suspected vigilante – out in the Long Earth. 'Sally Linsay, right? That's at least one of the names you're known by.'

Sally shrugged. 'And I know about you, Captain Margaret Dianne Kauffman. Oh, it wasn't hard to find out about your military career – anybody concerned about Long Earth politics knows all about the *Franklin* and its officers and the rest of the fleet and their galumphing Starfleet-type mission. Actually I'm kind of glad it was you who showed up; you're evidently one of the less stupid of the Captain Kirks running around out here.'

'Thanks.'

Sally eyed Maggie shrewdly. 'Listen – since you're here. And since you're evidently not some military-issue psycho.'

'Praise indeed.'

'I do believe in serendipity. Grabbing opportunities. There's an idea I've been playing with, about law-enforcement.'

'That's not our role, strictly speaking . . .' Somehow Maggie was back on the defensive. 'What are you talking about?'

'You may be less stupid than your peers, but what a dumb mission you're engaged in. It really is like bloody *Star Trek* – a handful of ships patrolling an infinity of worlds. Look, if you want to manage the Long Earth then you have to get holistic.'

'I've no idea what you're suggesting.'

'I'm suggesting you need an ally that's spread as wide as the Long Earth itself.' She looked directly at Maggie. 'I'm talking about trolls.'

That took Maggie totally by surprise. '*What?*'

'Use the trolls. Take a couple on your ship, even. Look, they are, or were, being used all over the Long Earth already, wherever people want a friendly hand. Why not the military too? They have an extensive communications system, coupled to a huge folk memory—'

'The long call.'

'Yes. Not to mention being somewhat physically intimidating.'

This was too much for Maggie to take in. It occurred to her that her mission had evolved a hell of a way from that tough-love speech by the President, to *this*. On the other hand maybe she *should* be making some kind of response to this business of the trolls. 'I'll need to think about it . . . Why would *you* want this?'

Sally shrugged. 'I'm on the trolls' side. How better to protect them than to have them work *with* the soldiers? Also, maybe it will help them learn to trust us again . . .'

They reached the clump of forest. Maggie followed Sally into the shade, where they found two dead trolls – the third Sally mentioned had presumably left a corpse off on some stepwise world – and a live juvenile still trying to cuddle up to one of the bodies.

'You say you have these scientist characters stashed somewhere near by.'

'You'll find them. You better had, in fact, before the other trolls get here.'

'What other trolls?'

Sally gave her a knowing look. 'At twilight, young though it is, this orphaned cub will attempt to join in with the long call. That will summon other trolls. And when they turn up – look, trolls are comparatively merciful. More than most human parents would be. But they are protective of their cubs.'

'Point taken.'

They began to walk back to the fire.

'Listen,' Sally said now, apparently on impulse. 'There's something else. Since I believe you have the right stuff, Captain Maggie, take a look at this.' She rummaged under a small heap of gear, and pulled out a piece of shining tech.

It was a tube encrusted with keypads, vaguely resembling some kind of musical instrument, but technologically advanced. It was like an ocarina redesigned by Einstein, Maggie thought.

'This is a troll-call.'

'A what?'

'Call it a two-way translation device for talking with trolls. I'm pretty good at it by now, I can call for help, or to signal danger. I mean, our language is nothing like theirs – this is just a prototype – and you can't get across much more than basic concepts. But for now it's the best we can do. With a few trolls on your ship, and one of *these* . . .'

'How do I get hold of one?'

'Oh, it's not for sale,' said Sally. 'But I could get one for you from the manufacturer.'

'Who *is* the manufacturer?' asked Maggie.

Sally just smiled.

Maggie took a leap into the dark. 'OK – get me one. That way I keep my options open. And I will consider what you've said.'

'Good.'

'How will I find you? . . . Oh. You'll find me, right?'

'You're getting the hang of this.'

Any dirigible crew, when on the ground, were routinely wired up and monitored; Maggie's officers had of course overheard every word.

Nathan Boss thought they should have apprehended Sally Linsay, or at least tried to.

And Joe Mackenzie thought she was crazy even to be thinking about taking trolls on board.

'I don't know, Mac. We do need new ways of working out here. I've learned that much in the past month. I mean, she's right, once you are more than ten steps from the Datum, it's like interstellar space. You can't control the Long Earth like it was some occupied city in a war zone. Or even Datum New York. Freedom's a mess, isn't it? Listen, Mac – do some research for me. Find me some troll experts . . .'

22

THE *GOLD DUST* and its accompanying fleet crept through the Low Earths, the last couple of dozen stepwise worlds before the Datum. The skies were pretty crowded over these relatively heavily developed worlds, and as the ships were stepped through collisions were a real threat. In the last few worlds they actually had to follow a scout on the ground, who would step forward, check out the route, and then come back when the way was clear.

But even the clutter of West 3 or 2 or 1 was as nothing compared with what they found when they finally crossed over to the Datum. They looked down on the landscapes of West 1, and then with that last step it was as if somebody had exploded a daisycutter bomb, scything away the greenery for miles around and replacing it with concrete, tarmac and steel, staining the shining river a turbid grey and penning it in with reinforced banks and bridges, all under a grubby, colourless sky. Joshua thought you couldn't have had a better demonstration of what humanity could do to a world, given a few centuries and a lot of oil to burn.

The *Gold Dust* herself seemed diminished as she settled gingerly towards her docking apron. And the very first detail Joshua saw as he disembarked, on the wall of an old brick warehouse, was a giant portrait of President Cowley, standing there glaring with his arm held out and palm upraised, as if to say: Keep Out!

Sally, following Joshua, glared around dismissively. She was back with them, however briefly, from her latest jaunt. Long as he'd known her, Joshua still knew little of the various channels through which she kept in touch with what was going on out in the Long Earth, a vast domain which, in some sense, she seemed to feel responsible for policing. Now she said grimly, 'Welcome home.'

The disembarked passengers were decanted into an immigration hall, a huge processing area full of snaking lines and checkpoints and screening booths, Homelands goons visored so you couldn't see their faces, threatening instruction posters on the walls, enigmatic banners:

GENESIS 3:19

Like what he recalled of airports, Joshua saw now, this twain station had brightly signed links to other transport networks: planes, trains, buses, cabs. Transport had been one of the few big growth industries on the Datum since Step Day. To make a long-distance journey across a Low Earth, it was still generally easier to jump back to Datum Earth, catch a bus or plane, and step back once you'd reached your destination. But to access those services you had to get through immigration. Joshua checked over his little party as they waited in line. Dan, who had never had an experience like this in his life before, was confused. Helen looked stoically patient, as ever. Bill was still paralysed by his latest hangover, after his send-off by the crew of the *Gold Dust*. Sally just rolled her eyes at the endless stupidity of humanity.

And as they waited in their line a man approached them, small, intense, dressed in a black cassock, dog collar and crested hat. Dan flinched back as he drew nearer. The guy carried a Bible, and a small brass globe on a chain from which the rich scent of incense wafted. He was evidently working the waiting crowd.

Coming right up to them he pressed a leaflet into Sally's hand. 'In the name of the Lord, now you have returned home, *stay here*, on the Datum Earth – the one true Earth.'

Sally glared at him. 'Why should we? Who are you?'

He said earnestly, 'There is not a shred of evidence, either scientific or theological, that the discarnate soul can travel crossways through the worlds. Let your children die *there*, out in the wilderness, and their souls will *never* find their way to the bosom of the Lord.' He crossed himself. 'And as you know the Day of Judgement is approaching. Even now, on all those so-called stepwise worlds, at the heart of all those godless copies of the true America, fire and brimstone are spreading sulphurous fumes across Yellowstone—'

Sally just laughed, and told him in crisp Anglo-Saxon to go away, more forcibly than Joshua would have dared. The man shuffled off in search of easier targets.

'Well, *he* was a bit mad,' Bill said.

At last they reached the front of the line. Here their bags were opened and searched meticulously, and each of the party was put through a whole-body scanner. Joshua and Sally were first through. On the other side they were both issued with wristbands, brightly coloured and no doubt studded with tracker technology, that they would have to wear at all times until they left the Datum.

As they waited for the others Joshua murmured, 'I don't get this. All this processing and screening – all new since the last time I came back. But what's the point? I know there are stepwise hazards for the Datum: infectious diseases, invasive species. But all these barriers – the Long Earth is an open frontier. Here we are obediently riding in on a twain and arriving at a transport hub, but we could step back *anywhere* on the Datum, with a backpack full of long-horned beetles. There's no logic.'

Sally rolled her eyes. 'It's all symbolism, Joshua. You never *do* get stuff like this, do you? This is President Cowley saying to his voters, look how I'm protecting you. Look how terrible these travellers are, what a threat they are.' She glanced at the banks of security processing gear. 'Also there's a lot of federal money to be earned by the companies that manufacture gear like this. Fear generates big profits.'

'You're very cynical.'

'Joshua, cynicism is the only reasonable response to the antics of humanity. Especially on the Datum.'

At last Dan, Helen and Bill came through. Dan was wide-eyed and bewildered, but not actively scared, Joshua was relieved to see. Reunited, they picked up their luggage and moved through a crowded outer hall, looking for a cab rank. Joshua noticed a feature that was new since he'd last come through a place like this: small patches of the crowded sidewalks marked off by yellow hatching, reserved as stepping areas that you otherwise tried to keep clear, so as to allow an unimpeded flow-through. Only on the Datum would you need such controls; he felt an uncomfortable claustrophobia just thinking about it.

And now another man approached them, this one in a smart-looking business suit, carrying a plastic shopping bag. Evidently they weren't to be left alone for a minute. Aged maybe thirty, this guy had thinning hair, spectacles, and a winning smile.

He stood directly in their path, so they had to stop. Joshua thought he was probably another religious nut. Then the man said, clearly and calmly, 'Welcome to Earth, mutants.'

And he reached into his bag.

Joshua lunged forward, putting his body between the man and his family. From the corner of his eye he saw Sally pick up Dan and step away in an instant with a pop of imploding air. And the man pulled out a blade, short, heavy, wicked. In one movement he hurled it.

The knife hit Joshua above the right breast. He was thrown back, pain flooding him.

He saw Helen charge forward and ram her fist into the man's face. She was a midwife, and strong in the upper body; he was laid flat out. Cops and other security people came running.

For Joshua, the world greyed and fell away.

23

'YOUR WOULD-BE killer is called Philip Mott,' Monica Jansson said, as she poured Joshua's coffee. 'A junior attorney working for one of the big railroad combines. No previous record, no significant contact with the police. He's not a phobic, as far as we know, and he's not a home-alone – that is, never dumped by a family stepping away, a common trigger for this kind of behaviour.'

Joshua knew all about that syndrome. Helen herself was the sister of the Madison-bomb accomplice Rod Green, a homealone gone rogue.

'But,' Jansson said, 'Mott doesn't own a Stepper box. He's hardly ever stepped at all as far as any of his character witnesses testify. He has been running with President Cowley's Humanity Firsters for years, some of the more rabid elements, which even Cowley now officially disowns . . .'

Joshua shifted in the sofa, which was a little too deep for him to feel comfortable. A couple of days after the attack his shoulder was healing, but was still strapped up, and was prone to deliver stabs of fresh pain if he didn't favour it. Sally sat beside him, cradling a coffee mug, perched on the edge of her seat. As ever she looked as if she was about to bolt through the door, or out of this reality altogether. Dan, meanwhile, was outside, playing basketball with Bill, using a rusty old hoop fixed to the wall of Jansson's house. Joshua could hear them running around in the sunshine, Dan jabbering out some imaginary commentary.

And Helen, incredibly, was in custody, on assault charges.

They were staying with Joshua's old sparring partner, former MPD Lieutenant Monica Jansson. Jansson's house, here on the outskirts of Madison West 5 – to which the residents of Datum Madison had been rezoned after the nuke – was typical Low Earth architecture, a massive structure of wood of a quality that would once have been impossibly expensive on the Datum. Jansson's personal past showed in the way the place was studded with bits of high-tech gear: a widescreen TV, cellphones, a laptop.

Jansson was in her fifties now, but looked older, to Joshua's inexpert gaze. She was thinner than he remembered too, her hair greyed and cut short. And he'd noticed a line of medicines, in small white plastic bottles, on the mantelpiece over the big fireplace – and just above the mantelpiece was Joshua's sapphire ring on its leather loop, hanging in pride of place from a picture hook on the wall. Encouraged by Helen, he'd brought the ring here with the vague intention of showing it, one of his few impressive trophies of his travels, to a few discreet friends.

On the TV, some geologist was crawling around a bubbling mud pool in a copy of Yellowstone, on some Low Earth or other. Apparently there had been similar disturbances at Datum Yellowstone and at some of its Low Earth footprints. The jokey commentator was talking about geysers failing, wildlife fleeing and such, and how it was actually *good* for business at the National Park, with people coming in to rubberneck the latest chthonic turmoil in the stepwise copies. Maybe that religious nut at the twain port had been right about the fire and brimstone at Yellowstone, even if he made the wrong interpretation.

Sally said now, 'So this Mott guy has never pulled a stunt like this before?'

'Not on the record, no. But a lot of the Firsters are like that nowadays. Their strategies have evolved. They soak up the propaganda, they stay quiet, under the radar, they take to carrying around stakes—'

Joshua asked, 'Stakes?'

'That's their jargon for the weapon he carried. Like staking a vampire, you know? A stake of iron, for a stepper. Very hard to police. And then, out of the blue, they find themselves in some situation where they're presented with a target of opportunity. Such as near a twain terminal, but outside the security barriers so nobody knows what he has in the bag – where this guy met you, Joshua.'

'And recognized your face,' Sally said dryly.

'And – bang. He would have been aiming for your heart, by the way. Even if he missed the heart, he might have caused you problems if you tried to step away with a chunk of steel sitting in your chest.'

Sally grunted. 'I'm hearing that there are countries on the Datum where governments are doing that kind of thing purposefully. Surgically fixing iron clips to your heart, or an artery.'

Jansson said, 'Yeah. They call it stapling. Look, don't worry. Mott's still in custody; he'll be charged. Datum law-enforcement isn't what it was in my day, but you don't get away with attacks like that.'

'And nor does my wife, it seems,' Joshua said bitterly. 'I can't believe they charged Helen with assault.'

'Well, she did lay the guy out. Quite a haymaker. She'll get off with a reprimand, it was self-defence—'

'She's still in custody! They took away her Stepper, won't even give her bail. How long will we have to wait to get her out?'

'That's the policy now with non-residents of the Low Earths or the Datum, I'm afraid.'

Sally shook her head. 'The Datum's become a world full of paranoids, run by paranoids. No wonder we never come back.'

'Well, you came back this time for a reason,' Jansson said to Joshua. 'Your meeting with Senator Starling, right?'

'To talk about this issue of the trolls, yes.' He shrugged, making his shoulder ache anew. 'Thanks to you, Jansson – I know you opened a few doors to set that up. But now I'm doubting the wisdom of coming here at all.'

'You have to try,' Sally snapped. 'We went through this back at Hell-Knows-Where.'

He said tiredly, 'Sure. But now we're here it's obvious that the issue of the welfare of trolls isn't going to be at the top of the Datum political agenda.'

Jansson nodded. 'You may be right. But the case of Mary out at the Gap has made the news even on the Datum. It's such an exceptional case, such obvious cruelty and injustice, in the middle of a space programme, for God's sake. It couldn't be higher profile, and presents an opportunity for change. Which is why I did what I could to help set up your meeting with Starling.'

Sally said, 'Exactly. Joshua, what's the use of your having a famous face if you don't use it for good?'

171

He grunted. 'All my "famous face" has done for me so far is get me stabbed, my wife put in custody, and my kid scared out of his wits.'

Jansson glanced out the window at Dan. 'Oh, I think that little pioneer's tougher than that.'

Joshua grimaced. 'President Cowley would say he's a little mutant.'

Jansson smiled sadly. 'Also a sinner.'

Sally nodded. 'Genesis 3:19. We saw the posters.'

Joshua closed his eyes, remembering Bible classes at the Home. 'What God told Adam and Eve after the expulsion from Eden. *In the sweat of thy face shalt thou eat bread, till thou return unto the ground; for out of it wast thou taken: for dust thou art, and unto dust shalt thou return.*'

'That's it,' Jansson said. 'God has put us on this world, or worlds, to work. You comber types, happy to just wander around – or at least that's how you're painted here – are a bunch of slackers. Without work mankind can't progress . . . and so on.'

Joshua sighed. 'And so, pushed by such madness, we slide into war, or something.'

Jansson sipped her coffee. Joshua thought he saw her shiver, though the day wasn't cold.

He asked gently, 'And how are you, Monica?'

She looked up. 'Best to stick to Lieutenant Jansson, don't you think?'

'You're settled here in West 5?'

'Well, nobody's allowed to stay long back in Datum Madison even now. They might let you back for a while, Joshua, if you want to see it. I could pull a few strings. It's an eerie place to see. The wildlife is flourishing. Prairie flowers sprouting in flash-burned rubble.

America's Chernobyl, they call it. It's slowly healing, I guess.'

He said carefully, 'And are you?'

She looked at him tiredly. 'Is it that obvious?'

'Sorry.'

'Don't be. It's leukaemia. My own stupid fault. I was too eager to go hopping back and forth to the Datum after the blast. But it's manageable with drugs, and they're talking about gene therapy.'

'You always tried to put things right,' Joshua said abruptly. 'That's what I always recognized in you.'

She shrugged. 'That's a cop's job.'

'But you took it a bit further than most. I always responded to that.' He reached over, wincing as his shoulder ached, and touched her hand. 'Just don't give up yet. OK?'

Sally stood up impatiently. 'If you two are going to get all mushy on me I'm out of here.'

Joshua turned. 'You're not going already?'

She winked. 'I always have chores, Joshua. You know me. I'll be back. So long, Lieutenant Jansson.' And she disappeared with a soft pop.

Jansson raised her eyebrows. 'I'll make some more coffee.'

24

MARLON JACKSON, Senator Starling's aide, was determined to take the meeting with this bizarre Valienté pioneer-type character on the chin.

Jim Starling was mostly manageable, in Jackson's experience. Regrettably the Senator had a good if erratic memory, which could make him devilishly difficult to steer in the way a decent aide should be able to. But at least the Senator's tantrums were generally short and futile, and in that the man was not unlike Jackson's great-grandfather's description of Lyndon B. Johnson: 'A goddamn tornado until he ran down, and then you could get the work done.' Jackson's forebears had been behind-the-scenes toilers for democracy for generations.

But great-grandpa had never had to deal with modern technology. Such as a diary system into which an appointment for this Joshua Valienté had got inserted, even though everybody with access denied putting it there. Even when Jackson managed to delete the entry, it *got put back again*. Evidently Valienté had some kind of support; Jackson, an old hand in DC, knew the signs.

And it *would* have to be someone like Valienté, who last time Jackson had seen him in person had been stonewalling a Senate board of inquiry about his spectacular but mysterious jaunt across the Long Earth, in an apparently *pilotless ship*. Driven by apparently *covert technology*, some of which was subsequently gifted by the Black Corporation to the nation, much to the silent fury of the nation's political classes. Valienté, a walking talking symbol of the Long Earth, backed by some kind of hidden hand – Valienté, who had forced his way in here, more or less, to face a senator whose main support base despised the new colonies and everything about them. A clash of minds occurring just as the political situation vis à vis the colonies had never been trickier, what with the Valhalla declaration on top of all this crap about trolls . . .

In Jackson's world this was a small incident, but one out of control and fraught with danger. Like a hand grenade rolling across the floor. If he just got the chance to smooth out the Senator's more idiotic brain dumps into something that sounded like constructive dialogue, then everything would be fine. You just had to hope, in this business.

He gulped down one of his ulcer pills.

In fact Joshua Valienté and his buddy, both dressed in *Bonanza*-type dung-coloured pioneer gear, were a few minutes late when security finally showed them into the office. To Jackson they looked like an irruption from America's semi-mythic past into the clutter of this mid-twenty-first-century office.

After a curt introduction, Valienté went straight on the attack. 'Seven minutes late because of your security protocol. Are you afraid just of me, or all your voters?' Before Jackson had a chance to respond, Valienté looked around at the hunting trophies on the office walls. 'And what decor. Looks like they're all either inedible or from a protected species, or both. Nice symbolism.'

His companion guffawed.

Jackson hadn't yet said a single word. He was struggling here; he felt as if he'd been hit by some primal force. 'Why don't you take a seat, Mr Valienté, and Mr—' he glanced at his briefing '– Chambers?'

At least they complied to that degree.

What *was* this Valienté? Jackson's briefing had suggested some kind of retard with nothing more than a gift for stepping . . . He was evidently more than that. His very voice was strange, Jackson thought as he tried to size up this man, a voice which laid down words as a poker player laid down cards, with finality and decision. He seemed slow rather than fast, but relentless. As hard to stop, once he came rolling at you, as an oncoming tank.

As for the trophies on the wall, Jackson knew that the tiger head had been acquired by Starling's grandfather who'd bought it from a dealer in Chinese aphrodisiacs, but most of the rest were the result of the Senator's own efforts. All these trophies were a signal – Valienté was right to spot the symbolism – to inform any visitors that the Senator had an impressive and well-oiled armoury and was not shy of using it. But then, practically everybody who voted for him was a firearms enthusiast. Jim Starling was *not* a man to take any notice of latter-day eco-tards wetting their pants because they thought somebody was killing Bambi out in some dismal stepwise Earth. Which, of course, was the background to this whole business.

Anyhow this was not Jackson's problem; he just had to get through the next hour or whatever until these guys were shown the door. 'Coffee, gentlemen?'

176

Chambers said, 'You wouldn't have a cup of tea at all?'

Jackson made a call; the drinks arrived in a couple of minutes.

Then, to Jackson's relief, he heard a flush from the bathroom. The door opened and the Senator came in with, fortunately, for once, everything safely stowed away.

Starling, a burly fifty-something in shirtsleeves, evidently in the middle of his working day, looked disarmingly welcoming. The colonists stood up, and looked a little less, well, *bristling*, as the Senator shook their hands. This was what Starling was good at, working people even from the first second he walked in a room.

And Jackson could see it shook Valienté up when Starling asked for his autograph, as they sat down. 'Not for me, it's for my niece. She's a big fan.'

Valienté seemed to feel the need to apologize as he signed a card. 'I didn't vote for you. Postal votes don't get out as far as Hell-Knows-Where.'

Starling shrugged. 'But you're still my constituent, according to the Aegis definition and the electoral records.' Joshua maintained a legal address at the Home in Madison West 5. 'And you're in politics yourself now, right?' He flipped through the paperwork on his desk. 'A mayor in some pioneer-type community. How admirable.' The Senator flopped back in his big chair and said, 'Well, now, gentlemen, you came all the way back from your distant Earth, you came all the way in to DC, you wanted to see me urgently. So let's get to it. I believe the issue is game preservation in the subsidiary Earths, yes?'

'Yes, sir,' said the Irishman, Bill Chambers.

'No,' said Valienté, back on the attack again. 'Trolls

177

aren't *game*. And there are no such things as *subsidiary* Earths; every Earth is an Earth, a whole world. That's a very Datum-centric point of view, sir.'

Jackson drew breath to intervene at this point. But the Senator took this with good humour. 'I stand corrected. But the Earths that interest me are the ones containing US citizens, under the Aegis. And my concern is to ensure that our citizens are allowed those liberties that our Constitution demands.' He shuffled his paperwork, glancing over it again. 'I believe I understand why you're here. But why don't you put it in your own words?'

Valienté was no orator, evidently, Jackson saw, despite his own political experience. Haltingly, as best he could, he tried to summarize the concerns gathering across the Long Earth over the treatment of the trolls.

'Look – when I heard about this notorious case, of Mary and her cub at the Gap, I was dismayed. But it's only the tip of the iceberg where the trolls are concerned. At Hell-Knows-Where, you know, we protect our trolls under a citizenship extension.'

'What? You're serious? So how far do you take that? Oh, don't answer that. Look, whatever hayseed laws you pass in Who-Knows-What—'

'*Hell*-Knows-*Where*.'

'Don't amount to a hill of beans back here, as your type might say. Let's get to the point. These trolls are humanoids. Right? Humanoid, pre-human if you like, but *not human*, no matter what ordinances you pass in your hick *Blazing Saddles*-type town. They are animals, and, according to my best advice, dangerous animals. So we have these creatures out there, powerful and aggressive creatures, who, according to you, should not be killed or otherwise inconvenienced, yes? I have read the paperwork, even though my assistant probably thinks I haven't,' and he winked at Jackson. 'Powerful, aggressive animals, and now killers.'

Valienté said, 'Powerful, yes. Even a female troll will weigh as much as a sumo wrestler and can punch like a heavyweight boxer . . . Aggressive? Only if they're pushed. Mostly they're helpful.'

'Helpful?'

'Senator, humans and trolls work together. It happens all across the Long Earth, even in the Low Earths – hell, you must be aware of that, the economic value-add of troll labour . . .'

The trolls had become an ever-present in the worlds colonized by mankind. To pioneers bereft of heavy machinery, trolls were willing and clever workers who would clear your field, tote your bales of hay, even help you put up the schoolhouse. Nowadays, in the more developed societies in the Low Earths and beyond, trolls were put to work on the vast sheep farms that covered many parallel Australias, even shearing and spinning the wool, and in the tremendous rubber plantations of stepwise Malaysias. They even worked in the assembly lines of factories in some Low Earth Americas.

'That's as may be.' Starling riffled the paperwork. 'But here I have a sheaf of reports of attacks by these trolls of yours on humans. In one case leading to a man being paralysed, in another a small child traumatized and its mother left lying dead. And so on. What do you say to that?'

'Senator – trolls are only dangerous in the way that bears in a national park are dangerous. I mean, every so

179

often some dumb tourist wants to get a picture of his toddler sitting nicely with a cute little cub . . . That kind of ignorance is bad enough back in the original USA, but it's deadly on the stepwise Earths, which are all more or less wild. We tell people this all the time. In most stepwise worlds, being dumb is a prelude to being dead.

'And the situation's going to get worse, Senator. The trolls have something called the long call, which means that eventually every troll in every world gets to know what every other troll knows. It takes a while to permeate. But sooner or later, if humanity treats trolls as ferocious animals, then our relationship with them everywhere will be fundamentally altered—'

Starling laughed out loud. 'And that, sir, sounds like a lot of wu-wu tree-hugger bull hickey to me. The *long call*? You'll be warning me about the wrath of Eywa next. Bottom line, Mr Valienté: our citizens must be protected, even from being dumb, which is not a crime. Good heavens, if it was, the jails would never empty. Especially here in DC. Ha!'

Valienté pressed his point. 'All I am asking for, sir, is some kind of declaration that the United States gives the trolls the status of a protected species throughout the Aegis.'

'That's all, is it?' Starling spread his hands. 'But you must know that the situation regarding animal protection is complicated in this country as it is. We have federal laws, but a lot of legislation is at state level. Who exactly is it you want to define these laws, let alone enforce them? And in any event, as with so much concerning the so-called colony worlds, there's endless debate about how our Datum laws extend out there.' He glanced again at his briefing. 'I see you've floated the idea that these trolls of yours could be considered an exotic species. If so they would fall under the Department of Agriculture Animal and Plant Health Inspection service. But there's a counter-argument that they aren't exotic at all, but endemic – I mean, they're native to all the other Earths, aren't they? So the old categories don't necessarily apply, legally or morally, it seems to me.

'As regards the specific case of this base at the Gap, if it was under the US Aegis they would need a Department of Agriculture permit to justify the trolls' use in research. They should have gone through a process of obtaining such a permit, and maybe there's some control to be applied through that route. But you see, Mr Valienté, though US citizens are involved in this work, as I under-stand it this Gap base isn't even in the US footprint. Somewhere in England, right? Maybe you should be argu-ing your case in London, not here.' He shrugged and pushed away his paperwork. 'Look, the legal position is vague, and the issue lacks moral clarity to me. I am listen-ing, gentlemen, but I don't consider the case made. At best, all I could do is bring your concerns to the Senate. But I don't believe I'm minded to do that. And besides you're missing the wider issues.'

'What wider issues?'

'Whether you like it or not, Mr Valienté, there are questions of national security involved here. This isn't about animals, for cripes' sakes. I'm talking about *threat*. That's what concerns my constituents, here on the Datum. The threat of the unknown. It wasn't so bad when all we had to think about was aliens coming at us from another planet, like in the movies! Shit, at least we'd get warning, you'd think. At least we'd have a chance of shooting them out of the sky. But now we have open borders, it seems to me. Now the aliens could just walk in!'

The Irishman – Jackson had to check the name again, Bill Chambers – spoke for the first time, all but. 'Senator, you're talking about these mad military twains you've sent out all over the place, aren't you?'

Starling leaned forward.

Jackson tensed, ready for trouble; he knew the warning signs when his lord and master was getting pissed.

'Yes, sir,' said Starling. 'That's one response. Somebody must plan for the worst eventuality. That's the job of a responsible government.'

To Jackson's horror, Chambers actually blew a raspberry. 'Ah, come off it, Senator. Are you kidding? This is just another boondoggle, a spending free-for-all, like the missile gap after Sputnik, like 9/11, like Madison. The vaguer the threat the more money you get to chuck at it, right? Look, I live out there, and here's what I say. I say you can't have one government for a million Americas, and this proves it. It just can't work, it would be one god-awful bureaucracy. Well, so it is already. Hell, after all those centuries the fecking English never even managed to run Ireland properly. How are you lot going to manage *this*?'

Valienté laughed. 'You'd better not go repeating that when those Navy airships show up over our town hall, Bill.'

'Yeah. Maybe you should hold that thought, pioneer guy.'

But Chambers wasn't quite done. 'You know, before Step Day one world was enough for you characters. Because you didn't even know the rest existed, did you?

Now we've gone out there and made something of it all, and you lot who stayed at home want a piece of the fecking pie. Suddenly one world is no longer enough for you. Can't you just leave us alone?'

Starling just looked at the man, steadily. Then he sat back and turned to Valienté, to Jackson's relief; at least it didn't look as though there'd be any actual physical violence, not this time.

'You know, Mr Valienté,' Starling said now, 'I have nothing to say to your companion here. I'm kind of disappointed in *you*, however. I understand you are known to be a truthful man, a careful man. I have seen depositions commending you for valour when you were younger, on Step Day. Quite a number of young people owed their lives to you. Then came that episode when you went charging off into the Long Earth – going where no one had gone before, right? All very admirable. Now you come in here with these ridiculous demands, this bullshit about these animals . . . I'd have thought you'd see a bigger picture. Ah, what the hey.' Then he grinned, unexpectedly. This was often Starling's way, Jackson knew, to become good-old-boy expansive having mauled his opponent to his satisfaction.

'Listen. Let's not part on bad terms. I believe you to be brave but naive, just as you probably believe that I am a mere tool of the military-industrial complex. Nevertheless you have spoken your piece and done it well, and I enjoyed disputing with you. I suspect your Sister Agnes would be proud of you, if I may say so.'

That caught Valienté short, as no doubt it was meant to. Jackson was impressed Starling had read that far in his briefing.

'Oh, I know all about the Home that used to be on Allied Drive, Mr Valienté. It's become part of your legend, for better or worse. And I met Agnes once, when she came into this office to harangue me about a different issue. I was very sorry to hear about her death. I know she meant a great deal to you and other former inmates.'

Valienté actually smiled, which was a measure of Starling's charisma. 'Well – thank you. She had a calm death. There was even a representative of the Vatican at her funeral.'

'A nod of respect to a worthy foe, I imagine, from what I understand of her career.'

'Yeah. Even though they used to say she was the worst Catholic since Torquemada, or so she claimed. You know, Mr Starling, I don't exactly miss her. Somehow it's as if she never died . . .'

25

HELEN WAS WAITING for him when he got back to Jansson's house in Madison West 5. To their shared relief she was out of custody now, but under house arrest, here at Jansson's.

She listened to his frustrated account of his meeting with Starling.

Then, to distract him, she showed Joshua correspondence they'd been sent on the Black Corporation's latest iteration of its 'colony in a box' package. This was a technology they'd been prototyping at Hell-Knows-Where, in fact, evidently hoping to exploit Joshua himself as a poster-boy face for the programme. It had now developed into a neat integrated concept: a one-stop drop at a new colony site by one of the larger twains containing technological manna from heaven, such as satellite navigation supported by no fewer than three microsats injected into synchronous orbit by a compact launcher, enough equipment to seed a first-class hospital, a kit for a basic online university complete with a choice of virtual professors, and comms gear from old-fashioned landline telephony to shortwave radio packages and comsat aerials. More exotic items included a few bicycles for fast transport before the horses arrived, advice on mail-order marriage partners . . . The most sophisticated bit of kit was a matter printer, able to convert basic raw materials into complex parts. But such gadgets, Joshua knew, were prone to breakdown – and with the general stalling of technological development after Step Day, there hadn't been much advance in areas like nanotech. What was likely to be more useful to the average colonist, he thought, was the miniaturized set of basic how-to manuals, encyclopaedias, even a pharmacopoeia.

A basic thrust of the package was that you were encouraged to link up, initially through the shortwave, with other colonies sharing the same stepwise world; no one colony alone might be able to support a decent college, for example, but share your resources around the scattered townships of a whole world and you might just manage it.

'That was my idea in the first place,' Joshua said. 'The lateral link-ups. I like the idea of folk thinking of themselves from the outset as citizens of a whole planet, of a world growing sideways rather than just stepwise – a new world without borders from the beginning.'

'You're just a latter-day hippie.'

'Identities change. The old concept of nationality just melts away . . . Maybe we'll see an end to war through initiatives like this. A new start for all of us.'

'And *now* you sound like Dad. *Bliss was it in that dawn to be alive*,' Helen said, only mildly sarcastically. 'Shakespeare, I believe.'

'I think you'll find it was Wordsworth. Sister Agnes used to come out with that line a lot.'

His wife watched his face. 'You still miss her, don't you? Agnes. You've mentioned her a couple of times since we've been back here.'

Joshua shrugged. 'Well, here we are back in Madison. And Senator Starling mentioning her threw me. As he intended, I suppose. Agnes was the best thing that could have happened to me when I was a kid. Same for all of us. They want me to go back sometime, you know. To the Home.'

'Will you go?'

'Maybe. Not to be the great Joshua Valienté, alumnus made good, now an icon of the Long Earth and a mayor . . . and blah blah. As long as they let me just *talk* to the kids, about stuff like, I don't know, knife usage, field medicine for beginners. How to make the night sky your ally, with the Big Dipper a place to hang your hat, and Orion your friend to guide you home. That's what *I* would have wanted to hear, back then . . . I do wish she could have seen *this* blissful dawn. Agnes, I mean. I ought to get some flowers for her grave.'

'Was she the type who would want flowers?'

Joshua smiled. 'She always *said* no to flowers. Then she'd accept them, and grumble about a wicked waste of money, and would keep them in her study until the petals dropped off.'

Helen kissed him on the cheek. 'Go now.'

'What?'

'Just go see her. Never mind some invitation from the Home. Go for yourself. You'll feel better for it. And don't worry about us. We're not going anywhere. I'm not, anyhow . . .'

He slept on that.

Then, the next day, he went.

In Madison West 5, this new city that was growing up to replace the bombed-out hulk of the old – based on a new post-Step Day urban development where, as it happened, Helen had briefly lived with her family before their step-wise trek – the Home had been duplicated meticulously, aside from having various flaws fixed; Joshua himself had given over some money to see to that. Sister Agnes had lived to oversee the rebuilding.

And then she had died, in the autumn sunlight of a new Earth. She had been buried in the sight of plenty of important people – some of whom, Joshua knew, would frankly have liked to see her dead a lot earlier.

For now, her body had a brand new cemetery all to itself. It was a clear, bright May afternoon when Joshua arrived with his bouquet and placed it dutifully on the stone, in this small plot outside the Home. There were flowers here already, from the Sisters themselves, and from other grown-up inmates who had benefited from Agnes's indefatigable patience, her thoughtful love.

He lost track of time, alone for once, not moving. If he was spotted by anybody within the quiet Home, he wasn't disturbed.

He was surprised to notice the shadows starting to lengthen, the afternoon drawing on. He left the little graveyard, to start the long walk back to Jansson's.

And he saw a figure standing across the road. A woman in a nun's habit, just standing, apparently watching him. He crossed the road. He couldn't see her face; she looked youngish. 'Can I help you, Sister?'

'Well, I've been away . . .' Her voice was a soft brogue. 'I only learned of Agnes's death recently . . . Would you be Joshua Valienté, by any chance? Your face is familiar from the news. Oh dear me, where are my manners? I am Sister Conception. Agnes and me, we went back a long way. In

188

fact we took our vows together. I knew she would become a force in the world, always knew it, even though she could be a mouthy madam . . .'

Joshua stayed silent.

'Sister Conception' took a long look at Joshua's face. 'It isn't working, is it?'

'Well, if you want me to think that you aren't who you really are, no. I'd know her in the pitch dark. I can remember her walking through the dormitory every night, before standing at the door and turning the light out. The click of that old Bakelite switch, held together with glue because there was never any money for a rewiring. The way she made us all feel safe . . . Besides, she never was a good liar. *Or* any good at an Irish accent.'

'Joshua—'

'I think I can work it out. Lobsang?'

'Lobsang.'

'A stunt like this is just like him. And it was me who brought him in to see Agnes when she was dying. All my fault, probably. And now – well, here you are.'

'Joshua—'

'Hello, Agnes.' He threw his arms around her, until she burst out laughing and pushed him away.

26

For Agnes, it had begun with a wakening. She had felt a gentle warmth, and a certain sense of *pink*.

She thought this over for an indeterminate time. The last thing she remembered was her own bed, in the Home, the murmuring of a priest. She said, more cautiously than hopefully, 'And I am in heaven?'

'No. Heaven can wait,' said a male voice calmly. 'We have more urgent matters to consider.'

Sister Agnes whispered (although she wasn't sure *how* she whispered), 'And will there be a band of angels?'

'Not exactly,' said the firmament. 'But top marks for getting in a reference to the works of the late Jim Steinman in your first *minute* of revived consciousness. Now, alas, you must sleep again.' And darkness returned to cover the firmament, and as it faded the firmament said, 'Amazing . . .'

What was most amazing was that all this was spoken in Tibetan. And that she *understood*.

More time passed.

'Agnes? I have to wake you again for a little while, just for calibration . . .'

That was when they showed Agnes her new body: pink, naked, raw, and very female.

'Who ordered *those*?'

'I'm sorry?'

'Look – even before my bosom headed south for the winter, I assure you it wasn't that size. Can you please tone it down a little?'

'Don't worry. All things are mutable. If you will bear with us, we will eventually be able to present you with a suite of bodies for all occasions. All prosthetic, of course. You'll certainly pass as human; things have got a lot more sophisticated since I began my own experiments. Although quite a lot of you, technically speaking, will *not* be human. Incidentally you are being attended by a number of surgeons and other medical personnel in the pay of a little-known subsidiary of the Black Corporation. They have no idea of your identity. Fun, isn't it?'

'Fun?' Suddenly Agnes knew exactly who was doing this to her. 'Lobsang! You bastard!'

The dark rose up again. But her anger stayed: the anger she had always looked on as an ally, anger that filled her up. She clung to that heat now.

Eventually the pinkness returned.

And the voice of Lobsang spoke again, gently. 'My apologies once more, but this is a very delicate procedure – what you might call the endgame. I have been working on your revival for three years, and now it's nearly done. Sister Agnes, dear Agnes, you have nothing to fear. Indeed I expect to meet you in person after breakfast tomorrow. While you wait, would you care for some music?'

'Not more bloody John Lennon.'

'No, no. Knowing your taste – what is your position on the works of Bonnie Tyler?'

Sister Agnes woke up yet again, bewildered. Bewildered, and smelling coffee and bacon and eggs.

The scent emanated from a tray close by the bed on which she lay, evidently placed there by a young lady – bespectacled, friendly, Asiatic, perhaps Japanese. 'There is no hurry, madam. Take your time. My name is Hiroe. Please ask for anything you desire.'

In fact coming back to life seemed to get easier as it went along. With Hiroe's help she made her way to the bathroom of what appeared to be a bland hotel suite, took a shower, stared at her perfect teeth in the mirror, and voided her bowels of nothing very much.

Hiroe said, 'You should find physical matters easy. We took your body through many basic processes while you were in deep sleep. Training it, so to speak. Would you be so kind as to walk up and down for a while, and tell me what you feel?'

Sister Agnes did indeed walk around, and gave her report. She tasted the coffee, which wasn't bad at all, and was surprised to find that the bacon was crisp to the point of charcoal, just as she had always liked it.

And then there was a closet full of clothing, including a habit of the kind she had worn for so many years. She hesitated. As a Catholic nun somewhat estranged from her Church's orthodoxy, if she had been uncertain of her theological status before all *this*, she was bewildered now. But she had made her vows long ago, and she supposed they still applied, so she donned the garment. And as she dressed she smiled, enjoying the surcease of old-age pain in every joint, a feeling of liberty of movement long forgotten.

She said to the Japanese girl, 'I imagine I have an appointment with Lobsang himself?'

Hiroe laughed. 'Well done! He said that you would be quick to get to the point. If you would kindly follow me . . .'

Agnes followed the girl along a steel-walled corridor, passed through a series of doors which opened and closed with a certain automated panache, and was ushered into a room full of books and antique furnishings – it might have been Charles Darwin's study, down to the blazing fire in an antique hearth. But it was a place Agnes recognized, from Joshua's description of a similar experience. Lobsang chic, it seemed.

Across the room was a swivel chair, heavily stuffed, with its back to her.

She snapped, 'It's fake, isn't it? The fire. Joshua told me about it. He said it wasn't randomized properly.'

There was no answer from the swivel chair.

'Now listen to me. I don't know whether I should be incredibly grateful, or incredibly angry—'

'But this is what Joshua asked for on your behalf,' a cultured voice replied at last. 'Or so I inferred. I was brought to see you when you were ill – do you remember? In the Home, in Madison West 5. You had already been given the last rites. You were suffering, Agnes.'

'I'm not about to forget that.'

'And Joshua asked me to ease that suffering. Surely you would have wanted that—'

'Joshua. Of course he'd come.' Of all the children she'd cared for in her years in the Home, Joshua Valienté had always been the most – remarkable. It was typical of him never to have forgotten, not to have stayed away – to have come back when she needed him most, as her life, after too many decades, guttered like a fading candle. Come back to try to put things right. 'Joshua would ask for help. I suppose you weren't about to refuse him.'

'No. Especially as he asked me through gritted teeth; we did rather fall out after the Madison incident.'

'But he was surely merely asking you to ease my way. I would never have expected this – blasphemy!'

Now at last the chair swivelled, and Lobsang faced her, in an orange robe, his head apparently shaved. She'd seen him in person only once before, and she remembered that face – eerie, not quite the human norm, of no clearly identifiable age, like the reconstructed face of a burns victim perhaps. She remembered her own reflection; her new mechanical carcass was better quality than *this*. Evidently she was a later model.

He asked, 'Blasphemy? Must we talk in such terms?'

'Then in what terms do you want to talk?'

'Perhaps about the reason I . . . brought you back.'

'Reason? What reason could there possibly be?'

'Oh, a very good one. I would be very pleased if you would rise to this unusual occasion and consider a proposition – a new purpose, which I believe will accord with your own disposition. Will you hear me out?'

Sister Agnes took a seat in an almost identical overstuffed chair, opposite him.

'How are you finding your body, by the way?'

She raised her hand, looked at it, flexed her fingers, and imagined she heard the whirring of tiny hydraulic motors. 'I'm finding you've turned me into Frankenstein's monster.'

'Actually Frankenstein's monster was considerably

more learned and worthy than his so-called master. Just a thought.'

'Get to the point. What do you *want*?'

'Very well. Agnes, knowing a great deal about you from Joshua, and from other sources including your own diaries – and knowing your most excellent sympathy for an irrevocably flawed humanity – I have shanghaied you, so to speak, on behalf of said humanity. I have a mission for you. It is this: I need an adversary.'

'A what?'

'Agnes, you know me. You know what I am. I span the world! Indeed, the worlds. I wield an enormous amount of power, starting with the ability to fix parking tickets and working on up to a scale that no tyrant in all of history has been able to boast. I have no master. I report to nobody save myself. Even Douglas Black is only a patron, a facilitator. He could not *stop* me. And that's what worries me.'

'It does?'

'Of course. Shouldn't it? I need an adversary, Agnes. Somebody to tell me when I am out of order. When I'm being inhuman. Or being too human, even. It seems to me, given all that Joshua has said about you, that *you* are uniquely placed to be that person.'

'You brought me back to life to be your conscience? This is ridiculous! Even if I agreed – how could I stop you from doing anything that you want to do?'

'I will give you the means to shut me down.'

'What? Is that even possible?'

'It's tricky,' conceded Lobsang. 'There are now a number of iterations of myself scattered across the world, the Long Earth, and even various locations around the solar system. You can't have too much backup . . . But, yes, I can find a way to make it happen. To have *me* deleted from all those places.'

'Hmm. And in all those places,' said Sister Agnes, 'where is your soul?'

'Here, talking to you like this, in these new bodies, surely we can agree that the soul has no boundaries?'

'Do I have a choice in any of this?'

'Of course. You can walk away now and you will be taken anywhere on the planet that you wish. You will never hear from me again. Or – well, you too have an off switch, Agnes. But I know that you are not going to take those options.'

'Oh, you do, do you?'

'You see, when I came to visit you with Joshua that day, and I asked you if you had any regrets – do you remember? You whispered, "So much left to do." Now you have the chance to do more. What do you say? Will you be Boswell to my Johnson, Agnes? Watson to my Holmes? Satan to my Miltonic God?'

'Your nagging wife?'

He laughed, an eerie, not quite human sound.

Sister Agnes was uncharacteristically silent for some time. The loudest noise was the not-quite-authentic fire. In this womb of a room, she felt stuffy, enclosed. She longed to be out of here. Out on the open road – 'What happened to my Harley?'

'Joshua had it stored properly: off the ground, tyres over-inflated, fuel drained from the tank, everything greased up.'

'Will I be able to ride it? I mean, will I be physically capable—'

196

'Of course.'

'And will this wretched alchemy of yours allow me to drink beer?'

'Most certainly.'

'Where the hell am I, by the way?'

'In Sweden. At the headquarters of a wholly owned subsidiary of the Black Corporation's medical division. It's a nice crisp day outside.'

'Is it?'

'There are bikes. I thought ahead, you see. Not Harleys, but . . . Would you like to go for a ride?'

It was tempting. To be young again. Young, and on the road . . .

'In a moment,' she said firmly. 'How's Joshua?'

27

So Joshua found himself sitting with Sister Agnes reincarnate, in a shabby coffee shop in Madison West 5.

It was an odd atmosphere. Two people trying to get a grip on this inexplicable new world: a world where the dead could rise and sit cheerfully sipping a coffee while talking of old times . . . Two people not quite finding the words that needed to be said. As it was, however, for now, the smiles were doing the job.

Agnes sat upright, a bit primly, sipping her coffee. Maybe her features were just a little too regular, her skin a little too smooth, to be convincingly human.

But as far as Joshua was concerned, too many of the regulars in this coffee shop, mostly Low Earth construction workers, took a much too irreligious interest in Agnes's new curves. 'They ought to have more respect for the wimple.'

'Oh, hush. All men are rudimentary creatures who respond to symbols a lot more basic than a habit and a crucifix.'

'I can't quite believe this is happening.'

'Neither can I. And it's hard to even believe I'm here to do the disbelieving, if you know what I mean.'

When he looked up she was smiling, that flagstone-cracking beam of a smile that had always made her look twenty years younger. Agnes's smile wasn't the kind of smile that the regular world would associate with the word 'nun'. It was a smile that had always contained a touch of mischief, and also a terrible rage, kept in check until it was needed. This was what had enabled her to sustain the Home, and her many other projects, in the face of opposition from the Vatican on down. The smile and the rage.

She sipped her coffee quite convincingly, just as Lobsang's ambulant units always had; he tried not to think about the internal plumbing that made this possible. Now she lowered her cup and looked on him with pride, it seemed. 'Ah, me. And here you are, a full-grown man, a father, a mayor—'

'Lobsang did this to you.'

'He did,' she said warningly, 'though he used some careless talk from you as an excuse to do it, young man. We'll have to have a serious chat about that.'

'How? I mean—'

'Either I was downloaded from my poor dying brain via some kind of neural scan into a bucket of gel, or I was brought back by Tibetan monks chanting the Book of the Dead over my already interred corpse for forty-nine days. Lobsang tried both ways, he says.'

Joshua smiled weakly. 'That's Lobsang, all right. "Always have a backup." I came to your funeral, you know, but he kept the rest from me, I guess. I didn't know about the reincarnation. Or the monks. They must have driven the Sisters crazy . . . Does anybody else know you're back? I mean, at the Home—'

'Yes, I got in touch with the Home as soon as I could. I asked for Sister Georgina, she was the least likely to go bananas when she picked up the phone and heard my voice, or so I thought. I got a note from the Archbishop, if you want to know. The Church picks up more secrets than Lobsang himself. But I'm not public knowledge yet. Of course I'll have to come out, so to speak, some time, if I'm to assume my place in the world again. At least, thanks to Lobsang, I'm not the first, umm, *revenant* in silicon and gel, even if he is wrapped in a cloak of mystery. Enough people are aware of his origins; at least my basic existence might be accepted.'

'What place in the world?'

She pursed her lips. 'Well, Joshua, as you ought to know if you ever paid any attention, before my final illness I was deputy chief executive of the Leadership Conference of Women Religious, which represents most of America's Catholic sisters. I was actually in the middle of a terrific fight with the Vatican itself, its Congregation for the Doctrine of the Faith. That's the Inquisition, to you. About a book by a Sister Hilary in Cleveland.'

'A book? What about?'

'The spiritual benefits of female masturbation.'

Joshua sprayed coffee. The male heads turned again.

Her eyes glittered, as if she was ready for the fight. 'We've been at war with the Pope and his cardinals since the Second Vatican Council. Just because we think social justice is more important than opposing abortion or same-sex marriage. Just because we reject their patronizing patriarchy – which is why nuns become nuns in the first place, one way or another. Oh, I can't wait to get back into the fray, Joshua. And with this new body I'm never going to run out of steam, am I? I'll be the Energizer bunny of militant nuns.'

'What's an Energizer bunny?'

'Oh my dear child, you have so much to learn.'

'Tell me why Lobsang brought you back. Not for my benefit, I'm guessing?'

She snorted. 'Maybe that's ten per cent of it. Apparently, I am to serve as a moral compass for Lobsang himself.'

'Hmm. That's not necessarily a bad idea.'

'Maybe so, but I remain astonished that he doesn't realize that the pointer of *my* own moral compass is severely bent around the stop.'

He grinned. 'I remember when you hit that papal nuncio with a shoe. We all enjoyed that, even though we knew nothing about the scandal that guy was wrapped up in at the time. Then about two years afterwards the cover-up was exposed, and we all wished that you had hit him with *both* shoes.'

'Of course, at first, I hated Lobsang for bringing me back from the dead. What a cheek. While at the same time, if you can understand me, I was beside myself with gratitude that he did so.' She looked down at her body, at her hands.

'But he gave you the choice of not going along with this, right? You could have gone off and led some independent – umm, life. Or—'

'Or have him show me where my off switch is.'

'How did he convince you?'

She looked thoughtful. 'Well, I'll tell you the truth. It was one particular conversation we had. Lobsang said about something or other, "Does not compute." "Right," I said . . .'

201

* * *

'That was an ironic allusion, by the way,' Lobsang had added.

They had been in a kind of gym, both in more or less incongruous tracksuits, where Lobsang was helping Agnes develop her physical reflexes.

'*What* was an ironic allusion?'

'The phrase "does not compute" was used in an ironic sense to imply bewildered exasperation,' said Lobsang patiently. 'It was not used unthinkingly as an error message in response to insufficient or contradictory information.'

'Lobsang?'

'Yes?'

'What the hell are you talking about?'

'You persist in thinking of me as a computer. I am trying to dispel that illusion. Why are you shaking your head?'

'Sorry. It's just, well, you're trying too hard, I think.'

'You may call me "Lobby". Perhaps pet names will break the ice, do you suppose?'

'Lobby . . .'

('Joshua, he kept pausing, waiting for me to carry on talking. Have you ever spent time with a foreigner who wants to practise his English on you? Lobsang was like that, in those first few days, anxiously trying out his humanity on me . . .')

'Look,' Agnes said, 'you're going about it all *wrong*. You're not a human. You can't *be* a human. You're a very intelligent machine. You're *more* than human. Can't you live with that? Being human isn't about the brain, it's all tied up with messy things like – well, organs and juices and instincts.'

'You are describing your body, not yourself. In fact your former body.'

'Yes, but—'

'Externally you were an animal, but that was not your *self*. Externally I am a machine, but you should not judge by appearances.'

'OK, but—'

'We could try the Turin test,' said Lobsang.

'Oh, machines have been able to pass the Turing test for years.'

'No, the *Turin* test. We both pray for an hour, and see if God can tell the difference.'

And she had to laugh.

'That was it? He made you laugh?'

'Well, it was the first time he actually seemed authentically human. And he did keep on. It was like being licked to death by puppies. He wore me down in the end.'

Joshua nodded. 'You know, if this works out even ten per cent, he's going to be lucky to have you.'

She snorted. 'You'd better ask him that. I'm learning to crack the whip . . . Joshua, I know you've had your differences with him.'

'You can say that again. When I called him in to help you it was about the only time I've spoken to him since the Madison nuke.'

'I think he misses you, you know. He spans the world, but he has few friends. If any.'

'Which is why he has to manufacture them, right?'

'That's rather harsh, Joshua. On both of us.'

'Yes. I'm sorry. Look, Agnes, as far as I'm concerned, however you got here, it's just good to have you back.'

Now she looked oddly concerned. She took both his hands in hers, as she used to when he was small and there was something difficult she needed to tell him. 'But you and I know the real question, Joshua.'

'What question?'

'I look like Agnes. I think like her. I can carry on her work. I *feel* like I'm her. But can I *be* her? I'm a nun, Joshua. Or Agnes was. And enough of a nun to know that there's no place in Catholic theology for Tibetan-style reincarnation.'

'Then what?'

She looked away, which was not characteristic of her. 'My death, Joshua . . .'

'Yes?'

'I . . . *experienced* it. What we call the Personal Judgement, or something like it. *And God shall wipe away all tears from their eyes.* I encountered God. Or so it feels. So I believe.' She raised her hands again and turned them over, inspecting them. 'And now here I am in this miraculous new form. *For this corruptible must put on incorruption, and this mortal must put on immortality.*' She twinkled a smile at him. 'Don't worry, I won't ask you for chapter and verse. Maybe I'm some sort of electronic ghost – not Agnes at all, or at best a blasphemous mockery of her. Or maybe, instead, I'm here to fulfil the will of God, in a new way – in a world transformed by technology, to fulfil that will in a way that was never possible before. I feel I'm ready to accept the latter interpretation for now.'

He stirred the last of his coffee. 'What does Lobsang *want*, do you think? What's he trying to become? The guardian of the whole human race, maybe?'

She thought about that. 'I rather believe that he might be more like a gardener. Which sounds nice and bucolic and harmless, right up to the time you remember that a gardener must sometimes *prune* . . .'

He stood. 'I have to go back. My family have had a lot of problems since we got back here.'

'I heard.'

'About the nature of your new existence – well, I did spend a lot of time with Lobsang. I'm no theologian. My advice is, just get on with it. Do the good that's in front of you. That's what you always said.'

'That's true. Actually at some point I'm hoping for a bit of theological guidance from those fellas in fancy dress from the Vatican.'

'I don't care about the Vatican. As far as I'm concerned you're *my* Agnes.'

'Thank you, Joshua.' She stood and hugged him. 'Don't be a stranger.'

'Never.'

28

SALLY RETURNED TO Monica Jansson's home, arriving without any warning, without any explanation of where she'd been.

Jansson had been alone in the house. She had been waiting for Joshua to return from his visit to the Home, Helen was off talking to cops and lawyers about bail conditions, and Dan was happily playing softball with Bill Chambers, who was monumentally hungover, as ever.

They sat over coffees. Two oddballs thrown accidentally together, Jansson thought. Sally seemed restless, as usual. Her pack was waiting at the door, and she wore the multi-pocketed sleeveless jacket that was the basis of her field gear. They tentatively talked, about life, and what they had in common: the Long Earth, and Joshua.

In an odd way, Joshua had always been at the centre of MPD Lieutenant Monica Jansson's experience of the Long Earth, as it had opened up on her watch, and ultimately defined her career path, indeed her whole life. Now she told Sally anecdotes about the old days.

Like about the repeated attempts she had made to recruit Joshua.

* * *

There was one time, seven months after Step Day, when Jansson had arranged to talk to Joshua at the Home, then still located in Datum Madison. The talk had been chaperoned, and that was fair enough, Jansson had thought, sitting on a sofa with a Sister or two, as the old song went. After all, Joshua was still just fourteen years old.

And his suspicion of her had been so solid it was like an extra person, crowding on the sofa with Jansson and the Sisters.

He'd said, 'Do you want to study me?'

'What?'

'Hand me over to the professors at the university. Put me in a cage and *study* me.'

She felt shocked. 'No, Joshua. Never that. Listen. You've become notorious. A legend, whether you like it or not. But right from the start, from Step Day, I've done my best to keep you off the official record.'

He thought that over. 'Why?'

'Because it would be bad for you. You can do as you please. But I want you to think . . . well, about working with me. Not *for* me. Put your abilities, and all that positive energy you have, to good use. I can get you assignments. Ways to help people. I'm talking about paid work. Like a Saturday job – it won't get in the way of your school work. Joshua, I promise that if you work with me I'll continue to protect you.'

He flinched. 'But if I won't work with you, you won't protect me.'

'No. No! Joshua, that came out wrong. Look, I'll protect you come what may—'

But he had just vanished, a pop of displaced air, gone, leaving the two Sisters exasperated.

Jansson had looked on the bright side. He hadn't actually said no.

She had kept on trying, until, grudgingly, he became an ally.

And he had been an ally ever since.

'Nice story,' Sally said. 'And that was really your way of protecting *him*, right?'

'A friend for life, that's Joshua. He does seem to surround himself with strong women. You, Helen, Sister Agnes—'

'And you too, retired Lieutenant Jansson.'

'I'll take that as a compliment. Must be difficult for Helen sometimes, however. She is his wife.'

Sally looked away. 'I'm profoundly uninterested in Helen. A gloomy little stay-at-home. Although she did throw a good right hook at that nutjob in immigration.'

'That she did.'

Sally kept glancing at her watch.

Jansson asked cautiously, 'So where are you going next?'

'The Gap.'

'Really? Because of Mary the troll, I guess.'

'Yeah.'

Jansson smiled. 'What will you do, wave a placard?'

'Why not? It's better than letting the poor creature be put to death, out of sight and out of mind.'

'True enough. It was a shocking incident. When I saw it I wrote a few mails myself, you know . . . That was how I got the leverage to have Joshua meet Senator Starling. I wish I could go with you.'

Sally faced her. 'Are you serious?'

That took Jansson aback; she'd spoken on impulse.

'What? Well – yes, I guess. If I could. Why do you ask?'

'Because you're useful, that's why. You're Joshua's "Spooky" Jansson. You can get things done in the human world where I can't.' Sally looked diffident, as if she hated to admit the slightest weakness. 'Maybe together we could do some good. Or at least scare the spacesuit pants off those dweebs up at the Gap. Joshua said you put things right. That's your strength. Well, because of this whole business with the trolls, there's soon going to be something "not right" with the whole of the Long Earth. Come with me. What do you say?'

Jansson smiled weakly. 'What, just like that? It's kind of Thelma and Louise, isn't it? And at my age, and my condition? I'm not supposed to be more than a couple of hours from my hospital. I suppose I could self-medicate. But I've never been nearly that far stepwise. It's two million steps to the Gap, right? I don't think I'd make it.'

'Don't be so hasty.' Sally winked. 'Remember who you're speaking to. I know a couple of short cuts . . .'

'It's crazy. It's impossible. Isn't it?'

29

As JANSSON AND Sally were preparing to leave Madison West 5, Maggie Kauffman was just arriving.

'Find me a troll expert,' Maggie had told Joe Mackenzie. What the Captain wanted, the Captain got.

It had taken a couple of days. No outernet search was quick, by the nature of the outernet's very infrastructure, although the closer you got to the Datum the faster information was swapped around. But Mac soon turned up a number of universities that had investigated trolls in the wild. He showed Maggie some of their reports. Trolls were found to be inquisitive, convivial, and quick learners. It was generally agreed that they were at least pre-sapient, but a minority of scholars declared that they were in fact truly sapient, though their intelligence had a different perspective, a different basis from human minds. Clearly they learned at a phenomenal rate . . .

All this seemed a little dry to Maggie. She asked Mac to find somebody who knew trolls better than as test subjects or specimens. Somebody who lived with them.

Which was why she left her command briefly, and, without letting her superiors know – stuffed shirts like Ed Cutler would have squashed this initiative before it had begun – she dashed on a fast commercial twain back East, ending up on a world five steps West of the Datum, at the new city of Madison, Wisconsin . . .

A few miles outside the city, Dr Christopher Pagel and his wife Juliet, among other activities, ran a rescue centre for maltreated big cats, animals bought illegally by drug barons and other slimeballs and displayed for the machismo, then abandoned when they were no longer cute. The business pre-dated Step Day – when it was set up the victims had included lions and tigers – but since then, thanks to the opportunities opened up for new kinds of trophies through access to the Long Earth and its kaleidoscope of unspoiled worlds, the roomy cages had also housed such beasts as a sabre-toothed smilodon, and even a cave lion: *Panthera leo atrox*.

And the Pagels were using an extended family of trolls to help with the business.

The Pagels, elderly but elegant and remarkably kindly, told Maggie that the trolls helped with more than just heavy labour. Their very presence seemed to calm the cats. Dr Chris described how the male of the local family of trolls had a very good way of dealing with one potentially troublesome tiger, who after one attempted attack on its keeper was gripped at the neck by a big troll hand and pushed slowly and carefully to the ground, at a speed and pressure that made it clear to the big cat that ending up underground was just a possibility if he didn't get with the programme . . .

Maggie learned a lot of other details about the trolls from the Pagels. Such as, what they wanted from humans, it seemed, was entertainment: variety, new concepts. Show even a juvenile troll something like a lawn mower, with bolts big enough for troll fingers to work, and he or she would carefully take it apart, keeping all the bits neatly in a line, and then put it back together again, for the sheer joy of it. Juliet Pagel had experimented with human music; a good gospel choir would have trolls sitting in rapturous silence, as would 1960s close-harmony groups like the Beach Boys.

Maggie's decision about the trolls was slowly solidifying. As far as she was concerned, she had to be mindful of the fact that her command was tasked to be an ever-present symbol of the United States Aegis. As such, it wasn't enough for the *Benjamin Franklin* to tour these outer worlds like an old-fashioned dreadnought, projecting vague threat and handing out leaflets about how you had to pay your taxes. Her mission had to symbolize the nation's positive values. And that meant, in this age of the Long Earth, living in harmony with the other inhabitants of the stepwise worlds, in particular with the trolls. Sally Linsay had been right, she'd decided on reflection: how better to show that than by having trolls actually aboard her ship?

As a twain Captain, Maggie had been granted a great deal of latitude in her decision-making out here. Still, she spent time trying to make sure she had got the support of at least a majority of her crew for this experiment. And she had no intention of telling her superiors what she was up to, until she absolutely had to.

So, when she returned to her ship, she brought three trolls with her. They were a family, parents with a juvenile: the Pagels had called them Jake, Marjorie and Carl.

As soon as they boarded, despite all Maggie's

groundwork in advance, the arguments started once more. She let them run; the trolls weren't going anywhere.

In the event it was only a week before the crew of the *Franklin*, as they drifted through the skies of countless stepwise Americas, became accustomed to stopping work at twilight, when the big loading bay doors were flung open, and the trolls joined in the harmonies and undertones of the long call as it echoed across the reaches of world after world.

'I mean,' Maggie said to Mac and Nathan, 'in *Star Trek* they put a Klingon on the bridge.'

'And a Borg,' said Nathan.

'Well, there you go.'

'Not a Romulan, though,' Mac said. 'Never a Romulan.'

'The trolls are staying,' Maggie said firmly.

30

IT TOOK NELSON Azikiwe a couple of months after that talk with Ken, when he'd let the cat out of the bag about his resignation, for him to tidy up his affairs in the parish, dispose of extraneous belongings, and brief his successor – including on the temperamental toilet – before he was ready to depart on the next phase of his life, in search of the Lobsang Project and other mysteries. He took his time. He had always led something of an itinerant life, but believed in making time to say his goodbyes properly.

He decided to travel to America by plane; his generation wasn't used to the slow-boat nature of twain travel. But there weren't as many aeroplanes around these days, Nelson discovered, not since the Long Earth had begun to be serviced by the twains. It was the new worlds, of course, for which the twains were so well suited: airships didn't need airports, they could set you down easily almost anywhere. But even for lateral, cross-Earth travel, even on the Datum, airships had come back into vogue. For one thing helium, a safely non-flammable lift gas, was a whole lot easier to obtain now, the Datum's natural stock having been badly depleted before the resources of the stepwise worlds had been opened up. And the stately pace of airships certainly worked for cargo: sacks of corn and mineral ore didn't mind how long it took to get there, and rarely complained about the in-flight movie.

But an industry like the traditional airlines would take some time to die, and for now, on the Datum, the planes still flew – even though for this trip Nelson had to put up with delays, as many US flights were grounded because of ash clouds arising from an event at Yellowstone, some kind of minor eruption there.

The plane Nelson finally caught swung out from England, crossed the north Atlantic, flew down over the Canadian Shield, and at last reached the endless farmland of Datum America, which spread beneath his window like a glowing carpet. If you had the eye for it, he realized, there were occasional gaps to be seen in that grand panorama of cultivation, scraps of recovering wildness in the summer green where a homestead or a farm had been abandoned, almost certainly because the owners had decided to step Westward. (And it *was* West for most Americans, despite the assurances of the experts that the stepping labels 'West' and 'East' were purely arbitrary.) Off they stepped, in search of more land, a better life. Or, he mused, possibly they went simply because, well, the new worlds were *out there*, and there was something in the genes of an American, and perhaps even a Canadian, that impelled you always to move on. It was a frontier with apparently no end, and while there wasn't exactly a step-wise stampede these days the Long Earth still drew in the pioneers.

His own destination was more modest: O'Hare. He'd stop in Chicago a while. Then he had plans to visit a new university being built in Madison, Wisconsin, West 5, as part of the city's post-nuke recovery. He had friends there, and interests. Madison was where Willis Linsay had first posted the plans for a prototype Stepper box on the internet, a glorious, destructive gesture that had changed the world for ever – indeed, the worlds. And Madison had been the boyhood home of Joshua Valienté himself. Nelson, on the track of the Lobsang Project, had an inkling that Madison was a place where he might find some things out, get some questions answered.

As it turned out, this tentative plan didn't even survive his leaving the airport.

Nelson was always glad to get out of the cramped enclosure of a plane. He was a large man, the kind of man who had trouble fitting into an airline seat, but who could walk through any neighbourhood anywhere without having to worry overmuch about his security. Sometimes the deference accorded to him simply because of his size bothered him. But by and large, he reflected as he patiently queued his way through the landing process, he had to admit it was useful to get your way without even asking.

His size had certainly saved him from all but a few scuffles in the South African townships of his boyhood. All such troubles had however evaporated when he found the local library and discovered a universe of ideas into which his young consciousness rose faster than a Saturn V into the Florida sky. That wasn't to say he had simply soaked up the lessons of authority; almost from the beginning he was identifying problems to solve, and indeed solving them. One teacher remarked that he had a genius for connectivity.

His life had changed utterly, for better or worse, the day he had first applied his analytical skills to the concept of the Almighty. Even if you dismissed the traditional notion of God, it had always seemed to him that without a First Cause of some kind there was a philosophical void, a space to let. His buddies in the nerdosphere populated that void with the Illuminati, maybe, or the staring eye in the dollar-bill triangle . . . After Step Day, after the opening-up of a universe vast, fecund and accessible to mankind, it seemed to him that the need to fill that void had only deepened. Which was essentially why he had decided to devote the next phase of his life to an exploration of that void, and related mysteries.

Anyhow, this morning at O'Hare, Nelson's intimidating size, backed up by his problem-solving ability, certainly helped him thread his way through the maze of US immigration.

And at the final customs barrier, after Nelson had cleared through, a clerk chased him and produced a leaflet. 'Oh – this was left for you, Mr Azikiwe.'

The leaflet was an ad for a Winnebago. Nelson was planning to fly to Madison; he didn't need a Winnebago. But when he looked up again, the clerk was gone.

Nelson felt a thrill of connectivity, like solving a Quizmasters puzzle. 'I get it, Lobsang,' he said. And he pocketed the leaflet.

By an hour later he had rented a top-of-the-line Winnebago, with plenty of generator capacity for his tech, and a bed, a big one, *just* the size for him.

He drove out of the airport parking area in this home on wheels and, having no further instructions he could discern, picked a direction at random and hit the freeway. Just the experience of driving on such roads was glorious. He wondered if this, in the end, was the ultimate expression of the American dream: to be in transit, all problems left behind like discarded trash, nothing in life but follow-the-horizon movement, motion for the sake of it.

He drove west for the rest of the morning.

Then he parked up in a small town, shopped for fresh food, and logged on for a quick inspection of the latest sweepings of the online world, including the findings of his buddies in the Quizmasters. He'd had them working twenty-four seven on his problem since he'd tantalized them with the barest hint: 'Say, we have all seen that clip of the *Mark Twain* being towed into Madison and the girl talking about a cat that spoke Tibetan, haven't we? Is there a clue there? But a clue about what? Looks like someone is playing with our heads . . .'

Given Nelson's starting hint, the Quizmasters had been going crazy, speculating, inferring and pattern-matching. Standing in the Winnebago, making an elegant curry from fresh-bought ingredients, Nelson watched messages and tangled hypotheses flicker across his screens, and thought it all over.

When the curry was ready he largely ignored the screens. Nelson had learned to love the manners of the English past, as he'd known them in St John on the Water, when people used to *address* their food; there was something about the phraseology that made the boy from the townships smile. But while he ate, he saw from the corner of his eye how the Quizmasters were beating themselves up, putting out theories at the rate of one a minute, some of them completely outlandish.

And then up came one trace that drew his attention: thanks to an oddity of TV scheduling, by hopping among various channels, starting just about now it would be possible to watch the classic movie *Close Encounters of the Third Kind* continuously for the next twenty-four hours.

He murmured, 'So: Devil's Tower, Lobsang? It's been done before, a bit unoriginal. But I've never been there, I've always wanted to see it. I won't ask how to find you; I rather believe you will find me . . .'

Nelson finished his curry and cleaned up. His sat-nav told him it was around a thousand miles north-west from Chicago to Wyoming. A dream ride in a vehicle like this. He'd take his time, he decided, and see the sights; he was nobody's puppet.

Maybe he'd even catch one of those iterations of *Close Encounters*.

31

THEIR FINAL FALL through the soft places, the longest of all, brought Sally and Jansson to a world only a dozen steps or so from the Gap itself. Soft places transported you geographically as well as stepwise. They landed in England, the north-west, near the Irish Sea coast – a location Sally knew was close to the footprint of GapSpace, home of the new space cadets.

Monica Jansson arrived exhausted, bewildered. Sally had to help her lie down on the soft grass of this latest hillside, wrapped in a cocoon of silvery emergency blankets.

It had taken a week for them to traverse the two million worlds to the Gap through the soft places – a lot faster than any twain, but a gruelling journey even so. Sally had to scry out the soft places, using motions like a kind of tai chi. They seemed to cluster in the continental heartlands, away from the coasts. They were easier to find at dawn or sunset. Sometimes Jansson could even *see* them, a kind of shimmer. Weird stuff. But they would take you wherever you wanted to go, in four or five steps.

Jansson, for her part, had never complained as they travelled, and it had taken a few transitions for Sally to work out just how hard it was for her. A soft place was a flaw in the Long Earth's quasi-linear pan-dimensional geometry. Finding soft places was the unique skill Sally's genetic inheritance had given her. And it was a hell of a lot easier than plodding all the way out, step by step, the way that dull little mouse Helen Valienté had once walked through a hundred thousand worlds with her family to set up their pioneer-type log cabin. But nothing came for free, and the soft places did take something out of you. It wasn't an instantaneous transition, like a regular step; there was a sense of falling, of deep sucking cold, of a passage that lasted a finite time – that was how you remembered it, even if your watch showed that no time had passed at all. It was gruelling, energy-sapping. Plus Jansson was already ill, even before they set off. But Jansson wasn't the type who would complain, whatever you did.

Sally bustled around, collecting wood for a fire, unpacking their food and drink. Then, in this late afternoon, a warm enough late May day in this particular stepwise England, she sat quietly beside her fire, letting Jansson sleep off the journey.

And Sally watched the moon rise.

It wasn't the moon she was used to. In this world, only a few steps from the Gap itself, Luna was liberally spattered with recent craters. The Mare Imbrium, the man in the moon's right eye, was almost obliterated, and Copernicus was outdone by a massive new scar, a brilliant splash whose rays stretched across half the visible disc. It must have been something to see, she thought, on this world and its neighbours, when Bellos and its stepwise brothers had made their shuddering close approach – missing this particular Earth, but passing near by – and the ground below would have convulsed from bombardment by random fragments, while the face of the moon above lit up like a battlefield in the sky . . .

Jansson stirred now, and sat up. Sally had set a pot of coffee on the little stand over the fire. Jansson took a tin mug gratefully in gloved hands, and looked up at the sky, in a vague way. 'What's wrong with the moon?'

'We're too close to the Gap, is what's wrong with it.'

Jansson nodded, sipping the coffee. 'Listen. Before we get there. Just imagine I'm a dumb cop who knows more about bloodstains and drunks than about cosmology and spaceships. What exactly is the Gap? And what's it got to do with space cadets?'

'The Gap is a hole in the Long Earth. Look, the alternate Earths go on for ever, as far as we know, all broadly similar though differing in detail. But the Gap is the only place so far found where the Earth is missing altogether. If you were to step over you'd find yourself floating in vacuum. There was an impact. A big rock – maybe an asteroid, or comet, or something like a rogue moon – came calling. The space cadets call this hypothetical object Bellos.'

'Why Bellos?'

Sally shrugged. 'Some dumb old movie reference, I think. Joshua might know. And Lobsang's probably *got* the movie . . . Everything that can happen must happen somewhere, right? Bellos, or copies of it, came swimming out of the dark, and completely missed uncounted billions of Earths. A few, like *this* one, were close enough to its path to be sideswiped by fragments, and suffered varying amounts of damage.'

'Like what?'

'Like splattering new craters over the moon. Like stripping away lots of atmosphere from the Earth. Or changing the pole positions. Or messing with continental shift. Generally making the extinction of the dinosaurs look like a street fight. But not wiping out the planet altogether.'

Jansson nodded. 'I can see where the story is going. And one Earth—'

'One Earth was taken out entirely.'

Jansson whistled. The idea seemed to frighten her. 'It could have hit *us*,' she said.

'Datum Earth was way up the other end of the probability curve.'

'Yes, but if it hadn't been – even if we'd been living on one of these nearby worlds—'

'Earthquakes, tidal waves, that kind of fun. Oh, the dust winter would probably have killed us off. Us, or our primate ancestors, more likely, it was that long ago.'

'Nasty.'

'No, it's just statistics. It happened, that's all.' Sally poured more coffee. 'It couldn't happen *now*, at least. Not that way. The extinction of mankind, I mean. We've spread out. The Long Earth is an insurance policy. Even a Bellos couldn't take out all of us.'

'OK. And this Gap is useful because—'

'Because you can just step into space. You see, on world Gap Minus One, you put on a spacesuit, step over – and there you are, gently orbiting the sun. No need to ride a rocket the size of a skyscraper to fight Earth's gravity, because there ain't no Earth there. And once you're out there, you can go anywhere. That's the dream, anyhow. Access to space.'

Jansson's head was drooping. 'Can't wait to see it. In the morning, yes?'

'In the morning. You sleep. I'll put the tent up before it gets dark. Are you hungry?'

'No, thanks. And I took my meds.' She lay down again, pulling the blankets over her.

'Goodnight, then.'

'Goodnight, Sally.'

As Jansson slipped back into sleep Sally sat silently, perhaps the only awake, sapient mind on this planet.

And as the light dimmed, and the battered moon brightened, she felt as if someone had knocked out the walls of her mind. The landscape, a grassy hillside stretching away before her, seemed to acquire depth, otherness in a direction she could almost see. It was bottomless, multi-dimensional, endless. She had once dreamed that she had found out how to fly; it was absurdly easy, all you had to do was jump into the air and *jump again when you were up there.* Now she chased the tantalizing feeling that all she needed was the trick of it and she could step away, not into one world at a time, but spread *across* the Long Earth, a whole thick band of worlds, all at once. The very air around her felt prickly, the land as insubstantial as smoke.

But then Jansson coughed, and moaned softly in her sleep. Sally's infinity high evaporated as quickly as it had come.

32

SLOWLY THE CREW of the *Franklin* got used to their troll crewmates.

That didn't apply to all the colonies they visited, though.

New Melfield was a grubby and unprepossessing farming community in the Corn Belt. The whole township turned out when the *Franklin* descended – and seemed uniformly astonished when a family of trolls followed the human crew down the lowered gangway.

The trolls and the rest strolled around while Maggie chatted to the local mayor, passed over Datum documentation, and generally engaged the man and put him at his ease. Indeed he evidently needed his ease putting at, for her briefing had pegged this place as yet another nasty little locus of spite towards trolls, not to mention humans and other dumb animals. Well, change had to start by degrees.

So by mid-morning this mayor had three trolls in his office, actually sitting on chairs; trolls just loved chairs, especially if they swivelled. And when Maggie had finished the coffee she'd been offered, she said clearly, 'Wash up, please, Carl.'

The young troll, holding the mug like an heirloom,

looked around the room, spotted the open door to the little coffee station and sink area in the room next door, carefully washed the mug in the sink, and placed it just as carefully in a rack. Then he walked back to Maggie, who gave him a peppermint.

The mayor watched this in blank astonishment.

That was the start of a couple more days at this township, days devoted to seducing hearts and minds, with younger kids being given rides in the *Franklin* to see their homes from the air for the first time in their lives, and older kids – heavily supervised – playing with the trolls.

But on the second day the crew went on the alert, when a second twain showed up in the sky above New Melfield.

The ship was a merchant vessel. That evening the captain himself, with an aide, crossed to the *Franklin* and met Maggie in her sea cabin. And they came bearing a package.

Maggie glanced quickly at Nathan Boss, who'd accompanied them aboard. 'We scanned the parcel,' Boss said. 'It's clean.'

The merchant's captain, young, overweight, grinned at Maggie. 'You must be very important, Captain Kauffman, we were detoured a hell of a way to bring you this. You have the assurance of Douglas Black himself—'

'Douglas Black? Of the Black Corporation? *The* . . .' Wow, she thought. Sally Linsay has contacts.

'Yes, Captain. *The* Mr Black assures you that nothing in this package is to the detriment of either you or the *Benjamin Franklin*. Instructions can be found inside. I know nothing more . . .'

Maggie felt ridiculously like a kid at Christmas, eager to unwrap the gift.

As soon as the guy was gone, at Nathan's cautious suggestion she took the package outside the ship to open it, just for extra security. And inside she found, carefully wrapped, a curious instrument faintly resembling an ocarina. A troll-call – Sally Linsay had come through. She toyed with the controls; it looked more complex than the gadget Sally had shown her, maybe some kind of upgrade. And there was a brief page of instructions, signed by hand: 'G. Abrahams'. The name wasn't familiar.

She couldn't wait to try it on the trolls.

She dismissed Nathan, who went off grinning and shaking his head. Then, alone, she made for the observation deck, where the trolls preferred to sleep, perhaps because of its cooler temperature. The trolls were huddled together, grooming gently, half-asleep, communicating in their usual soft, barely audible tones.

Maggie quietly switched on the ocarina, pointed it at Jake, and listened carefully.

And was surprised when from the direction of Jake a clear voice said, 'I am fed / satisfied; this is fun; I yearn to return to / meaning not understood / . . .' It emerged as a human male voice, firm, reasonably pleasant, if rather synthetic.

So the troll-call worked, even if it did seem to be more like an exchange of concepts than a true translation. Those nerds at the Black Corporation – or whoever 'G. Abrahams' was – must have *loved* working on the development of this thing.

Now she pointed the troll-call at Marjorie.

'Female here / watching / no mate female / meaning not

227

understood: tentative translation, a female choosing for her own purposes not to have a mate . . .'

They meant her! 'Everybody's a relationship counsellor,' Maggie grumbled to herself. Plucking up her courage, she raised the troll-call and said clearly into its mouthpiece, 'My name is Maggie Kauffman. Welcome aboard the *Benjamin Franklin*.' A liquid warble accompanied her words.

The trolls seemed to snap to attention. They stared at her, mouths open, eyes wide.

She pointed to herself. 'Maggie. Maggie . . .'

Marjorie gabbled back, apparently attempting to find a label for her. 'Friend / grandmother / interesting stranger . . .'

It was 'grandmother' that flabbergasted Maggie. *Grandmother!* How human was that? And was that how they saw her relationship to her crew, that she was the old woman looking after all the little children? Well, they *were* mostly a lot younger than her . . .

She boldly walked up to the trolls, where they sat huddled in a corner of the cabin, and sat on the carpet with them. 'I'm Maggie. Maggie . . . Well, you're right. I have no husband. No mate. The ship is my home . . .'

It seemed to her that Marjorie, the female, was looking at her sorrowfully, with soulful brown eyes. With extreme care, a hand like a leather shovel gently touched Maggie's. Maggie felt she had no choice but to move closer, and she felt huge arms close around her.

Carl, meanwhile, got hold of the ocarina and experimented until he found a way to say, 'Peppermint.'

That was how Maggie was found in the morning,

coming awake as a crewman very, very gingerly unwound his Captain from the snoring trolls.

Breakfast was somewhat embarrassing. Every last crew member knew how she'd spent the night. But she never had been one for standing on her dignity.

She spent a day letting the crew experiment with the troll-call, under supervision. And she had Gerry Hemingway from Science study its workings, or anyhow its inputs and outputs.

That night she had to order the crew to put the call away, to leave the exhausted trolls to their slumbers on the observation deck.

Then, at breakfast the next day, she called the crew together. She looked carefully around them, and picked out Jennifer Wang, one of the marine detachment, whose grandparents, she knew, had come from China. 'Jennifer, you spent a long time with Jake yesterday. What did he say to you?'

Wang looked around, somewhat embarrassed. But she cleared her throat and said, 'A lot I couldn't understand. But it was along the lines of, "far from home". It creased me up! I mean, I'm a Chinese American and proud to be a citizen, but it's in the blood. How did the big guy know?'

'Because he's smart,' Maggie said. 'He's intuitive. He's *sapient*.

'You know, people, we were sent out here to find sapience in the Long Earth, among other goals. Right? And now here it is, on this ship, living among us: sapience. And that, by the way, will be my defence at the court-martial.

'I'm proud of you all for how you're dealing with your new shipmates. But if this room isn't cleared and you're not at your posts in two minutes, you're all on a charge. Dismissed.'

33

THE LAST STEP across was a sudden transition from a dune field, just inland from a grey ocean, the local copy of the Irish Sea, into what looked like a rudimentary industrial park, a place of gleaming tanks, rusty gantries, smoke stacks, blocky concrete buildings. There was nothing very space-age about it as far as Jansson could see at first glance.

'Come on.' Sally shifted her pack and led the way.

Jansson followed, walking steadily across grass-covered ground that gradually gave way to lumpy dunes. The morning was dry and bright in this world, one step away from the Gap. She could smell salt and rotting seaweed in the wind off the sea. She tried to visualize where she was: tried to imagine that there was vacuum, space, a void, just one tap of the Stepper at her waist away from this mundanity. Tried and failed.

They hadn't covered a hundred yards when the landscape was illuminated by a blinding light, coming from the rim of the development ahead, like a droplet of sunlight brought down to the Earth.

Without hesitating Jansson pushed Sally to the ground, lay on top of her, and pulled her jacket hood over her own head. Jansson had been in the world next door when the

Madison nuke went off; she hadn't forgotten. The noise of the explosion hit them, then a hot wind, and the ground itself shuddered. But it passed over quickly.

Cautiously Jansson rolled off Sally, wincing as her enfeebled body protested with a chorus of aches. They both sat up and looked west. A cloud of white smoke and vapour was rising up from the explosion site.

'Not a nuke,' Sally said.

'Not this time. Some kind of chemical factory blowing up? Sorry to jump you.'

'Don't be.' Sally got up and brushed away sandy soil. 'This place is going to be a playground for tech-boy nutjobs, who may or may not know what the hell they are doing. Let's watch our backs.'

'Agreed.'

They walked on, eyes wide open, alert for more problems. A fire guttered at the destroyed plant; as they approached they could see steam rising from amateurish-looking attempts to douse it.

There was no security here that Jansson could see, not even a fence. But as they entered the sprawling facility they were noticed. Jansson saw workers staring at them.

At length a man walked out to greet them. In his fifties perhaps, he was not tall but very upright, wiry, tanned, with greying crew-cut hair. He wore a blue jumpsuit with a faded NASA logo and a name tag: WOOD, F. He grinned at them, welcoming enough. 'Ladies.'

'Gentleman,' Sally snapped back.

'The name's Frank Wood. Formerly of NASA, and now of – well, whatever you want to call us here. GapSpace will do; we're incorporated under that name. Can I ask why you're here? We don't get too many casual visitors this far out. Are you volunteers? If so, give me a hint of your technical specialities and I'm sure you'll fit right in. Journalists?' Ruefully he glanced over his shoulder at the rising cloud of steam and smoke. 'You'll see we just had an incident with a lox storage tank, but that's not so unusual.'

Jansson flashed her badge and warrant card. 'I'm police. Madison, Wisconsin specifically.' He glanced at it, but she put it away before he had a chance to figure out she was long retired, and shouldn't have kept the shield anyhow.

'Oh.' He looked disappointed in her. 'Frankly, Lieutenant Jansson, that kind of Datum authority doesn't have a lot of purchase out here. Even if we were in the US Aegis, which we're not. I guess you're here about the troll thing, right?'

'Afraid so, Mr Wood.'

'Call me Frank . . .'

'I think I recognize you,' Sally said.

'You do?'

'The video clips. It was you who stopped those techs putting the troll down on the spot.'

He actually blushed, and looked away. 'Well, I never wanted to be famous. Look, the guy you want to see about all that is called Gareth Eames. Nearest thing to a chief executive we got here. English guy. If I'm honest with you, if not for the fuss in the outernet – yes, we get the news even out here – the troll *would* have been put down by now. But even guys like us take notice when we're in the middle of a flame war. Come on, I'll take you to Eames—'

'No need,' Sally said briskly. 'I'll find the way.'

Wood looked dubious, then shrugged. 'OK.' He pointed to a low, squat concrete building. 'That's the admin block, or the nearest we have to it. We build everything like a blockhouse here; living with rockets you learn to be cautious. You'll find Gareth in there. And that's where we're holding the troll too, in the calaboose.'

'Great.' Sally turned to Jansson, and whispered, 'Let me get over there and scout it out, without Buck Rogers here hovering over me.'

Jansson was doubtful, but this was Sally's modus operandi, she was learning. Always keep the other guy off balance. 'OK. And as for me—'

'Distract this guy. Let him show you his toy spaceships, or whatnot. I think he has his eye on you, by the way.'

'Garbage. Also, let me remind you, my personal rocket ship takes off from a different launch pad.'

'So he's no more perceptive than most men.' Sally winked. 'Undo a button or two and he's your slave for life. See you later.'

34

'WE DON'T THINK of this world as Earth West Two Million Plus Change, or whatever,' Frank Wood said. 'We think of it as Gap East 1. Because the Gap is the centre of our universe, not the Datum. And a strange kind of world this is, right? Almost empty of humans. Whole continents nobody's even set foot on. We basically live off fishing and a bit of hunting – while we build spaceships. We're a tribe of hunter-gatherers with a space programme! . . .'

As Frank Wood rambled on, Jansson inspected GapSpace. The facility was like a fannish reconstruction of a half-remembered Cape Canaveral, she thought, having visited that old wonderland once as a tourist – and it was there, at the Cape, it turned out, that the GapSpace people had recruited Frank Wood himself. She recognized basic facilities such as kilns churning out bricks baked from the local clay, and forges, and manufacturing plants. Then there were the traditional attributes of a space centre, like huge spherical tanks whose walls were frosted because, Frank told her, they held great volumes of super-cold liquid fuels. The company even had its own logo, a roundel with a thin crescent Earth cupping a star field, the GapSpace name below, and above, a corporate slogan:

THERE IS SUCH A THING AS A FREE LAUNCH

Joshua had once told Jansson that that was a line of Lobsang's. And, most thrilling of all, even to a hardened old heart like Jansson's, there were spacecraft. There was one capsule-like craft that stood on four robust-looking legs, and a gantry that held a rocket booster, a tank maybe sixty feet tall topped by a flaring nozzle that pointed oddly *up* into the sky, as if the rocket were preparing for a launch down into the Earth. It was a stand for static test firing, Frank explained.

The workers here were mostly male, mostly around thirty to forty years old, mostly overweight. Some were dressed in protective gear, or coveralls like Frank's, but others wore shorts, sandals, and T-shirts bearing slogans from long-forgotten TV shows and movies:

YOU DIDN'T HEAR ABOUT THE POLAR BEAR?

One guy bearing a sheaf of blueprints came right up to Jansson, looked her in the face, and said, 'Neo, huh? It's like one unending con here, man. Am I in heaven?' And he walked off before she had a chance to reply.

Frank raised his eyebrows, as if sharing a joke with Jansson. 'Look, this isn't a corporate operation. Not yet. You can see that. These guys are all volunteers. Hobbyists. We have amateur rocketeers, radio hams, astronomers, and disappointed space cadets, like me, I guess. A few folks back home are funding us privately. The big corporations don't yet see the value of this. Why go to all the trouble of crossing space to some desert world like Mars when there are a billion habitable Earths a walk away? But they'll learn, and no doubt they'll muscle in when we start getting results.'

'And you'll all get rich.'

'Maybe. Anyhow, as you'll have guessed, social skills aren't exactly high on the list of selection criteria here. You'll get used to it . . .'

For Frank Wood, she learned, the Gap had turned out to be his chance to recover the Dream.

Before he was recruited by Gareth Eames, Frank hadn't even heard of GapSpace. But he had been working at the Kennedy Space Center, what was left of it, and it was sad. In the rocket garden, the open-air museum, they weren't even taking care of the precious relics any more, he told her. You could see corrosion from the salty air eating its way into papery cylindrical hulls, gaping rocket nozzles. They still flew unmanned satellite launches, but for a man who would have flown in space himself such routine shots had all the drama of a garage sale.

Frank remembered when he was a kid and had watched bright-eyed men on TV explaining how they were going to put mass drivers on the moon, and break up asteroids for their metals, and build tin-can worlds in space, and set up beanstalks, ladders into the sky from the surface of the Earth. Who wouldn't want to be a part of that?

And then the Steppers were invented. Frank was thirty-one years old on Step Day, already an Air Force veteran, and had just been accepted into NASA's astronaut corps. But now you had the Steppers, and the Long Earth. Mankind suddenly had all the space it wanted, a cheap and easy route to a trillion Earths.

Once Frank Wood had dreamed of flying to the planets, if not the stars. Now the spaceships of the future stayed on the launch pad of the imagination, and as he worked towards retirement in what was left of KSC, an astronaut candidate reduced to driving a tourist bus, he had felt like an early mammal scuttling around the bones of the last dinosaurs.

Then Gareth Eames, a smooth-talking Brit, had shown up, gabbling about something called the Gap. A kind of Long Earth loophole for space cadets, it seemed to Frank, who at first had barely understood.

And then Eames showed Frank a photograph of a spaceship.

What struck Jansson most in this brief tour wasn't the space technology, nor the nerdish workers, but the trolls. They were everywhere, labouring in the factories beside clunky assembly-line robots, lugging heavy loads to and fro – such as enigmatic structures of brick, arches and dome segments – and, in one place, mixing and laying down concrete to build what was evidently going to be a broad apron, like a landing pad. This particular party were singing as they worked, and she strained to hear; their song, softly sung, was a round based on what sounded like some old pop song with lyrics about wishing you were a spaceman, the fastest guy alive . . . No doubt they'd picked it up from the local nerd population.

Frank Wood didn't even mention the trolls, as if they were invisible to him.

After their walkabout Wood led her to a kind of rough open-air coffee bar, beside the big inverted rocket booster. Jansson sat with relief.

'This is a genuine space launch facility,' he said. 'I'm sure you figured out that much. But we're in a unique position here, next to the Gap, and the way we work is like nothing that's ever been done before.'

She instinctively liked Frank Wood, but she was quickly growing tired of the fan-boy bragging. 'It seems simple enough to me. All I have to do is take one more step and I'll be in space. Right?'

'True,' he nodded. 'In the vacuum. Of course you'd be dead in under a minute if you weren't in a pressure suit. Then you'd find yourself being flung off into space at hundreds of miles an hour.'

'Really?' She tried to visualize why, failed.

'The Earth's rotation,' he said. '*This* Earth. If you're standing at the equator you're being rushed around at a thousand miles an hour. The gravity holds you down, *here.* Step next door, and the gravity's gone, but you take that momentum over with you. It's like I whirled you around my head on a rope, and the rope broke, and you just went flying off into space. Of course we can use that velocity vector if we're clever, but mostly it's just a nuisance. The only stationary points are at the poles, and it's not convenient to work there. That's why we're at a relatively high latitude, here in England. The further north the better. Or south, of course.'

'Of course,' Jansson said uncertainly.

'Which is opposite to the wisdom of launching from the Datum, where the lower the latitude the better, to get a boost from that rotation . . . What you have to do is step over in a spaceship.' He pointed to the capsule she'd spotted before, like an Apollo command module on four legs. '*That* is our shuttle. Adapted from twain technology, a stepping vehicle, but wrapped in a rocket ship re-engineered from the old SpaceX *Dragon.* All iron and steel components excluded, right? What you do is step over into the Gap – you have to pick the right time of day, when the turning Earth brings you to just the right spot – and the shuttle fires its rockets to take off the spin velocity and bring you to relative rest. Then you dock at the Brick Moon.'

'The what?'

'That's what we're calling the permanent station we're building at the location of the Earth, in the Gap. Brick and concrete are easy to make over here, and easy to step in great sections over there, as long as you use mortar and stuff that can withstand the conditions of the vacuum. Even trolls can churn out great chunks of it.' Which was the very first time he had even mentioned the humanoids. 'The station is going to be a kind of honeycomb of sub-spheres in a cluster two hundred feet across. Quick and dirty, but we can do what we like here, whatever we can carry over, you haven't got to cram everything into the nose-cone of a converted ICBM and subject it to multiple gravities . . . A brick structure won't take pressure, but we can install inflatables or ceramic shells within the frame. When it's done, *that* is where we're going to launch our space missions from.' He pointed now at the inverted booster. 'I guess you recognize this baby.'

'I wish I could say I did,' she said sadly.

'It's a re-engineered S-IVB. That is, a Saturn V third stage. You know, the old moon rockets? Old technology but reliable as hell. This is just a test article; we're reworking it in steppable materials.

'Here's the beauty of the Gap. From the Datum, you needed a thing the size of the Saturn V itself to get to the moon and back. Right? Because of the need to escape

Earth's gravity. In the Gap, all you'd need to get anywhere, Mars even, is no bigger than *this*. We've already launched one test shot, a mission to Venus with a ship we called the *Kingfisher*. In future we're looking at nuclear rockets, which will offer a much better delta-vee. That is—'

'I believe you. I believe you!'

He stared at her, and laughed. 'I think we're going to get on, you and I, Lieutenant Jansson. Sorry. I know I get carried away. Look – did you ever read Robert Heinlein? Basically it's like that here. You really can build a backyard rocket ship and fly to Mars. What's not to love about that? All these worlds are ours, *including* Europa . . . Sorry again. Another nerdy reference.

'Listen, Ms Jansson. Given the reason you've come out all this way – you mustn't think badly of the young guys here. They *are* mostly guys, they mostly lack social skills, they're kind of driven. Many of them have some kind of personality disorder, probably. But their hearts are in the right place, generally speaking. They may be thoughtless to trolls, but they aren't deliberately cruel.' He looked distracted. 'By contrast – have you ever met anybody who was? I mean, a *really* bad person. I served in the Air Force. I saw some sights, in postings overseas.'

'I was a cop,' she said in answer.

He glanced over and grinned. ' "Was"? So when you flashed your badge at me, Lieutenant Jansson—'

'OK, you got me. Call me Monica, by the way.'

His grin widened. 'Monica.'

A guy in a Bart Simpson cap came wandering over. 'You're Lieutenant Jansson?'

'That's me.'

241

'Your friend Sally Linsay sent me to fetch you. Oh, and she had a message.'

'What message?'

'"The trolls are gone."'

'That's it?'

The guy shrugged. 'You coming, or not?'

35

JANSSON WAS ESCORTED over to the big admin block, where Sally waited for her, and – Jansson couldn't quite figure out how she did it – within thirty seconds Sally had given Bart Simpson the slip.

They hurried through cramped, badly lit, roughly walled corridors. 'Come on,' Sally said. 'There's things you need to see in this dump.'

They passed what looked like offices, study rooms, labs, even a kind of computer centre. A few people glanced at them, curiously or not, but nobody stopped them or questioned them. They must be used to strangers here. Jansson was getting the impression that this was indeed a loose organization, a bunch of fan types getting together, and no doubt with people coming and going as enthusiasm or other commitments allowed. No security to speak of.

They came to a staircase that led them down into an underground complex, a warren of roughly walled corridors and rooms. Jansson remembered what Frank had said about safety bunkers. And she remembered, too, the speculation about why Mary the troll hadn't just stepped away from her tormentors; keeping her underground would be the simplest way, so she couldn't step at all.

And now, as they hurried along, Jansson started to hear music, of a jagged, discordant kind.

'So,' Jansson said. ' "The trolls are gone." What does that mean?'

'Just that,' said Sally grimly. 'Not from here, particularly, not yet, but I bet the drift away has started – here like everywhere else – they're abandoning the Long Earth in general. Look – you know about the long call. All the trolls everywhere sharing information. Well, it seems they've reached some kind of tipping point.'

'Tipping point about what?'

'About us. About humans. Our relationship with them. All over the Long Earth, *they're leaving* – leaving the human colonies anyhow, it seems, any world where there's a significant human presence. They're not dumb animals, you see. They learn, and they modify their behaviour. And now, they've learned all they need to know about us.'

Jansson barely understood this, couldn't comprehend an event of such strangeness, of such magnitude. 'Where are they going?'

'Nobody knows.'

Jansson didn't bother asking how Sally knew about any of this. She'd seen herself how Sally could move around the Long Earth, and she was somehow tuned into the trolls too, and their long call. To Jansson Sally was like a homespun embodiment of some all-pervasive intelligence agency, or a ubiquitous corporate presence, like the Black Corporation maybe. *Naturally* Sally Linsay knew what was going on, across all the worlds.

And Jansson knew Sally held the cause of the trolls close to her heart – well, they wouldn't be here otherwise. So she was cautious when she asked, 'Does it really matter?'

Sally winced, but stayed civil. 'Yes, it matters. The trolls *are* the Long Earth, as far as I'm concerned. Its soul. They're also integral to the ecology. Not to mention damn useful. This fall, on a thousand farming worlds, without troll labour they'll be struggling to bring in the harvest.'

'So,' Jansson said, 'of course *we're* going to do something about it.'

'Of course we are,' said Sally, grinning fiercely.

'Starting with what?'

'Starting with right here. This is the place . . .'

They had come to a door with a jokey hand-painted sign: SPACE JAIL. The discordant music, if you could call it that, leaked out of the room, sharp, unpleasant, and Jansson resisted the temptation to cover her ears. And when Jansson looked through a spyhole in the door she saw, cowering in the corner, a troll, a bulky female. She sat slumped, immobile, yet somehow the misery seeped out of her. She had nothing in there save a bowl of water.

'Mary,' Jansson breathed.

'Our heroine. *I will not.*' Sally made the signs as she spoke.

'Well, we're underground.' She thought about what Frank had told her. 'But we are at the Gap. Solid rock in one stepwise direction but not the other. She *could* step out into vacuum, I guess, to try to reach the cub. She isn't stapled, is she?'

'I don't think so. But she must recoil from the vacuum instinctively. Also they're using that noise to keep her confused and unhappy. You should meet Gareth Eames, the supervisor here. A Brit. What a slimeball. For some reason he hates the trolls with a passion. He has a background in acoustics, and he said he started his own interaction with them when he found out how to drive them away with discords. Now he's developed that into a weapon, a trap, a cage. But the other thing that's holding her here . . . Come see.'

A little further along the corridor was another locked door, this one with a small window. When she looked through this time, Jansson saw something like a crude nursery, or maybe a chimp enclosure at a zoo, with climbing bars, ropes, big chunky toys. There was a solitary troll in there, a cub, playing in a desultory fashion with a big plastic truck. He wore an odd silvery suit, with his head, hands and feet bare.

'Mary's infant.'

'Yes,' said Sally. 'The handlers call him Ham. You can see what they're doing. That's some kind of experimental pressure suit he's wearing. You saw the images. They wanted to use him as a test subject.'

'They didn't mean to harm him—'

'No. But Mary must have had some sense of the danger they were taking him into – the Gap is surely a place a troll would avoid – which is why she protested.'

Jansson knew Sally well enough by now. 'You have a plan, don't you?'

'We're only going to get one chance.'

Expecting the answer, dreading it, Jansson asked, 'To do what?'

'To bust them out of here. We take this kid to his mother, we all step away—'

'And then what?'

'We go on the run. Hide out somewhere, until we can find a proper sanctuary. Maybe wherever the rest of the trolls are going.'

'I knew you were going to say something like that.'

Sally grinned. 'And I know you're going to help me. All cops want to cross over to the dark side once in their lives, don't they?'

'No.'

'Anyhow I need you, Jansson.'

'To do what?'

'To begin with, to get these doors open. You were a cop; you can do that. Look, I don't know how much time we have. Can you open this door, or not?'

Jansson could, and she did, and she was committed.

36

THREE WEEKS AFTER Sally's stunt, when the news of it percolated back through the outernet to Datum Earth, Lobsang summoned Joshua for a face to face meeting. Their first for years, the first since Agnes's funeral, in fact.

Lobsang.

As was his way, Joshua spent twenty-four hours thinking about it.

Then, reluctantly, he went along.

The transEarth Institute facility to which Joshua was directed, a couple of miles from the footprint of Madison on Earth West 10, turned out to be a low, blocky, sprawling structure of the ubiquitous Low-Earth-architecture stone and timber, standing alone on a deserted stretch of road that cut through banks of prairie flowers. Of course Lobsang would have set up this office of his own part-owned subsidiary of the Black Corporation at a stepwise Madison, to be close to Agnes and the Home. A Low Earth it might be, but this was still a different world, with a subtly different late-afternoon sky. Back on the Datum, on a June day like this, the horizon would have been tinted orange-grey, the beautiful and deadly colours of combustion. Not here; this sky was a deep, flawless blue. In a way such comparative emptiness, such cleanliness, even so close to the Datum, gave Joshua a renewed sense of the sheer immensity of the corridor of worlds that was the Long Earth.

Inside the facility, Joshua encountered the usual office clutter: deceptively uncomfortable chairs, stricken rubber plants, and a determinedly pleasant young lady who did everything but check his chest X-rays before allowing him to pass on. There seemed to be a camera in every angle of the walls, each watching him steadily.

At last he was directed through a self-opening door into a white-walled corridor. As Joshua followed the corridor another camera swivelled, following him, its lens glittering with paranoia.

The door at the far end of the corridor opened and a woman stepped out. 'Mr Valienté? So glad you could make it.' She was small and dark, Asiatic, and wore the largest spectacles Joshua had ever seen. She held out her hand. 'My name is Hiroe. Welcome to transEarth. You need to wear this badge.' She handed him a badge on a lanyard, with the transEarth name and chessboard-knight logo, and his name, mugshot, and a scrambled code that could represent anything from his shoe-size to his DNA sequence. 'Wear that at all times, or our security killer-robots will zap you with their laser-beam eyes. Just kidding!'

'Really.'

'Oh, sure. You may be interested to know that you've already cost Selena Jones a dollar. You remember Selena?'

'I remember Selena. Is she still Lobsang's legal guardian?'

'Under some jurisdictions, yes. She wagered me you wouldn't come, that you wouldn't respond to Lobsang's call for help.'

'Did she now?'

'But curiosity is a wonderful thing, is it not?'

That and a fool's residual loyalty, he thought.

'This way, please.'

Hiroe led Joshua now into a big, low-ceilinged room, with picture windows looking out over a stretch of prairie. There were monitor screens all around the place, and a worn keypad on the desk, which was a slab of oak six inches thick. It was the kind of office that might belong to someone who enjoyed their work, and didn't do much else *but* work.

More interesting was the stone trough in front of one window. The plants in it were trumpets fully five feet high, a pale green with red and white ribbing. They clustered together as though they shared a secret, and gave Joshua an uneasy feeling that it wasn't just the air currents that were making them move.

'*Sarracinea gigantica*,' said Hiroe. 'They're carnivorous, you know.'

'They look it. When's feeding time?'

She laughed prettily. 'They're only interested in insects. They secrete a nectar, a drugged bait, that's got interesting commercial possibilities. We got the original seeds from one of the stepwise alternates, of course.'

'Which one?'

'You couldn't even begin to afford to buy the answer to that question,' she said pleasantly, motioning him to a chair. 'Just a moment, please, while I process you through the final stages of security . . .' She tapped at the keypad.

'That's our trade, you know, here at transEarth. We buy and sell commercially useful information.'

So this wasn't *just* a Black-funded playpen for Lobsang, then, Joshua thought cynically. He supposed it would be characteristic of Douglas Black to demand a profit.

'There: you're in the system. Please do wear your badge at all times. So are you ready to meet Lobsang?'

Hiroe took him out of the building, and they walked in the grounds. The evening was gathering now, on this world as on all the others. A few streetlights sparked on the local horizon, and the sun hung low in the sky.

But there was a faintly sulphurous smell in the air. The news today was that this world's copy of Yellowstone was a little more restless than most of its brothers. Reports of trees being poisoned by acid seeps, for instance. Evidently there was ongoing geological unrest at the Yellowstone footprint across most of the Low Earths. On the Datum itself there had been an explosion that had killed a hapless young park ranger called Herb Lewis: not a volcanic eruption, the scientists emphasized, a hydrothermal event, an explosion of trapped, superheated water. All minor events. *Minor*: even from here, a thousand miles away from Yellowstone, Joshua thought he could smell this particular world's *minor event*, and, remembering the apocalyptic nutjob who had accosted them at the Datum twain station about fire and brimstone at Yellowstone, he felt a prickle of unease.

Hiroe sat down on a slab bench carved out of one great baulk of timber. 'Please. We will wait here for Lobsang.'

Joshua sat stiffly.

'You are nervous about meeting him again, aren't you?'

'Not nervous, exactly . . . How can you tell?'

'Oh, the little things. The gritted teeth. The white knuckles. Subtleties like that.'

Joshua laughed. But he glanced around before replying. 'Can he hear us out here?'

She shook her head. 'Actually no. In this place he has limits on his capabilities. Sister Agnes says that's good for him. Not to be omnipotent, in at least one place in the world. Or, the worlds. Why do you think I brought you out here before speaking this way? I didn't want to hurt his feelings.'

'You're more than an employee, right?'

'I do think of myself as a friend. He is everywhere, and yet he is very alone, Mr Valienté. He does need friends. Especially you, sir . . .'

An old man approached through the afternoon light – that was Joshua's first impression. He was slender, tall, with a shaven head, and he wore a loose orange robe. His sandalled feet were dirty, and he carried a kind of rake.

Joshua stood up. 'Hello, Lobsang.'

Hiroe smiled, bowed, and gracefully slipped away.

'First things first,' Lobsang said. 'Thank you for coming.'

The features of this particular ambulant unit reminded Joshua of some of the guises, the bodies Lobsang had donned before. But he had allowed himself to age – or at least, Joshua thought, he had programmed some suite of nano-fabricators to carve wrinkles and inflate jowls and make him look somewhere over sixty. His posture was bent, his movements slow, and the hands that clasped the rake had slightly swollen joints and skin pocked with liver spots. Of course it was all artifice. Everything about Lobsang was artifice, and you had to keep reminding yourself of that. But it was impressive artifice even so; if Lobsang was going to do 'elderly monk' he was going to get every detail right, down to the frayed hem of his grubby orange robe.

Joshua, resolutely unimpressed, didn't feel much like small talk. 'Why did you want to see me? Because of that stunt Sally pulled?'

Lobsang smiled. 'In cahoots with your old friend MPD Lieutenant Jansson, I'll remind you. *Cahoots.*' He repeated the word, forming the syllables with exaggerated motions of his lips. 'Lovely word, that. The kind of word that's necessary to use, purely for the pleasure of saying it. One of the many unexpected joys of incarnation . . . What were we saying? Oh, yes, Sally Linsay. Well, her tunnelling-out with the troll Mary and her cub has made the news across the worlds.'

'Tell me about it,' Joshua said ruefully. Thanks to the old footage of the return of the *Mark Twain*, and the liberal use of face-recognition software, Joshua was now famously known as an associate of Sally. He had been badgered by the media, and by groups adopting various positions on the trolls and the issues surrounding them.

Lobsang said, 'Sally's stunt has brought the issue of the trolls and their relationship with humanity to the top of the news agenda, yes. But the whole business has been bubbling up into a crisis for some time. I'm sure you're aware of that. And now the trolls have started to take action of their own. Action with direct consequences for us all.'

'I heard. Trolls just clearing off all over, right?'

Lobsang smiled. 'Let me show you. Or rather, let my trolls show you.'

'*Your* trolls?'

'There's a pack of them a dozen or so steps away. My holding here extends stepwise, across several worlds.' He held out his hand, as if in invitation. 'Shall we go see?'

There were perhaps twenty trolls in the group. Females sat lazily grooming in the shade of a sprawling tree – the early evening was warm in this particular world – while cubs played, a few young males wrestled in a desultory way, and at the fringe of the pack adults flickered in and out of existence. And as they worked or played or dozed, they sang, a lively sing-along overlaid with complex hooting harmonies, the melody line repeated in canon to form an unending round.

Lobsang led Joshua to a small fenced-off garden area. There were a couple of benches, a water fountain. And, under the broken canopy of a scattering of trees, the ground here was covered in moss, not grass, moss that glowed bright green in the low sunlight.

'Take a seat if you like,' Lobsang said. 'Help yourself to water. It's clean, from a freshwater spring. I should know; I have to clean the pipes.' He got down stiffly on to his hands and knees and began to work his way across the moss lawn, plucking out stray blades of grass, like removing weeds. '"The Rare Old Mountain Dew",' he said.

'What's that?'

'The song the trolls are singing. An old Irish folk song. You know, it's possible to date the first contact with humans of any given troll pack by the songs they sing. In this case, to the late nineteenth century. Do you remember Private Percy? I have carried out such an exercise, tentatively; the result is a kind of map of natural steppers in the pre-Willis Linsay era. Though of course it's not always possible to track back the trolls' own wanderings.'

'What did you mean by *your* trolls, Lobsang?'

He shuffled forward, working at the lawn patiently. 'A figure of speech. I found this pack in a Corn Belt world; I invited them to follow me here, as best I could. There are other groups here. Of course they are no more *my* trolls than Shi-mi was *my* cat, on the *Mark Twain*. But I have created a reserve here, and on the neighbouring worlds, many square miles in extent and many worlds deep. I have kept out humanity and done my best to make the trolls, this pack and others, feel welcome. I have been striving to study them, Joshua. Well, you know that I have been pursuing that project for ten years, since our journey on the *Twain* and our visit to Happy Landings. Here I can watch them in conditions approaching their wild state.'

'And is that the reason for the humble pose, Lobsang? You, a superhuman entity that spans two million worlds, reduced to this?'

He smiled, not interrupting the rhythm of his work. 'Actually, yes, it does help with the trolls. I am a constant presence but not an alarming one. But I would not use words like "reduced". Not around Sister Agnes anyhow. In her eyes I am expanding my personality.'

'Ah. This was her idea, was it?'

'I'd got too big for my boots, she says.'

'That sounds like Agnes.'

'If I wanted to be part of humanity, I had to become embedded in humanity. Down in the dirt, at the bottom of the food chain, so to speak.'

'And you went along with it?'

'Well, there wasn't much point going to all the trouble

of reincarnating the woman if I'm not going to listen to her advice, was there? This is why I felt I needed her, Joshua. Or someone like her. Someone with the sense and moral authority to whisper doubts in my ear.'

'Is it working?'

'I've certainly learned a lot. Such as, how much less ornamental an ornamental garden seems if you're the one who has to sweep up the leaves. How to handle a broom, which requires a certain two-handed dexterity and a kind of rolling energy-conservation strategy. And it's remarkable how many *corners* you discover there are in the world. Some pan-dimensional paradox, perhaps. But there are chores I particularly enjoy. Feeding the carp. Pruning the cherry trees . . .'

Joshua imagined Agnes laughing her reincarnated head off. But he didn't feel particularly amused.

Lobsang was aware of his stillness. 'Ah. The old anger still burns, I see.'

'What do you expect?'

It had been ten years since Joshua had returned from his journey with a lost avatar of Lobsang to the reaches of the Long Earth, to find Madison a blistered ruin, destroyed by a fanatic's backpack nuke. He had barely been able to bring himself to speak to Lobsang since.

'You still believe I could have stopped it,' Lobsang said gently. 'But I was not even there. I was with you.'

'Not all of you . . .'

Lobsang, by nature a distributed personality, had always claimed that the essence of himself had travelled with Joshua into the far stepwise worlds – and that essential core of him had not returned. Whatever Joshua spoke to now was *another* Lobsang, another personality locus, partially synched with the residual *Mark Twain* copy thanks to memory stores Joshua had brought back. Another Lobsang – not the same – and not the Lobsang Joshua had known, who presumably still existed far away. But *this* was the Lobsang who had witnessed the destruction of Madison, and had stood by.

'Even then, when the *Twain* returned, ten years ago, you were . . .' Joshua groped for the old religious word. '*Immanent.* You suffused the world. Or so you claimed. Yet you let those nutjobs walk into the city with a nuke, you let Jansson and the other cops run around trying to find them, while all the time—'

Lobsang nodded. 'All the time I could have snapped my metaphorical fingers and put an end to it. Is that what you would have wanted?'

'Well, if you could have, why didn't you?'

'You know, throughout the ages people have asked the same question of the Christian God. If He is omniscient and omnipotent, why would He allow the suffering of a single child? I am not God, Joshua.'

Joshua snorted. 'You like to act that way, broom and sandals or not.'

'I cannot see into the souls of men and women. I only see the surface. Sometimes I find I have not even imagined what was lying within, when it is eventually revealed through word or action. And even if I could have stopped those bombers – *should* I have? At what cost? How many would you have had me kill, in order to avert an action that would have remained entirely hypothetical? What would you have thought of me then? Humans have free will, Joshua. God will not, and I *can*not, stop them harming each other. I think you should talk to Agnes about this.'

'Why?'

'She might help you find it in yourself to forgive me.'

Joshua thought he could never do that. But he had to put it aside, he knew. With an effort he focused on his surroundings. 'So, the trolls. What have you learned about them?'

'Oh, a great deal. Such as about their true language. Which has nothing to do with the crude signing and point-at-the-picture pidgin humans have imposed on them when they want to give them orders.'

'But even that's pretty powerful, Lobsang. You see clips of Mary saying "I will not" everywhere. On posters, in graffiti, online, even on animated T-shirts.'

'That's true, but it's irresponsible for the tax rebels of Valhalla to mix up their symbols with those of the troll issue – conflating two separate conflicts, each of which spans the whole of the Long Earth.' Lobsang sat back on his heels, convincingly sweating. 'You know that their music is the heart of the trolls' true language, Joshua. Surely that's no surprise. After contact with humans they pick up our songs, but they make them their own, spinning endless variations . . . Music is a way for them to express the natural rhythms of their bodies, from their heartbeats, their breaths, the periodicity of their strides when they walk, even the sparking of the neurons in their heads, perhaps. And they use the rhythm of the song as a timing device, when they want to step together, or hunt. Galileo did that, you know.'

'Galileo?'

'He used music as a kind of clock to time his early experiments in mechanics. Pendulum swings and so on. And of course the trolls' songs carry information. Even a simple disharmony can carry a warning. But there's much more to it than that. Watch them now; I think they're planning a hunt . . .'

The flickering of the stepping trolls, around the core group, was becoming more intense. The returning trolls would add a new line to the ongoing harmonies, loudly or softly, boldly or subtly; the song as a whole was evolving, adapting, and the other steppers seemed to react.

'I plant food sources around the reservation,' Lobsang said. 'Across the stepwise worlds, I mean. Honeycombs, for instance, and animals for them to hunt, deer, rabbits. The pack works as a kind of single organism in seeking out such resources. Stepper scouts spread out across the worlds, and if one finds a promising resource, a deer herd say, he or she will return and, well, sing about it.'

'They're still singing about getting drunk on Irish moonshine as far as I can tell.'

'The core song is only the carrier wave, Joshua. I've done some acoustic analysis; there are variations in pitch, rhythm, even the phasing of the song scraps, that carry information about how far away the find is, how high a quality the food is. Other scouts will pick up on that, go and check it out, and come back with a confirming report, or maybe a contradiction. It's an efficient way for the pack to explore *all* the local possibilities, and soon they'll settle on a selection – often they'll switch to another key, or another song altogether, to signal unanimity – and then they step away. Honeybees work this way; when they need to find a new location for the hive they send out scouts, who come back and dance out the data.

'Trolls individually are not much smarter than chimps, but collectively they have evolved a way for the group to make intelligent, robust decisions. But it isn't like human decision-making, or democracy. Even the kind of democracy you practise out in the boondocks.' He smiled at Joshua. 'I heard they made you a mayor.'

'Sort of.'

'Tightly contested election, was it?'

'Oh, shut up. My main job is to moderate the town meeting. Hell-Knows-Where is still small enough for all the capable adults to gather on the common land, and debate the issues. We use Roberts's *Rules of Order*.'

'Very American. But maybe there's something of the trolls' collective wisdom in what you're practising. Sooner that than suffer the errors of a single wrong-headed leader. The trolls almost always get it right, Joshua, even when I set them some pretty intricate puzzles to solve.'

'Nobody's observed this before, have they?'

'Nobody's had the patience. People always focus on what the trolls can do for them. Not on what the trolls *want*. Not on what they can *do*.'

'How come *our* chimps don't work that way? I mean, the ones on the Datum.'

'I suspect it's an evolutionary adaptation to stepping. Out in the Long Earth, where your food source may be near by geographically but a few worlds away stepwise, you need different search and cooperation strategies. The scouts have to spot the food, and return quickly with the news; the group must decide to move in on it rapidly, or not . . . It's an environment which encourages efficient scouting, precise, detailed communication and quick, robust decision-making. Just as we see here.

'But again, there's still more to the music of the trolls than the needs of the moment. The long call, the essence of which is spread across the worlds, is a kind of encoded, shared wisdom. The call can last a *month* before it repeats, and is laden with ultrasonics, beyond human hearing altogether. But even more than that, it's like a smearing out of consciousness – like nothing humans experience. I've been making efforts to decode it. You can imagine the challenge. I'm making some progress; I have a kind of translation suite, in various prototypes.'

'If anybody can achieve that, you can, Lobsang.'

'That's true,' Lobsang said complacently. 'But right now, Joshua, the long call is vibrating with bad news for the trolls. Bad news because of us. Watch this.' He stood, stiffly, and held up his hands. 'I am trying to study the trolls in their natural state. I made of this group one basic request, though: that in return for the sanctuary I offer them – protection from humans – they stay here, until I release them. Verbally, I mean, they aren't physically restrained in any way. Simple as that.'

'And?'

'And now, Joshua, I *will* release them.' He clapped his hands, once, twice, sharply.

The trolls stopped singing – they stopped stepping, once the scouts had returned – and every head, save for the smallest infants', turned to Lobsang. After a few heart-beats of silence they broke into a new song, a lilting ballad.

' "Galway Bay", ' Lobsang murmured to Joshua.

And then they began to step away, mothers with cubs first, males last for protection from predatory elves. In less than a minute they were gone, leaving only a scuffed patch of ground.

Joshua understood. 'Gone with the rest, just as the reports say. All over the Long Earth.'

'It's true, Joshua. And that is what I wanted to speak to you about. Come. Let's walk. I'm getting stiff from my weeding . . .'

Across the worlds, June skies remained clear, suns set in unison like synchronized swimmers diving, and dark gathered softly, slowly. On one world an owl hooted, for reasons best known to itself.

And Lobsang spoke further of the trolls.

'They've become vital to the economy of the whole of mankind – including the Datum, if only indirectly. So the corporations, including the Black Corporation, are putting on a lot of pressure, wherever they can apply it, to get the trolls back.'

'And back at work.'

'Yes. Also there are security implications. Worse than the trolls disappearing, if they were to be seen to become an active threat to mankind, if a coordinated military response were provoked – we need to avoid *that*.

'But there are other, more fundamental issues. The more I study trolls the more convinced I am that they are central to the ecology of the wider Long Earth itself. Like the elephants of the African savannah, they've been out there for millions of years, and for all that time they've been shaping the landscapes they inhabit – if only by *eating* so much of them. Sally Linsay taught me this; she's studied them in the wild, in her way, far longer than I have. If you remove the big beasts from an ecology you can cause something called a trophic cascade. Knocking out the top of a food chain causes destabilization all the way down – booms and crashes of populations – and that can even cause a rise in greenhouse gases, and so on. A tremor of extinctions and eco-collapse all across the Long Earth, or at least as far as the trolls reach. And all because of us.'

Joshua grunted. 'Makes you proud.'

'The trouble is, Joshua, there's no particular reason for the trolls to return. Before Step Day they had a long and deep contact with humans, and they were treated decently, and in turn they treated us decently.'

Joshua thought again of the story of Private Percy Blakeney, a veteran of the First World War trenches, lost and bewildered in the stepwise world into which he'd unconsciously tumbled, who had been kept alive by trolls for decades.

'But since Step Day it's been a different story. The exploitation of that cub for experiments at the Gap was only the tip of the iceberg.'

Joshua said, 'Seems to me we'll only get the trolls to come back if we can somehow persuade them that we will respect them. That we will listen when they say, "I will not," as Mary did. Not an easy concept to convey to a humanoid . . .'

'I know you tried to convince Senator Starling to campaign for them to be protected under US Aegis law. Even that's not an insignificant challenge.'

'Yeah, animal protection legislation is a mess.'

'Not just that, Joshua. For one thing we'd have to decide what the trolls *are*.'

'What do you mean by that?'

'Well, they don't comfortably fit the old categories, do they? Of human versus animal, the distinction through which we believe we have dominion over nature. It's as if, I think, we'd found a band of *Homo habilis* – something between us and the animal. In some ways the trolls are animal-like. They don't wear clothes, they have no writing. They have no language that's quite analogous to our own. They don't use fire, as even *Homo habilis* probably did. And yet they have some very human traits. They make simple tools, out in the wild – poking sticks, stone hand-axes. They have strong family bonds, which is why it's so easy to trap a troll mother, if you have her cub. They show compassion, even to humans. They do have their own language, in their use of music. And they laugh, Joshua. They laugh.

'The distinction between human and animal is the clincher, you see. You can own an animal; you can kill it with impunity, aside from feeble anti-cruelty legislation. You can't own a human, not in any civilized society, and killing a human is murder. So should we extend human rights to trolls?'

'We have, kind of, in Hell-Knows-Where.'

'Yes, but you're more sane there than most. The basic quandary is: should we embrace them in our own category of being?'

'Which is a challenge to our pride. Right?'

'And more,' Lobsang said. 'A challenge to our very self-image. Meanwhile, there are others who argue that the trolls can't be human because they have no sense of God. Well, not as far as we can tell. What would the Catholics, for instance, do about that? If trolls have souls, then they must be fallen, as we are – that is, tainted with original sin. In which case it is the duty of Catholics to go out and baptize them, to save them from limbo when they die. But, you see, if the trolls are actually animals, to baptize them is blasphemous. Apparently the Pope is preparing an encyclical on the subject. But in the short term the religious debates are just stirring everybody up even more.'

'What does Agnes say?'

'"Trolls like ice cream, and they laugh. Of course they're bloody human, Lobsang. Now go get your broom, you missed a bit."'

'That's Agnes, all right . . . Let's get to the point. Sally dragged me out of my home and all the way to the Datum because of this. Of course Sally found us in the first place, ten years ago, because of a disturbance of the trolls. When they fled from First Person Singular. Now you want me to go out again, don't you? Out into the Long Earth, beyond the High Meggers. To do what? Find Sally and Jansson with Mary, I guess. Then what? Find where the trolls are hiding? Persuade them to come out, to join the human world again?'

'That's pretty much it,' Lobsang said. 'Sounds impossible, doesn't it? And it doesn't help that we're already in the middle of so much upheaval from the Valhallan independence demands.'

'You want to restore the balance.'

'You and I always did share the same instincts, Joshua.' Lobsang bent to remove a single dead leaf from an otherwise immaculate lawn. *Will you do it, Joshua?* He didn't ask the question, but left it hanging in the air.

Joshua thought it over. He was in his late thirties now. He had a young wife, a kid, a role in society at Hell-Knows-Where. He was no longer a mountain man, if he ever had been. And now here was Sally, charging off into the Long Earth through her soft places, as if challenging Joshua to follow. Here was Lobsang, like a ghost from the past, snapping his fingers once more. Was Joshua just going to jump as commanded?

Of course he was. Even if he wasn't the man he used to be. But then, even Lobsang wasn't who he once was, quite.

They walked on, stepping occasionally from world to world, from sunset to sunset. The troll songs hung in the richly scented air of each world – but Joshua wondered if they were diminishing, even as he listened.

Tentatively he said, 'Having met you now, I can see your instinct was right.'

'What do you mean?'

'You did need Sister Agnes.'

Lobsang sighed. 'But I think I need you too, Joshua. I often think back to our days together on the *Mark Twain*.'

'Watched any old movies recently?'

'That's another thing about Agnes. She won't let me show any movies that don't have nuns in.'

'Wow. That's brutal.'

'Something else that's good for me, *she* says. Of course there aren't that many movies that qualify, and we watch them over and over.' He shuddered. 'Don't talk to me about *Two Mules for Sister Sara*. But the musicals are the worst. Although Agnes says that the freezer-raiding scene in *Sister Act* is an authentic detail from convent life.'

'Well, that's a consolation. Musicals with nuns in, huh . . .'

A voice rang out across the park, a voice Joshua remembered only too well from his own past. 'Lobsang? Time to come in now. Your little friend will keep until tomorrow . . .'

'She has loudhailers everywhere.' Lobsang shouldered

266

his rake and sighed as they trudged across the grass. 'You see what I'm reduced to? To think I hired forty-nine hundred monks to chant for forty-nine days on forty-nine mountain tops in stepwise Tibets, for *this*.'

Joshua clapped him on the shoulder. 'It's tough, Lobsang. She's treating you like you're a kid. Like you're sixteen, going on seventeen.'

Lobsang looked at him sharply. 'You can pack that in for a start,' he snapped.

'But I've got confidence you can overcome these difficulties, Lobsang. Just face up to every obstacle. Climb every mountain—'

Lobsang stalked off sulkily.

Joshua waved cheerfully. 'So long! Farewell!'

37

JOSHUA MADE HIS way out of the transEarth facility through the reception building in Madison West 10. Of course he could have stepped away anywhere, but it seemed polite to go back out that way. Besides, he had to give Hiroe his badge back.

Bill Chambers was waiting for him in the foyer.

'Bill? What are you doing here?'

'Well, Lobsang sent for me. He figured you would need a companion for the trip.'

'What trip?'

'To find Sally, and the trolls. What else?'

'But we only just spoke about it . . .' He sighed. 'What the hell. That's Lobsang for you. OK, Bill, thanks.'

'Fair play to him, he says he'll give us some kind of translation gadget, so we can talk to the trolls.'

'If we can find them at all. If I'm honest I've no idea where to start.'

'I do.' His ruddy face creased in a wide smile. 'Which is, I guess, why he sent for me. We have to start with Sally. Figure out where she might have gone.'

'How do we do that?'

'Well, Joshua, you're as close to her as any member of the human race, like it or not. There must be *something* she's done or said, some clue we can follow.'

'I'll think about it. OK. What else?'

'Then we need to track down them troll lads. And I've an idea about that. Look at this.' He dug an item out of his jacket pocket, and handed it to Joshua.

It was a tape cassette, a bit of technology fifty years obsolete, or more. Its plastic was worn and grubby, and the label unreadable. The cassette *smelled* strange, Joshua discovered now as he handled it. Half rutting goat, half patchouli, half chemical. It smelled, in fact, of clear nights in the High Meggers. 'Who the hell plays cassette tapes, outside of a museum? What is this, Bill?'

'A lure.'

'A lure for what? Or who?'

'Somebody who's going to help us. You'll see. So – what first?'

'I'm going to see my family. Try to explain all this to Helen.'

Bill looked squarely at him. 'Ah, she already knows, man.'

And Joshua remembered that fragment of poetry Helen had quoted at the very beginning of all this: *A woman with the West in her eyes, / And a man with his back to the East.* 'Yeah. Probably.'

'As for me, I'm off to get bladdered while I've got the chance. See you in the morning.'

38

THE *BENJAMIN FRANKLIN* was summoned to the town of New Purity, a hundred thousand worlds East of Valhalla, where there had been an ambiguous report of yet more trouble with trolls.

Joe Mackenzie stood by Maggie on the observation deck, looking down on the community. From the air it had a look of competence: town hall, neat fields, and, of course, what looked like a large church. 'New Purity, huh?' he said. 'What's the name of this sect again?'

Maggie checked her briefing. 'The Uncut Brethren.'

'Well, you'd expect a church. But there's no stockade.'

'No. And look over there.' She pointed at what looked like a charnel pit.

Even as the twain descended, Maggie's instincts started pressing alarm buttons. *The Uncut Brethren.* Maggie had been home-schooled by avowed atheists – actually not that avowed, they had argued that an outright funda-mentalist atheist was just as bad as the worst fire-and-brimstone spittle-dribbling Bible-puncher, and as an adolescent Maggie had been fascinated by both extremes. So, as a connoisseur of believers and un-believers, she thought she recognized the Uncut Brethren's type on sight, as they gathered before the

Franklin party: uniformly dressed, both male and female, in drab woollen smocks, with long queues of hair down their backs.

Still, they seemed hospitable enough – right up until Jake the troll and his family stepped down the ramp from the hovering twain, after the human crew.

One young man promptly approached Maggie. 'We don't allow these creatures on our premises, our homes, our farms. They are unclean.'

Maggie looked into his face, irritated. But she saw tension there. Even grief. Something bad had happened here. 'Unclean how? Also, Jake is not a creature.'

The man's face worked. 'Very well, let *him* tell me that.'

Maggie sighed. 'Actually that's possible, just. What's your name, sir?'

'My name is immaterial. I speak for all, it is our way.'

Maggie felt a gentle but persistent pressure on her arm. It was Jake. She beckoned to Nathan Boss, who carried the troll-call. 'This alive person / close to dead / gone away / person was and is not / song of sadness.'

Hearing these scratchy words coming out of the instrument, the Brethren stared at the troll.

Maggie faced the young spokesman. 'What happened here? Just show me.'

For answer, he led her away from the neat buildings to that pit they'd spotted from the air.

It was indeed a hole in the ground, full of corpses. A dozen bodies in total, she guessed, maybe more. There were no human remains here that she could see, but many humanoids: trolls, and another species Maggie recognized from her pre-mission briefings. *Elves* – one of the more vicious varieties, if she remembered the detail.

271

Maggie turned again to the young man, and said with a note of command, 'I think you need to tell me your name, son.'

He blushed and said, 'Brother Geoffrey. Auditor of the Uncut Brethren. We are a contemplative order; we believe the prepared soul can overcome all hostile circumstances . . .' His voice faltered.

The story she extracted from Brother Geoffrey, in between his sobs and *mea culpas*, had been repeated all over the Long Earth. Every stepwise Earth was a new world, a world for free, a blank slate on which you could write a wonderful life, if you dreamed a strong enough dream and watched your back. Here, the Brethren had built a decent open township, along, according to Geoffrey, Athenian lines. Their philosophy seemed to be a melange of the teaching of figures that Maggie, in her vague theological understanding, generally identified as the good guys, Jesus, the Buddha and Confucius among them. But they had not listened to basic warnings that must have been given them by more experienced hands, even before they left the Datum.

And the peril that had befallen them, out of many possible out here, had been elves.

Mac approached her. 'We've done a little forensic analysis on that pit. Captain, it was the elves did the attacking. Defensive wounds only on the trolls. The elves evidently stepped in, targeting the humans . . .'

In her briefings Maggie had seen records of such bewildering attacks, launched out of nowhere by stepping hunter-killers. 'A stockade would have been no use against steppers.'

'No, but cellars would, and I don't think this lot dug

272

those either. The trolls got caught in the crossfire – hell, they may have just been passing through, they may even have been trying to help. Damned unlucky for them, since trolls are getting so thin on the ground. And it didn't do the trolls themselves any good. *These* guys don't know the difference between trolls and elves, I figure.'

'So the colonists turned their guns on trolls and elves indiscriminately.'

'That's about the size of it.'

'Thanks, Mac.'

Geoffrey still stood beside her. 'My mother – my own mother has been taken. And—'

'I know. But it wasn't the trolls. Look.' She pointed at little Carl, playing with kids' toys, much to the joy of the few children here in their drab smocks. '*That* is what trolls do. You need to understand the reality of the Long Earth if you're to survive here. And in your case, if there are elves in the stepwise vicinity, that means accepting the trolls. They will help you clear your fields, put up barns, dig wells. And, best of all, they'll deter the elves.'

He seemed to struggle to absorb that. But his next response was positive. 'How do we do that? Bring the trolls here, I mean.'

A difficult question, or at least bad timing, since the trolls seemed to be withdrawing from the human worlds all over. She shrugged. 'Be nice to them. To start with, I suggest that with the help of my crew you bury the corpses of those trolls alongside those of your own people. Pretty soon every troll on this world, and all the other worlds, will know about that bit of respect. Oh, and we'll help you dig some cellars before we go.

Anti-step precautions, right? *And* a stockade for good measure . . .'

They worked through the rest of the day.

That evening, as the sun went down, the community gathered to listen to the song of the *Franklin*'s trolls. Soon the replies started coming, like echoes from beyond the dim horizon, the ones far away eerily mingling with those near by, the calls flowing and floating over the landscape and melding into one great symphony.

Yet there was a certain emptiness to the sound. This world, like all the human-occupied worlds of the Long Earth, was becoming bereft of trolls, and a silence was falling across all the Long Earth, as if there had been an extinction event, some terrible plague. What a strange phenomenon it was, Maggie thought. She could think of no precedent, nothing like this before – it was as if all the elephants were withdrawing from Africa, maybe. A rejection of mankind by the natural world. Even her own trolls seemed oddly restless, and she was determined to release them if they showed serious signs of wanting away.

The next thing, she thought with resignation, would be demands on her from various homesteaders to bring back their troll labourers, how it was about time the government *did* something . . .

The *Benjamin Franklin* hovered over New Purity for two more days, before riding high into the air and vanishing stepwise.

39

SALLY KNEW THE world they had arrived at. Of course she did.

And of course it was new to Jansson. All of this, like the Gap, like every world beyond the Lows, was new to her.

It had taken three weeks of travelling, since the Gap, to get here, with regular stepping and falls through the soft places. Sally could have got here quicker, Jansson suspected, but she had worked to keep them hidden as well as on the move – and you couldn't move trolls on too quickly; those big frames took a lot of feeding, every day.

They emerged from the latest soft place into a land-scape that was almost but not quite desert. They stood in a broad valley, with cliffs on either side pocked by caves. On the valley floor were a few stunted trees, the remnants of a broken stone bridge, and a building, one vast cubical mass of shaped black stone. The air was so dry it seemed to suck the moisture out of your flesh, and Jansson instinctively searched for shade. Sally remembered this place well. And the radiation threat, she said. They would be safe enough as long as they stayed well away from that building.

This was the world they had informally called Rectangles, when Sally had found it with Joshua and

Lobsang, ten years ago. A world of failed intelligence, it had seemed, and death. The world where Joshua had found a single beautiful artefact, a sapphire ring. A world that seemed unchanged a decade on, save for the detritus of more recent visitors: boot prints in the dirt, campfire scars, archaeologists' trench-marker flags – even some trash, plastic cartons, ripped bags.

The troll and her cub wandered off, looking for water, food, shade.

Sally got Jansson comfortable in the shade of one of the struggling trees, on a rough bed of their piled-up gear and covered by a single silver emergency blanket. Then she briskly built a fire – they didn't need the heat, but it might keep any critters away.

Jansson said, 'So you've been here before. With Joshua, all those years ago. And we're here because the trolls are here . . . or near by. Hiding out. That's your guess, right? Whatever *that's* based on.'

Sally shrugged, non-committal.

Jansson thought she understood, by now. During the journey Sally had kept disappearing, for a few hours at a time, a day, sometimes for longer periods. Plugging herself into whatever network of contacts and information she had built up out here. Jansson suspected Sally herself would find it hard to sum up the various whispers she'd been hearing, from various sources. If she came *here* she'd find trolls, or trolls would find her; that was the sum of her instincts. Jansson just had to hope Sally's scraps of information and gut sense added up to a good guide . . .

Jansson gave up thinking about it. It would certainly do no good to ask Sally. Taciturn nature or not, a selective silence was one of Sally's most irritating habits.

When Jansson had drifted off to sleep, Sally went hunting.

The valley bottom itself was suspiciously flat, Sally thought, just as had been her impression the first time she was here. As if it was all one slab: another artefact, maybe, like the building itself. There were slopes of scree at the base of the canyon walls, and here and there green extremophile-type plants, lovers of heat and dryness, struggling for life. At first glance there was no sign of movement, no animals or birds or even insects. That didn't bother Sally. Where there was greenery of any kind there were going to be herbivores to browse on that greenery, and carnivores to browse on the herbivores. It was a question of patience. All she had to do was wait. She never carried food – not in the endless larder that was the Long Earth. A lizard or two would do. Something like a naked mole rat, maybe. A deep burrower.

By the steep valley wall, in the shade of a rock face, she settled on her haunches. This was how Sally had lived her life for a quarter of a century now, ever since she'd left Datum Earth for good not long after Step Day, when her father had made his ambiguous gift of Stepper technology to mankind. And of course she'd had plenty of practice out in the Long Earth in the years before that. Living off the land on the move was easy, but it was a fantasy to believe that animals that had never met man were naturally tame. An awful lot of good things to eat were too used to running from *anything* strange. You had to wait . . .

This place was just as she remembered, save for the more recent boot prints, she saw as she relaxed, and took in her surroundings. Of all the discoveries Joshua and

Lobsang had taken back to the Datum from their voyage of exploration a decade ago, this was probably the most sensational: evidence of intelligent dinosaur-like creatures more than a million and a half steps away from the Datum. It had done Lobsang no good to protest that the colony-organism that had called itself First Person Singular was far more interesting and exotic, because nobody *understood* that. Nor was it any use to point out that the creatures whose remains they'd found here, though reptilian, could not *really* be dinosaurs in any meaningful sense . . .

There had been a clamour to know more. The universities had received a flood of funding to send out follow-up parties. For a few years researchers had crawled over this site, though the radioactivity made the work hazardous, and they had sent out drone planes and balloons equipped with infrared sensors and ground-penetrating radar to take a look at the rest of this world.

It had surprised nobody to learn that the pyramid, this valley, was only the visible tip of a worldwide culture: ancient, long fallen, buried in the sands of this arid world, which Lobsang and the *Mark Twain* had not been equipped to explore properly, or even detect. In and under the dust there were traces of cities, roads, canals – not human-like in layout, clearly the product of *different* minds, but otherwise eerily familiar, and all very ancient.

No, these were not dinosaurs, but their ancestors might once have been dinosaurs – just as humans had had ancestors in the dinosaur age, furtive squirrelly quadruped mammals . . . Perhaps in this world the tremendous asteroid impact that had destroyed the dinosaur-dominated ecology of the Datum had worked out differently; here it might have taken out the big beasts and left behind their smaller, smarter, more agile cousins. The Rectangles creatures were remotely descended from raptors, perhaps.

But, much later, they had evidently suffered their own extinction event. Maybe there had been war, or plague, or another asteroid fell unluckily . . . In the aftermath, a community of survivors, or their descendants, their technology lost, their civilization smashed, had been drawn here by the strange phenomena surrounding a nuclear pile, possibly natural, a chance concentration of uranium ore under that building. It had been a god, a temple that had slowly killed them.

That was one theory, at any rate: a *chance concentration* of the ore. But from the beginning there had also been speculation that this pile was not some natural phenomenon but the ruined and still toxic remnant of a much older and higher technology. The remnant radioactivity came from an abandoned core, or maybe a waste dump. This hypothesis was the subject of much debate, but it fitted Sally's own first impressions when she'd come upon this place.

It was kind of satisfying that the answers weren't simple or clear. Like all worlds, this one was no neat, finite theoretical model but the product of its own long and unique evolutionary history. Sally, moreover, had been through college herself in Madison; she understood enough science to know when a house of theorizing started to totter on foundations of inadequate data, and ignored most of the guesswork.

She was pleased that Joshua had never revealed the existence of the one tangible souvenir they had brought back from this place: the exquisite ring, it could almost have been crafted by a human jeweller, that they had found on the fleshless finger of one post-dinosaur. Pleased that Joshua had kept it all these years.

Well, the research money had run out, the Long Earth was always full of other study targets of various kinds, and the archaeologists had long since sealed up their digs and gone away. And Sally, now, in hunting mode, was glad of it. Glad of the solitude. Nobody here but us shadows on the rock . . .

A hot breath on her neck. *The hunter hunted*, she thought immediately. She hadn't been paying attention. She whirled, reaching for the knife at her belt.

A wolf: that was her first impression. Huge, fur bristling, mouth open, tongue hanging, eyes like windows into Arctic waste. It looked as heavy as she was, more. And it had got close enough to *taste* her, practically, before she'd even noticed.

She forced herself not to just step out of here, her first reaction. She wasn't alone on this trip; she had to think of Jansson. She wondered if she had time to shout a warning to Jansson, and whether it would do any good.

But the animal didn't attack.

It stepped back, one pace, two, raised itself up – and *stood*, on its hind legs, not balancing like a dog doing a circus trick, but standing easily, naturally, as if it were designed to stand like that. Now she saw it had a kind of belt around its waist, from which tools hung – including a very technologically advanced-looking pistol made of some kind of metal, that looked like nothing so much as a Buck Rogers sci-fi ray gun, and was totally out of place. When the wolf spread its empty paws to her, she saw that the digits were long, flexible, the paws almost like thumbless hands encased in some leathery glove. Surprise heaped on surprise.

And then it spoke.

'Sally Linsss-ay.' Its voice was a growl, a rasp, a kind of crudely shaped whisper, but understandable, and the human words were backed up by subtle posture changes: a raise of the head, a twitch of the snout. 'Coming he-rrhe, we knew. Kobolds-ss say. Welcome.' And it lifted its magnificent head and howled.

40

IN THE WEEKS since they'd left behind the Low Chinas, the airships *Zheng He* and *Liu Yang* had forged steadily East, their stepping pace gradually increasing, though, Roberta learned, still far short of their design maximum. Worlds washed below the twains' bows in great bands, cold or temperate, moist or arid, this Eastern stepwise geography roughly matching the mapping made by American explorers to the West, punctuated by Jokers of various kinds, like random flashbulbs.

They made periodic stops, and members of the crew went down to the surface, suitably protected, to observe, measure, retrieve samples of the geology, flora, fauna, even exotic atmospheric traces. They followed the Long Earth exploration strategy established by Joshua Valienté a decade earlier, with surface pioneers supervised by controllers on airships above. Roberta, watching from above, made methodical notes.

They passed the milestone of two million steps from the Datum.

And now they approached a particular world where, it was planned, Roberta herself was to descend to the surface, with Lieutenant Wu Yue-Sai.

The Chinese had reached this world before, and it had

been studied at least to some extent. This first descent was intended as a learning experience for Roberta, she was told, and she accepted that. She had already spent a lot of time in a kind of training chamber with Lieutenant Wu Yue-Sai, who showed her how to don her jumpsuit, and use her individual Stepper box, and the small monitor sets they would wear on their shoulders: how the Captain would speak to them through unobtrusive earpieces, how to use the med packs and emergency rations and silvery blankets in the event they got stranded – how to use the ceramic-and-bronze handguns they were issued. Roberta took each piece of equipment, each procedure, asked relevant questions, and practised over and over.

Yue-Sai tried to lighten up the process. She cracked jokes in her imperfect English, and tried to invent games and contests to help the practice go by. Roberta would simply wait until these moments had passed, and then would carry on with her own patient exercises.

With time she felt Yue-Sai give up on her, in a sense, and withdraw. Roberta had observed this many times before. It was not that Roberta Golding did not understand people; rather, she understood them too well. Yue-Sai's attempts at fun had been transparent exercises in motivation, which Roberta saw through immediately. Besides, with her own sense of inner purpose she needed no external motivation. Yet that was not enough of a response for Wu Yue-Sai, and Roberta saw that too.

Aged fifteen, Roberta was a person who *saw* things. That is, she saw them more clearly than those around her. She certainly saw her own limitations, for instance now, as she prepared to face a remote stepwise world for the first time. She could be killed by her own ignorance, or by sheer mischance, in the blink of an eye. She saw this, and accepted it with a calm that seemed to chill others around her. But what was the purpose of self-delusion?

The career towards which she was heading was entirely a matter of stripping away delusion, she sometimes thought. What was the nature of the universe into which she had been born? Why did it exist at all? If it had a purpose, what was it? These seemed to her the only questions worth exploring. And the only valid technique evolved by humans for exploring such questions was the scientific method, a robust and self-correcting search for the truth. Yet it had become obvious to her since about the age of twelve that science as it had progressed so far – physics, chemistry, biology, all the rest – had only inched towards grappling with the true questions, the fundamentals. *Those* questions had only been addressed by theologians and philosophers, it seemed to her. Unfortunately, *their* answers were a mush of doubt, self-delusion and flummery that had probably done more harm than good. And yet that was all there was.

For now she had devoted herself, nominally at least, to theology and philosophy, as well as to explorations of the natural sciences, such as on this expedition. She had even received grants to help support this mission to the step-wise East from the Vatican, the Mormons, from Muslim orders, and various philosophical foundations. Dealing with such bodies, she had quickly learned when *not* to share her view that organized religion was a kind of mass delusion.

She had to work with what was available. She some-times imagined she was like the scholars of the European Middle Ages who had worked their way through the ranks of the Church because there was no other organized scholarship around. Or, perhaps, as if she had been dropped even further into the past – as if she were trying to use stone blades and lumps of ochre to build a radio telescope. Still, she persevered, for there was no choice.

Despite her unsatisfactory education, Roberta Golding saw the world clearly. And she saw people clearly, more clearly than they could see themselves. Humanity, she once said in an answer in a philosophy exam taken when she was eleven years old, was nothing but the thin residue left when you subtracted the baffled chimp. Responses like that made her a promising scholar, and in Happy Landings, where there were many bright children like her, she had never had any trouble getting picked for the net-ball team. But here her lack of response, her habit of speaking in brief lectures, her corrections of simple errors, didn't make the crew warm to her. Not even the forgiving Yue-Sai.

The airships settled over a suitable location, and in a methodical fashion sent up sounding-rockets and weather balloons to gain a broader picture of this world. Then Yue-Sai took Roberta down to the elevator deck, they checked over their equipment one last time, and descended to the surface of Earth East 2,201,749.

They were standing at the fringe of a forest, close to a sprawling river estuary. From the cover of the trees Roberta was able to look out over the open plain of the estuary and the wetlands that fringed it, to a sharp ocean horizon. She was distracted by huge flying creatures that swept low over the ocean water, a flock of them, each with filmy wings outspread – the largest flyers Roberta had ever seen. Something like pterosaurs? Something like bats? Something evolved from a different root altogether? Silhouetted in the sparkling light off the sea they swooped lower, graceful necks dipping, and huge fish, or fish-like creatures, were plucked from the water and gulped down into long beaks.

This was a warm, watery world, a world of high sea levels, of shallow oceans that washed far into the hearts of the continents. A world that could support such fantastic visions. And a world, Roberta understood from her studies, with dangers of its own, unknown on drier Earths like the Datum: not least exotic climatic catastrophes, such as the hypercane already brewing out on the local copy of the Pacific Ocean . . .

Shadows shifted across the forest.

Yue-Sai waved her hand. Roberta made sure the speaker feed from the monitor on her shoulder was off, and stood stock still and silent in the cover of the trees.

Immense forms moved through the forest, heading for the estuary and the fresh water. Roberta glimpsed compact, muscular bodies, on all fours but with massively powerful hind legs – they were something like kangaroos, she thought, but beefed-up – and with their ears flaring into tremendous coloured crests, stiffened with cartilage. There were several of these animals, the adults taller at the shoulder than Roberta, calves running alongside, and one infant being carried in a pouch at its mother's belly.

Silent as a cat, Yue-Sai slid through the forest, tracking the herd.

Roberta followed as best she could. She wasn't as quiet as Yue-Sai, but the whirring lenses of the shoulder monitor pack were noisier than her footsteps, and she took some pride in that.

They came to the edge of the forest, by a braid of fresh water. Across the estuary's damp plain huge flocks of birds, or bird-like creatures, strutted, squabbled and fed. With marsh flowers in abundance it was a mass of colour, under a deep blue sky. Roberta thought she saw the characteristic ridged backs of crocodilians sliding through the deeper water.

And, by the water's edge, the creatures of the forest came to drink.

The most obvious, the most spectacular, were those big bulky roos with their colourful sail-like ear-crests. The creatures were so huge and heavy, they moved so slowly and patiently, they looked as if they were carved from living rock. And they were so massive that those great hind legs must surely be evolved for kicking, not for jumping like a Datum kangaroo. But their ear-crests were oddly fragile-looking, almost translucent in the light of the sun, evidently just skin and tissue stretched over frames of cartilage. The crests were alight with brightly coloured patterns that shifted and dissolved as Roberta watched.

Yue-Sai murmured, 'Are you getting this, Captain Chen, Mr Montecute?'

'Yes, Lieutenant,' replied the Captain in their ears. 'Try to keep these crests in view. Why so complex a display? I'll have our scholars try passing them through pattern analyser suites . . .'

Yue-Sai touched Roberta's shoulder and pointed again, further along the river bank.

More beasts drinking. These were like big flightless

featherless birds, Roberta thought, walking almost daintily, balanced on two big back limbs but with two small grasping arms in front. Their heads were long, almost snake-like, but with wide duck-like beaks. When they dipped to the water, sucking noisily, long muscular tails waved behind them.

Roberta asked, 'Birds, or dinosaurs?'

Yue-Sai shrugged. 'They're all the same big family. Don't expect anything, Roberta. Don't be surprised by anything . . .'

Roberta understood the principle. The histories of the parallel worlds of the Long Earth had been shaped by similar processes, but differed in the detail. You had to imagine you were travelling across a kind of probability tree, where you found worlds on which some long-past event had turned out differently, thus reshaping life's subsequent history and providing novel raw material for natural selection to mould . . .

'For example,' Yue-Sai said, 'those duckbills look bird-like, or dinosaurid. But those big crested beasts are mammals. Some kind of marsupial, it seems. And *there's* something you'd never have seen back in the Cretaceous.' She pointed.

Elves.

Stepping humanoids. There was a pack of them, maybe twenty, including children and nursing infants. They had found a spot away from the big herbivores, and far enough back from the deep water to be safe from the crocodiles and any other threats. They were scooping up water with their hands, and digging into the mud for roots and worms and molluscs. A few of the younger males were bickering; with irritable pant-hoots they flickered between the worlds, so that to watch them was like trying to follow a badly edited movie.

'There are other sorts here too,' Yue-Sai said softly. 'I spotted them in the deeper forest—'

The conversation was cut short by a sound of thunder.

Yue-Sai and Roberta shrank back into deeper cover. Some of the duckbills kept drinking, but the big adults looked up suspiciously. The crest-roos dipped their great heads and backed into a rough circle.

There was a crash, the splintering of wood, a groan as a young tree was felled, and the forest parted like a flimsy stage set as a tremendous animal burst into the open. Its body must have been fifteen yards long, balanced exquisitely on two striding legs. Its arms were small, comparatively, but longer and more muscular than Roberta's own legs, and the right arm had some kind of creeper wrapped around it. Its skin was covered with feathers, brilliantly coloured, like the costume of an Aztec priest. The head was a gaping nightmare of teeth and blood, and when it opened its mouth to roar Roberta imagined she could smell raw meat.

It strode forward, huge, purposeful. It seemed more mechanical than animal, a killer robot, an automaton, and yet it breathed and pawed the earth. The herbivores were already fleeing, following the water's edge, galloping and bellowing.

But the elves did not run, not immediately. They scattered into a loose arc, facing the creature, the adults to the fore with stone blades in their hands, the young behind them, but even the young were snarling defiance. It was like another movie scene, Roberta thought.

Stone-tool-wielding man-apes against the dinosaur.

Yue-Sai was staring, as if unwilling to miss a second of the spectacle. 'A dinosaur, all right. Or its sixty-five-million-years-later descendant. Tyrannosaur-like, or something else evolved to fit the same niche.'

'Of course China had its own magnificent dinosaur lineages,' Captain Chen reminded them sternly. 'There are other comparisons to be used, Lieutenant.'

'Yes, sir,' Yue-Sai said absently. 'It could even be a flight-less bird. If it is like a tyrannosaur, the odds are this is a female. They had ranges a few miles across; the males were sparser, one every few tens of miles. But what's that on its arm? . . .'

The predator's roars and the humanoids' responding snarls and gestures were reaching a climax. Abruptly the predator charged, right into the middle of the elf group.

The young with their parents scattered. The adult elves started flickering in and out of existence, faster than the predator could catch them, though she ducked her head, snapped her huge teeth, and swept empty space with her arms and tail. One elf materialized in mid-jump right beside the predator's head, and took a swipe at her right eye with his blade before stepping away again, without ever touching the ground. The precision was remarkable, and the predator's eye was saved only by a chance duck of the head.

Bloodied, enraged, the predator stood at the centre of the band of humanoids, unable to land a killing blow on any of them. She roared again, sweeping her huge tail, snapping her teeth.

But the humanoids had had enough. They stepped

away now, mothers carrying their children, as far as Roberta could see leaving nobody behind.

'You have to hand it to those little guys,' Jacques said in their ears. 'They stood up to their Grendel.'

Yue-Sai shrugged. 'Eventually the beast will learn not to tangle with humanoids, especially steppers. And anyhow they were never her main target. Look.'

Now the predator was heading down the beach after the big crest-roos. They had a head start; the roos, alarmed, tons of flesh and bone on the move, were like a retreating tank division. But one mother hung back to shepherd her calf.

'They've got too much of a start,' Jacques said.

'Are you sure?' Captain Chen murmured. 'Look at what she is doing with her arm.'

Roberta could see that the predator was using one agile hand to unwrap the vine from her arm. The vine was maybe six feet long, and was weighted at either end by something like a coconut. And now, even as she ran, her legs pounding the beach and her spine and tail almost horizontal, the predator whirled the vine and released it. It flew across the intervening space and wrapped itself around the big back legs of the lagging mother crest-roo. The vine snapped immediately, but it was enough for the mother to be brought crashing to the ground. Her calf slowed beside her, lowing mournfully, clearly afraid.

And it had a right to be, for the predator was on the mother immediately. It ran by and ducked its head to rip a huge chunk out of the crest-roo's rear right leg, then almost casually swiped its head against one magnificent flaring ear, crushing the cartilage so the crest folded like a fallen kite. The mother bellowed in pain.

But she was able to stand, though blood dripped from the gaping wound. She even nudged her infant to move on, as they shambled up the beach after the rest of the herd, which had already cut into the forest.

The predator stood and watched them go, by the water's edge, breathing hard. The crest-roo's blood stained her mouth. Then she ducked to the water, took a mighty drink, shook her head, and trotted after the mother and calf. It was a pursuit that could have only one outcome.

'That predator used a bolas,' said Roberta.

Yue-Sai said, 'Yes . . . It looked as though it could have been a natural object. A vine-like growth with fruit. But there was nothing "natural" in the way she used it.' Yue-Sai looked delighted, in her quiet way, to have made this staggering discovery. 'I told you, Roberta. We're far away from home now. Have no preconceptions.'

'I'll second that,' Captain Chen said. 'And I should tell you that our signal-processing experts here inform me that there was data content in the patterns that flared across the crests of those roo-like beasts. *They were talking*, through the visual means of their crests! Sentience! Our onboard scholars must make all this clear when they joint-author their paper: "A mammal–reptile assemblage of tool-making intelligences beyond Earth East two million". How marvellous! What a great discovery for China!'

They began to walk back to the pick-up point.

Chen, evidently enthused, went on, 'We Chinese, you know, Roberta, have a utopian legend of our own. There is a story that dates back to the fifth century after your Christ, of how a fisherman found his way through a narrow cave to the Land of Peach Blossom, where descendants of soldiers lost from the age of the Qin dynasty lived in a land sheltered by mountains, in peace with each other, in peace with nature. But when the fisherman tried to reach it a second time, he could not find the way. So it is with all utopias, whose legends proliferate around the world. Even in North America, where the natives' dream of the Happy Hunting Ground was displaced by the European settlers' fables of the Big Rock Candy Mountain. Do you think if we travel far enough we will find such a land, Roberta? Are such legends a relic of some early perception of the Long Earth itself?'

'There is no sensible content in this discussion,' Roberta murmured in reply. 'And as to the papers you're planning – none of this matters.'

Yue-Sai turned to her.

'How's that?' Jacques asked.

Roberta gestured at the landscape around her. 'The coming hypercane will destroy all this. I've been studying the climatic theory of these worlds, with their high sea levels. They are prone to tremendous hurricanes, extracting heat from the shallow oceans. Storms that can span continents, with thousand-miles-per-hour winds; water vapour is thrown up into the stratosphere, and the ozone layer is wrecked . . . I've also been studying the records of the weather balloons you launched from the twains. There's such a storm forming right now. Ask your meteorologists. It's unmistakable. It will take a few more weeks to reach full strength, but when it does this complicated little community will be right in its path. It's been an interesting experiment, a stepwise mixing of different species. But it will soon be terminated.'

There was silence.

'"Terminated"', said Captain Chen at last.

Roberta was used to this kind of reaction to her choice of words, and found it irritating. As if a child were covering its ears to avoid hearing bad news. 'All life is terminated, ultimately. I'm only telling the truth. It's trivially obvious.'

Again, nobody spoke.

Yue-Sai looked away. 'Captain, I think it's time we returned.'

'Agreed.'

41

THE *ZHENG HE* and *Liu Yang* lingered for some days in the vicinity of Earth East 2,201,749. The scientists catalogued their observations and specimens, while the engineers crawled over the airships, testing their systems, carrying out routine maintenance.

Then they moved on, into realms of the Eastern Long Earth never before explored by Chinese crews, or any other. Into the unknown.

Shortly afterwards the ships made a longer stop, next to Earth East 2,217,643. Here they found a Gap: a break in the chain of stepwise worlds that made up the Long Earth, where the relevant Earth had been removed. Roberta quietly pointed out to Jacques that the first Western Gap discovered, by Joshua Valienté, had been at around Earth West two million. No doubt, from the similarity of those numbers, there was some conclusion to be drawn about the nature of the great tree of probabilities that was the Long Earth.

Valienté's airship had been wrecked by the step into vacuum that was the Gap. The Chinese ships were better prepared. Their crews had their ships hop back and forth across the Gap, dropping off hardened automatic probes, which, given the momentum of the spin of the neighbouring Earths, went sailing off into the Gap world's empty black sky. Jacques stared without much interest at the images returned – stars that looked much like the stars as seen from any world, planets that seemed to circle in their usual orbits with smug indifference to the absence of an Earth. The crew, though, were fascinated, as they had not been by humanoids and dinosaur descendants. Jacques reminded himself that this mission had been mounted by a space agency; no wonder the crew were intrigued by glimpses of the wider universe.

And Roberta, too, seemed to be interested. She requested that the probes be made to study the neighbouring planets, Mars and Venus, to look for any difference in their atmospheres, their surfaces.

With this initial investigation of the new Gap complete, Captain Chen, with a rather boyish and excited grin, came to his passengers and urged them to be at the observation deck the next morning. 'That's when the real journey will begin . . .'

When morning came Jacques and Roberta joined Lieutenant Wu before the big prow windows, Jacques cradling a coffee, Roberta a glass of water. The airships hung in the sky of this latest world, two sleek fish of the sky over a sprawling blanket of forest. There was a river in the middle distance, a glassy stripe, and further away the extensive shallow sea typical of these warm worlds, blue to the horizon.

The stepping began without warning, and worlds flapped by, slowly at first, then ever faster. Soon they were travelling at a step a second, a rate they were all used to by now, and weather systems came and went to the beat of

Jacques's pulse: sun, cloud, rain, storms, even some snow. The detail of the forest flickered – once a tremendous, evidently recent crater appeared right under the prow of the *Zheng He*, before being whipped away like a stage prop – and occasionally a world flared, or darkened, and Jacques knew that the ships' systems would be recording yet another Joker.

Chen joined them, and grasped the polished wooden rail that ran before the window. 'You might want to hold on.'

Behind them, the trolls began to sing 'Eight Miles High'.

The stepping rate increased. To Jacques the passage of the worlds was suddenly visually uncomfortable, as if a strobe light were flashing in his face at increasing frequency. He tried to focus on the position of the morning sun, which remained constant in the multiple skies, but masks of cloud flashed across its face, and the sky flickered white, grey, blue. They all grabbed the rail now, even Roberta. Jacques thought he heard a thrumming of engines, and he sensed the airships driving forward even as they stepped. He could see the silvery hulk of the *Liu Yang* flex, a mighty plastic fish swimming through the flickering light of world after world.

Behind them, a crew member threw up.

'It will pass,' Yue-Sai said. 'We have all been tested for a tendency to epilepsy, and the nausea medication has been carefully applied. The discomfort will pass in a moment . . .'

Faster and faster the stepping came, faster and faster the weather systems flickered past their view. Jacques forced himself to keep watching, and focused on the rail in his hands, the vibrations of the ship's engines transmitted through the floor under his feet.

And then the flickering seemed to fade away, the worlds merging into a kind of continuous blur. The sun, paler than usual, hung in its patient station, in an apparently cloudless sky that took on a deep blue colour, like early twilight. The landscape below was misty and vague, the shapes of the hills grey and dim, littered with patches of forest that seemed to grow, shiver, pass away. The river that had been writhing jerkily across the landscape now spread out, as if flooding a wide band of ground with a silvery grey, and the ocean coast too became a broad blur, the boundary between land and sea uncertain.

'We have passed the flicker fusion threshold,' Roberta murmured.

'Yes!' Chen cried. 'We are now travelling at our peak rate, an astounding *fifty worlds per second* – worlds passing faster than the refresh frames in a digital screen, faster than your eye can follow. At such a rate we could traverse the great treks of the first pioneers of the Long Earth in little more than half an hour. At such a rate, if we kept it up, we could traverse more than four million worlds per *day*.'

Jacques asked, 'But we're moving laterally too, right? Why's that?'

'Continental drift,' Roberta said immediately.

Chen nodded approvingly. 'Correct. On Datum Earth the continents drift with time. The rate is something like an inch per year. Thanks to those cumulative effects there is also some drift as you move stepwise. So we move laterally, the great engines working to keep us over the heart of the tectonic plate on which South China rides. Sooner that than get lost altogether.' He winked at Jacques. 'Our Chinese airship technology has, incidentally, also set air-speed records.' He checked his watch. 'Now if you will excuse me I have engineers who need praising, or calming down, or both. Duty calls . . .'

Jacques noticed that the lower digits on the Earth counter mounted on the wall of the deck had become a blur, like the worlds they were tracking, while higher, grander, slower-changing digits marked the tremendous strides they were making, off into the unknown.

The trolls, meanwhile, sang on.

42

Vignettes from the continuing mission of Captain Maggie Kauffman, as the summer wore on across the Long Earth:

The voyage of the USS *Benjamin Franklin* progressed in a rather disorderly, zigzagging way. The colonists of the Long Earth didn't organize themselves consciously, either geographically or stepwise, and yet a kind of organization was emerging nevertheless, Maggie noticed, with clusters of homesteads growing up in neighbouring worlds. Gerry Hemingway of Science was developing a mathematical model of this, of a percolation of mankind into the Long Earth which resulted in a distribution that he described as 'on the edge of chaos'. Maggie, wearily, thought that summed it up pretty well.

Once, on the Atlantic coast in a temperate Corn Belt sky, they encountered a British dirigible called the *Sir George Cayley*, returning from a mission to Iceland. At such locations as Iceland, incoming steppers rummaged through the parallel worlds looking for beneficent weather. If you got the choice, you would go to a world with the local climatic optima – change your world, change your weather. In Iceland's case, you sought out analogues of the relatively benign first-millennium country first discovered and colonized by the Dark Age Vikings. (Dressing up to play the part was apparently optional.)

Parties from each ship visited the other. British ships always had the best booze, in Maggie's experience, including gin-and-tonics raised in toasts to His Majesty – and the Brit crews, charmingly, always stayed seated for the loyal toast, a tradition going back to Nelson's day, when there had been no room on those crowded wooden ships to stand.

However, such pleasing adventures, for the *Franklin* crew, were not the norm.

More typical was a call to a world some seven hundred thousand steps from the Datum where a hopeful silver miner, who seemed to have got his ideas about excavation techniques solely from the movies, had turned his wannabe mine shaft into a death trap. Getting him out was a technical challenge, but luckily one of the crew, Midshipman Jason Santorini, had misspent some of his early years caving; he just *loved* worming his way into the rubble heaps.

When the dispiriting rescue was over, Maggie gave the crew a couple of days' shore leave before moving on.

On the second day, as Maggie sat eating lunch with her senior officers, on the ground in the shadow of the *Franklin* – with Midshipman Santorini being rewarded for his efforts with lunch at the Captain's table – another twain, a small commercial vessel, drifted in from the horizon. It lowered a stairway a little way away in the scrub, and two people alighted stiffly: an elderly woman, a middle-aged man.

And a cat, that followed them down the ramp.

Maggie and her officers stood to greet the couple. Joe Mackenzie eyed the cat suspiciously.

The man said, 'Captain Maggie Kauffman? I'm pleased to meet you in the flesh, having heard so much about you! It took us some time to arrange a rendezvous, as you can imagine . . .'

'And you are?'

'My name is George Abrahams. This is my wife, Agnes. My title is Doctor, though that need not concern us.' His accent sounded vaguely Bostonian, the name naggingly familiar to Maggie. He was tall, slim, a little stooped, and wore a heavy black overcoat, and a homburg over silver hair. His face was oddly neutral, expressionless – unmemorable, Maggie thought.

The cat, slim, white, looked around, sniffed, and set off in the general direction of the *Franklin*.

Mac nudged Santorini. 'Keep an eye on that damn flea bucket.'

'Yes, sir.'

Maggie invited them to sit, courteously enough, and Mac, evidently acting out of a kind of reflexive politeness, even poured them coffee.

Then Maggie said more sternly, 'Tell me how you found us, Dr Abrahams. This is after all a military vessel. And what do you want of me?'

How he had been following her seemed innocent enough: through outernet accounts posted by civilians, of the *Franklin*'s various interventions. All of this was public. As to the what, that concerned the troll-call.

Maggie snapped her fingers. 'Of course. Yours is the name on the instruction sheet.'

'I *am* its designer,' he said, not particularly modestly,

and his wife rolled her eyes. 'From all accounts you got the measure of it very quickly – amazingly so, if you don't mind my saying it. Well, I come bearing gifts. I have fifteen more translators for you and your crew. Of course, they are still only prototypes, though refined versions. As we develop them further both parties are learning to use the gadgets – trolls and humans, I mean. As I'm sure you've found out, trolls are patient and they learn just as fast as humans, oh my goodness how they learn, and of course they remember; they remember everything.'

'Well – thank you,' Maggie said, nonplussed. 'We'll happily take possession of the troll-calls, after security checks . . . You know Sally Linsay, I take it. And – I have to ask – are you associated with the Black Corporation?'

'Oh my dear lady, two interrogations in one sentence! Of course I know Sally – a remarkable judge of people. And as harsh as a hanging judge when she's in the mood! As for the Black Corporation—' He sighed. 'Yes, of course they are involved. Captain, I am independent, I have my own workshop – yes, I am in partnership with the Black Corporation, but they don't own me. They did fund my work, and arranged delivery of the prototype to you.'

'Once again Douglas Black is giving away technological treasures for free?'

'My impression is that Douglas Black believes that to release such a technology should in the long term have a beneficial effect on humanity's career in the Long Earth. And in the short term it may heal our fractured relationship with the trolls. I of course have worked closely with the trolls in the course of my studies. What wonderful beasts they are! Don't you think? And so soulful! Anybody who has ever owned pets *knows* that animals have something which equates to a soul . . .'

The wife nudged him. 'You're preaching, George. And what's more, to the converted. We've done what we came to do. Now it's time to wave goodbye and let these good people get about their duties.'

That seemed to be that. Slightly bewildered, Maggie and her officers arranged to collect the troll-calls, and rose to wish the couple goodbye. The wife, who seemed oddly elderly compared with the husband, fussed as they retreated to their ship: 'Do get on, dear. Remember your prostate!'

'Don't ham it up too much, Agnes . . .'

It was only after they had gone that Mac looked around and said, 'What happened to that damn cat?'

Their next assignment was in a stepwise Nebraska, on the way back to the Corn Belt, where the hunter-gatherer-type wandering inhabitants of nearby parallel Americas periodically got together for what they described as a 'hootenanny'. A mixture of marriage market, farmers' auction, rock concert and Hell's Angels gathering, these events were magnets for trouble. But for the *Franklin* the assignment was routine, the ship's very presence a deterrent to disorder.

Maggie took the opportunity to have her chief engineer, Harry Ryan, run a comprehensive overhaul of the ship's systems; it had been a while since the last maintenance break. Among other small issues, he quickly reported problems with the *Franklin*'s two remaining winged aircraft, microlites capable of air launches for fast response; they had already cannibalized a third craft for spares . . .

As she was scanning Harry's report in her sea cabin, Maggie became aware of a steady gaze.

It was a cat. *The* cat, George Abrahams's cat, standing patiently on the carpet, gazing at her. Slim, white, healthy-looking, she was a breed indeterminate to Maggie, who was no cat person. Her eyes were eerie green sparks. Sparks like LED displays, Maggie saw, looking closer.

And the cat spoke, a liquid string of syllables in a female human voice, quite incomprehensible.

'What? *What?*'

'I apologize,' the cat said. 'George and Agnes Abrahams used me to practise their Swahili; it became my default setting. I am aware that you are running a systems check . . .'

Maggie, floundering, found a memory floating to the surface of her mind. 'Joshua Valienté. He had a talking cat, didn't he? So the story goes.' Then she realized that not only was the cat talking, she was *engaging the cat in conversation.*

'I am fully equipped to support your current activity. The systems analysis, I mean. Turbine number two is developing metal fatigue. Also the flush in the aft crew bathroom is malfunctioning. Rodent infestation is negligible but not zero, by the way.'

Maggie stared at the cat. Then she came around her desk, grabbed the cat, and set her on the desktop. The beast was heavier than she had expected, but she felt comfortably warm.

She thought over what the cat had said. Then she slapped a comms panel. 'Hey, Harry.'

'Here, Captain,' the engineer replied promptly.

'How's the rear crew head?'

'What? . . . Umm, let me check my roster. A faulty flush, as it happens. Why do you ask, Captain?'

'How about turbine number two?'

'No faults reported.'

'Would you check it over again? Call me back.' She stared at the cat. 'So – what the hell *are* you?'

'An artificial life form. Well, evidently. Including top-of-the-line artificial intelligence. The nice thing about artificial intelligence is that at least it's better than artificial stupidity. Don't you think? Ha, ha.' Her voice was fully human, but diminished, as if issuing from a small loudspeaker.

Maggie stayed stony-faced. 'That couple, Dr and Mrs Abrahams, left you behind.'

'I am another gift, Captain. Forgive the subterfuge. It was thought that you would refuse me reflexively. Yet I am capable of supporting your mission in a variety of ways. A mission to which I am fully committed, by the way.'

'You have a name?'

'Shi-mi. Which is Tibetan for cat. I am an upgrade of previous models . . .'

Maggie's comms unit blipped: Harry Ryan. 'Don't know how you guessed it, Captain, but there *is* a flaw in number two turbine. Metal fatigue in the bearings. We'll need to strip it down within seven weeks max – best to do that in dry dock. It's a very fine imbalance; it wouldn't have shown up for a few more days' running, but there is a rising chance of failure. Captain, I'm embarrassed we didn't spot it.'

'Forget it, Harry. Ask Nathan to put together an itinerary to take us home.'

'Yes, Captain.'

Shi-mi said modestly, 'The turbine didn't sound true. Easy to spot. It was however only one cat's opinion.'

'But you're not just a cat, are you?'

'No, Captain. *I* was built to the finest standard specifications of the Black Corporation's robotics, prosthetics and artificial intelligence divisions. Whereas your turbine was built for the government on a low-bid contract. Thank you very much, and I hope I have passed the audition. Incidentally – would you be offended if I brought you an occasional mouse? It is rather traditional . . .'

'No.'

'Yes, Captain.'

'And stay out of Joe Mackenzie's way.'

'Yes, Captain. Does that mean I can stay aboard?'

'Just get out of here.'

'Yes, Captain.'

43

LOBSANG PULLED STRINGS at the Black Corporation and secured Joshua and Bill the use of an airship, for the purposes of their quest in search of Sally Linsay, and the trolls. It was a relatively small, nimble craft, with a translucent solar-capture envelope a couple of hundred feet long, and a gondola the size of a truck trailer, with walls of ceramic panels and big viewing windows. Primarily used as a scout to accompany the great stepwise convoys on the Valhalla run, the ship had no name, only a corporate registration number. Bill promptly named it the *Shillelagh*.

Bill, for reasons he'd yet to share with Joshua, said he wanted to fly, not out of the usual Mississippi-ports, but from the Seattle area in the Pacific north-west. The quickest way to transport the airship from its base at a Low Earth Hannibal to Seattle was to break it down, ship it by rail across the Datum, and then reassemble it on an apron at SeaTac airport. That took a week. The travellers used the time to prepare, to gather supplies and kit for the journey.

Regarding the trolls, Lobsang provided them with what he called a 'troll translation kit', downloaded into a neat jet-black slab, small enough to fit into a backpack.

As for Sally, Joshua did some snooping as Bill had requested, visited the hotels she'd stayed at, even Jansson's home, looking fruitlessly for leads as to where she'd gone.

And he had to face the family he was leaving behind, as he disappeared on yet another jaunt into the remote Earths – once again leaving at Lobsang's behest, once again pulled sideways by Sally, Helen's enigmatic rival. Little Dan was jealous, pure and simple; he wanted to go exploring too. Helen, who was struggling to get permission to visit her Madison-bomber brother in prison, was ominously silent. It wasn't a happy family that Joshua left behind, and not for the first time, and it tore his heart in two.

But off he went anyhow.

And on an impulse he took the sapphire ring, his one souvenir of his first Long Earth quest a decade ago: took it from where it had been hanging on Jansson's wall, and hung it up in the gondola lounge. He wondered if Sally would expect him to do that.

Thus, on a bright June morning at Datum SeaTac, Joshua found himself sitting in this compact gondola, laid out just like a travel trailer with a tiny galley area and lounge, foldaway bunks and tables – in fact, he learned, it had been designed by Airstream – while Bill took his place in the small wheelhouse at the gondola's prow.

The *Shillelagh* lifted easily. Soon Joshua had a fine view of the airport and the crowded development around it, and of Puget Sound.

All of which was whipped away as they began to step, to be replaced by the increasingly sparse facilities of SeaTac West 1 and 2 and 3, with their ribbons of road and rail tracks and small settlements cut into the enduring forest, each world glimpsed in the space of a heartbeat – until soon, after only a very few worlds, there was barely a sign of mankind at all, only the forest and the Sound, and the Cascades piled up in the distance. The ship rose steadily as it stepped, and Bill directed it laterally towards the mountains, which persisted more or less unchanged as they passed through the worlds. The sky flickered, though; the weather was never identical from Earth to Earth, and on this June day they passed from sun to cloud to showers.

In the first few worlds there was nothing much to see but tree tops. Joshua knew there were bears down there in those forests, and beavers, and wolves. And people too, although further out than the Low Earths there was only a long but thinning tail of colonization. More rats than people, probably, now that the twains with their roomy holds and cargoes of foodstuffs flew so thick. What else was down there was guesswork. There was a programme to map the Low Earths from orbit, with small fleets of pole-to-pole satellites that would fly over a turning world, inspecting its continents, oceans and icecaps with cameras, ground-penetrating radar, infrared and other sensors, before stepping on to the next world, and the next . . . Even such coarse imagery, which would show few details smaller than a reasonably sized car, was only available for a hundred or so of the lowest worlds. Further out than that, save for particular worlds which had been subject to closer study, nobody knew, really.

They were climbing the flank of Mount Rainier itself by the time they hit the first Ice Age world. For a few seconds they rode high over the crumpled white sheets that coated the ground. And then back to the endless forest green.

Joshua sat back, watching the scenery blankly. Already he missed his family. He wondered how he was going to pass the time.

'Bill?'

'Yes?'

'Just checking. How is everything?'

'Cracker.'

'Good.'

'I just need to concentrate on the piloting. Not my usual occupation, but the Black Corporation lads gave me a decent run-through. It's simple enough . . . But not like driving a car, I'll tell you that. Or even riding a horse. After all the ship has to be sapient, to a degree, and it's smarter than a damn horse in fact. It's like you have this constant dialogue with the thing. Y'know, I once rode an elephant on this farm in the African bush, a rescue sanctuary. An African elephant isn't tamed like the Indian sort; he's a big strong smart animal that knows where he wants to go, and if you're lucky that might happen to be the same way you want to go. Otherwise you just have to kind of hang on. This is the same. All a bit mad, isn't it? But we'll get there. Wherever "there" is.'

'Fair enough.'

And that was that. It was just like the journey of the *Mark Twain* all those years ago – but at least this time Joshua got on better with his crewmate.

By sunset they had sailed out of the Ice Belt, as it was called, the sheaf of sporadically glaciated worlds around the Datum, and were passing over the more arid worlds of the Mine Belt. The view got even more dull. Joshua made a meal – of field rations warmed on a single gas ring, no gourmet kitchen on *this* ship – and took a portion to Bill, who was camping out in the wheelhouse.

Then he turned in, looking out through the gondola's windows as the dying rays of midsummer sunsets glowed on the gasbag.

The dawn brought more of the same.

By mid-morning of the second day they had crossed into the Corn Belt, a hundred thousand steps from Datum Earth, a thick band of warmer worlds lush with forests and prairie, and now studded with human farming communities – including Reboot, at Earth West 101,754, founded by Helen and her family of trekkers, and the place where she and Joshua had married.

Then, in the late afternoon, Joshua sensed the airship slowing. The strobing of the skies slowed, and the more or less identical landscapes below flickered gently, coming to a standstill.

And an angry buzzing filled the air. Suddenly the gondola was dark, the light excluded by a swarm of dark heavy insectile bodies that slammed continually against the clear windows, chitinous wings clattering. Joshua glanced at the gondola's compact earthometer: this was West 110,719.

He had to yell over the noise. 'Hey, Bill!'

'Here.'

'I recognize this place.'

'You should. Classic Joker. In fact you discovered it, during The Journey with Lobsang.'

'Yeah, and we passed straight on through. What are we doing here, Bill? Those bugs are going to choke us if they get in the air vents.'

'Patience, grasshopper.'

The airship lifted now, Joshua could feel it, though the world remained hidden by the swarming, angry bodies of the flying insects – they were like huge locusts, perhaps, an impression he remembered from that first visit.

Abruptly the *Shillelagh* rose into sunlight. Joshua saw he was still hovering over the flanks of Rainier, or this world's copy of it. Evidently this world was warmer than the average, for forest rose up almost all the way to an eroded summit – it was oak woodland, mature trees rearing out of a luxuriant tumble of fallen trunks and thickets. He spotted a stream down there, bubbling down the steep slope of the mountain. As he watched, something blundered through the undergrowth and crashed away east, and a few roosting creatures took fright and rose up – they weren't birds, they were like huge, fat dragonflies – and fluttered noisily away to safety.

When Joshua looked away from the mountain summit, he saw a landscape cloaked by swarming insects, a pulsing, gleaming carpet of them that seemed to extend all the way to the ocean shore, visible in the distance. The land crawled with them, like black rivers coursing between sparse patches of green, and clouds of flyers rose up everywhere. But nothing flew as high as this summit, and not as high as some of the other mountains of the Cascades, whose flanks rose out of the swarms like green-clad islands in an insectile sea.

'They're altitude limited,' Joshua observed. 'The insects.'

'Yeah, most of the larger species. Not all. Enough to make the summits survivable.'

'Survivable by who?'

'By us, Joshua. Well, specifically, by you.'

'We're stopping here?'

'Yeah. Not long, maybe overnight.'

'Why?'

'We've an appointment to keep up here. This is why I wanted to start us off in the Cascades. I'll drop an anchor, deploy the ladder. The grassy stretch by that stream down there looks a good place to camp. Take the tape. The cassette, you know.'

Somewhat reluctantly Joshua began to pull his kit together: a sleeping bag, food packets, fire-making gear. Bug repellent spray! 'I'm going down alone, am I?'

Bill sounded embarrassed. 'Look, Joshua, I don't want to sound like a fan-boy here. Your Journey's famous – and of course I know the inside story. The idea of you going down into all them unknown worlds all alone, while Lobsang stayed tucked up in the airship. Comedy gold.'

'Well, that's a consolation for all the scars.'

'But the strategy actually makes sense. You go down, do the exploring thing, make contact.'

And Joshua wondered, contact with what?

'Meanwhile I'll stay aloft, ready to help out when it all goes tits-up.'

'*When?*'

'If, mate. If. Slip of the tongue.'

Not for the first time in the course of his adventures in the Long Earth, and against his own better judgement, Joshua went with the flow.

Bill insisted that he carry a two-way radio, and a small shoulder unit with TV and sensor links. Joshua agreed, despite unpleasant memories of Lobsang's shoulder-riding parrots, and for his part packed a handgun.

The climb down into the undergrowth was easy. Immediately he was on the ground the ship rose, taking the ladder with it.

Alone, Joshua turned around slowly. In this open space that the stream had carved between the trees, it was pleasant enough. The air smelled of damp wood and the leaf mould of millennia, and he heard the remote buzz of the lapping ocean of insect swarms below this summit. Over his head squadrons of some insectile equivalent of bats hurtled after things like flies.

He had nothing much to do but wait. He began to make his camp, spreading out his blanket roll and sleeping bag. He thought about a fire, but the air was warm and moist enough without it. With his travel rations he didn't need to cook.

He began to relax. It was almost like he was on sabbatical. He toyed with the idea of doing some fishing, just for fun, if the streams on this summit supported any fish . . .

The radio clicked into life. 'Josh, can you hear me, mate?'

'No.'

'Ha ha. How you doing down there?'

'Making a restaurant reservation.'

'Funny you should say that. If it does all go tits-up and you need supplies quickly there's a cache, only a mile or so downstream.'

'A cache? Of what?'

'Survival stuff. A little shelter, a bit of food, knives, tools. Spare laces for your boots. Left by combers, for combers.'

Joshua sat on his sleeping bag. 'Bill, what is this place?

Why did we stop here? I mean, in a *Joker*? Who the hell stops in Jokers?'

'Combers do. That's the point, really. You want to know the story of this world? How Earth West 110,719 got its locusts? Our best guess is that pterosaurs never evolved on this world.'

'Pterosaurs?'

'And other flying dinosaurs. Back on the Datum, before the pterosaurs, big insects ruled the skies. Got as big as they could, in fact, exploiting the high oxygenation of the air. Then when the pterosaurs came along the big insects got hunted down, and only the little ones survived, and they never got so big again. After that the skies belonged to the pterosaurs, and later the birds. Here – no pterosaurs, for whatever reason. And later, the birds didn't have a chance to grow large either. So here it's not swallows chasing flies; here huge rapacious dragonflies hunt down birds the size of big moths . . .'

'Not a world for humans, then.'

'No chance.'

'But the combers come here.'

'Of course. And to survivable refuges in other Jokers. Joshua, a Joker is a whole world, and it isn't going to be the same all over; there are always going to be safe places, refuges like this. You get to know them.'

'How?'

'Through other combers. There's a whole subculture that people like you, and even Lobsang, know nothing about. And we like it that way.

' *You* think the story of the Long Earth is about colonies like Hell-Knows-Where, or Helen's Reboot, or cities like Valhalla, and wars of independence and whatnot. All the mad old stuff from Datum history projected into the new worlds. Well, that *isn't* the story, Joshua. It's about a new way of living – or maybe a very old one. The combers haven't *colonized* the Long Earth, Joshua. Nor have they *adapted* it to suit themselves. They just live in it, as it is.'

This lecture surprised Joshua, who had grown up with Bill, and now shared a town with him, and thought he knew him. 'How do *you* know?'

'Oh, you know, you have your sabbaticals. I take off for a bit of an old stroll meself from time to time. I always come back. Too fond of my home comforts, that's my problem. And of the odd drink. But it's always a grand vacation. Anyhow I know how these fellas think.'

Joshua thought that over. 'And we need comber thinking now to find the trolls, right?'

'Because trolls live in the Long Earth too. And they know the secret places, the places to hide out, like combers are learning . . . It's getting dark.'

'I noticed.'

'Joshua, you're happy down there for the night? There are various exotic horrors lurking, needless to say.'

'But you've got infrared sensors, sonar motion sensors. You'll spot any moving bodies, hot-blooded or cold-blooded. Right? Wake me if you need to.'

'No worries. Sleep tight, buddy.'

'And you.'

He woke up in a grey, moist dawn.

Even before he opened his eyes he was aware of an uneasy prickling at the back of the neck, the product of a million years of animal sensitivity trying to kick its way past the doorkeeper of the cerebrum.

He was being watched.

And he heard words: '*Path-less-ss one . . .*'

Still in his sleeping bag, he sat up.

The elf was leaning against a tree trunk a few yards away, blending into the shadows so perfectly that Joshua might never have noticed it if it hadn't turned its head and grinned. Low dawn sunlight fell on two rows of perfectly triangular teeth.

Then the elf stepped out into the open light, reaching the sleeping bag in a couple of strides.

It was no more than four feet tall, and was squat and strong, with a face that owed something to a solemn baboon and a punk-rock hairstyle that owed everything to a cockatoo. It wore a sort of leather loincloth, and carried a leather pouch at its waist. It was bootless, showing feet that were quite human except for the talon-like toenails. Joshua looked for other weapons and couldn't see any.

He was oddly reminded of a mole, its paws equipped for digging. This was like nothing so much as an overgrown, vaguely human-shaped, upright, clothes-wearing mole. An upright mole *wearing sunglasses.* The lenses were cracked and scarred, and the creature's ears, folded flat against its blunt skull, didn't look up to the job of support, so the shades were fixed in place with a band of grubby elastic.

The elf grinned again. Joshua could smell its breath from here.

His gun was inside the sleeping bag. Joshua got a distinct impression that attempting to reach it would be the single most stupid thing he could possibly do.

At such times, thought Joshua, there had to be a more

useful opening than: 'A star shines on the hour of our meeting.' But that was what crackled out of the radio on the ground by the sleeping bag. Bill was evidently watching.

The elf grinned again and said, 'I wish-sh you a good death-th.'

English. It spoke English! It *was* an elf, obviously, a member of one of the many slim, gracile species of humanoids that had come to be known as elves across the Long Earth. But though he'd never seen one before, Joshua immediately knew what subspecies this must be.

'He's a kobold.'

'Evidently,' murmured Bill from the radio. 'Some folks call them ringtails. Or "urban foxes", according to the fecking English.'

'I thought they were a comber legend.'

'Don't tell him that, he might get the hump. I have him on infrared,' said Bill. 'I see his weaponry. He won't harm you. Well, probably not. Tell me how you'd describe him.'

'Can you imagine Gandhi meets Peter Pan?'

'No . . .'

The kobold grinned, showing those sharp teeth. 'Not worry, little mann. I protect. Be ss-safe. Be friend.'

'Great. My name's Joshua.'

He nodded gravely. 'Know. Lobsang ss-send you.'

'Lobsang? You know about Lobsang? . . . Why aren't I surprised?'

Bill said, 'You're all over the kobold grapevine, Joshua. Especially since I started putting out feelers about Sally on your behalf.'

'You got ss-tone that sing-ss?'

'The stone that sings?'

319

'Yah. Stone that eats soul of mann, sings. The holy music. Menn that ss-sing after death.' The kobold paused, moving his lips as he thought hard, and added, 'Like Buddy Holly.'

'Say yes,' said Bill.

'Yes.'

'Flip, Joshua, do I have to spell it out to ye? Give him the cassette.'

'Oh – the "stone that sings". I get it.' Joshua reached for his jacket, which he had been using as a pillow, found the battered old cassette tape in the pocket, and handed it over.

The kobold reached across and took it like a devout worshipper handling a relic. He sniffed at it, held it to his ear and shook it gently. 'Bill was-ss here before. We talk. He give me mus-ssic. He give cof-ffee. He give machine that drinks-ss sunlight and plays-ss holy mu-ssic.'

'You mean a cassette machine?'

The kobold turned the tape over in his long fingers. 'Kinks-ss? . . .'

'It's the album you wanted,' Bill said from the radio. '*The Kinks Are the Village Green Preservation Society.*'

'Good . . .' The kobold dug a battered old tape-drive walkman from the pouch at his waist, held up a glittering solar-cell surface to face the sunlight, pulled ancient-looking headphones around his neck, and pushed the tape into a slot. 'Extra-ss?'

'You've got the twelve-track mono version released in Europe, and then the fifteen-track UK edition in stereo and mono, and some rarities. An alternate mix of "Animal Farm". An unreleased track called "Mick Avory's Underpants" . . .'

But the kobold was no longer listening. He backed up against a tree, the worn foam of the headphones pressed against his ears.

Bill said softly, 'That's it. He's out of it for a couple of hours while he checks that out. Joshua, if you need breakfast, now's a good time.'

'The Kinks, Bill?'

'A great 1960s band from the UK, who made it big in the US with—'

'I don't care. No disrespect to the Kinks. What's with the tape?'

'Trade goods, Joshua. Kobolds like human culture. Some of 'em are big on music. This one was hooked when he first heard "Waterloo Sunset". He's a kind of snitch. An informant. I get him the music he wants; he gives me – information.'

'Yeah, but who uses a cassette machine?'

'Well, he's older than he looks, Joshua. He's been doing trades like this for years. And he's a humanoid with an evolutionary path that split off from mankind's millions of years ago. He's not likely to be a technology early adopter, is he?'

Joshua pushed his way out of his sleeping bag. 'I need a coffee.'

44

THE FIRST STEPPERS, exploring the Long Earth, had found no trace of modern man away from the Datum.

Oh, they had found a few stone tools. They had found fossil hearths in the depths of caves. They had even found a few bones. But no great leap forward – no cave paintings, no flower-adorned burials, no cities, no high technology. (Well, none that was human.) The spark of higher intellect must have been lit behind beetling pre-human brows on a million worlds, just as on Datum Earth – but it hadn't caught anywhere other than on the Datum. Whatever the reason, the alternate universes into which Earth's pioneers poured out were mostly dark, quiet worlds. Worlds of trees, many of them, Earths like great tumbled forests. The Datum itself was just a clearing in the trees, a spark of civilization, one circle of firelight beyond which the shadows spread to infinity. There were humanoids out there, descendants of lost cousins of humanity, but people knew they would never encounter a humanoid that was anything like as smart as they were. Never a humanoid that could speak English, for example.

The only thing wrong with this generally accepted picture was that it was totally incorrect.

Professor Wotan Ulm of Oxford University, author of the bestselling if controversial book *Moon-Watcher's Cousins: The Humanoid Radiation Across the Long Earth*, gave the context for the species known as 'kobolds' in an interview for the BBC.

'Of course, such is the patchiness of our exploration of the Long Earth so far that we can come to only tentative conclusions. The evidence for kobolds themselves is little more than legend and anecdote. Nevertheless DNA analysis of samples returned by early expeditions, including a tooth found embedded in the boot of Joshua Valienté, confirms that the humanoids of Long Earth diverged from Datum Earth stock several million years ago, probably at the time of the rise of *Homo habilis*, the first tool-making hominid. This supports my own hypothesis that it was the increased cognitive skills of *H. habilis* that enabled some members of that species to step sideways into the other Earths: the ability to imagine the tool in the stone, perhaps, is related to the ability to imagine another world entirely. And then to reach out for it . . .

'After this divergence – the departure of the steppers, with the Datum inhabited by the descendants of the residuum who could not step – humanoids radiated into the Long Earth, evolving in a variety of niches. And across four million years natural selection has proved remarkably inventive.

'One fundamental boundary among the humanoid species is whether they retained their ability to step, or not. Some did, as we know, like the form known as the trolls. Others did not. Having found an Earth of suitable habitability these groups settled down, *lost* their ability to step, in some cases also lost the intelligence that under-pinned that stepping ability, and began to populate their single Earth. This should not surprise us. The juvenile sea squirt is mobile, with a central nervous system and a brain. Once it has found a suitable rock, it settles down, opens its mouth to begin a life of sedentary feeding, *absorbs its brain*, and turns on the TV. Similarly birds having colonized an island free of predators will lose their ability to fly. Flight, like intelligence, is energetically expensive and may be selected out if not used, if no longer necessary for survival. Similarly, presumably, with stepping.

'A second evolutionary boundary among the nomadic species is whether they have had extended contact with humanity on Datum Earth, or not. If they have *not* had contact they may have evolved into forms quite un-familiar from experience on the Datum, such as the trolls.

'If they *have* had contact with mankind, you might think we would know about it. Well, in a sense, we do. It's remarkable how much human folklore can be explained away if you postulate humanoid races that can move stepwise at will.

'As for the human-contact humanoids themselves, their subsequent evolution must have been affected. They may grow to look like us, for cover. They may look threatening or cute, to disarm us. Or, most interestingly, they may have evolved speech mechanisms like ours in order to deal with us, in some way. Even intelligence might have been promoted, in competition with us.

'And so we come to the kobolds. These creatures may indeed be the "kobolds" of myth, the source of German legends of mine spirits, which are also known as types of gnome or dwarf, or *Bergmännlein*, "little mountain men". They would infest metal mines, and would be heard rather than seen. They could be helpful: their knocking could guide human miners to rich ore seams, or warn them of danger. In Cornwall, England, they became known as "tommy-knockers". And they would sometimes steal human artefacts, gewgaws like mirrors, combs; they were evidently fascinated by human material culture, though they could not emulate it.

'It has to be said that the observed kobolds' robust anatomy, their aversion to bright light, their hands and feet evidently adapted for digging into the earth, are all features consistent with an underground origin. Perhaps they evolved in the subterranean Datum, or at least adapted to it, their ancestors having stepped away and returned. And perhaps in recent centuries the rising human population finally drove them away, leaving them separated from humanity until our own stepping diffusion began. The word "kobold" incidentally is the source of the name "cobalt" . . .

'Oddly enough, though these creatures are in many ways the most human-like of the humanoid species, and in some ways the most cognitively advanced, they are among the most secretive. Perhaps that's because of the derogatory names humans tend to give them. Or perhaps it's just because they know humans.

'It may be surprising to a layman that there are any *sedentary* Long Earth humanoids who have been shaped over evolutionary timescales by contact with humans. This can only come about, of course, if that species returned to Datum Earth and *then* lost its stepping ability. Well, there is one Datum species that may fit this category, though the genetic evidence is controversial: the bonobo chimps. In retrospect, who could ever have imagined that these gentle creatures belong on the same planet as the likes of us? Not to mention their cousins the common chimps, who are almost as unpleasant as we are. No wonder the bonobos' ancestors got out of here as soon as they could steal a car. And bad luck for the present-day bonobos that their more recent ancestors came wandering back.

'Is that enough, Jocasta? Then perhaps you could tell the long-haired kobold lookalike in the production booth that eating a burger all the way through my interview was *even* more off-putting than you might expect . . .'

45

'Y<small>OU HAVE MORE</small> Kinks-ss?'
'Some,' whispered Bill through the radio.
'Give.'
'No.'
'What is your name?' Joshua asked at last.

The kobold grinned. At least, his teeth grinned. 'My name to menn is Finn McCool.'

'I thought of that,' Bill said. 'Seemed to fit.'

'I give no name for menn. Not *my* name.'

'Finn McCool will do,' Joshua said.

'People of the pathless-ss world stranger than trollen,' Finn McCool said, studying Joshua and his bits of kit. 'How live? No weaponn?'

'Oh, I have a weapon.'

'But one only. You are pathless-ss. We are many.'

'Many? Where? Where are the rest of you?'

The kobold held out his hand. 'You give. This-ss the way, as all know. You give, I talk.'

'Ignore him,' Bill said. 'We've given already. He's just trying to drive a hard bargain.'

Joshua studied the kobold. 'You trade, right? You trade with other humans?'

'Other humans-ss. And with other, not-humann, not kobold-ss . . .'

'With other types of humanoid? Other races?'

'And *they* trade with others-ss. Others-ss, ff-rom far world-ss.'

'How far?'

'Worlds-ss where there iss no moon. S-ssun different colour . . .'

'Horse shit,' said Bill. 'No such worlds. He's just trying to wheedle more out of you, Joshua. Aren't you, Finn McCool? You can't shit a shitter, you little shit. Listen, Joshua, you have to understand what we're dealing with here. These are slippery little buggers. They get around quick, they seem to be able to use soft places, they talk all the time, and they trade, with us and each other. But *they're not human.* They don't do business the way we do, grubbing for wealth, making as much profit as we can. They're more like—'

'Collectors?'

'Something like that, yeah. Like nerds who collect comic books. Or like magpies, fascinated by human stuff, shiny gewgaws that they can steal and stare at but they never understand. There's no logic to it, Joshua. It's just about the stuff they want, that's all. Once you understand that they're not hard to handle. Big fecking ugly magpies with trousers on. That's you, Finn McCool.'

The kobold just grinned.

'Well, I guess you know why we're here, Finn McCool,' Joshua said. 'What we want. *Where are the trolls?*'

'You give—'

'Cough up, you little gobshite,' Bill snapped.

Finn McCool hissed, and said grudgingly, 'Trollen in *here.* But not *here.*'

Joshua sighed. 'Textbook enigmatic. Any time you want to jump in, Bill—'

'Finn McCool. Are you saying the trolls are hiding out in a Joker?'

'Not *here*.'

'A Joker, but not this Joker. As I guessed. But which one?'

Finn McCool seemed to Joshua to have no intention of answering.

'That's it?' Joshua said. 'That's all we get out of you in return for that magnificent, umm, old tape?'

Suddenly McCool stood straight. He sniffed the air with his flat, chimp-like muzzle, and laughed.

'Joshua,' Bill said urgently. 'I detect nine, correction ten – no, eleven hotspots converging on you. I now have visual confirmation. Hmm.'

Joshua spun around. A morning mist swirled now between the trees, and the stream was lost to view. Anything could be out there. Water dripped off the leaves of the trees. 'What do you mean, *hmm*? What do they look like?'

'Well . . . Purposeful.'

There was a flash of teeth, Finn McCool faded for an instant, and was gone. Joshua could have been wrong, but it seemed that McCool's grin was the last bit of him to go.

And out of the mists . . .

The rising sun sent spears of reddish light across the grassland, and the altitude of this summit lent a faint chill to the breeze. A few shreds of mist stirred down among the trees that marked the stream.

And there were shapes among the trees.

They began as mere suggestions of motion in the mist, and then solidified. The general effect was of a wheel slowing from turbine speeds to stillness. When they were still—

They were not much taller than a man, but the bean-pole thinness gave an exaggerated impression of height. Their skin was greyish, and they wore their ash-blonde hair Afro-style. They could have passed muster in some of the badly lit discos Joshua had, if rarely, attended in his youth back in Madison.

Except for the ears. Which were large and pointed, and constantly flicking back and forth as though seeking the faintest sounds. And except for the eyes, that glowed a very faint green. They carried long thin double-bladed weapons of wood – swords, for want of a better word. They weren't yelling, or waving their weapons. They just looked quietly determined.

Any child could have put a name to them. *Elves.* Not relatively friendly music-loving conversationalists like Finn McCool. The elves of nightmare.

And they were closing on Joshua, from every direction.

Joshua had nowhere to run. He had encountered various species of elves before. He knew that stepping wouldn't help, not when faced with an enemy that was a *better* stepper than he was. His gun was somewhere in the scuffed-up sleeping bag. Only the radio was in reach, a plastic block the size of his fist. Not much of a weapon . . .

The first elf to reach him brought back its sword for a killing arc – and hesitated, as if relishing the moment.

Joshua, frozen to the spot, stared back. Close to, the creature looked like something out of a book on pre-history, though a Neanderthal would have considered it ugly. Its face was a network of wrinkles. It wore a short fur tunic, some sort of knapsack, and an expression of calculation. Maybe it was hesitating as it tried to work out which way he was going to step, so it could follow him and kill him anyway.

All this in a heartbeat. Then Joshua's reflexes took over.

He ducked, grabbed the radio, and brought it around in a rapid swing that was interrupted by the elf's jaw. Bits of glass and plastic erupted in a shower of golden sparks. As the elf staggered back, Joshua's leg came up for the classic strike favoured by women's self-defence teachers every-where, and a high-pitched squeal of agony added to mankind's tiny stock of anatomical knowledge of Long Earth humanoids.

And suddenly there was action all around Joshua.

McCool was back, he had brought more kobolds, and they were already fighting. The cavalry, Joshua thought with a rush of gratitude. But this was a cavalry that *stepped*, like its opponents. Suddenly figures from both subspecies were flashing past Joshua's view, like fragments of nightmare.

Joshua got out of there. He ran head-down for the ladder which came dangling from the descending ship. He had to knock one fighter out of the way; he couldn't tell if it was a good guy or a bad guy.

Only when he got to the ladder, and, with the security of an alloy rung in his hand, was already rising in the air and out of the battle, did he look back down.

The elves favoured swords, while the kobolds tended to fight barehanded – which showed rather more intelligence in Joshua's view, because if you were grappling with your opponent he couldn't step without taking you with him. Besides, the kobolds seemed to have elevated unarmed combat to the point where weapons would merely get in the way. He saw one kobold vanish momentarily as a blade nearly beheaded him, then reappear, grab the sword arm and with balletic grace send a kick into the elf's chest that must have killed immediately. As usual with a humanoid fight, it wasn't a battle so much as a series of private duels. If a fighter was victorious he sought out another opponent, but would be quite oblivious to the fact that a colleague was being backed into a corner by overwhelming odds.

And then Joshua saw Finn McCool downed by a wooden sword thrust through his arm. Maybe he tried to step, but he was stunned, confused. His elf opponent dodged a disembowelling swipe from McCool's horny toes, and withdrew the sword for a second thrust.

Again this elf paused before the moment of the kill. His back was to Joshua.

And Joshua had a chance to intervene.

'Damn it!' Joshua let go of the ladder and his chance of safety, dropped heavily to the ground, picked up a fallen branch, and ran across. It wasn't that Finn McCool had endeared himself to Joshua. But if Joshua had to choose, he'd take the side of someone who hadn't actually tried to kill him. Had, indeed, come back to fight on his side.

Still running, he hit the elf across the neck as hard as he could. Joshua had anticipated a satisfying thunk of timber on flesh. Instead there was a soft necrotic splat, as the rotten branch disintegrated in an explosion of fungus spores and angry beetles. The elf, totally unharmed, turned slowly, its face puckered in astonishment.

Finn McCool's good hand flashed out once, twice, and

where it hit there was a sharp crack of bone. The elf folded up on itself, and stepped away before it died.

Blood was dripping from McCool's arm, but he wasn't paying it any attention. McCool stood up, face to face with Joshua – and Joshua realized that something had gone very wrong. 'Pathless-ss one! I kill you many!'

The war around them was ceasing. Elves and kobolds alike had paused in mid-slaughter to watch them. 'Now look—'

Finn McCool flung back his head and screamed. The flying kick he launched could have killed Joshua in a second.

But Joshua had already set off running, heading for that ladder again. He threw himself into the air and grabbed a rung, and to his credit Bill raised the ship immediately. Joshua looked down from a few yards up, to see Finn McCool sprawled cursing under a tree, his injured arm leaking blood.

Then Joshua was rising up through the sparse canopy and into the sunlight, and the montane forest, the messy, sprawling battleground, receded from view.

He climbed up the rest of the ladder, through the hatch and into the sanity of the gondola, stood up, and cracked his head on the ceiling. He started pulling up the ladder in great tangled armfuls.

'That is you, isn't it, Joshua?' Bill asked anxiously. 'I've been out of touch since you used the radio to bust that elf's jaw—'

'Just go, go!'

Only when the ladder was up did he let himself sag down on to a couch, fighting for breath. There was no sound up here but the squeaks and groans from the gas-bag as it warmed up in the morning's heat. Below him the *Shillelagh*'s shadow drifted peacefully across the forest roof, as if all sorts of hell weren't going on down there in the gloom.

He kept seeing Finn McCool's face, a contorted Noh mask of fury and hatred. 'I saved his life. McCool. Somehow that made me a deadly enemy. Where was the logic in that?'

'It's kobold logic, Joshua. Like human honour, but in a distorting mirror. You shamed him by saving him, when he was supposed to be saving *you*. You want to go down and have a bit of an old chat about it?'

'Just get us out of here.'

The forest below blinked away.

46

Nelson's first stop in Wyoming, where he had driven in his rental Winnebago on the trail of the Lobsang Project, was at Dubois, cowboy country.

Alas there was a shortage of cowboys nowadays, Wyoming folk having been particularly quick to head for the new stepwise worlds where land was free and government interference infrequent. It was almost reassuring for Nelson to read on a truck bumper sticker, 'In this Neighbourhood we don't just Watch.'

He found a LongHorn, and ordered a beer and a burger. The TV in an upper corner, largely ignored, was showing images of continuing geological problems in Yellowstone, in another part of the state. Swarms of minor earthquakes, an evacuation of some small community, landslips, roads cut. Dead fish in Yellowstone Lake. Bubbles, rising languidly in some pool of hot mud. But many of these incidents, Nelson slowly gathered, were in fact occurring in stepwise versions of Yellowstone in the worlds next door. The geologists, scattered over a band of worlds with instruments stripped from long-standing stations on the Datum, claimed to be learning a huge amount from comparative studies of the differing behaviours of the stepwise calderas. The newsreaders, vacant and pretty, mimed exaggerated relief that the still-overcrowded Datum itself didn't seem to be seriously affected, and cracked silly jokes.

Nelson looked away, retreating into his own thoughts. It had taken him a month to get here from Chicago, a slow, rambling journey, and a very pleasurable one. He had needed the time to shed his past, the very intense experience of his years as a priest in St John on the Water. He had been like a deep sea diver decompressing, he imagined. In the meantime, the world's mysteries could wait . . .

To his mild irritation, just outside Nelson's window was an animated billboard fixed to an iron rail fence. It cycled through various distracting messages, which he did his best to ignore. Distractions everywhere: that was the modern world, on the Datum anyhow. Then one message caught his eye: 'Can you see the humour of this iron railing?'

He nearly dropped his burger, which would have been a wicked waste. 'A G. K. Chesterton quote? *Here?* . . . Good afternoon to you, Lobsang. So I'm on the right track.'

The Winnebago wasn't the fastest machine on the road, but once out of Dubois Nelson floored it.

He said aloud, to anybody listening, 'Strictly speaking I am doing an amazingly dumb thing. I might be dealing with a madman. Well, I've met one or two of those, but very few of them quoted me the works of one of the best writers Britain ever produced . . .' Gazing down the empty road Nelson wondered how long it was since anyone other than a scholar had read the works of G. K. Chesterton. He'd not even read much himself since he'd devoured the best of them in his teens, after a chance discovery in a public library in Joburg.

Devil's Tower was visible on the horizon ahead when a motorcycle cop pulled him over.

The cop wore a dark visor, carried a massive gun in a holster at his hip, and, as he sauntered over, he had an all-round air of menacing dominance. 'Mr Nelson A-zi-ki-we?' He took a lot of care with the name. 'I've been expecting you. Show some ID, please.'

Nelson drew breath. 'No, sir! Show me your ID . . . Here we are, two strangers on an empty road, both uncertain of the other's identity – and allegiance. A quintessentially Chestertonian moment, don't you think?'

The cop's eyes were invisible behind the visor. But he grinned and said, 'In the breaking of bridges—'

More Chesterton. Automatically, the words coming straight up from the obsessive reading of his adolescence, Nelson said, 'Is the end of the world.'

'Good enough, friend. No further credentials necessary. Unfortunately a genuine patrol officer is on the horizon, so excuse me for running. You'll find coordinates in your sat-nav.'

Thirty seconds later his motorbike was lost on the horizon.

Of course the kosher cop, when he arrived, was inquisitive. Nelson went into innocent-and-mildly-disorientated-tourist mode, and managed to stall him until *three* Winnebagos, all with *California* plates, zoomed past doing somewhere over eighty, low-hanging fruit that couldn't be ignored by any Wyoming cop.

Nelson drove on.

* * *

It was the middle of the following day when he drove the Winnebago into the forecourt of an electronics factory, and faced locked, unmanned gates, marked with the logo of the transEarth Institute. A small speaker on a pole by his driver-side door demanded, 'Identify yourself, please.'

Nelson thought it over. He leaned out and said, 'I am Thursday.'

'Of course you are. Come right inside.'

The gate swung open silently. Nelson took a moment to run an online search on that name: *transEarth*. Then he drove through the gate.

47

HE FOUND A door, which revealed a short corridor, which led to an elevator.

'Please walk forward,' said the voice – Lobsang's voice? 'Take the lift; it will operate automatically.'

Of course it could be some kind of trap. But had the voice purposefully called the elevator a 'lift', British style, to put him at his ease? If so, cute, but strange.

He walked ahead willingly. The elevator sealed up around him and descended.

Even now that disembodied voice spoke to him. 'This facility used to belong to the US government. Since being bought by transEarth, somehow it's slipped off the map. Governments can be so clumsy . . .'

The elevator door opened to reveal a kind of study, perhaps a rather English design, complete with fireplace and dancing flames – obviously artificial, but crackling fairly realistically. He might almost have been back in one of the grander of his parishioners' houses in St John on the Water.

A chair shifted, set beside a low table. A man of indeterminate age stood to meet him, wearing a monk's orange robe, head shaven, smiling – and holding a pipe. Somehow, like the fire, he had an air of artificiality.

'Welcome, Nelson Azikiwe!'

Nelson stepped forward. 'You are Lobsang?'

'Guilty as charged.' The man waved the pipe vaguely towards another chair. 'Please sit.'

They sat, Nelson taking an upright chair opposite Lobsang.

'First things first,' Lobsang said. 'We are safe and discreet in this place, which is one of several such support facilities I own across the world – indeed, the worlds. Nelson, you are free to walk out of here any time you wish, but I would prefer it if you never spoke about this meeting – well, I believe a fellow Chestertonian will be discreet. Grant me the liberty of confirming your favourite novel – *The Napoleon of Notting Hill*, was it not?'

'The source of the railings quote.'

'Exactly. Personally my pick is *The Man Who Was Thursday*, still an excellent read and the precursor of many spy romances over the years. A curious man, Chesterton. Embraced Catholicism like a security blanket, don't you think?'

'I found him as a kid, when I was digging around in a Joburg library. A stash of ancient books, a relic of the days of the British presence. Probably not been read since apartheid . . .' Nelson ran out of steam. He supposed the idea of a *bongani* like him sitting in a dusty library absorbing the adventures of Father Brown had been surreal enough, but this situation took the biscuit, as his parishioners might have said. What to ask? Where to begin? He essayed, 'Are you part of the Lobsang Project?'

'My dear sir, I *am* the whole of the project.'

Nelson reflected on various searches he'd run. 'You know, I recall gossip about a supercomputer that

340

endeavoured to get its owners to accept that it was human, a soul having been reincarnated into the machine at the moment it was booted . . . Something like that. The nerdosphere consensus was that it was a red herring.' Nelson hesitated. 'It was, wasn't it?'

Lobsang dismissed the question. 'By the way, would you like a drink? I understand you're a beer man.' He stood and crossed to a walnut drinks cabinet.

Nelson accepted the drink, half a glass of a heavy, flavoursome brew, and persisted with his questions. 'And are you somehow connected to the *Mark Twain* expedition?'

'You have me there. That was the second time I found myself close to the glare of public scrutiny, after the circumstances of my miraculous birth, and it was rather harder to escape. I'm afraid poor Joshua Valienté ended up taking more of the resulting attention than he wanted. Or deserved, actually. While I receded to the comfort of the shadows.'

'And isn't transEarth some kind of subsidiary of the Black Corporation?'

Lobsang smiled. 'Yes, transEarth is partly owned by Black.'

'Tell me why I'm here.'

'Actually you came to me, remember. You're here because you solved the puzzle. Followed the clues.'

'The link between you and the *Mark Twain*?'

'Quite. But of course you have your own underlying personal connection to Black, since your scholarship days. You won't be surprised to find that the Black Corporation has been watching you for some time. You're one of Douglas Black's longer-term investments, in fact.'

Lobsang leaned over his table, tapped its surface so that a screen flipped up, and Nelson watched disturbingly familiar images of himself, his family, his life slide past one by one, beginning with his own smiling face as a two-year-old.

'Born in a Johannesburg township, of course. You first came to our attention when your mother put you forward for Black's "Searching for the Future" programme. Scholarships and various other contracts followed, though you were never directly employed by Black. Then came your rise to modest prominence as a palaeontologist of the Long Earth. Exploring the stepwise past, yes? It was something of a surprise when you took your own sideways step into the Church of England, but Douglas Black believes in allowing those he values to find their own way. He trusts them, you see. And now here you are, well spoken of by Douglas's good friend the Archbishop of Canterbury – yet seeking new directions.' He smiled. 'Did I miss anything significant?'

Nelson felt needled at the idea he was being manipulated. 'And what are *you*, sir? Are you anything more than another "long-term investment" of a rich and powerful man?'

Lobsang was oddly hesitant. Nelson was reminded, surprisingly, of some of his more theologically doubting parishioners. 'In a way. In fact, literally, *yes*. Technologically speaking I am a product of Black technologies, beginning with the gel that supports my consciousness. Legally speaking I am a business partner, a co-owner of a Black Corporation subsidiary. Yet beyond that Douglas gives me great – well, untrammelled freedom. What *am* I? I *believe* that I am a reincarnated Tibetan motorbike repairman. I have clear if somewhat erratic memories of my former life ... Some call me a deranged if highly intelligent supercomputer. But I *know* I have a soul. It's the bit talking to you, correct? And I have dreams – do you believe that?'

'That's all rather muddled. Are you in need of counselling?'

Lobsang smiled ruefully. 'Probably. But more specifically, I need – companions – in my quest.'

'What quest?'

'Simply put, I am researching the Long Earth phenomenon and all its implications for mankind, and I have come to understand I cannot do it by myself. I need different perspectives – such as yours, Reverend Azikiwe. Your unusual mix of the rational with the mystic ... You can't disguise that you too have always searched for truth. One only has to glance at your online activities to perceive that.'

Nelson grunted. 'I suppose there's no point in discussing my right to privacy.'

'I have a mission for you. A quest, a journey across the Long Earth – and indeed across this one. We will be travelling to New Zealand, on Earth West number – well, the numbers scarcely matter, do they?'

'*New Zealand?* And what will we be travelling to see?'

'You saw the records of the *Mark Twain* expedition, I believe. Those that were made public at least.'

'Yes . . .'

'Did you come across references to the entity known as First Person Singular?'

Nelson stayed silent. But his curiosity was like a fish-hook in his flesh.

Lobsang shifted in his chair. 'What do you say?'

'It's all a bit sudden, isn't it? I need to think about it.'

'The twain will be here tomorrow.'

'Fine.' He stood. 'I'll sleep in my vehicle overnight. That will give me time to consider.'

Lobsang stood too, smiling. 'Take all the time you need.'

That night there was a thunderstorm, a real humdinger coming in from the west, and rain that made the Winnebago sound as if it were a target on a firing range.

Nelson lay in his bed listening to the barrage, and considering the world in general and his current situation in particular – including a sidebar on the nature of souls. It was strange how many people he'd met who had no use for orthodox Christianity yet nevertheless unthinkingly believed that they had a soul.

It was stranger still to think that perhaps you could *create* a soul. Or at least, create a body that could store a soul . . . Suddenly he was eager to begin this journey with Lobsang – if only to get to know Lobsang himself.

And yet there was residual suspicion. He remembered what Lobsang had said, somewhat enigmatically: *Actually you came to me, remember. You're here because you solved the puzzle. Followed the clues . . .* True, but who had planted those clues in the first place?

The next morning he called to arrange pickup for the rental Winnebago.

At noon, the promised twain dropped soundlessly out of the sky. Nelson had travelled on twains many times before, but this one seemed rather spartan, a two-hundred-foot envelope over a compact, streamlined gondola.

The twain lowered a safety harness and pulled him up into the air. He was deposited in an area near the stern.

Once out of the harness he made his way through a cramped interior to a lounge cum galley that evidently doubled as an observation deck. He felt rather than heard motors start up.

And suddenly, through big picture windows, he saw he was in storm clouds, with rain battering the windows – and then hot sunshine that caused the hull to steam. Stepping already, then. He had taken anti-nausea pills, recommended by Lobsang, and despite his usual aversion to stepping felt little discomfort.

A short staircase led him to a door to a wheelhouse above the lounge – a door which appeared to be locked. As he tried the door handle a screen on the wall lit up, showing a smiling, shaven-headed visage. 'Glad to have you aboard, Nelson!'

'Glad to be here, Lobsang.'

'I am, as you may guess, the pilot of this craft—'

'*Which* Lobsang am I talking to?'

'I invite you to understand that Lobsang is not simply a single presence. To call me ubiquitous doesn't do the trick. Remember the movie *Spartacus*? Well, all of me are Spartacus. It does require regular downtime to synch us all, *me* all . . . You're alone on the ship, but should you require a physical presence, for instance for medical reasons, I can activate an ambulant unit. We will make for New Zealand, stepping more or less continuously to find the most auspicious winds, world by world. Believe it or not, on a twain I like to do it the gentle way.'

'I'll try to relax and enjoy the ride, then.'

'Do that. Relaxing was one thing Joshua Valienté never managed . . .'

'Valienté certainly didn't look very relaxed on the clip I found of him returning to Madison. A clip that led me to this point, in fact, to you. A clip you probably sent me yourself, right?' He'd committed himself to this peculiar quest, but his resentment at the idea that he had been controlled, drawn into this situation, started to morph to anger. 'How far back does your influence extend? I don't suppose you had anything to do with establishing a chat group called the Quizmasters? . . . Were you, in fact, behind the entire trail of breadcrumbs that led me to you?'

Lobsang smiled. 'From now on, no more tricks.'

'I hope not. Nobody likes being manipulated, Lobsang.'

'I don't think of it as manipulation. I think of it as the setting out of an opportunity. It's up to you whether you take that opportunity or not.'

'Yesterday you called me an investment.'

'That's Douglas Black's language, not mine. And remember, Nelson, as I pointed out, *you* came to *me*, in the end. Look, whether we end up working together or not, welcome aboard, and enjoy the ride. If nothing else, think of it as a vacation, if you like.'

'Or an audition.'

'If you will.'

Nelson smiled back. 'But, Lobsang, who is auditioning whom?'

48

THE BEAGLE AND the kobold approached, walking out of the dusty distance.

In their rough camp, Jansson and Sally stood, wary. As the creatures drew near, Jansson was very aware of an emptiness at her belt where her cop-issue Stepper box ought to be. The beagle, the dog-man, had confiscated it on the day they'd arrived. And so she, at least, without Sally's aid, had been stuck here ever since, on this peculiar world with its strange inhabitants.

It was the first time they'd been visited in the week or so that they'd been here, since they'd been met in the Rectangles world and brought to this Earth a couple of dozen steps further West – to a world full of trolls, as Sally said she could feel, hear, as soon as they arrived. The beagles were waiting, they were told, for the return of some kind of ruler from . . . someplace else. It would be this ruler who would deal with the humans.

Jansson supposed it gave them time to get their bearings, for her to recover somewhat from the journey so far. Even that first jaunt, from Rectangles to here, had been a grotesque experience, because the beagle who had met them couldn't step; it had had to be carried on the back of the squat, ugly humanoid Sally had called a 'kobold'.

It had all been a rush of strangeness for them both. Even Sally, Jansson had learned, the great explorer of the Long Earth, had known nothing of this place before being brought here, lured by the gossip of the kobolds. To Sally this world had been just another Joker, just another desert world in a band of such worlds which, apparently, had lost much of their water through some calamity during the turbulent epoch of planetary formation. On such a world geological activity was going to be reduced, life restricted . . . That was the theory. In fact, as Jansson was learning, on many Jokers there were habitable refuges.

On this world there was an island of green, of moisture – from what the kobold had said, Sally had guessed it could be the size of Europe. Unnoticed by dismissive previous explorers, including Joshua and Sally, who had come rushing through this world too hastily. Unnoticed by the teams of researchers who had followed that first expedition to Rectangles: they had been Datum-raised workers with Datum-trained expectations, who thought in terms of one world thick, and never looked stepwise.

Well, here they were, in a world that hosted these dogs, these strange sapients – and, evidently, the trolls, in great concentrations.

For a long interval there was silence. The dog beasts seemed to like to stare, to study, to think before speaking; the grammar of their interactions was not like the human. Jansson and Sally just stood there, waiting. The kobold had a wounded arm, Jansson noticed now, roughly bandaged with a soiled rag. He cackled, evidently enjoying the moment.

The trolls who'd travelled with them didn't seem bothered in the slightest. Mary sat on a knoll, humming a tune that was naggingly familiar to Jansson, while Ham happily raked the ground with his strong fingers, periodically popping grubs into his mouth. As if, Jansson thought, being approached by a bipedal dog wearing a ray gun happened every day.

The beagle stood before the women, eyes unblinking, that mobile wet nose quivering as, evidently, he *smelled* them. He must have been nearly seven foot tall, and he towered over both Jansson and Sally. But that, and the ray gun, weren't the only reasons he was so intimidating, Jansson realized. There was something fluidly *animal* about him, a sense of honed perfection, right down to the way his fine fur coated his flesh in smooth streamlined layers. And there was intelligence in his eyes, a bright hard directed intelligence.

His teeth, eyes, ears, muzzle, nose were all very dog-like, even though, Jansson saw, the overall shape of his skull, with a bulging brow, might have been humanoid. His face sometimes looked human, sometimes wolf-like, like a shifting hologram. His ears were too sharp, his eyes too far apart, his grin too wide, his nose too flat with that blackened tip . . . And his eyes, yes, it was like looking into the eyes of a wolf. He made Jansson feel shabby, incomplete. But there was also something unreal about him, as if he were a movie CGI special effect. He just didn't fit into Jansson's cosy, parochial, Datum-nurtured consciousness.

He couldn't step. And presumably none of his kind could, either. Jansson had to cling to that thought, that she could do something he couldn't—

She coughed, and shivered, a wave of weakness passing over her.

The beagle turned on her. 'Your name?'

His language was distorted, a mix of dog-like growls and whines. *Hrr-your-rrh ne-rr-mmhh?* Yet he clearly spoke English, his words understandable. Another astonishing conceptual leap for an ex-cop like Jansson to absorb.

Jansson tried to stand straight. 'Monica Jansson. Formerly Lieutenant, Madison PD.'

The beagle cocked his head on one side, evidently puzzled. He turned to Sally. 'You?'

'Sally Linsay.'

The beagle raised his fore-limb, his arm, and pointed at his chest. Jansson saw that his paw, his hand, had four extended finger-like appendages, nothing like a thumb, and he wore a kind of leathery glove over his palm. Protection for when he went on all fours, perhaps. 'My name,' he said now. 'Snowy.'

Sally clearly tried not to, but burst out laughing.

Jansson turned to the kobold. '*Snowy?*'

The kobold grinned nervously. 'Other pathless-ss ones came befo-rre . . . Gave na-mme.'

Sally said, 'And I know your name. Finn McCool, right?' She glanced at Jansson. 'One of the smarter of his breed. Good with humans. I might have known you'd be involved in this, chasing some angle.'

The kobold just grinned. 'Josh-shua.'

Sally scowled. 'What about Joshua?'

But the kobold would not reply.

Snowy studied them. 'You,' he said to Sally, 'crotch-stink human-nn.'

'Thanks.'

'Smell same as befor-rre. Like othe-hhrs of your kind. But-tt *you* . . .'

He came closer to Jansson. She tried not to flinch as, his eyes half closed, he sniffed her breath. He smelled of wet fur and a kind of musk.

'St-hhrange. Sick. You smell sick-hrr.'

'Very perceptive,' murmured Jansson.

He stepped back, raised his head and howled, a sharp, supremely loud noise that made Jansson wince, and Sally cover her ears. It was answered within a few seconds by another howl coming from the east.

Snowy turned and pointed that way. 'My Den. Smell of my litter-hrr. Name, Eye of Hunter-rrh. Cart coming, ca-rrhy you. Granddaughter of Den, name Petra. Sh-she see you. Granddaughter back from Den of Mother, fa-hhr from here.'

Sally asked, 'Does this Granddaughter know about us?'

'Not yet. Surp-hhrrise by Snowy.' He pulled back his lips to reveal very canine teeth in a kind of smile. 'Rewar-rrd for Snowy, for gi-ffft.' He sounded breathless, agitated.

Sally murmured to Jansson, 'Don't look down.'

'Why not?'

'If you do you'll see how he's already anticipating the reward he's going to get from this Granddaughter, who-ever she is.'

Snowy walked away, to Jansson's relief, a big priapic animal backing off and looking out for the cart.

The kobold was still here, grinning at them.

Jansson said wearily, 'So am I allowed to ask questions?'

Sally laughed. 'If you can figure out where to begin.'

Jansson jabbed a finger at McCool. 'I know of your kind. The police agencies across the Low Earths keep records of you. Partial sightings, fragmentary reports, scratchy CCTV images . . . What are you doing here?'

McCool shrugged. 'Hel-pp you. For price.' *Prei-sss*.

'Of course, for a price,' Sally said. 'I knew that the kobolds were always going to know where the trolls are hiding out, Monica.'

'So you went to them and asked—'

'They all know each other. They swap information. The trolls have their long call. With the kobolds it's more like the long snitch. Anything they know is swapped around and sold to the highest bidder. So I followed the rumour trail, one scrawny kobold to the next. At last I found one who told me to bring Mary to the Rectangles. And then – well, you know the rest. From there we were brought here, to this arid world, this Joker, full of these dog-like sapients.'

'Beagles,' McCool said. 'Called beagles-ss.'

Jansson asked, 'Who by? Why beagles?'

'Who? Other pathless-ss ones, here before. They call them beagles-ss.'

Sally said, 'Somebody's having a joke. I bet we can blame Charles Darwin for *that*.'

Finn McCool shrugged. It was an unnatural motion, Jansson thought, less like a human gesture than a monkey performing a circus trick.

Jansson asked, 'And is that how he got his "name"? Snowy?'

Another shrug. 'Human na-mme. Not true name. Beagles-ss not speak true na-mme to human-nn. Kobolds not ss-peak true name to pathless-ss ones.'

'How is it he speaks English at all? Learned from humans?'

'No. Kobolds here first. Kobolds sell beagles ss-tuff.'

Jansson nodded. 'You already spoke English. So the

beagles were the first to learn your language rather than the other way around.'

'Beagles are smarter than kobolds, then,' Sally said with a satisfied grin.

McCool looked away, edgy, nervous.

There was a plume of dust, coming from the east. Snowy spotted it, sniffed the air, howled again. There was an answering howl from off in the distance, and what sounded like a throaty caw to Jansson, like the cry of some tremendous bird. Jansson shivered again, having no real idea what she was getting into.

She turned back to McCool. 'Tell me one more thing. That beagle, Snowy, was carrying a stone-tipped spear – and a ray gun.'

Sally grunted. 'Actually it looked like a compact laser projector.'

'We just got here. But I don't see any cities, any planes in the sky. How did some kind of Stone Age warrior get a laser gun?'

Sally said to McCool, 'From some other world, step-wise. From you kobolds. Right? So is that your angle here?'

The kobold grinned again. 'Beagles not ss-tep. Smart but no toolss. Only ss-tone. Buy tool-ss from us-ss, all kinda stuff.'

'Including a weapon,' Sally murmured, 'that looked like it came from a society more advanced even than Datum Earth. Where *did* you get it, monkey boy?'

'Dug up,' Finn McCool said simply, and he grinned, and would say no more.

That approaching dust plume resolved into a cart, a heavy frame of wood running on four solid wooden wheels that seemed to be rimmed with rusty iron. Another beagle, perhaps slighter than Snowy, stood on the cart's bed, wielding reins. Taller than Jansson, taller even than Snowy, the bird things had fat feathered bodies with stubby wings, muscular legs, feet tipped with claws like sickles, long pillar-like necks, and heads that looked all beak. Yet they were harnessed up and appeared obedient.

'That would be an astonishing sight,' Jansson murmured. 'A dog riding a cart. Even if it wasn't being drawn by two huge birds. If you filmed that and put it on the outernet it would be a comedy sensation.'

Sally touched Jansson's arm, surprisingly sympathetic. 'Just let the strangeness wash over you, Lieutenant Jansson. Come on . . .'

Hastily they packed up their few bits of gear.

The cart slowed to a stop. The beagle driver jumped to the ground, and she – nude save for a kind of belt of pockets, you could see she was female – greeted Snowy. They ran around each other briefly, and Snowy even dropped for a moment to all fours, wagging a stub of tail.

'The females are dominant,' Sally murmured.

'What?'

'Look at the two of them. He's more pleased to see her than the other way around. Something worth noting.'

'Hmm. Maybe you're jumping to conclusions.'

Sally snorted. 'You could learn all you need to know about *human* males from one miserable specimen. Why not the same here? Listen, we need to find an angle of our own.'

'We came here to help Mary. We came for the trolls.'

'Yeah. But we weren't expecting all this complication.

354

We'll play for time – and stay alive in the process. Just remember, we can always step out, if it gets bad enough. I can carry you. These dogs can't follow, we know that now.'

With the greeting done, the female beagle approached the humans. She pointed to her own chest. 'Li-Li. Call me Li-Li.' She turned to the cart. 'Ride to Eye of Hunte-hhr.'

Sally nodded. 'Thank you. We need to bring the trolls we came with . . .'

But Li-Li had already turned away, and was beckoning to the trolls, singing a kind of warbled melody. Without any fuss Mary stood, picked up Ham and set him on her shoulder, and clambered aboard the cart.

The humans followed, with Finn McCool. Snowy snapped the reins, the bird beasts cawed like pigeons on steroids, and the cart jolted into motion, nearly knocking Jansson over. There were no seats. Jansson held on to the rough-finished wall of the cart, wondering how far it was to this city, and if she could make it all the way without collapsing.

Li-Li approached Jansson. Again Jansson had to endure a wet dog-like nose sniffing at her mouth, armpits, crotch. 'Sick,' Li-Li said without ceremony.

Jansson forced a smile. 'My body's going wrong, and I'm full of drugs. No wonder I smell strange to you.'

Li-Li took Jansson's hands in hers. Li-Li wore no gloves, unlike Snowy. Her fingers were long, human-like in that regard, but her palms had leathery pads on the underside, like canine paws. 'My jj-rrh-*ob*. Care for sick and injured. You lucky.'

'How?' Sally asked sharply. 'How were we lucky?'

'Snowy found-dd you.' She glanced up at the big beagle at the reins. 'Not ve-hhry clever but big spir-rrit. Always

355

truth-tells. B-hhrave. Good hunter, but kind. Takes you back to city, see Granddaughter Petra. Some hunter-hhrs, just take back head. Or ear-rrs.'

Sally and Jansson exchanged a glance. Jansson said, 'So we're lucky we got found by a beagle that didn't just kill us outright.'

'There's no higher morality,' Sally said. 'By the way,' she added more softly, 'I just jumped to another conclusion.'

'What?'

'She said Snowy's truthful. That implies that others aren't. These super-dogs know how to lie.'

Jansson nodded. 'Noted.'

49

SOON THEY MADE out a smear of smoke on the eastern horizon.

The trail they followed turned to bare mud scored by the ruts of traffic. The land seemed greener too, away from the open sward of scrubland into which they had stepped. They even passed by a few forest clumps. To Jansson, no naturalist, many of the trees looked like ferns, with squat, stubby trunks and sprawling, parasol-like leaves.

In one place she could see through a screen of trees to a shimmer of open water, a lake, and by its bank creatures had gathered to drink. They were rather like small deer, Jansson thought, but their bodies were a little too heavy, their legs a bit too stubby. Deer with a dash of pig, perhaps.

Li-Li was on the alert as the cart rolled through its closest approach to the lake. At his reins, Snowy stared fixedly at the deer things, his ears erect. Li-Li growled a phrase to him, over and over.

Finn McCool the kobold grinned his anxious, nervy grin at Sally and Jansson. 'She says, "Snowy. Remember wh-hho you a-are . . ." These dog fellows-ss run off four-legged after prey if they get chance. Sh-should be on leash-shsh . . .'

'Nothing would surprise me,' Jansson said, as the cart rolled on away from the water.

Sally said, 'We ought to remember that our hosts might look like dogs, but they're *not dogs.* That might lead us astray. Their ancestors never were dogs, because dogs probably never evolved here, not as we know them. These are sapient creatures carved from some dog-like clay. Just as we are sapients made from heavily modified apes . . .'

Jansson found herself longing for the concrete and glass of the Datum, the reassuringly grubby crimes of lowlife humanity. Perhaps all this, natural selection's arbitrary shaping of living things, was something you got used to out in the Long Earth. Not her, not yet. 'The plasticity of living forms.'

'What's that?'

'Nothing. A line from a book.'

Her reaction merely seemed to puzzle Sally.

Now they passed through farmland, a belt of it that evidently surrounded the beagle city. A scrawl of dry stone walls, none of them straight, divided the land into rough fields crowded with beasts browsing or grazing. Some of these looked like fatter, stupider versions of the deer things Jansson had spotted by the lake in the forest. Others were more like cattle, goats, pigs, even what looked like some kind of rhinoceros with lopped-off horns, and a few fat, feathery versions of the bird creatures that drew this truck. Dogs could be seen patrolling the herds. In one field, deer-like animals were being driven into an enclosure, perhaps for milking.

And here Jansson saw trolls, the first since they'd arrived in this world, save for Mary and Ham. A party of a couple of dozen, perhaps, were working their way along a dry stone wall, evidently making repairs. They sang as they worked, the usual beautiful multi-part harmony applied to a lively, jumping melody. Ham, who had been napping on Mary's lap, woke up now, and climbed up on his mother's shoulder to see. In his immature piping voice he sang back phrases, echoing the song.

Sally listened hard. 'I'd swear they're singing "Johnny B Goode". My father would have known.'

Jansson said, 'These are the farms of smart carnivores. Right? Nothing arable, no crops. Nothing but meat on the hoof.'

'Right. There'll be plenty of peptides in the arteries after they've fed us up a few times here, Monica.'

'The trolls seem happy, judging by that party we saw.'

'Yes.' Sally seemed oddly uneasy with that observation. 'These dogs are evidently sapient. We know trolls like to be around sapients. I guess that's why they're coming here, to this world, for refuge. Sapients, but non-human. So they're comfortable here.'

'You're jealous!'

'Am not.'

'Come on. Everybody knows you like trolls, Sally Linsay. You championed their cause even before this latest blow-up, even before we absconded from the Gap with Mary.'

'What about it?'

'Well, now you're finding out that, no matter how special trolls are to you, humans aren't all that special to trolls.'

Sally just glared back.

Suddenly Snowy stood bolt upright, staring out to the north, ears pricked again, the hairs on the back of his neck rising. Again Li-Li murmured words, or growled commands, and Snowy stayed in control of his reins.

'You can see why he's distracted,' said Sally. 'Take a look.'

When Jansson twisted to see, she saw small compact brown-furred forms bounding across the fields away from the cart, white tails bobbing. 'They look like rabbits,' she said.

'I think they are rabbits. Authentic Datum pedigree. I wonder how they got here.' And Sally turned to glare at Finn McCool.

He grinned, showing too many triangular teeth. 'Beagles-ss love them. Fun to chase. Good to eat.'

'What else have you sold these creatures?'

'As-side from rabbits?'

'Aside from rabbits.'

He shrugged. 'Not juss-st me. The wheels-ss. The iron . . .'

'You sold them *iron-making*?'

'Brought blacksmith-th. Humann.'

Jansson asked, 'And the fee you negotiated for all this—'

'The litters-ss of their litters will be paying in ins-sstallmentss.'

And, Jansson thought, paying for this 'gift' of the rabbits. Ask an Australian about rabbits . . .

The kobold had been leaning towards them, apparently keen to join the conversation. Distracted, the women abandoned their talk, and he shrank back. Jansson wondered if Finn McCool picked up some undertone of contempt, of dismissal. Now he dug his elderly walkman out of his pouch, lifted his headphones over his ears, and played his music, swaying to a beat Jansson could hear, tinnily. He smiled again, watching the faces of Sally and Jansson, making sure they were noticing him. The kobold was like a poor imitation of a human, and a needy one, Jansson thought: needing the regard of humans, whatever animal dignity his distant ancestors had once possessed long bred out by corrosive contact with mankind. Jansson turned away with a peculiar disgust.

And she saw, to her horror, that while Li-Li and Snowy were distracted, Sally had slipped the ray gun from its loose holster at Snowy's waist. She inspected it briefly, then put it back. 'Dead,' she whispered to Jansson. 'I thought it looked kind of inert. Another useful fact, Monica . . .'

50

THE TRAIL GREW wider as they approached the city. There was more traffic now, carts laden with butchered carcasses and cut leather and heaps of bones. Live animals on the hoof were driven forward too, things like bears, some even a little like apes, controlled in rough herds by beagle shepherds with sticks and whips that cracked. There was even a party of trolls being led by a beagle but under no apparent duress, singing what sounded like rockabilly to Jansson.

And there were many pedestrians: beagles, adults and pups alike, all sparsely dressed, with belts or jackets replete with pockets. Jansson saw no sign of adornment, nothing like jewellery, no hats or fancy clothing. But as the crowds thickened Jansson started to *smell* them, the sharp stink of wet fur and piss or dung, and she wondered if that was how these dog-like people decorated themselves: not with visual embellishment but with fancy scents.

The adults all walked upright. Maybe dropping to all fours was frowned on in the city, something you only did out in the country or in private – like a human going naked, maybe. But the young would get down and hop and gambol around their parents' legs like puppies around a new owner. Jansson was no anatomist, but she watched the beagles curiously, trying to see how a pre-sumably dog-like four-legged body plan had been adapted to a natural-looking upright stance – and how it had been arranged that slipping back to all fours was so easy. That was a difference with humans, she thought; even as a kid she wouldn't have lasted five minutes if she'd tried to knuckle-walk like her remote chimp-like ancestors. But she couldn't make out the detail.

She clung on in the rattling cart, letting the sights and scents wash over her. The gathering crowd might almost have been human, if you looked at it through half-closed eyes. The beagles' bodies, upright, were taller than human, and with the pelvis slung oddly low, so the torso was long, the back legs short. Not impossibly far from the human. But then she would see ears prick up, and cold wolf-like eyes stare back at her, and the pack scent of the dogs would wash over her, and she felt as if these creatures could not have been more alien.

Finn McCool was watching her. 'You strange to them-mm, but not that ss-strange. They think you kobolds-ss.' He laughed at that. 'We're all the ss-same to them, we human-nn f-folk. Ss-ame to stupid puppies-ss.'

'You and I,' Sally said with cold contempt, 'are *not* the same.'

It was a relief when the cart at last reached the city itself. The Eye of the Hunter was a wide brownish smear of wooden buildings set in a muddy plain, under a pall of smoke. The central development was bounded by a wide moat spanned by solid-looking bridges of wood and stone. The moat was evidently for defence, but there was no city wall that Jansson could discern, just a low, irregular dry stone barrier that looked as if it was intended to keep out beasts wandering from the fields rather than purposeful invaders.

Just before they reached the moat, they passed stockades into which farm animals were being driven for slaughter. Jansson, in a quick glance, saw the beagles working, polished stone blades flashing, blood spurting, and the animals fell one by one. Death and blood: universals on every world, it seemed, no matter how far you travelled. Jansson felt her queasy stomach churn.

In the city, the buildings, none more than a couple of storeys high, were robust but unadorned, wooden boxes with walls of stone or packed mud and roofs of timber or a kind of coarse thatch: irregular shapes, nothing of the squareness or roundness you'd associate with a human town. There seemed to be only a couple of traffic arteries, long, straight avenues running north–south, east–west through the heart of the city; the other tracks were winding, irregular. Whatever these dogs were, they weren't geometers – not in the style of human geometry, anyhow. Now the dominant smell was of wood smoke and a lingering raw-meat stench, overlying the rich dog-like scent of the beagles themselves. And this was a noisy place as well as a smelly one, with an unending chorus of barks and yaps and howls.

They didn't get much further before they were held up by a small pack of tough-looking male dogs. They surrounded the cart, and began to interrogate Snowy and Li-Li with rapid-fire yelps and growls.

'Cops,' Sally said. 'Or royal guards. We must be heading straight for the palace ... Some palace, however. Not exactly Paris, France, is it?'

'It's not even Paris, Texas.'

'But it's not built to impress *us*.'

Li-Li gave them a wolfish grin, and sniffed, with short chuffing sounds. 'Know this from rrh-kobolds. Humans can't smell. But city, city full of wo-rrds. Scent over there. *I he-hre, half day ago, seeking you.* And distant, distant – hear howls? *I, I have fine f-hhrresh meat from count-hrry, buy now, buy now . . .'*

Sally grinned. 'Think of that, Jansson. Imagine if you had the nose of a police dog. The city's full of information. There are scent markers everywhere, just like posters or graffiti on the walls, and the howls must be more long-range, like some kind of internet.'

They came at last to a building bigger than most, wider, but no taller, and no more elaborately constructed than the rest. Here the human party was told to wait with Snowy, while Li-Li jogged inside.

The strongest smell just here was wood smoke. 'Dogs discover fire,' Jansson murmured.

'Maybe that's how it started,' Sally mused. 'Dogs are smart animals. Intensely social, adaptable, easy to train. Here, maybe us clever monkeys never evolved to keep them in their place. And one day, in some starving pack out on the prairie, one bright young female comes home with a burning branch in her jaws, taken from some lightning-struck forest . . .'

'Or some bright young male.'

Sally grinned. 'Be serious.'

Li-Li returned, to say they would be taken in to see the Granddaughter immediately.

51

THEY WERE LED through narrow, twisting, confusing corridors – confusing unless you could follow scents, probably – to a large chamber, with long curving walls of stone and mud, a high ceiling, windows, and a fireplace, unlit.

The basics of the room might have been laid out by a human, Jansson thought, down to the detail of the fireplace built under what was evidently a chimney stack. Some things were universal. But the room, while well constructed, was drab to human eyes; there was no paint, no wallpaper, no tapestries, no art on the walls. What there was, however, was a rich melange of scents, which even Jansson's battered old cop's schnozzle could detect.

The princess of the beagles had no throne; she sat easily on the ground, on what looked like a patch of natural turf growing in the middle of the room. The princess was flanked by guards, who had stone-tipped spears and space-age blasters to hand. Jansson wondered how the grass got the light to grow.

The Granddaughter's title was not 'Granddaughter'. Her name was not 'Petra'. The adviser beside her, an age-ing male with a glum posture, was not called 'Brian'. But these were the best labels Sally and Jansson were given, courtesy of the kobold. The Granddaughter wore only a practical-looking pocket belt – that, and, Jansson saw, some kind of pendant on a loop of leather at her neck, what looked like handsome blue stones set in a ring of gold. It was an artefact that caught Jansson's eye; it looked naggingly familiar.

And there was a dog by her side! A *real* dog, an authentic dog, a Datum dog, a big Alsatian if Jansson was any judge. It sat up, watching the newcomers, its tongue lolling; it looked healthy, well fed, well groomed. Somehow it looked the most natural presence in the world, here in this room full of dog-people, and yet the strangest too.

All the beagles watched stonily as Jansson and Sally, hastily instructed by Finn McCool, showed submission to the Granddaughter by getting down on the ground and lying on their backs, arms and legs up in the air.

'God, how humiliating,' Sally murmured.

'You should worry. I'm going to need help getting up again.'

The kindly nurse type Li-Li came over to assist when the gesture was finished. Then Sally and Jansson, with McCool, had to sit as best they could on the hard-packed earth of the floor, while the Granddaughter murmured to her advisers.

'That dog,' murmured Sally, 'is a Datum dog. Something to do with you, McCool?'

'Not me . . . anoth-ther kobold seller-rr. Popular here. They lik-ke big males. Sex-ss toys.'

Sally snorted, but kept from laughing.

Jansson leaned over and whispered, 'Sally. That pendant she's wearing.'

'Yes. Shut up about it.'

'But it looks like—'

'I know what it looks like. Shut up.'

At length the Granddaughter deigned to consider them. She said, with the usual rough approximation of English, 'You. What you call hhrr-uman. From worr-ld you call Datum-mm.'

'That's correct,' Sally said. 'Umm – ma'am.'

'Wh-hrr-at you want her-hhre?'

Sally and Jansson went through a halting explanation of why they had come: the problems with the trolls across the human Earths, how Sally had learned from the kobolds that many of the trolls had fled to this world, how they hoped that the trolls they had brought here, Mary and Ham, would be safe . . .

The Granddaughter considered this. 'Trolls hrr-appy here. Trolls like beagrr-les. Beagles like trolls. Troll music fine. H-rruman music arse shit.' She perked her own ears. 'Beagle ears better-hhr than human. Human music ar-hhrse shit.'

'That's what my father kept telling me,' Sally said. 'All downhill since Simon and Garfunkel broke up, he said.'

Petra stared at her. 'I know noth-thing of this Simon and Garr-hrr—'

'It doesn't matter.'

'Beagles despise human music. Beagles despise h-hrr-umans.'

That blunt statement shocked Jansson. 'Why?'

The Granddaughter stood upright now and walked over to her, towering over the sitting women. Jansson did her best not to flinch, and to return that wintry stare. 'Why? You-hhr stink. *You* especially . . .'

But it seemed to Jansson that the Granddaughter's own scent was odd, unnatural, overlaid by some kind of perfume perhaps. Maybe, for a species to whom scent was so important, to mask your smell was to mask your thoughts.

'And,' said Petra, 'you-hhr dogs.' She pointed at the patient Alsatian. 'Once wolf. Now toy, like sc-hhrap of bone in mouth. *No mind-dd.* Hrr-umans did this.'

Jansson supposed that was true: dogs were wolves reduced to submissive pets. She imagined seeing a small-brained humanoid in a collar, on a lead ... Still, she protested. 'But we love our dogs.'

Sally said, 'In fact we co-evolved with them—'

'They have no rrh-ights. He-rre, walk on two legs, not four-rr. Except pups at play. And except hunt. We have cr-hrr-ime. Those who do wr-hrr-ong. We catch, we turn out of city. We hunt.'

Jansson returned her gaze. 'On all fours? You hunt down criminals, on all fours?'

The adviser, Brian, spoke up for the first time. 'We have many pups. Big litte-hhrs. Life cheap. Like to hunt . . .'

Petra seemed to smile. Jansson smelled meat on her breath. 'Like to hunt. Good for wolf-ff within.'

Sally snapped, 'So you despise humans for how we domesticated your cousins on our world. Fine. But *we've* done nothing to harm you, any of you. We didn't even know you existed before Snowy there showed up on Rectangles.'

'You offen-nnd me. Stinking elves gone w-hhrong. You, no hrr-ights here. Why should I not th-hhrrow you out for the hunt?'

Sally glanced at Jansson, and said desperately, 'Because

we can get you more ray guns.' She pointed to the nearest guard. 'Like those.'

Jansson, astonished by this claim, turned and stared at her.

Sally wouldn't meet her eyes. 'Those weapons look old to me. Run down, are they? We haven't seen one fired . . . I know they're dead. *We can get you more.*'

Petra looked over at the kobold, who in turn looked – angry? Alarmed? If he had been supplying the weapons, he was being cut out of the deal, Jansson reflected. But she couldn't read his expression, if he had one.

Petra leaned forward, her great head thrust at Sally's face. Her nose wrinkled, wet, probing. 'You l-lie.'

'That's for you to decide.'

The moment of judgement hung in the air. Jansson sat still, feeling every ache of her treacherous body. Sally did not yield before Petra's glare.

At last Petra withdrew with a frustrated growl, and loped from the chamber, her sex-slave dog at her heels.

Sally delivered a noisy mock sigh. 'We live to fight another day . . .'

As the guards milled around, talking among themselves in growls and yaps, Jansson leaned over to Sally. 'What are you playing at?' But even as she asked she was thinking it through. She was a cop; there were clues here; connections formed in her mind. 'Has this got something to do with that pendant she wore, that was the spitting image of Joshua's Rectangles ring—'

Sally pressed a forefinger to her lips, but she smiled.

They were taken to a kind of suite at one end of the palace, with a communal area and a central hearth, and small rooms that could be shut off behind flaps of leather.

Finn McCool was put in here with the women. Sally brusquely pushed him inside one of the rooms and told him to stay put. The kobold cringingly deferred, as he tended to when close up and personal with a human. But Jansson wondered what resentment burned in that strange soul, resentment at the treatment he received from these superior creatures that evidently fascinated and repelled him at the same time.

Jansson picked a room at random. A pallet of straw had been set out on the floor, with blankets laid over it. There was no lavatory or wash basin, but a kind of well in the floor contained water that seemed clean. Jansson dumped her travel pack and fingered the blankets curiously. They seemed to be of woven bark. How were they made? She imagined beagles stripping and weaving bark with hands and teeth.

She went back out to the communal area, where beagles were laying out bowls of food on the ground around the hearth.

Sally sat on the floor, comfortably enough, studying the food. She glanced up at Jansson. 'How's your en suite?'

'I've been in worse flophouses. Right now I feel like I could sleep on concrete.'

Sally leaned closer and spoke more softly. 'Listen, Jansson, while we have a minute alone. We need a plan. To get ourselves out of this.'

'We could always just step away. As you said you could carry me out—'

'Of course. They've been casual about that, haven't they? They did take your Stepper box. Maybe they think we're like trolls, who won't step away if they leave a cub behind. But I suspect they're imposing their different way of thinking on us. *They don't use prisons*; that's not in their mind-set. They spoke about this tradition of the hunt. They're happy for wrong-doers to escape, right? To run for their lives, rather than be confined. That's the way they think. So their instinct isn't to lock us up. I guess they think that even if we do step, they'll come and hunt us down anyhow, carried on the back of kobolds. We'll see, if they try.

'But we're not going anywhere. Our business isn't done here. We need to normalize relations between humanity and these sapient dogs. We can't have the likes of the kobolds playing us off one against the other.'

Janssen glanced over at Finn McCool's cubbyhole. 'I agree,' she said fervently.

'Also there's still the issue of the trolls. If they're all congregating here, everything is—' Uncharacteristically she seemed to struggle for words. 'Out of balance, across the Long Earth. Somehow we have to resolve that. First things first, however. We need to cut that kobold out of his grubby trade, and we need some leverage.'

'You're talking about the rings. The one the Granddaughter wore, the one you and Joshua brought back from Rectangles.'

'Right. That's significant somehow. It all has to be connected, doesn't it? A ring from a world next door – a world the kobold can reach, but the beagles can't – high-tech weapons similarly retrieved from a stepwise world . . .'

Jansson tried to think it through. 'We only know one possible source of non-human high tech around here. The world called Rectangles, that nuclear pile. Right? And that's where you found the ring, identical to the

Granddaughter's. The simplest theory is that *that* is the source of the weapons.'

'I agree,' Sally said. 'Occam's razor.'

'And a cop's instinct. OK. But for some reason the kobold can't access more guns right now. If he could, he'd be handing them over already, wouldn't he?'

'It must be something to do with the rings. Why else would the Granddaughter have that one on display, around her neck? Maybe McCool needs rings to gain access, for some reason. He can't use the Granddaughter's any more—'

Jansson smiled. 'I see what you're thinking. Maybe Joshua's ring would work for him.'

'This is all guesswork, but it fits together. My own kobold contact did send me to Rectangles, not straight here. I always thought there might be some more old high tech on that dusty planet – damn it. We need that ring if we're to make anything of this. I'm going to have to go get it, the ring, off of Valienté's living room wall.'

'Go get it? Oh. You mean, step out of here.'

'I'll have to leave you here for a while. You're too ill – you'd only slow me down – I'm sorry. Anyhow one of us at least ought to stay, to prove we're not escaping.'

Jansson grimaced, trying to hide her alarm at the thought of being left here alone. 'I'll cover for you. They won't even notice you're gone.'

'Sure. And I'm hoping that Valienté also won't even notice when the damn ring has gone. The last thing we want is *him* showing up here . . .'

'He will come, if he can,' Jansson said firmly.

Sally seemed to think that over. 'If he does, maybe we can use him.'

But there was no more time to talk, for in walked the beagle Jansson remembered as the Granddaughter's adviser, with the human-language name Brian.

'Pleas-se.' Brian waved his hand-like paw in a very human gesture of welcome. 'Dine with me. I hrr-ave selected meal-ss which hrr-kobolds chose befor-rre.'

'We're not kobolds,' Sally snapped.

Jansson went and fetched a blanket, folded it up, and painfully lowered herself down on to it. She glanced over the bowls that had been already laid out. They appeared to be of carved wood. No pottery here?

'Nothing but meat to eat,' Sally said brusquely, inspecting the bowls' contents. 'Don't ask where the cuts come from. At least it's all cooked, more heavily than the beagles prefer, I suspect.'

'Bur-hhrned,' growled Brian. 'Free of all taste . . .'

'All except that one.' Sally pointed to a central bowl, filled with fat, pinkish morsels.

'Those cannot be cooked,' Brian said.

Jansson summoned up the energy to deal with more strangeness. 'Thanks for your hospitality.'

'Thank *you*,' Brian said.

'For what?'

'For being he-hhre. I, I have strange r-hhrole. Fits my st-hhrange mind. My nose follows, hhr, unusual scents. Granddaughter Petra toler-hhrates me, for my sometimes useful nose. And I, I a slave to he-hhrr scent, just like handsome fool Snowy . . . Females hhr-ule males. Same with hu-manss?'

'Yes,' said Sally. 'Some human males know it too.'

'I, I am st-rrange for beagle. Fo-rrever grow bo-hhred, the same old scents. Same old talk. I hhr-elish strangers

374

and strangeness. Other, other—' he searched for the phrase '– other *points of view*. What more differ-hrrent than beagle and kobold?'

'We aren't kobolds,' snapped Sally again.

'Sorry, so-hhry. Wrong term. What a shame we have not found each other before. Two types of mind, two ways of scenting the wo-hrrld. How much hhr-icher.

'Ex-ssample. This city named for our goddess, who is Hunter-rrh. We believe She is the Mother of Mothers. Her pack the Pack of Packs. As-ss Petra is Granddaughter, and there are Daughters over he-hhr, and Mother-hhr of Pack above them. Pack Mother-hrr lives far from here, rules many Dens. Hunter, Mother of Mothers, gave bi-hhrth to world, rules all, even Mother-hhrs. And when we die, our spi-hhrits flee our bodies, to be hunted by the Mother of Mothers, and taken back. What a-hhre your gods?'

Jansson said, 'We have many gods. Some of us have no god at all.'

'You see us as ba-hhrbaric. One step f-hhrom the wolf. Is our religion c-hhrude to you?'

Sally looked blank. 'I have no opinion.'

'Some of us despise wolf in us. As you pe-hrrhaps despise your ancestor animal, its ma-hrrk in you. We hunt. Kill. Big litters. Life cheap, wa-hrr common. Great slaughters. Cities empty, Dens fall. Then more litters, more little soldie-hhrs.'

'A cycle,' Sally said to Jansson, evidently fascinated. 'Boom and crash. They have big litters, lots of unloved warrior pups running around, lots of Daughters and Granddaughters competing to become this Mother, head of the nation. They fight, they have wars – they kill each other off, and when the population collapses the cycle begins again.'

'Like inner-city gangs,' Jansson said.

'Maybe. It's got to impede their progress. Technological, social. Maybe it's no wonder they're stuck at the Stone Age. And why they're easy marks for weapons dealers, like the kobold.'

'L-look-khh.' Brian leaned forward and picked out a pink blob from the central bowl. 'Unborn hrr-rabbit. Cut from the womb of its mother, f-hhresh. Deli . . . *delicacy*.' He rested the embryo between his teeth, bit down, and sluiced the blood into his mouth, like a connoisseur savouring a fine wine. 'Some of us despise wolf in us-ss. But the tass-te, oh, the tass-te . . .'

Suddenly the stink of the meat disgusted Jansson. She stood, stiffly. 'I must rest.'

'You a-hhre ill. Scent on you.'

'I apologize. Goodnight, sir. And you, Sally.'

'I'll look in later.'

'Not necessary.'

The few paces to her room seemed a long way. She thought she could feel the gaze of the kobold Finn McCool on her, watching from behind his curtain.

She slept badly.

Her head ached, her gut, her very bones. She took an extra dose of the painkillers in her pack, but it did no good.

She dozed.

She woke to find a wolfish face over her, in a dark barely alleviated by the starlight from the window above her pallet. Oddly she felt no fear.

'I am Li-Li.' The beagle pressed a finger to her lips. 'You a-hhre ill. I saw it. In pain?'

Jansson nodded. She saw no point in denying it.

'Please, let me . . .'

So Li-Li helped her. She arranged bundles of warm cloth around Jansson's body, and applied poultices of what looked like moss and lichen chewed to softness, to her belly, her back, her head. And Li-Li licked her face with her rough tongue, her neck, her forehead.

Gradually the pain receded, and Jansson slipped into a deeper sleep.

52

ABOUT A WEEK after Maggie's meeting with George and Agnes Abrahams, the *Benjamin Franklin* approached the Low Earths, heading for the Datum.

Maggie detected relief in the crew of the *Franklin* that, thanks to their wonky turbine, they were heading for some unscheduled home leave. Their tour of the Westward Long Earth was wearying. Day after day they crossed world after world of numbing emptiness – numbing at least for the city kids who made up most of the dirigible's crew – punctuated by calls to resolve one idiotic situation after another.

And *the trolls were gone*: how strange it continued to be to experience, even as seen from within the walls of a military vessel, a peculiar existential shift that cast a shadow over every world they visited.

Still, as the *Franklin* swam through the increasingly murky skies of the industrializing Low Earths, Maggie – even though she herself was a country girl – felt a warm tug of recognition, and wondered whether city living had some merit after all. The news as they approached home, however, was extraordinary. There was some kind of geological disturbance going on in stepwise versions of Yellowstone, across most of the Low Americas. Maggie found herself staring at images from East 2, of a herd of cattle choked by carbon dioxide emissions, and from West 3, of people being evacuated from threatened townships by twains. Isolated in the reaches of the Long Earth, Maggie and her crew had heard only the vaguest outernet hints that all this was going on.

Strange times, she thought, times of unbalance in the natural world and the human, on Datum Earth itself and far beyond.

Back at the Navy dirigible service's graving yard at Datum Detroit, the technicians were soon swarming all over the *Franklin*, along with gleaming diagnostics platforms with robot arms like a waltz of praying mantises. XO Nathan Boss and Chief Engineer Harry Ryan watched all this like hawks – along with Carl. The young troll wasn't allowed off the ship, the presence of trolls being problematic anywhere on the Datum, and the trolls being uncomfortable in this human-crowded world anyhow, but Carl was taking considerable interest in every spanner, wrench and robot test pod.

Even now, looking at Carl, it was hard for Maggie to remember that he wasn't some kind of chimp or gorilla. He was smarter than that, even if you left out the long call and the trolls' strange group intelligence. His own communication was more complex than any chimp's, and he could make and handle tools that would have been beyond the imagination of Cheetah. It was more useful, Mac had advised her, to think of trolls as more like human ancestors. Something between chimp and human. But these beasts, Mac reminded her, weren't living fossils, but had enjoyed millions of years of natural selection since splitting off from the line that led to humans. They weren't primitive humans; they were fully evolved trolls. Maggie was just gratified that *her* trolls, for now, had chosen to stick around.

The cat too, Shi-mi, took to stalking around the flayed-open carcass of the dirigible with every air of ownership and inspection. Maggie never *saw* Shi-mi communicating with a worker, or even one of the robots . . . She wasn't sure whether to be reassured or appalled by the cat's presence.

What she *was* faintly appalled by was the omnipresence of the Black Corporation. Every one of those spanners and wrenches that so fascinated Carl was marked with the logo of Black, or one of its subsidiaries.

Black seemed to have moved into the support of the dirigible fleet, and the US military infrastructure in general, in a much bigger and more visible way than she remembered from even before the *Franklin*'s mission began a couple of months back. Or maybe it was just that much more in her face, now she had a ship of her own. Black's relationship with the military was long-standing. He had after all donated the twain technology in the first place by making it open source, and was a prime contractor for all the armed services. Since abortive attempts to militarize his operations under eminent domain arguments some years before, his relationship with the military high command and purse-holders seemed to Maggie to have become, not just contractually unbreakable, but institutionalized.

Even so, now she thought about it, now she was so blatantly immersed in it, the situation made her uncomfortable.

That feeling got sharper when the job was done, and the yard boss sought Maggie out to tell her that the offending turbine two had been replaced, gratis, by a more modern Black Corporation model. She instinctively protested, but got no support from her chain of command.

And she remained suspicious when the *Franklin* was released from dock and made trial runs in the murky Datum sky. The ship was purring along like a sewing machine, running overall distinctly better than before. But she had Nathan Boss and Harry Ryan run a fresh systems and security check, stem to stern, just to make sure the Black people hadn't left any little surprises aboard, such as tracking devices or control cut-outs or overrides. Nothing showed up.

Not unless you counted the cat, Maggie thought. The damn thing had taken to sleeping, or at least simulating sleep, in a basket in Maggie's sea cabin. Somehow Maggie didn't have the heart to kick her out.

Harry Ryan's scan came through clean. Still Maggie remained suspicious.

That night, the *Franklin*'s last on the Datum before resuming its mission, Maggie was woken at three a.m. by an urgent message. According to patchy outernet reports leaking down from the High Meggers and beyond, the *Neil Armstrong* was lost.

53

MORNING, ON EARTH East 8,616,289:
Following Yue-Sai, her monitor pack on her shoulder, Roberta stepped gingerly over ground coated with a kind of green moss. They crossed a more or less open plain, under a cloudy sky, with the Chinese airships hanging silent above. There was no tall tree cover; the only significant vegetation was something like a fern, no more than waist height, with broad leaves spread low over the ground. The morning was bright, but the air was cold. Roberta was wrapped up in a quilted one-piece coverall and boots lined with wool, but the chill air stung her exposed skin, her cheeks, her forehead. Already Yue-Sai had nearly turned her ankle when she fell into the burrow of some subterranean animal. The animals turned out to be squirrel-like, although Roberta suspected they had features more like primitive primates than true squirrels. Well, primates or squirrels or something else entirely, they were everywhere, and you had to watch your step. It was not a very welcoming world. The navigators said that on this Earth the tectonic raft that carried South China was at a high latitude, halfway to the north pole. The geographers, straining for glimpses of the rest of the world from the sounding-rockets they sent up, said

they suspected that there was a supercontinent on the equator: South and North America and Africa jammed together, the interior desiccated, the global climate distorted.

Roberta had endured the boredom of the preparation for this latest jaunt, the training, the suiting-up, and had written off the dull, relatively data-poor hours of exploration that lay ahead. She knew it was important to apprehend these worlds physically. The first space engineers, whose biographies she had studied closely when seeking role models for her own career, had spoken of the need for 'ground truth', a sampling of conditions down on the ground of some planet or moon, to confirm or refute hypotheses drawn up from orbital inspection, or through telescopic observations. Ground truth, yes. She saw the need for it. And this was a very remote world, an exotic world, despite the brevity of the journey here. They had crossed the six million worlds since the planet of the crest-roos in no more than a week, with the airships' powerful drives propelling them forward in bursts of acceleration.

Even so she longed to be in her room on the ship, with her books and tablets. Safe inside her head. But she was not there, not for now. She was here. She focused on the real, physical world around her.

They climbed a bluff, beyond which, they knew from a hasty aerial survey, was a dry valley, and the spectacle they had come to witness. The shallow climb, the effort of lifting her feet safely over the lumpy ground, soon made Roberta pant.

Jacques, monitoring her progress from the *Zheng He*, noticed. 'I hope you haven't been skimping your exercise routines.'

Roberta took a deep lungful of air. 'I suspect the oxygen content is low.' She could hear the trolls singing in the background, a murmur in her earpiece.

Jacques said, 'The ship has atmospheric scientists who monitor the air quality before they crack the hatch. Turns out they've been watching the oxygen content fluctuate increasingly, the further out we've travelled. But here it's well within breathable limits.'

Wu Yue-Sai said sternly, 'But it did not occur to them to factor in the effects of physical exercise. That's unfortunately typical: overspecialization of departments and insufficient communication.'

'I believe the Captain is having words,' Jacques said dryly. 'If you'd rather come back in—'

'No, we're nearly there,' Yue-Sai said. She glanced back at Roberta, who nodded.

And as she approached the summit of the rising ground, Roberta could hear a kind of orchestra of disparate sounds: a bass rumbling as of heavy traffic, even like tanks, mixed in with a chorus of mournful bellows, and a percussion section of impacts, of clanks and clunks. Excitement built in Roberta, and she grinned at Yue-Sai. They both ran up the remaining slope and threw themselves flat on the mossy ground, so they could look down into the valley.

Where the tortoises walked.

This was what they had landed to see. A two-way flow of the animals was packed into the valley, all lumbering along, those to the right heading north, those to the left heading south. The biggest of them were *huge*, like tanks indeed, or even bigger, with shells the size of small houses that were battered, scarred – some had birds' nests built into folds and cracks on the shells, and Roberta wondered if those passengers had some kind of symbiotic relationship with their hosts. But she could immediately see that the tortoises came in a spectrum of all sizes scaling down from the big monsters, to 'giants' that wouldn't have looked out of place on the Galapagos Islands, to miniature sorts like the pets Roberta had seen people keep, even dwarf kinds she could have held in her hand. The smaller ones ran around the tree-trunk legs of the big lumbering monsters. The noise was cacophonous, from the squeaks of the smallest to great blasts from the titans, like the fog horns of supertankers.

Yue-Sai pointed out the little ones, and laughed. 'The babies are so cute.'

Roberta shook her head. 'They may not be infants at all. There are probably many species mixed up in there.'

'I suppose you are right. And I suppose we will never know what is what.' She sighed. 'So many worlds. So few scholars to study them. If only we had laboratories to produce self-replicating scientists, to explore all the worlds. Ah, but we do! They're called university campuses.'

Roberta smiled uncertainly.

Yue-Sai said, 'You don't get the joke? I suppose it was a little laborious. But is my English so bad?'

'It's not that. It's just that, Jacques and other teachers tell me, I am too smart for most jokes.'

'Really,' Yue-Sai said, straight-faced.

'There is an element of deception in many jokes, and then a reveal, of a truth which is surprising. I spot the deception too early. Which is why the comedy I prefer is—'

'Slapstick. Anarchic humour. Those Buster Keaton

films you watch. I understand now. Anyhow, all these worlds—'

'And all these tortoises! . . .'

They had discovered a whole sheaf of worlds of this kind. The further they got from the Datum, the stranger the worlds they encountered, the stranger the ecologies. In a way, tortoise worlds might have been anticipated. On the Datum the tortoise-turtle body plan was an ancient, ubiquitous and very successful one. Why *shouldn't* there have been worlds where tortoise lineages dominated?

'In many worlds,' Yue-Sai said, 'even on the Datum, you'll find tortoises behaving like this. Forming lines to get to waterholes, like the lake higher up this valley. Drinking their fill, enough to last months.'

'But not a line a hundred miles long.'

'No,' said Yue-Sai. 'And not a line running on what looks like a road, with a metalled surface.' Not that they'd been able to get close enough to check that out. 'And not a line with traffic police . . .'

These were individuals about the size of Galapagos giants. They stood on raised islands in the middle of the two-way flow, or in bays cut into the valley walls. Some of them had belts wrapped around their shells, with pockets, pouches. They even had tools, like whips that cracked occasionally, and things that looked like simple horns to Roberta, to amplify their calls. The function of these individuals was clear: to keep the tremendous flow moving peaceably. They would dive in, horns blaring, if there was a clash, or the two-way lanes got mixed up, or a little one fell under the feet of the giants. Somehow, amid a chaotic clatter of shells, everything got sorted out.

'We might have expected intelligence,' said Yue-Sai. 'I

have been studying. On the Datum, people learned that tortoises could solve mazes. At least, that was when people gave tortoises a *chance* to solve mazes, as opposed to eating them, or stifling them in "hibernation boxes". Perhaps there are great cities elsewhere on this world. Tortoise armies. Tortoise colleges . . . That thought makes me want to laugh, but I'm not sure why.'

'I don't believe we'll find anything too advanced,' Roberta said. 'Not locally.'

'Why not?'

'Look at the wardens' tools. They have similar functions, obviously, but differ in detail. See? The stone *here* is shaped differently from *there*. The braiding on the whip handle—'

'So what?'

'Tortoise culture must be different from ours,' Roberta said. 'Their reproduction patterns are different. If you are a tortoise you emerged from one of hundreds of eggs; you don't know your parents; you received no parental care. Their young may not be guided through family backgrounds and formal education as we are. Perhaps they compete for a right to live, and part of that competition is learning how to make tools. But that means every generation must more or less reinvent the culture from scratch.'

'Hmm. Thus limiting their overall progress, generation to generation. Maybe. That is a lot of supposition based on just a little data.'

Roberta had learned not to say things like *It's too beautiful a theory not to be true*. Once Jacques Montecute, overstressed, had told her that she should have the slogan 'Nobody Likes a Smart Alec' tattooed to her forehead in reverse, so she could be reminded of it every morning in the bathroom mirror. She contented herself with saying, 'It does fit with the likely physiology, and the evidence of the non-uniformity of the tools. But, yes, the theory needs more testing. It would be interesting to know what's going on nearer the equator in this world.'

Yue-Sai did a double take. 'Why so?'

'Because those tortoises that solved the mazes back on the Datum were allowed to do so in warm conditions. Tortoises are cold-blooded; they shut down in the cold, to some extent.'

'Oh. So maybe the behaviour we're witnessing here, in the cold, is—'

'Limited by temperature. They may be achieving much more in warmer latitudes. Do you think Captain Chen would sanction a journey south, towards the equator?'

'And risk getting shot down by some super-tortoise? I do not think so.' Yue-Sai packed away her equipment. 'Time to get back to the ship.'

Before they left, Roberta glanced across the valley, to the far wall where erosion had exposed the strata of the local sedimentary rocks. She could clearly see a marine deposit, a chalky layer embedded with flints, below a bed of gravel, and then above that a few yards of peat, under the mossy ground surface. She could read the geology. This region, now elevated, had once been under the sea. Later, ice had come and gone, leaving behind the gravel, and then the peat had been laid down over millennia of temperate climates ... This world, like all other worlds, had a story of its own, a story billions of years deep and probably not quite like any other in the Long Earth ensemble. A story that probably nobody would ever get around to unravelling, and all she would take away from this place was a few snapshots of tortoises.

She could only turn away.

Back at the airship Captain Chen was excited, and not about tortoises. 'Finally – finally! – we have the results back from the probes we sent into the Eastern Gap. You remember, more than six million worlds back.'

'Of course I remember.'

'You asked us to inspect the planets, Venus and Mars. And the scientists found—'

'Life.'

He seemed crestfallen. 'You knew? Of course you would know . . .'

On the Mars of the missing Earth East 2,217,643, there was oxygen and methane in the air, chemically unstable gases that must have been injected by the processes of life. There seemed to be some kind of vegetative covering on the lower ground of the northern hemisphere. And in the clouds of that copy of Venus, high, cool, full of water, chlorophyll had been observed. Earth-like plants, drifting in the Venusian sky.

No, Roberta wasn't surprised. Any Gap that could be reached by a stepping animal, even the most foolish of humanoids, was going to be a place where bacteria and other living organisms were regularly injected into space, if only accidentally, through the hole where Earth should be. Most such reluctant pioneers would die quickly, including the hapless humanoids if they couldn't step straight back – but some hardy bacterial spores, having hitched a ride on the stepping humanoids, might survive the radiation, the vacuum. And of those spores, some might ultimately drift into the skies of other worlds, and seed them. This was panspermia, the transfer by natural processes of life between the worlds. It was thought to be possible even in the Datum universe. How much easier panspermia must be in a Gap cosmos, with a way for life to reach space so much more easily than being blasted off by an asteroid impact.

No, Roberta wasn't surprised. She filed the confirmation away in the back of her mind, where a kind of model of the Long Earth, and all its facets, was slowly being assembled, fact by fact, deduction by deduction.

54

UNDER THE PROW of the airship *Shillelagh* as it ploughed West, the worlds ticked by, one every second, with hypnotic regularity. Bill paused the journey at recognized Jokers: at the anomalous worlds, flaws in the fabric of the Long Earth, where on a conventional journey travellers would hurry past, unseeing, eyes averted.

Even in the relatively generous, relatively settled worlds of the Corn Belt, in which could be found Reboot, Helen's family's home, there were Jokers. Early in the journey Bill stopped briefly at Earth West 141,759, where the multichannel radio receiver he kept running constantly blared out warnings in a multitude of languages and code formats. *Quarantine*, Joshua gathered through blistered eardrums: because it was the source of some particularly virulent pathogen, this whole world was under a quarantine administered by the UN, along with staff from the US's Plum Island Animal Disease Center. Any travellers should keep away from designated areas; otherwise they would be arrested, any materials impounded and destroyed, and they would be kept in confinement until decontamination procedures had been completed . . . It was a relief to move on and leave it behind.

'Are they serious, Bill? Can you really quarantine a whole Earth?'

'You can try. But *how* serious they are is another question. We have come across a few nasty viruses out in the Long Earth. Populations of birds and pigs, or birdy creatures and piggy creatures, are always reservoirs of bugs likely to be able to cross over and infect humanity, just as it's always been on the Datum. And you'd expect humans to have no immunity to such a disease coming from a stepwise world. The greatest threat is to the Datum and the Low Earths, of course, with their dense populations and travel networks. But Cowley and his gang of eejits use fears like this to whip up hostility to combers and trolls, like each one of us is a Typhoid Mary. You know, on worlds like this, they get doctors to volunteer to go in there and support trapped travellers, only to have their Stepper boxes confiscated, and they find they're not allowed out again . . .'

On they swept, with regular stuttering pauses.

Jokers weren't a lot of fun. Many were scenes of devastation one way or another: usually a lifeless ground under a sky that might be either obscured by ash or dust, or else glaring and empty, ozone-free, cloudless, a fierce blue. Bill had Just-So back-stories for many of these shattered worlds, pieced together from travellers' tales, comber legends, and occasionally some actual science field work.

The most common cause of such collapses, Joshua started to learn, was an asteroid impact. On long enough timescales, it was as if Earth drifted around inside a cosmic pinball machine. Bill lingered briefly at one heavily damaged world, West 191,248. The impact, only a couple of years back in this case, in central Asia, had been far from here; life close to ground zero was devastated, but the world as a whole was suffering under an asteroid winter.

But there were other types of calamity waiting to pounce. Earth West 485,671: a world locked in an Ice Age that had turned into a runaway glaciation, perhaps caused by the solar system drifting through a dense interstellar cloud that blocked the sun's light. Here the oceans were frozen down to the equator; the ice-shrouded landscapes glared brilliant white in sunlight that poured down from a blue sky empty of clouds, save for wisps that Bill said were probably carbon dioxide snow crystals. But the depths of the ocean, warmed by the Earth's inner heat, would stay liquid, and life would survive in dark underwater refuges until the volcanoes warmed the world again.

Earth West 831,264: here Joshua looked down on a rust-coloured, Mars-like landscape evidently bare of life, save for occasional streaks of purple slime. The air itself was stained red by the dust raised by incessant windstorms.

'What the hell happened here?'

'A gamma-ray burster. Well, that's our best guess. Probably caused by a kind of massive supernova, the collapse of a super-massive star into a black hole. Could have happened anywhere within thousands of light years. A storm of gamma rays would have stripped away the ozone layers and then fried the surface life.'

'*Boundless and bare, the lone and level sands stretch far away.*'

'What's that, Josh?'

'Just a stray memory of Sister Georgina.'

'In the long term life always bounces back one way or

another. But there's always the chance,' Bill said with grue-some relish, 'that we might step over on to some world just at the moment the big rock falls, or whatever. What's that in the sky? Is it a bird, is it a plane – d'oh!'

Joshua, oppressed by these charnel-house worlds, didn't feel much like laughing. 'We're still searching for Sally, right?'

'We're doing our best,' Bill said. 'That kobold did say he believed the trolls were hiding out in some Joker or other. The bad news is there are a *lot* of Jokers. The good news is there are a *lot* of combers out in those Jokers already.'

'Hiding from the man. Just like Sally.'

'That's the idea. Before we set off I sent word on ahead. I'm still hoping that if she's spotted, somebody will put the word out. There are a lot of radio hams out here; it's a good way to keep in touch across an undeveloped world. We'd hear them as we pass through. Of course some worlds are so badly beat up there is no ionosphere, and *that* theory breaks down.

'You really can't plan too definitely when it comes to combers. It's the nature of the beast. Combers! Some call them ridge runners or jackpine savages or mountain men, or hoboes or okies. In Oz they call 'em bushwhackers, the Brits say travellers. Once, in some parts, they were called wanderers. And you were *the* Wanderer, back then. Though not any more, buddy, you betrayed your own legend when you settled down to bake bread with the missus.'

That irritated Joshua. He had never wanted a legend of any kind. All he had ever wanted was to live his own life, on his own terms. Was he supposed to pander to some fan base? He felt like poking back at Bill, but he resisted the temptation. 'I get the idea. I appreciate you're doing your best.'

'I'm doing all there is to do. Unless you can figure out where she's gone after all . . . Anyhow, enough gabbing, I'm out of me head with the thirst up here. You want to crack a tube? Bring up another six-pack and I'll tell you the stories of a few more Jokers. Unless you want to watch a fillum. Just like back in the day with yer man Lobsang! Ah, go on, let's see a fillum . . .'

Joshua was mostly sceptical about Bill's Joker stories.

Such as what Bill told him of a Joker he called the Cueball. Joshua had actually glimpsed this one; they'd discovered it on his first journey out with Lobsang, nestling in the relatively domesticated Corn Belt. A world like a pool ball, utterly smooth, under a cloudless deep blue sky.

'I know a fella who knew a fella—'

'Oh, yes.'

'Who camped out on the Cueball for a bet. Just for a night. All alone. As you would. In the nip too, that was part of the bet.'

'Sure.'

'In the morning he woke up with a hangover from hell. Drinking alone, never wise. Now this fella was a natural stepper. So he got his stuff together in a blind daze, and stepped, but he says he sort of stumbled as he stepped.'

'Stumbled?'

'He didn't feel as if he'd stepped the right way.'

'What? How's that possible? What do you mean?'

'Well, we step East, or we step West, don't we? You have the soft places, the short cuts, if you can find them, but that's pretty much it. Anyhow this fella felt like he'd stepped a different way. Perpendicular. Like he'd stepped *North*.'

'And?'

'And he emerged on to some kind of other world. It was night, not day. No stars in the clear sky. No stars, *sort of*. Instead . . .'

'Your storytelling style really grates sometimes, Bill.'

Bill grinned. 'But I've got ye hooked, haven't I?'

'Get on with it. What did he see?'

'He saw all the stars. All of them. He saw the whole fecking Galaxy, man, the Milky Way. *From outside* . . . Still in the nip he was, too.'

That was the trouble with combers, Joshua was concluding. They were just expert bullshitters. Maybe they spent too much time alone.

And the search for the trolls, Jansson and Sally went on and on . . .

Sally. Once, when they were tethered for the night at some equable world, he thought he *smelled* her. As if she had come and gone while he slept. In the light he searched the gondola, and the area on the ground around the twain, but found no sign of her presence. Just a dream, he thought. He resolved never to tell Helen about it.

55

'ONE OF THOSE troll creatures really messed up a couple of guys here, and folks really don't like that, but you know what? When it saw me the damn thing rushed up to me, and danced around me like it was a friend! . . .'

So the *Benjamin Franklin* had got yet another call, to yet another dumb incident concerning trolls. As Mac remarked, 'You wouldn't think there'd be enough trolls left around to trigger all this trouble.'

The place was called Cracked Rock. Judging from the transmitted report, there was a mayor, but he was resident at some stepwise companion community, leaving the local sheriff, a Long Earth tyro, in charge. The unfortunately named Charles Kafka was new to the job, a refugee from the big city – hoping for a nice easy ride to pension age, by the sound of it, in some Old-West-nostalgia-type small town. Now it had all gone wrong, and he was panicking.

Cracked Rock was a speck on an unprepossessing world some distance beyond the Corn Belt. Not many steps for the *Franklin* to travel from its last destination, but it seemed to take an age to cross a barren-looking copy of America before coming on the township's lights, bright in the dusk, by the bank of a river. Now Maggie looked down on a tent city – there was no shame in that, many a flourishing city had started out as tents and shacks – with a church, unfinished by the look of it, dirt roads scraped across the surrounding landscape of sparse scrub. The sheriff's office looked like the best-finished building in town.

As the twain descended, the sheriff himself came out to meet it, accompanied by a cocky-looking younger man – and a juvenile troll, in chains. Maggie wondered if they'd done something to the troll to stop it stepping away. A few more folk drifted in from the township for a look-see.

With Nathan Boss and a couple of midshipmen at her side, Maggie cut short the introductions and asked Sheriff Kafka to sum up what had happened.

'Well, Captain, some trolls were walking past the township, a band of 'em – they know enough not to go too close – but there were some boys who intercepted them, including Wayne here, just looking for some fun, you know how good ol' boys are, but they picked on a little one and the trolls fought back, and *this* one,' he indicated the beast in the chains, 'laid out Wayne's brother. And then—'

Maggie had heard the same dumb story twenty times on this mission. Impatient, infuriated, she held up a hand. 'You know what? I've had enough of this. Midshipman Santorini.'

'Captain?'

'Go back to the ship. Bring out Carl.'

Santorini wasn't the type to argue. 'Yes, Captain.'

They waited in silence in the gathering dusk, the five minutes it took Santorini to comply. When Carl arrived, accompanied by Santorini, he hooted softly at the young troll in the chains.

Maggie faced the cub. 'Carl, I hereby appoint you to the crew of the *Benjamin Franklin*. For now, you've the rank of acting ensign. Santorini, make a note. XO, when we get back aboard, make it so.'

'Yes, Captain.'

'And, Nathan – give me your mission patch.'

The emblem of Operation Prodigal Son was an astronaut-type shield showing the dirigible hovering over a stylized chain of worlds. Nathan ripped the patch off his uniform, and Maggie used her own dog-tag chain to fix it to the troll's arm. Carl hooted, apparently in pleasure.

'Nathan, try to tell him what we've done here. Although I think he knows already.'

Nathan deployed his troll-call – the townsfolk stared curiously at the instrument – and started murmuring to the troll about being part of the *Franklin* family.

Maggie stared around at the gawking hicks with distaste. 'That, citizens, is what *we* think of trolls.'

Sheriff Kafka looked utterly out of his depth. 'So what now? You want Wayne to give his testimony?'

'Hell, no. I want to hear the testimony of the troll.'

The hicks goggled as Nathan used the troll-call to converse carefully with the captive.

'He remembers the incident. Well, of course he does. They know to avoid cultivated fields. They weren't *in* the fields. But a couple of the young were lagging, and the band scattered. Then these boys found them. Throwing stones. Trying to trip up the young. The trolls didn't fight back . . . You understand, Captain, you don't really get a linear narrative out of a troll. It's more impressions, bits of emotion. I'm having to interpolate—'

'That's OK, Nathan. The picture is clear enough.'

Wayne snorted. 'What the heck is this? It's a joke. It's only a talking animal.'

That got roughly translated through the troll-call. And the speed with which Carl moved, grabbing Wayne's leg and holding him upside down by one hand, was remarkable.

Maggie smiled. 'Your point is refuted, I think. And your testimony. Sheriff, it's not your people who deserve respect from the trolls but the other way around.' She tilted her head to look at the inverted Wayne. 'As for you, I'll leave you in the hands of your parents, in the hope of a better future.'

The boy wriggled in the grasp of the placid troll, all but scraping his scalp on the ground. 'Screw you. Everybody knows about you and your damn ship. It's all over the outernet. Captain Troll Lover.'

She felt her blood rise. But she said calmly, 'Drop him, Carl.'

And she turned away, heading back to the ship, before the boy hit the ground with a cry of pain.

56

THE *BENJAMIN FRANKLIN* hovered over the township of Cracked Rock through the night.

Still fuming from the sideswipe from that kid Wayne – how could a slimeball like him in some dump world like this know so much about her? – Maggie called her chief engineer. 'Harry, who's the nerdiest geek you have down there? You know the kind—'

'Ensign Fox,' Ryan said without hesitation.

'Fox. Toby, right? Listen – send him up.'

As she waited for Fox she scanned his personnel file. He really was a geek, of the barely tamed variety: a wretched sailor, but an IQ of a zillion. Just what she needed.

When he arrived, Maggie demanded, 'Ensign Fox. How often do you guys do a serious systems scan? I mean, sweep for bugs, Trojans, all that hacker shit?'

Fox seemed distracted by the presence of Shi-mi, who was watching from a basket on the floor. But he looked hurt to be asked the question. 'Well, Captain, we in Tech run sweeps more or less all the time. Of course we're mostly running Black Corporation software; it's self-policing, though we do have some independent firewalls which—'

'Black Corporation software. I bet we uploaded even

more of it back in Detroit, right? System upgrades, replacements.'

'Well, yes, Captain. That's routine.'

'And I know I had Harry scan the ship from stem to stern after the refit. But still – how much control does Black software have of this ship? Give me a non-technical answer.'

Fox thought for a minute, his small face crumpled. 'Well, Black is the principal contractor. Their software – it suffuses the *Franklin*, Captain.'

Maggie said, 'The ghost in the machine. Seems to me we leak like a damn sieve, Ensign. Even if it is under our level of detection.'

He didn't seem too perturbed, as if that were known and accepted. 'Yes, Captain.'

'Thank you, Fox. By the way, how's the Aegis census going?'

Fox's small face worked as he sought a concise answer. She imagined Harry Ryan beating that kind of verbal skill into the head of a boy who must once have suffered from the hyper-volubility of the typical nerd. In the end he said simply, 'Frustratingly incomplete, Captain.'

'Well, keep at it. Dismissed, Ensign.'

'Captain.'

When he'd gone she came around the desk, grabbed the cat, and set her on the desk. 'That guy George Abrahams and his damn troll-calls.'

'Captain?'

'This is supposed to be a military mission. *This is my command.* I bet every communication we attempt with the trolls is relayed back to him.'

'I couldn't say—'

'You're probably riddled with bugs too, aren't you? Listen, kitty litter. I want you to set me up another meeting with Abrahams. Understand? I've no doubt you can do it.'

The cat only mewed softly.

The next day, she got through her business at the township as quickly as possible. That mayor from a couple of worlds over, summoned at last, seemed totally in awe of Maggie, promised to do his best to learn the lessons of the event, and offered the *Benjamin Franklin* crew the freedom of the local stepwise cities, which Maggie politely declined.

She had one more meeting with Sheriff Kafka outside his office. When he tried to apologize for his screw-up, she slapped him on the back. 'You did your best last night. You've got a lot to learn – but then, who hasn't?'

He nodded gratefully. 'Godspeed, Captain.'

And now for George Abrahams.

She couldn't keep her intention to meet him again a secret from her senior officers. So she wasn't very surprised when Joe Mackenzie showed up in her sea cabin with a couple of coffees, and sat, watching her like an X-ray machine. 'Patient confidentiality guaranteed.'

Maggie said, 'You know what the issue is, Mac. Do *you* trust the Black Corporation? . . .'

'What's to trust?'

'I think someone is up to something.'

Mac grinned. 'Well, *everybody* is up to *something*. And the military have been in bed with Black for years. Which is why he was on the podium with Cowley when our mission was launched.'

'Yeah, but does that give Black the right to monitor us routinely? This is a military expedition, Mac. I get the impression that everybody from the Pentagon on down is turning a blind eye.'

Mac shrugged. 'So Black has a lot of power. So have military contractors had all the way back to World War Two. That's the reality of life, I guess. I mean, there's no evidence of malice on the part of Black, is there? Or a lack of patriotism.'

'No, but . . . Now it's personal, Mac. This is my ship, my mission. *Me.* It's just a feeling – but it's like I have a search-light on me. Do you think I'm losing my way?'

'No. I think you're following your instinct, and it's never failed you in the past.'

'What, even about keeping the cat?'

'Except for that,' said Mac.

57

THE AIRSHIPS *ZHENG He* and *Liu Yang* steadily forged towards their target of twenty million worlds East of the Datum.

They passed more unprecedented milestones: ten million, twelve, fifteen million steps. Now they were crossing an extraordinary span of the Long Earth, of this great probability tree whose twigs and leaves were whole clusters of worlds; now they were reaching branches of that tree with a very deep divergence from those that led to an Earth anything like the Datum. It became impossible for the crews of the airships *Zheng He* and *Liu Yang* even to rely on breathable atmospheres in the worlds they visited. The oxygen levels fluctuated significantly, from, rarely, concentrations so high that spontaneous combustion, even of wet vegetation, must have been a hazard to unwary visitors, to, more often, worlds where the oxygen level was no more than a trace, and the land on the backs of the dancing continents was much less green. A more subtle danger, Roberta learned, was too high a concentration of carbon dioxide, ultimately lethal for humans.

And life had less of a grip on many of these Earths. They found whole bands of worlds where the land was bare altogether, where its colonization by plants from the sea had apparently never happened, let alone its later 'conquest' by wheezing lungfish. All but featureless, all but identical, these drab worlds passed, day after day, unchanging even at the airships' tremendous stepwise speed.

Drab or not, Roberta for one was fascinated by the evolving panoramas of land, sea and sky she glimpsed through the windows of the observation deck, and intrigued by the closer-up glimpses of the worlds they stopped at to sample in more detail – not that she was allowed down to the surface on these hazardous worlds. Yet something in her, something weak and to be despised, recoiled from the bombardment of strangeness. After all, from here, even the whole of the Ice Belt, the band of periodically glaciated worlds of which the Datum seemed to be a reasonably typical member, seemed very small, very narrow, and very far away, spanning much less than one per cent of the monumental distance they had already travelled.

She spent more time alone in her cabin, trying to integrate the sheer flood of data hitting her. Or she would sit with the trolls on the observation deck, listening to their crooning, even though this kept the rest of the crew away from her – even Lieutenant Wu Yue-Sai, though not the loyal Jacques Montecute.

For his part, Jacques watched Roberta uncomfortably. He even felt a stab of guilt; this expedition might be too much for her after all. The horror of the Long Earth, in the end: Roberta was just fifteen years old, and the very scale of it might overwhelm one so young, no matter how smart.

* * *

On July 6, 2040, the Chinese ships reached their nominal target of Earth East 20,000,000 – a world which turned out to be unprepossessing, barren, ordinary. They planted a stone cairn with a plaque, took a few photographs, and prepared to turn back.

Captain Chen assembled his senior crew and guests on the observation deck of the *Zheng He*, for a party to celebrate the moment. The trolls sang a new song, playfully taught them by Jacques – 'China Girl'. Chen even broke out the alcohol, for once. But Jacques advised Roberta not to make this the day she first tried champagne. Without regret, she stuck to her orange juice.

Lieutenant Wu Yue-Sai, in full dress uniform, neat and pretty, linked arms with Roberta. 'I am so happy to have achieved so much, with you, my partner in discovery.'

Captain Chen strutted over. 'Indeed. And no doubt we will learn even more during our long return journey to the Datum. So many worlds to revisit and sample. Twenty million of them!'

Roberta considered that carefully. 'I feel my time would be better spent integrating the data I have already accumulated.'

'"Integrating the accumulated data"! Is that all you wish to do?' Captain Chen walked up to Roberta, looked up into her face.

He was an impulsive, somewhat childish man, Jacques judged, and evidently he was angered by Roberta's humourlessness, her failure to laugh at his jokes, perceiving that his moment of triumph had been spoiled.

'Clever child, clever child. But what a pompous creature you are. Clever, yes. But do you believe you are better than us mere mortals? *Homo superior* – is that what you understand yourself to be? Must we make way for you?'

She did not reply.

Chen reached up and wiped a thumb over her cheek; it came away moist. 'And if it is so, why are you crying?'

Roberta fled.

She didn't come down to the observation deck the whole of the next day.

A little before midnight, as he was preparing for sleep himself, Jacques went to her cabin door and knocked. 'Roberta?'

No reply. He listened for a while, and heard the sound of sobbing. Captain Chen had discreetly given Jacques a pass key in case of emergency. Now he swiped the card and opened the door.

The room itself was as orderly as ever, the single lamp burning over her workstation, her little heap of tablets and a few precious printed books, her notes. Charts on the wall, showing their progress across the Long Earth. No photographs, paintings, toys, no souvenirs save for science samples – none of that for Roberta Golding.

Barefoot, wearing T-shirt and sports slacks, Roberta was curled up on her bed, face away from the door.

'Roberta?' Jacques went over. She was surrounded by scrunched-up tissues; she had been weeping for a while, evidently. And she had bruises on her temple. He'd seen this in her before; she would hit herself, as if trying to drive out the part of her that wept at night. He'd thought she'd grown out of it, however. 'What's wrong? Is it what Captain Chen said to you?'

'That fool? No.'

'Then what? What are you thinking about?'

'The crest-roos.'

'The what?'

'The reptilian-mammalian assemblage we found on East two million, two hundred thousand—'

'I remember.'

'All doomed to be eradicated by a hypercane. An accident of weather. Probably gone already. Scrubbed away like a stain.'

He imagined that dreadful perception building up in her head, all these long days. He sat on the bed and touched her shoulder. At least she didn't flinch away. 'Remember Bob Johansen's English class?'

She sniffled, but at least she stopped crying. 'I know what quote you mean.'

'Go on, then.'

'*Oh God, I could be bounded in a nutshell—*'

He continued, '*And count myself a king of infinite space—*'

'*Were it not that I have bad dreams,*' she whispered.

He knew how she felt. It was the way he felt himself, sometimes, if he woke in the small hours, at three a.m., a time when the world seemed empty and stripped of comforting illusion. A time when you *knew* you were a mote, transient and fragile in a vast universe, a candle flame in an empty hall. Luckily the sun always came up, people stirred, and you got on with stuff that distracted you from the reality.

The problem for Roberta Golding was that she was too smart to be distracted. For her, it was three a.m. all the time.

'Do you want to watch your Buster Keaton movies?'

'No.'

'How about the trolls? Nobody can be unhappy around a troll. Shall we go see them?'

There was no reply.

'Come on,' he said. He got her up, draped a blanket over her shoulders, and led her to the observation deck.

There was a single crewman on watch here, reading a book; she nodded to Jacques and looked away. The trolls were slumbering in a big heap near the prow. The infants were asleep, and most of the adults. Three or four were murmuring their way through a song about not wearing red tonight, because red was the colour that my baby wore . . . Silly, but with easy, pretty multi-part harmonies. The Chinese crew tended to keep their distance from the beasts. Or, perhaps, the trolls kept them away, subtly. But they welcomed Jacques and Roberta.

So Jacques sat on the carpeted floor with Roberta, and they snuggled up to the warmth of the big creatures' furry bellies. Immersed in the trolls' strong musk, they might have been at home in Happy Landings, if not for the strange skyscapes that swept past the windows.

'This is no consolation,' Roberta murmured, hiding her face. 'Just mindless animal warmth.'

'I know,' Jacques said. 'But it's all we have. Try to sleep now.'

58

CAPTAIN MAGGIE KAUFFMAN'S requested meeting with George Abrahams came to pass only a few days after her request of the cat, not particularly to her surprise. They arranged to rendezvous at a community further West, in a stepwise Texas, a town called Redemption – a location conveniently on the *Franklin*'s route to Valhalla, where all the Operation Prodigal Son dirigibles were now being summoned for the showdown with the Declaration-of-Independence 'rebels'.

Redemption turned out to be quite a large settlement, and one of the more grown-up ones – the kind with a sawmill boasting a zero-fatality record on a billboard. Maggie was sure the locals would already have registered their township's existence with the appropriate bureaux, and certainly would never have troubled the likes of the *Benjamin Franklin*. She happily ordered an R&R break for the crew, but made sure Nathan Boss had the MPs on the watch for trouble.

And then she waited. She even interrogated the cat: 'OK, where's Abrahams?'

The cat said softly, 'You don't find George Abrahams. Dr Abrahams finds you.'

After a couple of hours there came a ping from the duty

officer. A car was waiting for her by the access ramp.

It looked like a British Rolls-Royce, though curls of steam seemed to be seeping from under the hood. A man in black was standing beside an open door, with the air of a driver to the wealthy classes.

And in the car, when she climbed in, was George Abrahams. Somehow he looked bigger than she remembered, more imposing – no, *younger*, she thought.

He smiled as the car pulled away. 'The car's operated by the restaurant.'

'What restaurant?'

'You'll see. Nice sense of style, don't you think? Even if it is a steampunk limousine . . . Are you all right, Captain?'

'I'm sorry. It's just that you seem . . . younger.'

Abrahams smiled, and whispered, 'Well, it is all a façade, as we both know very well.'

Maggie found that faintly sinister, and it triggered something of the paranoia she seemed to be developing. Before disembarking, she'd slipped a locator into her uniform pocket, and now she was glad of it. 'I can't believe that you intend anything like a kidnap. I must tell you that my ship—'

'Don't be melodramatic, Captain. Look, we're nearly there. It really isn't a very big town, is it? Well, most Long Earth communities aren't, yet. Sometimes we forget how new all this is – that Step Day was just a generation ago.'

She was relieved to find they were indeed pulling up at a restaurant. Inside, she was impressed by the decor: heavy on stone and massive timbers in the usual colony-world style, but still elegant. Obviously some budding entrepreneur had realized that even in the reaches of the Long Earth people sometimes wanted a touch of class.

And the Chardonnay was excellent.

As they sat together in a booth for two, she raised a glass, ironically. 'So who should I be drinking to? Who are you, Mr Abrahams? Am I having dinner with the Black Corporation?'

'Actually, Captain Kauffman, the answer to your question is *no* – essentially. Though I do work with them and through them, I suppose – well, I told you that. I like to think of myself as working on behalf of humanity. And indeed on behalf of the troll nation, two fine species kept apart by stupidity. And that is why, Captain Kauffman, you have come to my attention, mine and that of a few others.'

She felt angry, exposed. 'What others? Douglas Black?'

'Certainly Douglas Black. Captain, you must think of yourself as a valued long-term investment. One of several, in fact.'

Fuming, she didn't reply.

Abrahams said now, 'You've certainly fulfilled the promise *I* saw in you.'

'What promise? When?'

'When they gave you command of the snazzy new *Benjamin Franklin* – despite a rather patchy official career record up to that point. Now, please don't be offended when I tell you that I had a hidden hand in that. I can tell you now that one of the selection panel disliked your outspokenness over your family's atheism, another even today has an antiquated view about women in senior positions . . .'

'I can't believe you had any influence over Admiral Davidson.'

'Not at all. But he needed support from the panel. Well.

413

All I can say is that, even in the depths of the Pentagon, levers can be pulled. Would you like another drink?'

'So I've been manipulated.'

'As for your handling of the trolls – did you know that you are actually featured in the long call now? "The woman who let trolls fly . . ."'

'Manipulated,' she repeated. 'My whole life, my whole career, it sounds like. How am I supposed to feel about that? Grateful?'

'Oh, not manipulated. Just – moved into the right position. It is up to you to take the opportunity offered, or not. After all, even within the parameters of your military mission, as a twain Captain you have had a great deal of autonomy. Your decisions are your own; your character is your own. You are who you are. Black, and I, and indeed Admiral Davidson, believe in giving the brightest and the best full freedom to operate. Anything else would be a betrayal.

'Of course you are *watched*. We are all watched, in this technology-soaked age. What of that? But as to perceived "manipulation" – we, all of us, all of mankind, face enormous challenges, an unknown and unknowable future. Isn't it better that we of good heart should work together, than not? Look, Captain Kauffman, all of this need make no difference to how you approach your work, when you go back to the ship after our conversation is over. Indeed, I would not expect it to.'

'I can't quit, can I?'

'Would you, if you could?'

She left that hanging. 'And are you going to tell me who you are?'

He seemed to think that over. 'The question has no real meaning, my dear. Now – shall we order?'

When the limo returned her, dropping her a short distance from the *Benjamin Franklin*, she saw the reassuring outline of Carl, standing by the access ramp. As she approached he actually saluted – quite professionally, too. She was careful to acknowledge.

It was late, and there was no alarm in evidence, so after a brief diversion to the bridge she made for her cabin. The cat was curled up beside the bunk. She was actually purring in her sleep – if indeed she was sleeping at all.

George Abrahams – not that Maggie remotely imagined that was his authentic identity. *Douglas Black*. Levers being pulled. No, strings being jerked, and Maggie Kauffman was the puppet. Well, there was little to do but accept it. That, she thought, or find a way to leverage her new 'partnerships' to her own advantage.

She got into bed without disturbing the cat.

59

LOBSANG LOVED TO talk – and indeed, to listen too, if you could keep up with him. In the weeks they spent crossing stepwise copies of the Pacific Ocean together, en route to New Zealand, Nelson came to understand fully that Lobsang was in a position to know *everything* that was worth knowing. He tried to imagine how the periodic synching of Lobsang's various iterations must feel – as if, metaphorically, they all met up in some big hall somewhere, all talking at once, communicating their disparate experiences with frantic urgency.

As a result the twain ride to a stepwise New Zealand passed pleasantly enough for Nelson. He even found he was able to put aside the idea that Lobsang, and the shadowy entities behind him, saw him as a 'valuable long-term investment' – along with many others, he supposed, a shadowy community of tentative allies, whose very names, he imagined, he might never learn.

Still, like all journeys, this one came to an end, sixteen days after their departure from Wyoming.

Nelson had visited Datum New Zealand many times. In this remote world, some seven hundred thousand steps West of the Datum, the Land of the Long White Cloud was evidently sparsely inhabited if at all, and its green mountains, its crystal skies, were unspoiled, and a magnificent sight from the air.

Heading west, the twain drifted away from the coastline and out to sea. Finally it slowed over a small island, a shield of green and yellow on the breast of this version of the Tasman Sea.

'So?' Nelson asked. 'What are we here to see?'

'Look down,' Lobsang's disembodied voice advised him.

'Something on that island?'

'It's not an island . . .'

Through the twain's excellent telescopes Nelson saw forest clumps, and a fringe of what looked like beach, and animals moving – what looked like horses – *elephants* – even a dwarf giraffe? An eclectic mix . . . And, more excitingly, people, on that strange beach. The seawater near by was turbid, mildly turbulent, and evidently full of life.

And this 'island' had a wake.

'It's not an island,' Nelson said at last. 'It looks *alive.*'

'You have it. A complex, compound, cooperative organism, a multiplex creature travelling north-east, as if determined to cross the Pacific . . .'

'A living island!' Nelson laughed, unreasonably delighted. 'An old legend, come to pass, if it's so. Saint Brendan, you know, crossing the Atlantic, is supposed to have landed on the back of a whale. That was the sixth century, I believe. There are similar tales in a Greek bestiary of the second century, and later in the *Arabian Nights*—'

'And now the reality. Nelson, meet Second Person Singular.'

The grammar made Nelson wince, although he picked up the reference to the notorious discovery of the *Mark Twain*. 'So what now?'

'We go visit.'

'We?'

The door to the gondola lounge deck opened, and in walked Lobsang, shaven head, orange robe – at first glance the Lobsang Nelson had met in Wyoming.

Nelson asked, 'This is your "ambulant unit"?'

'And fully waterproof. Come . . .'

They made their way to the stern of the ship, and the hatch through which Nelson had been winched aboard at the start of the voyage.

'We will be perfectly safe down there by the way,' Lobsang said now. 'Even should you choose to go scuba diving around the rim of the carapace.'

'Are you crazy? I've been in these waters before. Sharks, box jellyfish—'

'You'd come to no harm.' Lobsang pressed a button, and a dinghy folded itself out of a compartment, inflated, and dangled over the open hatch from a winch. 'I've visited this assemblage of life many times before, and I can assure you of that. Now, come make some new friends.'

Inside five minutes they were both clambering out of the dinghy, and on to the carapace of Second Person Singular.

Not that it felt like that. It felt as if they were climbing up a sandy beach. The 'ground' was solid under Nelson's feet, as if rooted deep in the rocky fabric of the Earth, like any island.

He looked around at a beach littered with sand and broken shells, clumps of forest. There was a fresh breeze; this hemisphere was emerging from its winter. He smelled salt and sand and seaweed, and a warmer, wetter scent of vegetation from the interior. The scents, the colours, the blue of the sky and sea, the green of the trees, were overwhelming, vivid. 'It's like Crusoe's island.'

'Exactly. But mobile. And – look there.'

A flap in the ground, earth underpinned by some kind of shell – yes, part of a tremendous carapace – opened up gently, like a yawning hatch, and a dozen or so humans emerged, grinning, climbing some kind of stair. Of all ages, they were naked and bronzed like athletes. A couple of children stared at Nelson.

One woman stepped forward, a red flower in her hair, still smiling, and said in good if oddly accented English, 'Welcome. What news of home? Please mister please, if you have any tobacco, please please . . .'

Lobsang was smiling indulgently.

Nelson managed to ask, 'Who the hell are these people?'

'Well,' said Lobsang, 'since this lost beast has evidently wandered into the oceans of the Datum itself, at least several, I suspect, are descendants of the crew of the *Mary Celeste* . . .'

Whether Nelson was supposed to take that literally or not, he got the idea.

Soon he found himself sitting awkwardly in a circle of very interested, very naked people, anxious to know about what was happening back on the Datum Earth. They sat close to what looked like a hearth – the fire was set on slabs of stone, no doubt in deference to the pain receptors of the back of their host, and Nelson quietly reminded

Lobsang that Saint Brendan had caused his whale-island to submerge with the sting of a carelessly lit fire . . .

The inhabitants' language seemed to be a Creole made up of mostly European tongues, but dominated by English, and not difficult to understand. Nelson told them what he could think of about recent developments on the Datum. They smiled and listened, bland, clean-shaven, well fed, stark naked.

For a break they were served halved coconut shells, brimming with milk.

Lobsang told Nelson that in the course of previous visits he had been able to make some direct contact with the island beast itself, it being similar in many respects to the original First Person Singular. *How* he achieved this contact he wouldn't say. The beast carried about a hundred human passengers. Some arrived as a result of a shipwreck or similar accident – and left by dying, or waiting until the end of the beast's 'cycle', as Lobsang called it, the length of time this apparently benevolent kraken took to do its rounds, when the people could disembark on some shore they might turn into a home.

But of course, as Nelson could see from the infants who sat before him staring with open curiosity, this little community was a living one. People were born here – and, presumably, some lived out their lives and died, all without ever setting foot, perhaps, off the back of this patient creature. They saw nothing strange about their itinerant home, or their way of life; it was only in discussions with Lobsang that he began to understand himself.

'These people are nurtured,' Lobsang said. 'Cherished. Every creature in the vicinity of Second Person Singular is docile in the extreme. It is as if this creature of close cooperation is surrounded by a looser cloud of mutual trust. Oh, one must eat, the occasional small fish might be snapped up, but Second Person Singular will not harm, or allow to be harmed unnecessarily, any higher creature. And in particular, no human.'

'If something this size ever got into major transport routes, especially on the Datum, there'd be trouble.'

'Oh, true. These beasts – I've called them *Traversers* – generally know enough to keep away from the Datum. As far as I can tell this particular specimen has got lost; it has strayed too close to the Datum, perhaps even passing into the Datum itself. At the moment it is trying to get to a place which I translate as "sanctuary" which, curiously enough, is close to Puget Sound. When we leave I intend to leave behind an iteration of myself, to navigate it to a place of safety. Most of its brethren, like First Person Singular, appear to dwell much further out from the Datum. Perhaps there is some – centre – in the remote Long Earth.'

'In the digests that were circulated about the beast that the *Mark Twain* travellers – well, *you*, I suppose – called First Person Singular, you suggested that the creature travels the Long Earth making a sort of audit. A stocktaking!'

'It's as good a first guess as any. There seem to be various different subspecies, none as large or as threatening as the original First Person Singular, however. Not all of them have this kind of shell-like carapace for example. All of them are themselves colony organisms, like Portuguese men o' war writ large – but they *grow*, they add to themselves by collecting specimens from the land and sea, some taking passengers as you see here, some incorporating them into the greater organism, like First Person Singular. And they are sapient, to some degree. Of course sapience implies purpose.'

'What purpose?'

Lobsang shrugged, a little artificially. 'Perhaps they are indeed collectors. Latter-day Darwins, or their agents, scooping up interesting creatures for – well, for science? To populate some tremendous zoo? Simply for their aesthetic appeal? You'll observe that most of the animals gathered here are of a similar body weight, within an order of magnitude or two – no blue whales, of course, and very few mice or rats. As if selectively sampled. But that may be too narrow a perspective. It seemed to me that the only goal of First Person Singular was to learn, to grow – goals shared with all minded creatures. But perhaps *she* was a special case . . .'

Whatever the purpose of all this, the human population considered it not a bad deal, as far as Nelson could tell. According to Lobsang, their living home looked after them even when it found it necessary to submerge: it took its animal and human passengers into air-filled chambers inside its carapace.

'Not that it submerges too often,' Lobsang said. 'Bad for the vegetation on its back, not to mention the layer of topsoil it accumulates . . . It's like an unending cruise, don't you think?'

'Hmm. The *Titanic* without the iceberg.'

'Lots of good company, plenty of seafood and occasionally other maritime fare including oysters and the occasional seal – but never dolphins, Nelson – oh, and plenty of sex.'

Nelson had guessed that, given the embarrassing

attention he himself was getting from a number of young women. 'And the people?'

'Nelson, there are billions in the suffering worlds of mankind who would think themselves blessed if they found themselves on this living shore.'

Nelson grunted.

Lobsang inspected him. 'Ah, you don't approve, do you? My dear Nelson, I see it in your eyes and in every expression. You, my friend, are a Puritan, privately aghast at the situation; you are thinking that mankind shouldn't live like this – there is a lack of striving which you find distasteful, yes? This is at the root of your unease about the Long Earth itself, I suspect. It's too easy. Mankind, you believe, should be always looking towards the stars, ever striving, learning, growing, *bettering* itself, challenging the infinite.'

Nelson stared at Lobsang's face, which showed deadpan with just a hint, a tiny scintilla, of humour. What was the human and what was the computer? 'You are disturbingly perceptive.'

'I'll take that as a compliment.'

60

THEY STAYED ABOARD Second Person Singular for some days.

It was a pleasurable enough interval, but Nelson did find it hard to relax into a lotus-eating lifestyle – maybe Lobsang was right that he had the soul of a Puritan – and the innocence of the beast's human passengers brought out something of the teacher, or the shepherd, in him.

The islanders were short on raw materials; they had a few handfuls of flint shards, bits of obsidian, metals, evidently garnered from the pockets of shipwrecked ancestors. They treated these as toys, tokens, ornaments. So, with scraps from the twain, Nelson taught them a certain amount of Metalwork 101. How to draw wire, among other things, allowing them to augment their meagre stock of treasured fish-hooks. He even left them instructions in the basics of crystal-set radios. Maybe some day they could use that technology to reconnect with the rest of mankind, whatever fraction of it passed through this world.

The islanders smiled and nodded, applauded when he assembled some intricate component, and used his bits of wire to adorn their hair.

Nelson spent some time too strolling in what he called

the jungle, the scrap of forest on the carapace. It flourished pretty well, despite periodic dunkings in the sea, but was an eclectic mix of species that reminded him more of a botanic garden collection than anything natural: from ferns to eucalyptus, and many species Nelson failed to recognize. As for the animals, Lobsang was right about there being a rough selection operating for size, in terms of body mass. The elephant types seemed to be a kind of mammoth, with curling tusks and ragged orange-brown fur. But they were dwarfed, no taller than a pony in St John on the Water, and very shy.

Another question that occurred to Nelson was how *old* this beast was. How long had it been sailing these stepwise seas? If he dug around in the forest, or in the dark spaces within its carapace, would he find the bones of antique beasts – the skeleton of a stegosaur?

Even Lobsang had no answer to such questions.

It was in the jungle, on the fourth day, with Nelson deep in thought, that Cassie trapped him. She was the woman who habitually wore a red flower in her hair, who had asked for tobacco when he'd landed.

He knew by now what she wanted. He tried to avoid eye contact with her, but, with the susurration of the sea all around them, he was cornered in her stare.

'Mister Lobsang say you are tight and sad and needing loving . . .'

The statement hung there, and Nelson could practically hear two value systems colliding in his head with a scream of stripped cogs. All right, he *was* a Puritan type; any male child brought up by Nelson's mother on the one hand and her version of God on the other would have turned out

425

that way. He had had relationships, including a long-term girlfriend with whom he'd had an 'understanding', a very old-fashioned term, but . . .

But then there were the islanders. He'd seen evidence of long-term relationships, like marriages, but among the young especially things were pretty relaxed. After all, everybody here knew everybody else – it was just like St John on the Water in that regard – and there was a kind of protective communal tolerance.

Besides, as Lobsang had told him, it was good for the islanders to have their gene pool replenished by passing travellers. Nelson almost had a duty to accept this invitation.

'Only a little wiggle, Mister Nelson!' She smiled, and laughed, and walked up to him.

And suddenly he was immersed in the moment, the analytical part of his mind seemed to dissolve, and his forty-eight years fell away. The world was alive with light and colour, the blue and the green, he could smell the sea and the vegetation and the animals of this place, he could smell the seawater-salt on the flesh of this woman as she approached him, and when she touched his lips with a fingertip he could *taste* her . . .

Nobody saw them. Well, save for Lobsang, probably.

Afterwards he stayed away from the jungle, and was *never* alone with Cassie, ever again.

On the fifth day, for a shower and a change of clothes, they returned to the twain, which shadowed the wake of Second Person Singular.

They sat together in the gondola, in formal western clothing that now felt stiff and confining. The living island drifted beneath them, complex, beautiful, fecund. It might almost have been designed to be viewed from the air.

'We haven't yet spoken of why you summoned me to your company in the first place, Lobsang.'

'Summoned?'

'You said we'd play no more games – that breadcrumb trail I followed was effectively a summons. Now you show me this Traverser . . .'

'An example of the remarkable fecundity, or inventiveness, of life in the Long Earth.'

'Why? Why bring me here, why show me this?'

'Because I believe you have a mind of a quality to appreciate a theory I have been nurturing since the opening up of the Long Earth.'

'A theory about what?'

'About the universe – mankind – the purpose of the Long Earth . . . This is all very tentative, yet crucially important. Would you like to hear it?'

'Is it conceivable that I won't? Or that I could stop you?'

'Reverend Azikiwe, I am impervious to sarcasm. Call it a feature of my self-programming . . .

'Consider this. *The Long Earth will save mankind.* Now that we're spread across the stepwise worlds, even the destruction of a whole planet, the creation of a new Gap, would not destroy us all. And indeed the Long Earth opened up just in time, some would argue. Otherwise we might have finished ourselves off. Soon we would surely have been scrabbling like chimpanzees in the ruins of our civilization, fighting over the last of the resources. Instead, we undeserving apes suddenly have the key to multiple worlds, and we are gobbling them up as fast as we can.'

'Not all of us. Your islanders on the Traverser are pretty

relaxed, and don't seem to be doing anybody any harm. And out in the Long Earth there seem to be plenty of drifters, "combers" they call them, who don't trouble anybody.'

'But look at this current situation with the trolls – pleasant, helpful and trusting creatures – of course we *must* dominate them, enslave them, kill them. Look at the tension over Valhalla and its quiet rebellion. I can't leave you to get on with your life, even a million steps away. I must tax you, control you!'

Nelson said carefully, 'Well, Lobsang, do you intend to do something about this? Of all the entities I know of in the human worlds, surely you alone have the power—'

Lobsang snapped, 'Indeed. In fact you may have some difficulty in understanding what you might call the range of my talents. My soul is the soul of a man, but I'm hugely enhanced beyond that, and distributed – not to put too fine a point on it, practically ubiquitous. By now one of my iterations should be heading out into the comets on the edge of the solar system. Nelson, I'm in with the Oort cloud!'

'Oh, good grief.'

'It made Agnes laugh . . . Maybe you had to be there. Look, Nelson, I am everywhere. But I'm not God, and *I don't interfere.* I don't believe in *your* God; I rather suspect that you don't either. But I also suspect you need to feel that there is some plan in the universe – something that makes sense, and gives meaning.'

'What kind of plan?'

'I may be no god but perhaps I have a godlike perspective. The Long Earth has made mankind immune to terrestrial catastrophes. But it has not made mankind immune to time. *I* consider long timescales, Nelson. I consider future ages, when our sun – all the suns of the Long Earth – have died, and beyond that the dark energy expansion, the Big Rip when the very atom will be torn apart, creating a new Ginnungagap . . .'

'Ah. The primeval void before creation. *There was not sand nor sea nor cool waves / Earth did not exist, nor heaven above—*'

'*Ginnungagap existed, but no grass at all . . .*' Lobsang nodded. '*Völuspá*: well remembered.'

'Norse mythology and Tibetan metaphysics – a heady brew!'

Lobsang ignored that. 'Humanity *must* progress. This is the logic of our finite cosmos; ultimately we must rise up to meet its challenges if we are not to expire with it. You can see that. But, despite the Long Earth, we *aren't* progressing; in this comfortable cradle we're just becoming more numerous. Mainly because we have no real idea what to do with all this room. Maybe others will come who *will* know what to do.'

'"Others"?'

'Others. Consider. We call ourselves the wise ones, but what would a true *Homo sapiens* be like? What would it do? Surely it would first of all treasure its world, or worlds. It would look to the skies for other sapient life forms. And it would look to the universe as a whole, and consider its cultivation.'

Nelson thought that over. 'So you believe that the logic of the universe is that we *must* evolve beyond our present state, in order to be capable of such great programmes. Seriously? Do you really believe a brave new species can be expected sometime soon?'

'Well, isn't it at least possible? At least logical? Nelson, there is much to learn – much to discover, much to do. We've discussed all this. You have left your parish. You are looking for a new direction, a new focus. I know you are seeking the same answers as me. What better than to work with me? I do need support, Nelson. I can see the whole world turning. But I can't look into a human soul.

'How do you feel? Have you seen enough here?'

Nelson smiled. 'Let's wait a little while longer. You should always leave enough time to say goodbye.'

61

A
S JOSHUA'S AND Bill's journey wore on fruitlessly, just
for a break, Bill lingered more often in what he said
the comber community called 'Diamond' worlds – the
opposite of Jokers, worlds with some unique attraction.

Earth West 1,176,865: this world came before they
reached the Valhallan Belt, the American-Sea worlds, but
here the Grand Canyon was drowned by a risen river: a
truly spectacular sight, as Joshua saw from above, which
drew tourists who camped along the canyon's elevated
rim.

Earth West 1,349,877: a world dominated by a strange,
even unearthly ecology, in which familiar terrestrial
creatures were surrounded by groves of green, twisted living
things that crawled and spread, defying classification,
neither animal nor plant – like slime moulds grown huge,
perhaps, of many diverse forms. No biologist had studied
this world. Visiting combers whispered of a Huge God, a
hypothetical alien monster that had crash-landed here
hundreds of millennia ago, leaving layers of flesh, bones and
fat from which these organisms, descendants of parasites or
some equivalent of stomach bacteria perhaps, had evolved.
Joshua found the crowded variety of strange life on
this world startling and in some way satisfying. As if

something had been missing and he'd never even known it.

And somehow that train of thought led him to the answer.

It came to him while he was asleep. He sat bolt upright, in the dark, in his cabin in the gondola.

Then he ran out to the galley cum lounge cum observation deck, and stared at a blank piece of wall.

'I've got it.' When there was no reply he hammered on the thin partition that separated this room from Bill's cabin. 'I said, I've got it!'

'Got what, yer mad eejit?'

'I know where Sally has to be. She's left me a clue, whether she meant to or not. It wasn't what she left behind, but what she took away.'

He heard Bill's muffled yawn. 'And that is?'

'*The ring*, Bill. The ring. Gold, set with sapphires. The one I brought with me and hung on this wall. It's gone, Bill. When and how she sneaked on board to get it I don't know. And how long it's been gone – Sally will be laughing her head off.'

'A ring. Ring-a-ding-ding. It's only taken you three weeks to figure it out, Joshua. So where do we need to head?'

'To Earth West 1,617,498 . . . To the Rectangles.'

'Fine. We'll start in the morning. Be there in three days. Now can I go back to sleep?'

62

IN PREPARATION FOR the approach to Valhalla, the Operation Prodigal Son airships assembled a hundred worlds to the East of the target, hovering like low clouds over the empty shore of this version of the American Sea, the best part of a million and a half steps from the Datum.

When the *Benjamin Franklin* took its place, Maggie was immediately hailed by the *Abraham Lincoln*, visible on the horizon. The *Lincoln*'s Captain told her that Admiral Davidson, commander of USLONGCOM, was aboard, and wanted to see her in person. The two ships closed, and touched down. Maggie changed her uniform, and waited for the Admiral in her sea cabin.

But then she got a summons from Nathan. 'You'd better get down to the access ramp, Captain. We've got a situation.'

When she got there, she found that Acting Ensign Carl the troll, wearing the armband that comprised his 'uniform', had been included in the party that had greeted the Admiral. Or maybe he'd included himself; that would be like Carl, always interested, always wanting to make new friends. Only now, Captain Edward Cutler, aide to the Admiral, was holding a gun to his head.

The Admiral himself, a spruce sixty-year-old, looked on with amusement.

Maggie made her way to Cutler and whispered in his ear. 'What are you doing, Captain?'

'Containing a dangerous animal. What does it look like?'

'Captain Cutler, this troll isn't dangerous. In fact—' Before this steely, intense man, she found herself embarrassed. 'Carl is a member of the crew.'

Cutler stared at her. 'Is this some joke?'

'No, Captain.' Maggie showed him Carl's armband insignia. 'I deposited the appropriate forms with the fleet.' That was true enough, though she'd done her best to keep the bureaucracy from focusing its attention on the situation. 'An experiment in cross-sapient cooperation.'

Admiral Davidson was openly grinning now. 'Call it symbolic, Ed.'

Cutler looked at Davidson, Maggie, the troll. Then he called, 'Adkins.'

A lieutenant trotted up. 'Sir?'

'Send a message to the White House, by the fastest means possible. Tell President Cowley that we are hereby surrendering to the hobo and okie types who infest the Long Earth. And in the process we are handing over control of our vessels to trolls, raccoons, prairie dogs, and any other dumb animals we happen to come across.'

'Right away, sir.'

'But just before I resign my own commission I think I'll put a bullet in the head of this little one—'

Maggie approached him again. 'Cutler. Are you a parent?'

'What? No, not yet.'

'Well, Captain Cutler, Ensign Carl won't hurt you whatever you do. But if you don't lower that weapon I will kick you so hard that your chances of *ever* fathering a child will be pathetically slim . . .'

It was a relief to get the Admiral into the relative sanity of her sea cabin. An ensign – not Carl – served coffee, and closed the door, leaving them alone.

Davidson leaned forward. 'So, Captain Kauffman.'

'Sir.'

'I've never been one to waste my time. You know that.'

'No, sir.'

'Let's get to it, then. In the short time you have commanded the *Benjamin Franklin* you have treated the ship as if it were your personal property, going well beyond the already loose parameters of your orders – to put it bluntly, making up the rules of engagement as you went along. Not only that, you have allowed possibly dangerous creatures to run free in the ship.'

'Yes, sir.'

'Resulting in such incidents as the humiliation of poor Ed Cutler, out there, over a troll.'

'Yes, sir.'

He grinned. 'Well done, Maggie.'

'Thank you, sir.'

'Personally, I particularly liked the way you handled the situation at New Purity. Having the dead of the trolls placed in the same cemetery as those poor pioneers. That went down well most every place that saw the record. You've done a great deal, and very visibly, to promote the kind of ideals that I, and others in the military – hell, even some in President Cowley's administration – believe should be guiding our behaviour in the Long Earth. I wanted you, all of you captains, to reach out your hand to these scattered new cultures. Not to wield an iron fist. Ours is not to police our people, or to moralize; our duty is to protect our own from external threat. But for us to do that we have to know who and what we are protecting, in this strange new landscape we face today. And for you to achieve those goals you had to be open; you had to listen, to learn. Which is what you've done. I could never have ordered you to do all this, Captain; you had to learn your way, which you have done, and I'm glad you did.'

'Thank you again, sir,' she said, uncertain.

'As to the future – well, somebody with your experience and particular skills should not be utilized simply to babysit every colonial group that hasn't read the manual. Captain, once this business at Valhalla is concluded, I'd like you to consider a new command: the USS *Neil Armstrong II.*'

Maggie caught her breath. The second *Armstrong* was a new dirigible marque, semi-secret, designed to explore the Long Earth far beyond the limits reached so far, even by the Valienté expedition, even by the rumoured Chinese venture.

'Your primary mission, as you'll understand, will be to seek out whatever became of the *Armstrong I* and her crew. We haven't even been able to send a ship out to search. Well, now we can. After that—' He gestured. '*Out there.* Of course you can select your own crew.'

She thought of Mac, and Nathan, and Harry – even Toby Fox. 'That won't be a problem, sir.'

'I thought not.' He glanced at his watch. 'Well, we have a heavy duty to fulfil when we get to Valhalla. I think we're done here.' He stood. 'But while I'm aboard, I think I would enjoy meeting your Ensign Carl, in a less confrontational situation . . .'

That night, Maggie lay half asleep in her bunk, lulled by the micro-sounds of the ship: every little click and creak and groan, so familiar after the voyage. Every sailor knew that a ship had a life of its own, an identity, idiosyncrasies – even moods.

She felt paws on the bed. She turned over. The cat's face loomed in the dark, green eyes glowing bright.

'You aren't asleep,' said Shi-mi.

'You really are a genius of perception, aren't you?'

'What are you thinking, Captain?'

'That I'll miss this battered old tub.'

'Yes. I hear congratulations are in order.'

'You would hear that, wouldn't you? And through you the whole of the Black Corporation, probably. In any event I haven't decided. You hear that, Abrahams, whoever you are?'

'You'll need a cat.'

'Oh, will I?'

'Personally I like the *Benjamin Franklin*. But I wouldn't mind roughing it with you. Think it over.'

'I will. I promise. Now get some sleep.'

'Yes, Captain.'

63

THREE DAYS AFTER his discovery that the ring was gone, when they got to the world they had informally called the Rectangles, there was only one obvious location for Joshua to make for.

He sat silently as Bill guided the airship over an arid, crumpled landscape to a dry valley, its walls honeycombed by caves, its floor marked with those familiar rectangular formations, like field boundaries or the foundations of vanished buildings – and that one monumental stone structure, like a sawn-off pyramid.

Even from the air the place oppressed Joshua. Here, ten years ago, with Lobsang and Sally, he had found sapient life, some reptilian form. How did they know it was sapient? Only because, in a jumble of dried skeletons in a cave, a relic of some last spasm of dying, Joshua had found a finger-bone wearing that ring he'd taken away: clean gold with sapphires. So these creatures had evidently been sapients, and were just as evidently long dead, and Joshua still felt the odd, existential ache of that near miss, as if he were stranded on some island watching a ship pass, oblivious.

And, oddly, he felt an echo of that strange experience in this new time, the Long Earth without the trolls. More worlds with something missing.

'Well, this is the site,' he called up to Bill. 'I kind of expected it to be swarming with trolls.'

He could almost hear Bill's shrug. 'And I never expected it to be that easy.'

'I guess not.'

'The world's a classic arid Joker,' Bill said. 'According to my instruments. Drier than my gob in Lent.'

'Take us down well away from that pile. It's hot.'

'Actually I thought I might make for the person on the ground down there waving to us.'

When Joshua looked away from the monument, it was obvious. Silvery emergency blankets had been spread over a rock bluff, positioned to be visible from the sky but not from the ground. And somebody was standing there in olive-green coveralls, waving both arms.

'Good plan,' Joshua said.

The *Shillelagh* descended smoothly. They both disembarked this time, with their boots on and packs on their backs – Bill was laden with a Stepper box, and Lobsang's troll translation kit – ready to explore.

Joshua wasn't particularly surprised at the identity of the person who had summoned them from the sky. 'Lieutenant Jansson.'

'Joshua.' Jansson was thin, pale, sweating, evidently a lot more unwell than when he'd last seen her. As they walked up she sat down on an outcrop of rock, clearly exhausted from all the waving.

'We came to the right world, then. We guessed correctly.'

'About Ms Linsay taking the ring? What it signified, where you were to come? Oh, yes. She complained about it being hard for her to find – the ring. "Trust that idiot to take it with him on his holidays," was her phrase, I'm afraid. Then she *hoped* you wouldn't notice its absence. And even if you did, you wouldn't follow her here. She hoped that, she said, but she did plan for you showing up . . . You took your time to work it out, Joshua.'

Joshua shook his head. 'You're still a cop, retired or not. Only a cop would call Sally "Ms Linsay". We need to be here, Monica. We have our own mission, from Lobsang. About the trolls.'

Jansson smiled. 'I think Sally anticipated that too. "That meddler Lobsang's bound to get involved in this"—'

'I know, I know.'

'I said she planned for you to come, Joshua. Whether she wanted it or not. That's why I'm here. She brought me over to wait for you. Call me a stalking horse. She did a complicated deal with the beagles over that.'

Joshua stared. '*Beagles?*'

'I know. Long story. Truth be told I think they were glad to have me stashed out of their sight, I smell bad to them . . . You know, it's been a month since we've been here, most of it playing for time, hoping something would turn up. Sally's patient. The instincts of a hunter, I suppose. It's been harder for me.'

He inspected her. 'I'm guessing you're self-medicating.'

'Yes, and I'm doing fine, so don't fuss. Now, just listen, Joshua . . .'

Jansson quickly told them that Sally was twenty-six worlds further over, and what the situation was: about the kobold, about the sapient canines.

'Finn McCool,' Bill growled. 'Playing both ends against the middle, I'll be bound. The little gobshite.'

440

For now, Joshua took in very little of this. 'Kind of complicated.'

'So it is,' said Jansson.

'That's what happens when Sally Linsay gets into your life . . . But, as I said, we have our own mission here. OK. Well, we're going to leave the airship here and walk over.'

'Fine. There's a certain time of day when they wait for me, stepwise, to meet me when I'm ready to come back . . . Listen, do you have any coffee while we wait? I ran out days ago.'

The final step into Earth West 1,617,524 was a jolt. Though he was warned by Jansson, Joshua had expected another arid Joker, like Rectangles. But it wasn't arid, not just here anyhow. Joshua had an immediate impression of green, of moisture, of freshness; he couldn't help taking a deep breath.

Then he observed that the green wasn't the usual riff on forest or prairie, but, evidently, *fields*, being grazed by creatures that might have been cattle but weren't, and tended by upright figures that might have been human farmhands, but weren't.

And then he took in the most important aspect of the landscape. The creatures standing before him, that might have been dogs, but weren't.

There were perhaps a dozen of the upright dogs, standing in neat ranks. The central two seemed the most significant, judging by the quality of the belts they wore at their waists – belts, on dogs. From which tools of some kind hung. And weapons. A thing like a crossbow.

And a ray gun! A gaudy toy, like a prop from some old TV show. Just as Jansson had described.

Their gender was very obvious; of the central couple, one was female, the other male. The male was taller, towering, a magnificent – *animal.* Yet not an animal. Even as he computed the peril they were all in, part of Joshua rejoiced. Sapients – an entirely new kind – and one *not* extinct for millennia, like over in Rectangles.

Bill gaped. 'I'm dreaming. I know you told us about this, Lieutenant Jansson.' He shook his head. 'But this is mad.'

The male turned to Bill, and pulled back his lips from a very wolf-like face, and Joshua was astonished anew when he spoke. 'No. You a-hhre not in d-hrream.' A dog-like growl, yet the English words were clear.

Jansson said, 'Joshua, Bill. Let me present Li-Li. And Snowy.'

Despite Jansson's briefing about all this, Joshua felt he was dreaming too. '*Snowy?*'

Jansson pointed to the humans. 'Joshua Valienté. Bill Chambers, his companion. Joshua is the one Sally promised.'

'"Promised"?'

'One of her schemes. Given you were bound to be coming anyhow, she spun it for her advantage. She bigged you up as an ambassador of a greater power . . .'

'Nice of her.'

Snowy studied Joshua. 'You are emissar-hrry of human Granddaughter-hrr.'

'Granddaughter?'

'He means ruler,' Jansson said.

'OK. Well, we don't have a Granddaughter – umm, Snowy. Not the way you mean. But – an emissary. I guess

442

that's the right idea. I'm here to put things right with the trolls—'

Before he could say any more Snowy, without moving a muscle, emitted a soft growl, and two of the dogs behind him moved forward in a blur. They were on Joshua before he could react, and they pinned his arms to his sides.

Joshua fought an instinct to step away. 'Hey. What are you doing?'

Snowy nodded.

And Joshua was thrown forward to the ground, his face pressed to the rutted dirt of the track.

His injured shoulder ached like hell. He made himself *not step out of this*, not yet.

He tried to lift his head. He found himself staring into the face of the female dog. Li-Li? She was unfolding a bundle of cloth that contained small wooden pots, blades of stone and iron, needles, thread. Like a crude field medicine kit. Her eyes were wolf-like, yet oddly tender.

He asked, 'Why – what—'

'Sorr-hrry.' She reached behind him, and he felt his shirt being ripped open.

Even now he forced himself not to step.

He heard Jansson, evidently distressed. 'Joshua? I'm sorry. Sally did talk about you as an emissary. They must have planned this. We never suspected they'd treat you like this—'

He heard no more, as what felt like a very heavy fist slammed into the back of his head, smashing his face into the dirt, and the option to step vanished anyhow.

And the pain began, slicing, piercing, and he fell into oblivion.

64

W HEN HE WOKE, he was sitting on some kind of hard chair, slumped forward. The pain in his back was exquisite, a tapestry.

A face floated before him. A dog, a wolf . . . It showed tenderness.

It was the one called Li-Li. She peered at him, lifted one eyelid with a leathery finger-like extension of one paw. Then she growled, 'Sorr-hrry.' She backed away.

Now Sally was here, standing before him.

Beyond her he could make out a room, a big chamber, stone walls and floor, well-built, roomy, drab, un-decorated. The air was full of the scent of dog. There were other people here. And dogs. His head was clearing, slowly; he felt like he'd been drugged.

'Joshua. Don't step.'

He focused on her with difficulty. 'Sally?'

'Don't step. Whatever you do, *don't step*. Well, you're here at last. You took some tracking down, you and the professional Irishman here, in your travel-trailer in the sky. But I see the clue I had to leave finally percolated through your brain.'

'The ring . . .'

'Yes, the ring.'

'Why's it so important, suddenly?'

'You'll see. Sorry.'

'Sorry? Why? And why the hell not step?' He was mumbling, he discovered.

She took his cheeks in her hands, making him face her. He tried to remember the last time she had touched him, save by the scruff of the neck to rescue him from some calamity or other, such as from the wreck of the *Pennsylvania*. 'Because if you do, you'll die.'

He guessed, 'My back?'

'It's a kind of staple, Joshua.'

That was Jansson. He looked around, blearily. He saw Jansson sitting on the ground by the wall, a beefy-looking dog standing over her.

He said, 'A staple? Like the North Koreans. An iron staple through the hearts of prisoners. So if they step away—'

'Yeah. In your case it's a cruder variant, of a type used by some warlords in central Asia, we think. Joshua, don't sit back. There's a kind of crossbow fixed to your back. It's just wood and stone and sinew, but it has an iron pin. You can walk around, you understand? But if you step away—'

'The pin stays behind, and *boing*. The bow fires, and the bolt goes straight through the heart, right? I get it.' He began to drum the message into his own head. *Don't step. Don't step.* He felt at his chest. Under the ruin of his shirt he found a stout leather band. 'What's to stop me just cutting this off?'

'First, that would set it off,' Sally said. 'And, second, they sewed the weapon to your skin. I mean it's supported by the strap around your chest, but . . .'

445

'They *sewed* it?'

'Sorr-hrry, sorr-hrry,' Li-Li said. 'Order-hrrs . . . here.' She brought Joshua a carved wooden mug, plain but smoothly shaped.

It contained a lukewarm, meaty broth. He drank gratefully. He found he was hungry, thirsty. He couldn't be that badly hurt. 'Orders, eh?'

'It's not her fault,' Jansson said. 'She's a kind of doctor, I think. She tried to do the work cleanly, competently. Gave you some kind of painkillers. If it had been left to others – Joshua, I'm sorry. I didn't know they were going to jump you like that.'

'Nothing you could have done, I suspect, Lieutenant Jansson.'

'We have a plan, of sorts. Or had one before you showed up. We've been trying to adapt . . .'

Sally said, 'We're second-guessing the motivation of non-human sapients. We weren't expecting them to treat you like this. Maybe this is what passes for diplomacy, among beagles. Just attack the ambassador when he shows up. However the staple is our technology, after all. Humans invented this stuff to control other humans.'

Joshua grunted, 'So I'm learning a moral lesson. But somebody brought it here, right? And somebody had to show these dogs—'

'Beagles,' Sally said.

'How to manufacture the iron components.'

'That would-ss be me. Hell-llo, pathless-ss one . . .'

Joshua looked around, more carefully, systematically. There was a row of dogs – beagles? – standing as if to attention over one of their number lying on a kind of scrap of lawn, green growing grass, like a carpet. Sally was standing before him, Jansson and Bill sitting on the floor, against one wall. And, in another corner, with a dog guard hovering over him—

'Finn McCool. I've seen you looking better.'

The kobold had evidently been worked over. He could barely sit up straight. His sunglasses were gone. One eye was closed, bruises showed down one side of his bare torso, and one of his ears had been *bitten off*; Joshua could see the marks of teeth, a crude stitching. Still, McCool grinned. 'It was all busines-ss. We told the beagles-ss of you, pathless-ss ones. Your ships flicker in the ss-ky of this world. You would notice beagles-ss soon. We told them, be ready. We taught them how to ss-taple the ss-teppers. We got good price-ss.'

'Did you have this done to me?'

The kobold managed to laugh. 'Not me. But I would hav-ve, pathless-ss one.'

Bill Chambers snarled. '*Pogue mahone*, gobshite.'

Joshua said, 'So what the hell happened to you, McCool? Contractual dispute, was it?'

'Or-hrrders again,' came another voice, canine, but with a more liquid quality than the rest. Female. 'My or-hhrders. Always my orders . . .'

Joshua turned to the group of dogs by the podium. He recognized the tall warrior – Snowy. He still had that ray gun dangling from his Batman-type utility belt, like a prop from one of Lobsang's old 1950s sci-fi movies, alongside crude blades of metal and stone. He stood at ease, but with an air of constant, competent alertness.

He was watching over another, a female, the one who lounged, very dog-like, on the grass. It was she who had spoken about orders.

Sally was studying Joshua with some sympathy, leavened by amusement at his probably obvious disorientation. 'Classic Long Earth set-up, isn't it, Joshua? A mash-up of three disparate sapient species – four if you count the Rectangles builders, off-stage – nurtured on separate Earths and now all mixed up together like this.' She nodded at the reclining female dog. 'Joshua, meet Petra. Granddaughter, ruler of this city – this Den, whatever – which is called the Eye of the Hunter.'

'Granddaughter?'

'Two down in the hierarchy from the Mother, I think. The big boss of this doggy nation is the Mother, then you get Daughters, Granddaughters—'

'*Petra?*'

'A human nickname, apparently. You'd probably ruin your epiglottis if you tried for their true names. Not that we mere humans are told them anyhow.'

'We're not the first to pass through here, then.'

'Evidently not. Those damn combers get everywhere, don't they? . . . Now pay attention. Petra's in charge, and she knows it.'

Joshua faced Petra. 'It was your orders to staple me?'

'Let me make it plain, Josh-shua. What is it we each-shh wann-t? You, the tr-hrrollss. Yes? Make peace.'

'That's why I came here.'

'Me too,' Sally said.

'Ve-hrry good. But I care not for you, or tr-hrrolls. Though t-hrroll music pleases. I care for *these*.' And she plucked the ray gun from Snowy's belt, hefted it in her graceful fingers, pointed it straight at Joshua's head – and pulled what was obviously the trigger.

He didn't flinch, though from the corner of his eye he

saw Jansson and Bill shrink back. Of course nothing happened. It wasn't the moment in the game for him to die, though he suspected that would come later.

The Granddaughter said, 'Weapons. Come from *him*.' She gestured at the cringing, grinning kobold. 'Where from? From scentless wo-hhrlds.'

Sally murmured, 'She means, stepwise. These canine conquerors can't step. Which is why they needed to staple you.'

'Weapons make Eye of Hunter-rhh strong Den. Stronger than foe dens.'

Granddaughter, Joshua thought blearily. Dogs had big litters. This granddaughter of the queen must have a lot of rivals.

Sally said, 'Joshua, you need to understand. As far as I can make out these canines don't care about us, or about stepping, the parallel worlds. All they care about is their own wars, their own agendas, their conflicts. We're just a means to an end.'

'We'd be the same, probably.'

'Right. And all they really want, right now, is weapons to fight their wars.'

'The ray guns?'

'But weapons die.' The Granddaughter threw the weapon, a kind of laser pistol, Joshua saw, contemptuously on the floor. 'That-tt one knows.' She pointed at the kobold. 'Whe-hrre weapons a-hhre. How to get. They dhrr-ibble into my hands, for ho-hrrible price, then die. Enough. We have per-hrrsuaded him to help.' She fingered something at her neck, a scrap of flesh dangling on a thong. It was an ear, Joshua saw. A kobold ear. And beside it, on a second thong, now he looked more closely – a ring, like his own, a Rectangles ring. 'But kobold has no weapons-ss fo-hhr us.'

'Prob-lemm for me,' hissed the kobold, his anxious grin showing bloody teeth, his gaze flickering over the humans' faces.

'I'll bet it is,' Joshua said.

Joshua couldn't figure it all out yet, not quite. But these rings, from the world a few steps away, were evidently crucial. As Sally had seen. And by retrieving their own ring she had sought some kind of advantage.

'Here's the deal,' Sally said quickly. 'The beagles want more ray guns. They are in caches, over in Rectangles.'

'They are *where*? In *what*?'

Sally gritted her teeth. 'Is this really the time for an archaeology lesson, Valienté? Just listen . . .' She spoke very rapidly, and he realized she was hoping the beagles, and the kobold, wouldn't be able to follow fully. 'The caches the kobold raided before are all exhausted. Locked up. To get at fresh ones he needs another key.'

Joshua's mind, unusually flexible for once – maybe it was the goad of the lingering pain – made the connection. '*The key is the ring we found in the cave of bones*. The ring I kept, the ring you took from the airship—'

'The ring I now have secreted on my person,' Sally murmured. 'But they don't know I have it.'

'I'm not surprised. And the ring the Granddaughter is wearing—'

'Opened a weapons cache that's now exhausted.'

'He needs a new key. He, or his buddies, must have combed Rectangles for the keys. How come he didn't find the one we did?'

'On the finger of a long-dead corpse? Some taboo,

maybe. Or instinct. He's not human, Joshua. He's not going to seek stuff out the way a human would.'

'OK. What now?'

'So here's the deal we made. The beagles can't step, right? So we go over to Rectangles – that is me, Jansson, the kobold. He shows us where the cache is, we open it with the ring, we come back with more ray guns, nicely charged up. That *was* the plan. But I've been playing for time, Joshua. For a month now. Time before I had to give away our only advantage. Time before I had to hand over high-energy weapons to these sapients we've only just met. I just hoped something would turn up, that we'd find some other way out. *You* were a wild card, Joshua. Once you got here – if you got here at all – I hoped I could use you to force a bluff, somehow. Get out of here, get to the trolls. Instead of which—'

'Here I am with a crossbow stitched to my back. Sorry to let you down.'

'Don't apologize,' Sally said without a hint of irony. 'Not your fault. Once again I didn't guess the non-human motivation right.' She sighed. 'Look. While you were out we talked, came up with a deal. I think we'll have to hand over the damn weapons. *If* they exist, *if* we can bring them back. The deal is that if we do make it back with the weapons, you get to speak to the trolls. But you've also become a kind of hostage, to make sure we won't just step away out of here.'

'Maybe you should do just that. Step away. Take Jansson, Bill with you—'

She sighed, irritated. 'You've always been an idiot, Valienté. If I left you here I wouldn't care, but Helen would kill me. Besides, it wouldn't do any good in the long

451

run. We have to handle this situation with the trolls here somehow. And resolve humanity's relationship with the beagles. We *come back*, and then, when everybody's got what they want—'

Joshua, his back twinging every time he moved, turned to the Granddaughter. 'Yes, what then, uh, Granddaughter Petra? Are we free to go?'

She *smiled*. Her lips pulled back over gleaming teeth. It was an almost human expression, if a chilling one. 'You will still be aliv-ve. And perhaps you will live on, if you display honour-rhh . . .'

Joshua tried to make sense of that.

Bill spoke up. 'Joshua. Remember, they're not human. "Honour" meant something different to that gobshite kobold, didn't it? I wonder what "honour" means to a sentient species descended from pack-hunting carnivores.'

'I have a feeling I'm going to find out,' Joshua said with dread. 'First things first.' He stood carefully, but his back flared with pain and he staggered, until Sally grabbed his arms. 'Where are the trolls?'

65

So, FULFILLING THEIR part of the deal, Jansson, Sally and the kobold stepped back to the Rectangles world.

Despite a strong dose of anti-nausea pills, the steps still felt like the usual punches in the gut to Jansson. When she got at last to the Rectangles, she folded over, groaning.

Sally stood over her, rubbing her back. 'Are you OK?'

'Never gets any easier. Not since the very first time I stepped.'

'On Step Day. I know. Out of my father's living room, with a Stepper he made, and left behind.'

Jansson, doubled over, thumped the ground, frustrated. 'It's not just the stepping. This damn illness, it gets in the way of doing stuff. You know?'

'I can imagine.'

The others waited the few minutes it took her to recover enough to stand straight. Sally was grave, patient. The kobold stood alongside her, restless, his own injuries obviously paining him. But he oddly aped Sally's stance, and he cocked his head as if in mock-sympathy, his gaze flickering from one face to the other, as if seeking approval. Jansson turned away from him, repelled.

She managed to stand up and look around. There was the airship hovering overhead, Joshua's *Shillelagh*, a massive, competent-looking, reassuring presence. Jansson took a deep breath. This world smelled of dryness, of baked, rusty stone. But it didn't smell of *dog*, and that was a huge relief.

Sally touched her shoulder. 'Look. I have to go back, with these reptile ray guns, whatever, for the sake of Joshua. Always assuming we find the guns at all. But the beagles can't reach you here; they can't step. You could just go, Jansson. Get into that airship and—'

Jansson smiled tiredly. 'And leave Joshua behind? Sally, I've known him since he was a boy. He is what he is, he's *where* he is, partly because I was in his life from the start. You know? Pushing him. Like you, I'm not about to leave him now.' She looked at the kobold. 'Though I have to admit I don't know why this one hasn't scarpered already. Why did you hang around to let them beat you up?'

'Drugs-ss,' the kobold said simply. 'They drugged poor Finn McCool. Could not ss-step.'

Jansson said, 'But you just stepped with us. The drugs have worn off now. Yet you're still here.'

Sally grinned, an expression that reminded Jansson uncomfortably of the beagles, the wolf-people. 'Oh, he knows that if he runs I will track him down. You won't be able to hide. Will you, you little prick? Wherever you go I will find you, and kill you.'

The kobold shrugged; he had already seemed nervous enough. 'Poor Finn McCool,' he repeated.

The heat, the dryness, were sucking at Jansson's strength. 'Shall we get on with this?'

'Good idea.' Sally glanced down the dry valley, at the

looming stone mass of the building there. 'Not too healthy for any of us, hanging around that thing.' Suddenly she had a ring in her hand. 'This what you need, Finn McCool?'

On the beagle world, the trolls had gathered by a river bank. Joshua and Bill walked towards them. Bill was carrying a backpack containing Lobsang's patent translation device.

Every step caused Joshua precise, relentless agonies. His lower back felt hot and damp, and he wondered if his stitches were ripping open as he carried the weight of the crossbow gadget. If so, the blood loss might kill him slow, even if he didn't step to give the weapon the chance to kill him quick. Even his dodgy shoulder was hurting, a grace note added to the symphony of agony from his back.

He tried to concentrate on his surroundings. The river was wide, strong, placid, and its banks were dominated by green fields and forest clumps. From the fields, the beagles' strange herd beasts had come to drink, sipping at the lapping water, lowering their misshapen heads.

And the trolls were here, by the water. A band of them had gathered at the closest point of the river to the Eye of the Hunter, where irrigation channels and open sewers cut across the ground to the town. As always the troll group, though sedentary in this world, was mobile in the Long Earth; at the fringe of the pack, scouts and hunters continually flicked away and returned, like ghosts.

There were hundreds of trolls, in this one band. Joshua could see they had been here for some time; the ground was scuffed and muddy, and there was a strong, unmistakable troll musk in the air. There were more bands like this, Joshua could see, spread along the river bank, and on the far side, and deeper into the country. The long call, unending, seemed to hang above them, a cloud of elusive memory.

Surely there were still trolls out there across the Long Earth; nobody had any real idea how many trolls there were in total. But this really did look to be where they were concentrating, he could see that. The centre of gravity of the troll population.

And the band before him was the very pivot of it all, as far as he was concerned. For there was Mary, the runaway from the Gap, and her cub Ham, unmistakable in the remnant of the silvery spacesuit the nerds at the Gap had dressed him up in.

As Joshua and Bill approached the trolls did not quite fall silent, but the volume of their song diminished. Ham sucked his thumb as he watched them, wide-eyed, apparently curious, like all young mammals.

Bill slipped the pack off his shoulders and unloaded it. It contained a tablet, blank and black, a couple of feet square, with a fold-out stand. Bill set this up, and placed the tablet to face the trolls.

Joshua glanced down. 'That's it? No on-switch, no boot-up?'

Bill shrugged. 'Black Corporation shit. It's not like the troll-call translators that Sally described, by the way, those trumpet things. Some kind of *new* Black Corporation shit. You figured what you're going to say here? How you're going to convince them that humanity loves them after all?'

Joshua had purposefully not thought this far ahead. He was no public speaker, and even preparing for town meetings back at Hell-Knows-Where tended to make him freeze up. 'I figured I'd wing it.'

Bill patted him on the shoulder, gingerly. 'Good luck with that.' He stepped back.

Joshua faced the trolls, standing straight, trying to ignore the liquid pain of his back. He was aware of them watching him, hundreds of pairs of those dark, unreadable eyes – backed up, he reminded himself, by hundreds of pairs of hairy arms, and fists like steam hammers. And he was the representative of a humanity that was probably still treating their kind as brute beasts across a million worlds. What the hell was he going to say?

He spread his hands. 'Good afternoon.'

'Actually it's still morning,' muttered Bill.

'I suppose you're wondering why I've gathered you all here today.'

'That's it. Start with a gag.'

The trolls were motionless.

'Whew. Tough crowd.'

'Shut up, Bill—'

'I didn't say that, Joshua.'

Joshua turned. A figure stood beside him, tall, erect, still, with shaven head, in an orange robe, and with a broom in his right hand. 'Lobsang.'

'I don't mean to steal your thunder, Joshua. But I figured you could use a little backup.'

'You can never have too much backup,' Joshua muttered.

Lobsang smiled, and for an instant he flickered, shuddering into a cloud of boxy pixels – Joshua could see the green prairie through his substance – before congealing again. A hologram, then, projected from the box.

Lobsang took a step forward, glancing back at the translator box. 'Hit it, boys.'

The thrilling sound of a mass choir burst from the translator box and filled the air, a pounding, repetitive chant, a thousand voices. To Joshua's ears it was not quite human, not quite troll, but a blend of the two.

The trolls looked astonished. They stopped grooming, stood up, all their faces turned towards Lobsang. And already, Joshua could hear, the song of the trolls was echoing the translator's riffs.

Lobsang raised his arms, brandishing his broom. 'My friends! You know me. I am Lobsang, who you know as the Wise One. This is Joshua. They call him the Wanderer. Yea, the Wanderer! And we have travelled far to speak to you . . .' As he spoke he backed up his words with rudimentary sign language, and his own voice sounded over the chorus from the translator box, thin, high, distinctive, like a Bach trumpet.

'Just when I thought my life couldn't possibly get any weirder,' Joshua muttered.

Bill said, 'I guess he can take this off around this world. Speak to as many trolls as he can get to. A hologram's not going to grow tired. The Lobsang world tour, 2040. The good thing is *we* haven't got to listen to it every time he does it . . .'

Sally handed Finn McCool the ring. 'Show us.'

'Eass-y,' said the kobold. He took the ring between his supple finger and thumb, set it on his upturned palm, spun it –

The ring blurred into the air, still spinning, shot past Jansson's face like a bright blue hornet, and made straight for the big stone building. It burrowed into the dirt at the base of the building's face, whirring like a drill bit, throwing up a spray of sand, until it had disappeared.

There was stillness, silence.

Sally seemed irritated. She glanced at the kobold. 'Now what?'

'Juss-t wait.'

Jansson smiled at Sally. 'You OK?'

Sally shook her head. 'I just get annoyed by stuff like that. Magic-ring crap. What a stunt. I mean, *I* could imagine how that could work: miniature accelerometers to detect the spinning that activates it, some equivalent of GPS to figure out where it has got to go, some kind of propulsion – magnetic? Even micro-rockets of some kind? Just a dumb trick, to impress the credulous, easily distinguishable from magic . . .'

The ground shuddered under their feet.

Jansson, queasy, stepped back quickly. Sand, thrown up from the foot of the building, settled back quickly in the dry air. What looked like a kind of lizard shot across the valley floor, seeking the shelter of a heap of rocks. Above them creatures like buzzards rose up, alarmed, cawing.

There was a grinding rumble.

And, to Jansson's blank astonishment, a whole section of the flat valley floor sank out of sight, down into the ground, revealing—

A ladder. Rungs cut into a stone wall.

'Ha!' Sally clapped her hands together. 'I knew it. Natural concentration of uranium my butt.'

The kobold came to Jansson. 'Watch.'

'Watch what?'

'No.' He tapped his wrist. 'Watch-ssh.'

Bemused, she handed over her old police-issue timepiece.

He held it up to the sunlight, trying to read its face. 'Eight minutes-ss.'

'I *knew* it,' Sally repeated, staring at the hole in the ground. 'The first time we came here I said so. There's a nuclear pile in that pyramid, or under it. It's *old*, old and abandoned technology, yet still hot. So old that later generations, who'd long forgotten the accomplishments of their ancestors, were attracted by the strange phenomena of the ancient waste. And were slowly killed off by it. Of course, this is the way the story was *supposed* to turn out. All ancient civilizations leave behind underground vaults of secret weapons. And each key works only once, I'm guessing . . .'

Jansson's cop instinct told her there must be more to this situation than that old movie cliché. This was all supposed to be millions of years old. What possible technology could endure such a time? And why would you set up such long-duration caches anyhow? For whose benefit? The only alternative was that these caches were somehow being *replenished*. But who by, how, why?

The kobold was still glaring at her watch, a caricature of a time-keeper, and now wasn't the moment for speculation.

Jansson turned on the kobold. 'Eight minutes until *what*, monkey boy?'

'Until tomb seals-ss again.' He studied the watch face, but numbers were evidently a mystery to him. 'Less-ss now . . .'

Sally turned. 'I'll go.'

'No.' Jansson grabbed her arm with all the strength she could muster. 'You said it's radioactive in there.'

'Yes, but—'

'I already bought the farm, Sally. Let me.'

'Monica—'

'I mean it. I feel like I owe Joshua.' She put on her determined face. 'What do I have to do, flash my badge?'

'Go, then. Go, go!' She actually pushed Jansson away.

It seemed to wear Jansson out just crossing the dry river bed to the hole in the ground. Was she going to be capable of doing this? What if she just got stuck down there, when the kobold's eight minutes were done? No help for that, if so. Get on with it.

To her relief the ladder cut into the wall was easy to climb down, with fat hand- and footholds. Getting back out might be more problematic . . .

'Sally, how much time?'

'Seven minutes. Less. I don't know . . . Shift it, Jansson!'

'I'm doing my best.'

At the base of the shaft she stood in a puddle of light from above. A kind of corridor, too low for her to stand upright, led off into the blackness. Only one way to go.

She carried a flashlight in her pocket, smaller than her thumb, with no iron parts so it worked when she stepped. She was an ex-cop; she always carried a flashlight. She flicked it on now, and followed a splash of light into the deeper dark. Joshua had always carried a flashlight, she recalled. Even as a thirteen-year-old, on Step Day. That was Joshua. This is for you, Joshua, she told herself as she drove herself on. To hell with trolls and beagles. For you.

The walls seemed to be of unpainted stone, no

markings, no signs. Yet they weren't smooth; they were ridged, in uncertain, uneven patterns. Tentatively she touched the markings, let her palm run over them as she hurried deeper into the corridor. She got the sense of meaning in the markings, like the time she'd attended a cop's familiarization class on Braille. Was this the writing of the reptile-folk who had built this place? Tactile, not visual?

'Jansson! You might want to move your ass . . .'

She came to a T-junction. Unbelievable. Maybe the markings gave definite directions, one way or another: THIS WAY TO THE MAGIC RAY GUNS. But they were useless to her.

She turned left at random, hurried down a corridor, hunching to avoid the low ceiling. Another junction! She took another left, what the hell. But remember the way back, remember the way . . . The walls were broken here by what looked like storage shelves. She saw pots, boxes, heaps of what looked like clay tablets, engraved. More records? Other kinds of stuff, equipment she couldn't even recognize . . .

'Jansson!' Sally's voice was very faint now.

Another T-junction. She went right, again at random. And now her flashlight picked up a ruby glint.

Rack upon rack of ray guns.

Lobsang apologized for the way humans, some humans, had treated trolls. He spoke of lobbies pressing the US government to grant trolls human rights, at least within the US Aegis, the long footprint of America across the Earths. It was only a start, there was no way to ensure that every human everywhere would behave as decently as they should, but it *was* a start . . .

'Maybe it's the best we can offer them,' Bill said to Joshua, speaking loudly to make himself heard. 'Kind of symbolic, but real nevertheless. Like the British Empire formally abolishing slavery in the early nineteenth century. Didn't get rid of slavery overnight, but it was a sea change.'

'He sounds like Martin Luther King with a heavenly choir. Typical Lobsang.'

'I wonder how much of this abstract stuff they can understand,' Bill said.

Joshua shrugged. 'Their collective intelligence is different from ours. If they get the basic message – *give us another chance* – that might be enough.'

'And what about giving these beagle beasts Dan Dare ray guns? Where's the morality in that?'

'Well, they're not our guns,' Joshua said. 'And we didn't provide them in the first place. If we live through this there'll be other parties to follow, proper contact. We can talk to the beagles then about peace, love and understanding.'

'Sure we can. After we've all had rabies shots. So you think this is going to work? This whole mad stunt of Lobsang's? And what then?'

To Joshua, all his life, the future had been nothing but a continual surprise. 'Tomorrow never knows.'

There was a soft tap on his shoulder. He turned, to look up into the cold eyes of Snowy.

'Talk to t-hrrollss. Going well?'

'I think so.'

'Good. Your work-k done?'

'I guess.'

'Josh-shua?'

'Yes?'

'Hrr-run.'

The rock hatchway had slid back into place, and save for a patch of disturbed earth there was no sign of the passage-way into the ground.

Only a heap of toy-like sci-fi blasters, retrieved from the cache.

Oh, and the ring, which had somehow been spat back out, to lie on the ground.

Jansson sat in the dirt, shivering despite the heat.

Finn McCool hissed, 'Have guns-ss. Now back to beagles-ss. And ss-ay goodbye to Josh-ssua.'

Sally snatched up the ring and harangued him. 'What did you mean by that, you piece of garbage?'

He backed off, hands raised defensively. 'Deal nearly finish-ss,' he said. 'Ray guns. Trollen. Now payback. Granddaughter honour Joshua. You say goodbye to him-mm . . .'

Sally glanced over at Jansson. 'You any idea what he's talking about? I'm guessing, nothing good.'

'Gang culture,' Jansson murmured, exhausted. 'Like that, maybe. The honour of the warrior. She's going to grant him a good death. Maybe that's what he means.'

'Shit. Then we have to help him.' Sally glanced around. 'What have we got? Think, think.' She pocketed the ring, and a ray gun that she slipped inside her sleeveless traveller's jacket. 'What else? You. Little Joe.'

The kobold cringed. 'What, what?'

'You got your walkman?'

'Stone that sings-ss?'

'Give it to me.'

'But, but, but, mm-mine!' He sounded like a child.

She grabbed his wrist so he couldn't step away without her. 'It's that or your left bollock. Hand it over. Now we go back. Get ready to step, Jansson . . .'

66

JOSHUA BACKED AWAY from Snowy, and from Bill, who scrambled to pack up the translation gear. Some instinct guided Joshua towards the river bank, the flowing water.

How the hell was he supposed to handle this? He was barely conscious as it was. The device on his back felt like a huge malevolent crab now, digging its claws deeper into his flesh with every pace. Maybe the painkillers were wearing off.

And Snowy followed. He wasn't moving as quickly as Joshua, so the gap between them opened up, yet there was a steady, purposeful, relentless quality to his gait. Then he dropped to all fours, becoming even more wolf-like. A huge, big-brained, weapon-carrying wolf.

Joshua was aware of the trolls watching, apparently curious, but none intervened. Other dogs watched too: Li-Li, the mordant Brian. More warrior types followed, it seemed, come to see the show.

Suddenly all the beagles howled, a pack in full cry.

'Come, Joshua-aahh,' Snowy growled. 'This fun-nn.'

'Get stuffed, Krypto.'

'And honour-hrr for you. Gift of Granddaughter. Life he-hhre, cheap.'

'Big litters?'

'Many born. All die. To die well is-s to have lived well-ll.'

'That's your culture. Not mine.'

'Head high on her wall. Honour-hhr of place.'

'Whose head?'

'Yours-ss.'

'Thanks.' Joshua, succumbing to the inevitable, turned and started to jog, parallel to the river. 'How can I win?'

'Die well-ll—'

'Any options aside from that?'

'*My* head on wall-ll . . . Play fair-hrr.'

'What?'

'I play fair.' The beagle stopped, stock still, and closed its eyes. 'R-run, human-nn.'

Joshua didn't hesitate further. He ran. He tried to think like a wolf, like a dog. Or rather, cliché scenes from every bad wolf-chases-man movie flashed through his head.

What the hell. He dived into the river.

Given this was generally such a hot, arid world, the water was surprisingly cold, the current strong, and it swept him downstream fast. Heavy in his clothes, he struggled to keep his head above the water. He considered kicking off his boots, then thought about running over open ground barefoot, and kept the boots.

As long as he didn't drown, this was a good plan, right? Throw the dog off the scent, like in the movies. But the pain from the lethal gadget on his back seemed even sharper in the cold water. And he felt like it was talking to him. *You could always just step away. End it in a second. A bolt through the heart – how bad can it be? Better than*

getting your throat bitten out by Deputy Dawg back there.
But he wasn't dead yet.

The river soon swept him away from the cultivated country, the fields, and into rougher terrain. He'd been brought into this place unconscious, and hadn't had a chance to scope it out. Evidently the Eye of the Hunter, the city of Granddaughter Petra's Den, really wasn't so large. He'd need to find a place to hide before Snowy caught up with him—

'Watch out-hrr.'

The voice came from downstream. He struggled to get his head out of the water. There was Snowy, sitting on a rock as if waiting to be fed by his owner, calmly watching Joshua get washed by.

He yelled back, 'Watch out for what?'

Snowy glanced further downstream. 'The hrr-rapids.'

And in a heartbeat Joshua had been swept past Snowy's rock, and over a low waterfall, and into the rapids. He was buffeted from one worn boulder to the next, a punch to the kidneys here, a slam in the chest there, as he tumbled through the rocks like a piece of lumber. He forced himself to give in to the surging, turbulent flow, to keep his limbs loose, to protect his head. But every time the pack on his back caught on some projection the pain was agonizing.

Then he was through, squirted out like an orange pip from a child's lips, and he was hurled even further downstream. When he glanced back, he could see no sign of Snowy. At least he might have gained some distance.

A fallen tree lay across the stream. With a mighty effort he plunged that way, grabbed the tree as he went past, and pulled himself out of the water on to a bank of gravel. He sat up to protect his back, panting, one breath, two, three.

There was nobody about. No Snowy. But now he had stopped moving he had time to concentrate on the pain in his back, a raking, ripping, tearing anguish. Worse, his lower back felt slippery again, and the damp gravel under him was stained red with blood.

Joshua Valienté had been travelling alone in the Long Earth since he was thirteen years old. He had been in some tight spots before, and he was still around. There was no reason why he couldn't get out of this one. *And you can always step, just step into a different sunlight, and it will be over in a flash . . .*

Not yet. *Think ahead.* Dogs and scent, right?

He pulled at his clothing. His shirt was a ruin anyhow; it fell apart easily. He threw one half into the water and let it wash downstream. Then he draped the other half over the tree that had saved his life. He stood, glancing around, and started to paddle down the river, sticking close to the bank, staying in the water.

'Nice t-hrry.' Snowy was right in front of him.

Joshua lunged to his left, away from the river, and ran across broken turf-like ground, not grass, something similar. The fallen tree that had saved him from the river was part of a shattered copse that looked as if it had been smashed apart by a lightning strike. He dived that way, rolled into the shadow of a big fallen trunk.

The huge form of the beagle padded silently across his vision.

Then he heard a human voice calling from far away, a male voice singing: a thin, wailing song, something about remembering Walter . . . The sound seemed to trigger a reflex in Snowy, and he bounded away.

Joshua knew he had been granted seconds, no more. No point running. He clambered out of his cover, his back aching, and he could feel blood trickling down his bare flesh. He cast around the clearing, picking up fallen branches, testing them. Here was one, thick and solid, too long – he smashed it in two on a lichen-covered trunk. He had a weapon.

A soft growl.

He turned. Snowy had the chewed-up remains of Finn McCool's walkman in his mouth. He spat the junk to the ground.

Without hesitating Joshua whirled, swinging the branch as hard as he could. It slammed into the beagle's heavy skull. It felt as if he'd tried to brain a marble statue. The impact shuddered up his arms, his aching back, and even his bad shoulder hurt like hell.

But the beagle stumbled, almost fell.

Joshua glimpsed knives of stone and iron in the belt at Snowy's waist. One chance. He leapt forward, his fingers grasping for a blade.

But Snowy stood straight, almost gracefully, almost kindly, and simply shouldered Joshua to the ground.

Now Joshua was flat on his back, with the crossbow gadget digging painfully into his spine. The man-wolf was on top of him, standing easily on all fours, his paws pinning Joshua's limbs, his heavy head above him, staring down.

A scent of meat on his breath. A glimpse of a wagging tail. Snowy actually licked his face.

'This won't hu-hrrt.'

No, it damn well wouldn't. Joshua braced to step, to put a clean end to this.

But that hadn't been Snowy's voice. He glanced sideways, in sudden hope.

Not a human. Another dog: Li-Li. She said, 'Granddaughter wants t-hrrophy. You want life. All can win-nnh.'

Snowy panted. 'I tell G-hrranddaughte-hhr I chewed your-hrr face off. Trophy head useless-ss.'

Joshua gasped, 'She won't be happy with that.'

'So I give he-hhr another-hhr trophy.'

'*What* other trophy?'

'Hold still . . .' Li-Li bent, and closed her mouth over Joshua's left wrist.

As the great jaws closed, severing skin and tendon and muscle and bone, Joshua screamed.

But he did not step.

67

GEOGRAPHICALLY VALHALLA was near the coastline of the inland ocean of this distant America, on Earth West One Point Four Million Plus Thirteen (stoner miscount correction applied, as Ensign Toby Fox solemnly told Maggie). The dirigibles of Operation Prodigal Son arrived in this world about midday of a sparkling late July day, and hovered in a blue sky as pure as a special effect in a computer game.

Admiral Davidson briefed his captains. They were here to assert the authority of the United States over these rebels, he said, but he wanted a show of goodwill, not a shooting match. His strategy was that a detachment of marines would accompany a group of senior officers, to be nominated by the respective captains, in a march on city hall. It was to be a good-natured, hearts-and-minds kind of event. However, he added, the marines would be armed.

And when Maggie heard that Captain Cutler from the *Lincoln*, the idiot who'd pulled a gun on Carl, was to be put in charge of this bizarre parade, she decided to nominate herself for the march.

At the drop point they formed up, fifty personnel in all, and walked through the streets of Valhalla – through this city of Earth West one-million-plus-change, this symbolic stronghold of the rebels of the Long Earth. At Admiral Davidson's orders the marines kept their weapons in sight but with safeties on. Meanwhile the silent dirigibles floated overhead, a menacing presence, full of watchful eyes, ready to act in a C2 role, as nodes of command and control – but, it was hoped, not as weapons platforms, not today.

And, this hot, humid noon, Valhalla was empty.

That was what they found as they walked on steadily from their mustering point. The marines stuck to the middle of wide, empty roads, with the officers walking behind, the only sounds their footsteps, and the calls of birds. There were a few abandoned vehicles in the empty streets, small hand-drawn carts. A couple of horses were tied up at a rail outside a Wild West-type saloon. There were even a couple of steam-powered cars, neatly parked up. No sign of people anywhere.

The dirigible crews reported that the picture was much the same as far as they could see from the air. Nobody at home.

Maggie walked beside Joe Mackenzie. 'Is it just me, Mac, or do you feel kind of ridiculous?'

The doctor said cynically, 'Well, we are military. You said it yourself; this operation can't all be about kittens stuck up trees. We have to do some soldier-type stuff from time to time.'

'True enough.'

At least Maggie felt relatively at home in this place, which unlike most stepwise communities felt like an authentic American city, with its scale, its streetlights, a few elements of traffic control, even posters for concerts and dances and lectures and such, although these were mostly hand-lettered in a small-town kind of way. It was definitely a Long Earth settlement, though, with the buildings massive blocks of timber and sandstone and concrete, the roadways crude lanes of tar, the sidewalks compressed river-bed gravel.

Then she heard the singing.

They came to a kind of square, really just the intersection of two main drags. Here, in the shade of a shop awning, were a dozen trolls, singing some kind of song about Mohawks and tea and taxes, as far as Maggie could tell. The marines, in the van of the party, slowed to a halt and stared.

Admiral Davidson and Captain Cutler had a quick conference.

Then Cutler gave the order that they were to take a break. It was a reasonable position from the point of view of security. They were in the open here, but were overlooked by no tall buildings, and had a clear view in four directions down these empty streets. As the rest dumped their packs and fished out water bottles, Cutler posted sentries to each of the square's four corners, and guys with Steppers were sent a world or two to either side also. It was a classic Long Earth security drill.

Maggie stood on the tarmac with Mac and Nathan. Nathan dug an MRE out of his pack, a meal ready to eat, popped it, and dug into a hot beef pie.

Mac looked on, seeming faintly appalled. 'Don't know how you eat like that at a moment like this, man.'

Around a mouthful of pie Nathan said, 'Takes years of dedicated training, Doctor. You got any salt?'

'No, I don't have any salt.' Mac dug a handheld

computer out of his own pack, and held it up to the trolls. 'I'm trying to identify that song they're singing . . . Aha. *Bring in your axes, and tell King George we'll pay no taxes on his foreign tea . . .* It's a Revolutionary War ballad. The Boston Tea Party. Whoever taught the trolls that is sending us a message. And has a sense of humour.'

Nathan said, finishing up his MRE, 'But where the hell is everybody else?'

Mac said, 'I'm guessing, in other parts of the city.'

'*What* other parts? . . . Oh.'

Mac was pointing at random, his fingers cocked at funny angles.

'Stepwise,' Maggie said. 'They've all gone stepwise?'

'Kind of. I visited, once. This city actually extends stepwise, in a way. I mean, it's not like a Low Earth footprint of a Datum town, like New York West 1 or East 5, or whatever. Here, the other worlds are more or less unspoiled, and therefore full of stuff to hunt and gather and eat. People live out there, at least some of the time. Together they support the city at the centre. It is kind of quiet today, isn't it? Usually there's some sort of critical mass of people actually *here*.'

'But not today.'

'Not today. Well, I guess they knew this invasion force was on the way. Who wants trouble? But not much of a war, is it, if nobody's interested in fighting? Not much *fun*.'

Captain Cutler heard that and turned, glowering. 'Fun, officer?'

'Sure, sir,' Mac said with a grin. 'War is fun. That's the terrible secret, why we've been doing it back to the Bronze Age, if not before. Well, now we have the Long Earth, everybody can have as much as they possibly want, there's always room to just walk away. No more need for war, right? Maybe it's a phase we need to grow out of.'

Nathan raised his eyebrows. 'Good luck with that as a guide to your career progression in the Navy, Doctor.'

A whistle blew. The break was over; time to continue their march. The marines began to pack up their kit, and sentries flicked away to summon back their buddies from their stepwise posts.

The city hall, according to the maps they had, was only a couple of blocks north of here.

Soon Maggie could see it, up ahead, over the shoulders of her officers. It was a squat colonial-era-mansion kind of structure, sitting on a bluff, a scrap of high ground. An open square sprawled before it, another road intersection. Two big flags fluttered from poles high above the building's frontage. One was the Stars and Stripes; the other was a blue field covered with a string of cloud-blue discs.

Mac grunted. 'I wondered when we'd get to see that new flag. There's a bunch of rebel colonies scattered across the Earths, starting with New Scarsdale back around West 100,000 and working their way all the way up to Valhalla, and beyond. They're the ones who backed the Footprint Congress here at Valhalla, where they composed their Declaration of Independence. And that's their flag. Multiple worlds, see? . . .'

Maggie heard a series of soft pops, like bubbles bursting: people stepping in. At last they had company.

Cutler started barking orders, relayed by the marine commanders. The marching formation broke up into a line. Maggie took her own position.

And she glimpsed people, men, women, children, most

476

dressed either like farmers or beach bums or a combination of the two, just popping into the world, all over the square before the city hall. They arrived sitting down, and when one landed on top of another the newcomer would fall away, laughing and apologizing. A babble of conversation started up, like a country fair.

All these people were filling in the space between the marines and the city hall. The dirigibles patrolled overhead, observing, impotent, their turbines growling.

Captain Cutler, red-faced, surveyed this scene. 'Bayonets,' he snapped.

'Belay that,' said Admiral Davidson mildly, but clearly enough for all to hear. 'We're here to *win* hearts, Captain, not to cut them out of warm bodies. And there'll be no firing either, except on my direct order. Is that clear?'

And still the people kept coming, filling in the square, like human raindrops covering the ground. Some brought picnic baskets, Maggie saw, bemused. Cake, bottles of beer, lemonade for the kids. Others carried gifts: baskets of apples, even strings of big, plump-looking fish that they tried to hand to the marines, and dumped at their feet when they refused.

Captain Cutler pressed Admiral Davidson. 'Our mission is to take that city hall and raise the US flag, sir.'

'Well, it rather looks as if Old Glory is already flying.'

'But it's the symbolism of the act . . . Let me try at least to clear a path across this square, Admiral.'

'Oh – very well, Cutler. But play nice, will you?'

At Cutler's barked orders, marines were sent into the crowd. Meanwhile the dirigibles began gliding over the square, loudhailers broadcasting orders. 'You are asked to disperse! Disperse immediately!'

Maggie watched marine Jennifer Wang, from the detail that had travelled on board the *Franklin*, wade in with her colleagues. Surrounded by these people in their country-work-type clothes, encased in her K-pot and turtle-shell body armour plates, she looked like some kind of alien invader beamed down from the sky.

Wang chose her target at random. 'Move, please, ma'am,' she said to one fortyish woman with a gaggle of kids.

'I will not,' the woman said clearly.

Her kids took it up like a playground chant. 'I will not! I will not!'

Wang just stood there, baffled.

They tried lifting people bodily out of the way, grabbing wrists and ankles and just lifting. But others, especially little kids, would come and sit on the person you were trying to shift. And even if you got a clean lift the person would just go limp, like a floppy mannequin, making him or her almost impossible to handle. Cutler, without referring back to Davidson, tried getting his marines to soft-cuff a few of the protestors. But the people involved would just flick away into another world, and come tumbling back where you couldn't reach them. Maggie found herself impressed with the coordination of this flash mob blocking the square, with the training they'd evidently had in this passive-resistance stuff – with their determination and discipline, almost military class, though with different techniques and objectives.

And gradually the chanting was breaking out all over: '*I will not! I will not!*'

Cutler stormed back to Davidson, frustrated, angry. Maggie thought his right hand hovered a little dangerously near his pistol. He said to Davidson, 'If we could identify the leaders, sir—'

'With a mob like this there may not be any leaders, Captain.'

'Then a couple of rounds above their heads. Just to scatter them.'

Without replying, the Admiral removed his cap, closed his eyes, and raised his lined face to the late summer sun.

Cutler snapped, '*No?* Then how the hell are we going to fulfil our mission here? *Sir.*' That last syllable was almost a snarl, and Maggie thought Cutler had to be close to in-subordination – if not to breaking down altogether. 'We cannot let these people mock us, sir. They do not under-stand us.'

'Understand us, Captain?'

'Admiral, they have never met anybody like us. Sir – you and I have served, we have been to the front line. We have taken fire, we have followed orders, and we have not yielded. And because of that these people were able to raise their kids, and come out to these dumb log-cabin type of worlds, and play at being brave pioneers . . .'

Admiral Davidson sighed. 'Well, the world has evidently changed around the two of us, son. In my view, the best kind of war is one that's resolved without a shot being fired. Keep your weapon holstered, Captain.'

'Sir—'

'I said, keep it holstered.'

And now a man stood up in the heart of the crowd, and walked towards the officers. He was maybe sixty, portly, dressed as a farm labourer like the rest.

Nathan murmured, 'I recognize that guy.'

So did Maggie. He was the guy with the favours, from a

community called Reboot. Maybe now wasn't the time to wave and say 'Hi', she suspected.

The man faced Davidson confidently. 'Fulfilling your mission all depends what that mission is, doesn't it, Admiral Davidson? If you're here to talk – well, that's fine. I very much doubt if you're going to achieve anything else today. Don't you?'

Davidson eyed him. 'And you are?'

'Green. Jack Green. I helped found a town called Reboot. Now I work for Benjamin Keyes, Mayor of Valhalla.' He held out his hand; Davidson shook it, to an ironic cheer from the crowd. 'If you want to talk, why don't you and your staff come to the mayor's office? I'm sure your marines will be looked after out here; you can see the picnickers have brought plenty for everyone . . .' He led Davidson away.

Captain Cutler, visibly livid, just stomped away, off into a side street.

Nathan glanced at Maggie. 'With your permission, Captain, I'll go keep an eye on Captain Cutler. Make sure he doesn't do anything stupid.'

'Good idea.'

Nathan hurried away.

Mac stood with Maggie. 'Ed Cutler needs therapy.'

Maggie thought that over. 'So will a lot of us, if you're right that war has suddenly become obsolete.'

'I am right, though, aren't I?'

'You usually are, Mac. You usually are.'

The shadow of a military-specification airship passed over the crowd. People looked up, shielding their eyes against the sun. 'Ooh,' they said, as though it were an advertising stunt at a football match. 'Aah.'

That was when Maggie knew the mission of the *Benjamin Franklin* was complete. That her own future was to fly the *Neil Armstrong II*, into stepwise worlds unknown.

That, for better or worse, without a shot being fired, the Long War was over.

68

AT THE BEGINNING of September 2040, with the military mission against Valhalla formally abandoned, and the trolls starting to show up in numbers again across the Long Earth, Lobsang and Agnes announced they would be hosting a garden party in the transEarth facility that Lobsang had turned into his reserve for studying trolls: a park spread several West worlds deep around Madison.

At first Monica Jansson demurred, but Agnes came to see her in person in Jansson's West 5 convalescent facility. 'Oh, you must come,' Agnes said. 'Wouldn't be the same without you. You were involved in the great adventure with those dog-people, weren't you? And after all, you are Joshua's oldest friend from outside the Home.'

Jansson laughed at that. 'Really? I was a gay junior cop busily making screwed-up career choices. Poor kid, if *I'm* all he had . . . Look, Sister, the journey's finished me off, with all that stepping, and the drugs.'

'*And* the dose of radiation you took in that dinosaur temple, or whatever it was, to spare Sally Linsay,' Agnes said sternly. 'She told me all about *that*. Look, Monica, you won't have to step anywhere. Not once we've got you to

West 11 anyhow. I've had Lobsang set up a nice little summer house there, and it's yours as long as you need it.' She leaned forward, confidentially, and Jansson saw how her skin, supposedly of a thirty-year-old according to Lobsang, was just a little too youthful, a little too free of blemishes, to be convincing. The young engineers who created such receptacles were never good at getting the flaws of age just right, she reflected. Agnes went on, 'I never could see the appeal of stepping myself, you know. Tried it once. Well, with the famous Joshua Valienté rattling around the Home, I could hardly not, could I? All *I* saw was a bunch of trees, and my own shoes that I was trying not to puke up all over, and no people, and where's the fun in that? And now, when I step – well, I don't feel anything at all. Lobsang designed me that way, the idiot. Anyway I can't see the point. Give me my Harley and an open road any day. Lieutenant Jansson, you must come, you're a guest of honour. That's an order.'

So, came the day: Saturday, September 8, 2040.

About two in the afternoon, and thankfully it was a bright, sunny, early autumn day here in Madison West 11, Jansson emerged somewhat shyly from the summer house Agnes had promised, which had turned out to be a decent little cabin with all mod cons. This location was on a height, and she had a fine view of grassy swards, dense clumps of trees, and patches of prairie flowers rolling down to the lake water. Agnes's barbecue party was scattered over this landscape, a few dozen people walking to and fro, kids and dogs playing noisily, and a knot of folk centred around a plume of rising white smoke over what was presumably the barbecue grill. A wash of music rose up from a knot of trolls down by the water, an elusive melody she couldn't quite place . . .

Just for a moment Jansson had a flash of disorientation. As if she saw the people as naked as the trolls, just a bunch of humanoids rolling around on this big lawn, empty-headed as young chimps. *Trolls. Elves. Kobolds.* She remembered the kobold who had called himself a human name: Finn McCool. Wearing bits of clothing, like a human, a man. And sunglasses! And how he'd gabble when Sally and Jansson were trying to sleep: just nonsense, but he tried to copy the rhythms of their talk . . . Now, sometimes, when she listened to some politician speechify on TV, or a priest yakking about God, all she saw was a kobold up on his hind legs, prattling nonsense just the way McCool used to.

Elves gone wrong – that was what Petra called humans.

She shook her head. Put it aside, she told herself. She walked forward determinedly, her exposed skin slopped with protective cream, a hat covering the increasingly patchy hair on her head, her gait as ramrod straight as she could make it.

She hadn't gone a dozen yards before Sister Agnes herself caught up with her, trailed by a couple of other nuns, one elderly, one maybe in her late thirties. 'Monica! Thank you for joining us. These are my colleagues, Sister Georgina, Sister John . . .'

'Sister John' looked faintly familiar to Jansson. 'Don't I know you?'

The nun smiled. 'My birth name is Sarah Ann Coates. I was at the Home, I mean a resident. When I grew up – well, I came back.'

Sarah Ann Coates: now Jansson remembered the face

484

of a twelve- or thirteen-year-old, scared, self-conscious, staring out of the file she had assembled on the incidents of Step Day in Madison. Sarah, one of the Home children Joshua Valienté had rescued in those frantic hours when the doors of the Long Earth had first creaked open. 'It's nice to see you again, Sister.'

'Come this way.' Sister Agnes linked her arm through Jansson's, and they started walking slowly towards the smoke from the grill.

'You're a great hostess, Agnes,' Jansson said, only slightly sarcastically. 'All these people here and you swoop down on me as soon as I show my face.'

'Call it a gift. But don't repeat that to Lobsang. He keeps badgering me to have avatars made. Iterations, like *him*. Copies of myself running around. Imagine how much I'd get done! So *he* says. Imagine the arguments I'd have, me, myself and I! So *I* say. I don't think so. Now then, Monica, I've assigned Georgina and John to look after you today, anything you need you just ask them – and any time you feel like disappearing, that's fine too.'

Jansson suppressed a sigh. Deny it as she might, she knew she needed the help. 'Thank you. I appreciate that very much.' The song of the trolls carried on the shifting, gentle breeze: the usual troll music, a human tune simply harmonized and turned into a round, with the melody line repeated and overlapping. 'What *is* that?'

'"The Wearing of the Green",' Agnes said. 'An old Jacobite marching song. Scottish rebels, you know. You can blame Sister Simplicity for that one. She always was one for her Scottish roots. That and prize fights on TV. It is good to have the trolls back, though, isn't it? Of course we had to restrict the guest list today to make sure there weren't too many people for the trolls to cope with. And Senator Starling has promised to put in an appearance later on. Suddenly a supporter of the troll cause, and suddenly he always was, if you know what I mean. Says he sings in a Sunday choir and wants to sing along with the trolls, if he can. Going to bring along a squad of Operation Prodigal Son sailors too, the USS *Benjamin Franklin* choir, just as a gesture of peace and harmony. Now then, let's find Joshua for you. It won't be hard, he'll be close to little Dan, and Dan will be close to the food . . .'

Agnes had appointed Lobsang as head chef. Jansson stared, bemused, at a Tibetan monk with a greasy apron over his orange robe and a chef's hat on his shaven head. A man she didn't know stood beside him, tall, fifty-ish, black, in a sober charcoal suit, wearing a cleric's collar.

Lobsang raised a greasy spatula. 'Lieutenant Jansson! Good to see you.'

Agnes more or less snarled at him. '*That* soya burger is raw, and *that* quorn sausage is on fire. Less blue-skyin' and more fat fryin', Lobsang.'

'Yes, dear,' he said wearily.

'Don't worry, Lobsang,' said the cleric beside Lobsang. 'I'll help. I'm a dab hand at chopping onions.'

'Thank you, Nelson . . .'

'Lieutenant Jansson.'

Jansson turned. Joshua Valienté stood before her, looking uncomfortable in a kind of smart-casual get-up: clean shirt, pressed jeans, leather shoes. He held his left arm to his chest, his clenched fist concealed by his shirt cuff. At his side was Helen, his wife, sturdy, pretty, cheerful. And little Dan ran past, dressed in a cut-down twain-pilot uniform, engaged in some noisy game with other kids, as oblivious of the adults and their society as if they were nothing but tall trees.

Jansson and Joshua stood there, facing each other awkwardly. Jansson felt an uncomfortable surge of emotion, having witnessed the dangers to which Joshua had exposed himself so far from home – and now seeing him like this, with his family. With Helen, looking as if she belonged nowhere but at his side. After all she'd been through with this man, Jansson didn't know what to say.

Joshua smiled, gently. 'It's OK, Lieutenant.'

'For heaven's sake,' Helen snapped. 'Give each other a hug!'

They leaned together, and she held him tight. 'With them, you're healed,' she murmured in his ear. 'Don't leave them again. Whoever comes calling.'

'Understood, Jansson.'

And yet she knew that was a promise he could never keep. She felt a stab of heartache for Joshua, the lonely boy she had known, the lonely man he would always be.

She pulled away. 'Enough. Squeeze too hard and I might break.'

'Me too.' Joshua reached forward with his left arm, revealing his artificial hand. It was a clunky, oversized creation with unconvincing pinkish skin; it whirred and whined like a movie prop when he unclenched his fingers. 'Bill Chambers calls it Thing. Like the Addams Family, you know? Funny guy. He's around somewhere, incidentally. Getting smashed with Thomas Kyangu.'

Jansson tried not to laugh. 'Joshua, surely they could have done better for you than that. Prosthetics these days—'

Helen said, 'He insists on wearing that horrible old antique.'

'Sooner this than one of the Black Corporation gadgets Lobsang offered me.'

'Ah,' Jansson said. 'With Lobsang inside.'

'You see the problem. I don't want to walk around with Lobsang in control of *any* of my extremities. I'd rather wait, thanks. Anyhow it doesn't bother Dan, so that's the main thing.'

Jansson said, 'Strange to think your own hand is nailed to the wall of that beagle princess's palace, a million worlds away.'

'Yeah.' Joshua glanced around, making sure Dan wasn't close by. 'You never got to see that, did you, Monica? There's a bit of the story you never heard.'

'He likes bragging about this,' Helen said wearily.

'You know those two beagles had got me pinned down, Snowy and Li-Li. I saw they were trying to save my life, in their way. But I wasn't exactly happy at losing a hand, even so. And, as Li-Li got her teeth into my wrist, I made a gesture . . .' He held up his robot hand, clenching a fist, and the middle finger extended with a whirr of hydraulics. 'And *that* is what is up on Petra's wall right now.'

Jansson snorted laughter.

'And *that*,' Helen said wearily, 'is what I can't stop Dan running around doing to all his little friends, every time his father tells that story.'

Joshua winked at Jansson. 'He'll grow out of it. Price worth paying, right?'

Jansson just smiled neutrally. An experienced cop knew better than to get involved in family arguments.

They were distracted by the approach of a short, slim,

wiry-looking man in his fifties. He looked vaguely familiar to Jansson. Somewhat shyly, he all but stood to attention as he addressed Joshua. 'Excuse me, sir. You're Joshua Valienté, right?'

'Guilty as charged.'

'Sorry to trouble you . . . I don't know anybody here and I recognized your face. I'm looking for Sally Linsay? I believe you know her.'

'Sure. And you are?'

The man offered his hand. 'Wood. Frank Wood. USAF, long retired, once of NASA . . .' There was a comedy moment; Wood had put forward his left hand to shake, but recoiled when Joshua's elderly cybernetic claw was produced in response.

Jansson snapped her fingers. 'I thought I recognized you, Mr Wood. I met you at the Gap. I was up there with Sally myself.'

He seemed startled to see her, then pleased. Evidently he hadn't recognized her through the increased decrepitude of her illness. 'Lieutenant Jansson? Good to see you again . . .'

More handshakes; Wood's hand was dry, firm. Jansson remembered, awkwardly, how she'd suspected this poor guy had had a crush on her out at the Gap.

Helen said, a tad reluctantly, 'I think Sally is down there, near the big group of trolls. With some Happy Landings types.' She led the way.

Jansson followed, accompanied by Frank Wood. When he saw how slowly and stiffly she walked now, he discreetly offered her his arm.

Just as discreetly she smiled her thanks. She said, 'Frank, just so you know—'

'I heard you were ill.'

'It's not that. I'm gay, Frank. And ill. Ill and gay.'

He took that with a self-deprecating grin. 'So our budding romance is doomed, huh? My radar never was too reliable. Probably why I never married.'

'Sorry about that.'

'Does being ill and gay preclude your being bought dinner, however?'

'It will be a pleasure.'

They found Sally with a bunch of trolls, and a few people dressed in what struck Jansson as a peculiar style even for colonial folk, kind of alternate eighteenth century. Sally herself wore her usual sleeveless travel jacket, as if she were about to leave any second for another urgent stepwise jaunt.

More introductions followed, and Jansson was able to match more names to faces. The oddly dressed types were from Happy Landings. A slim, shy-looking, youngish man turned out to be Jacques Montecute, headmaster of a school at Valhalla. A teenage girl, sober and serious, standing quietly at Montecute's side, was Roberta Golding, a student at the Valhalla high school who had made the news, along with Montecute, by travelling with the Chinese expedition to Earth East Twenty Million. They were here as guests of Joshua, it turned out; Dan Valienté would be starting at Montecute's school from next year. The Happy Landings folk seemed to stand a little way away from the rest, as if not quite part of the crowd.

And there was something particularly odd about Roberta Golding. A watchfulness, a stillness, that Jansson hadn't seen in such a young person since Joshua himself was that age. But she didn't detect Joshua's eerie calm about Roberta, nor his irreducible survival instinct. She had a look that Jansson, in her duty days, had associated with kids from damaged families. She had *seen* too much, too young. Jansson wondered uneasily what this flawed child might become, in future.

The trolls included Mary the runaway, and there was no mistaking the cub, Ham, who even now still wore bits of his silvery spacesuit. As soon as Ham saw Jansson he ran straight at her, making to hug her legs, and would have knocked Jansson clean over if Joshua hadn't intercepted him first.

Sally, being Sally, immediately homed in on Frank Wood. 'Well, well. Buzz Aldrin. What do you want?'

Wood nodded, graciously enough. 'I was hoping for a burger and a beer.'

Sally spat, 'Enough with the *Right Stuff* crap; you don't charm me. More trouble at the Gap, right?'

'Not at all. I came to thank you, Ms Linsay. And you, Lieutenant Jansson. For dealing with that business with the trolls the way you did. My colleagues up there are not bad people, but they are somewhat driven. I think we'd lost our moral bearings. Your actions helped us find them again.' He grinned. 'And now, on to the stars! We're already talking about probes to Mars, even a manned jaunt. And some neat visuals . . .'

He began to speak of something called a planetary alignment, occurring this very day: lots of Earth's sister worlds were lining up in one part of the sky, Mercury, Venus, Mars, Jupiter, Saturn, even the crescent moon. 'Of course it's visible from all the worlds of the Long Earth. But we're taking the opportunity to throw over probes, to

491

get decent images – to showcase the possibilities of the Gap, you see.'

Joshua said, 'You'll probably scare everybody to death. Aren't they saying this line-up is astrologically ominous?'

Helen pulled his sleeve. 'Don't tease the man.'

Sally snorted. 'But it's not as good from the Gap. You haven't got a moon!'

'*In the way*,' Frank said smoothly, good humoured. 'We don't have a moon in the way. All the better for seeing the real spectacle . . .'

The noise, the clamour, became too much for Jansson, all at once. The words being spoken around her seemed to dissolve into a jabber. She dropped her head and put her hands to her ears.

Frank Wood put an arm around her shoulders. 'Here, let's get you out of this.'

Agnes was immediately at her side too. She smiled into Jansson's face, took her arm, nodded to Sisters Georgina and John, and walked her and Frank away from the clamour. 'Come on,' Agnes said. 'Let's get some air. Then I'll call you a buggy – we have golf carts here – and get you back to your summer house for a break. How's that?'

'You're very kind.'

'I remember how it was to be ill, frankly. Lobsang didn't clean that out of my head, at least.'

They were heading towards the greater band of trolls down by the river. As they went about their business, eating, grooming, splashing in the water, flickering between the worlds, the trolls sang another gentle melody. A few humans stood by, clapping along, trying to join in.

Despite all the people present, Jansson felt a kind of

peace emanating from the contented troll band. 'That's another lovely song.'

Agnes squeezed her arm. ' "All My Trials". Outside of the Steinman canon, one of my own favourites since childhood.'

'Oh, yes. And how appropriate for me. *Soon be over . . .*'

Agnes squeezed her arm. 'That's enough of that.'

They had come to a bluff of higher ground, a shallow rise which Jansson climbed painfully, and here they paused. They looked out over the unspoiled lakes of this world, the sun hanging calmly in the blue sky, the young, still-small city rising on the isthmus – a ghost of Datum Madison.

Agnes said, 'I used to come up here when I was ill. Look at all this. The wider world that frames us all. The heavens, governed by their own eternal laws, the same on every world. Like Frank's alignment of planets, right? And the simple things, the play of sunlight on water, a universal across the Long Earth. That's where I found solace, Monica.'

'But when you've been out *there*, it all seems so fragile,' Jansson said. 'Contingent. It might not have been this way. It might not be this way tomorrow.'

'Yes,' Agnes said thoughtfully. 'And being close to Lobsang – well, I feel I see the world through his eyes, to some extent. The way he regards people – even his closest associates and friends, Joshua, Sally, that nice cleric Nelson Azikiwe, no doubt others – even me . . . He calls us "valuable long-term investments". I sometimes think he, or maybe his paymaster Douglas Black, is positioning us all like pieces on a chessboard, ready for the game to begin.'

'But what is the game?'

'No doubt we'll find out. Now, where's that buggy?'

There was a commotion behind them, raised voices. Reluctantly, Jansson, Agnes and Frank turned to look.

An airship had materialized, right above Lobsang's position. Lobsang himself seemed to freeze – no, Jansson thought, *he had gone* from his ambulant unit, gone in an instant, she could tell from his posture.

All around the grassy sward people's phones started to chime, and were pulled from pockets and purses. Soon the stepping started, people being simply deleted from the scene.

And Jansson heard two words on all their lips. The first, *Yellowstone*. The second, *Datum*.

Frank said grimly, 'Maybe Joshua was right about the planet alignment.'

69

JANSSON INSISTED ON being taken back to Madison West 5, no matter what pills she had to force down her throat to withstand the nausea. And once back at 5, she demanded to be taken, not to the convalescent home where she'd been staying, but to the new city's central police station.

The current chief, Mike Christopher, had been a junior officer in Jansson's time; he recognized her, let her in, and told her to sit tight in a corner of one of the offices. 'We're on alert, Spooky. There are already trickles of refugees showing up *here*, I mean in the Datum city.'

Jansson gripped Frank's hand. 'Refugees, Mike? In *Madison*? How far is Madison from Yellowstone?'

Mike shrugged. 'Over a thousand miles, I guess.'

'We're talking about an eruption. It must be an eruption, right? Will the effects of this really reach that far?'

He had no reply.

As she sat with Sister John, and Frank went to find coffee, Jansson tried to take in the images unfolding across the screens that plastered the walls of this office. Images taken from civilian news, police, military sources; images gathered on the ground, and from planes and twains, copters and satellites – all of them images from Datum Earth, down-

495

loaded on to memory chips and then hastily transferred by hand through the walls between the worlds, and retransmitted with only a slight delay.

After false alarms across the Low Earths, there had indeed been a significant eruption in the Yellowstone footprint – and it had been at *Datum Yellowstone itself*, she soon learned.

It had begun about one in the afternoon, Madison time. The evacuation of the Park had been going on since just before the eruption. About an hour later the great tower of ash and gas had started to collapse, all around the vent, a mass of superheated rock fragments and gases washing across the Yellowstone ground as fast as a jet airliner, smashing, flash-burning, crushing ... As excited geologists talked, unwelcome records started to tumble: this was already a worse eruption than Pinatubo, Krakatoa, Tambora.

Sleep seemed to be rising in Jansson's head, like her own pod of deep hot magma. She couldn't take in the words any more, the images. And those damn pills didn't seem to be helping with the pain.

She quickly lost track of time.

At one point she was faintly aware of a kind of conference going on over her head, involving Mike, the Sisters, Frank Wood, and somebody who had the air of a doctor, though she didn't know him. She gathered that they'd decided to move her, over her feeble protests, into a room at Agnes's Home for a couple of days.

Mike Christopher organized this briskly, a wheelchair, an ambulance. He winked at her. 'You get an astronaut to hold your hand, Spooky.'

She pulled her tongue at him.

And still the bad news came. Even before she was taken out of the police station new images were filling the wall screens, the tablets, the glowing smartphones.

A second eruption vent had opened up.

And then a third.

By the time they got her out of there, Yellowstone, imaged by brave USAF pilots in fast aircraft, looked like Dante's hell.

The next time she woke she was in a cosy but unfamiliar room, attended by Sister John. With brisk compassion the Sister helped her to the bathroom, and brought her breakfast in bed. She was in an adjustable bed, she discovered, like the one she'd been using in her convalescent home, there was a drip stand alongside, and her medications on a shelf by the door. Everything looked to have been moved over from the convalescent home. She felt a warm surge of gratitude for this kindness.

Then Sister John showed in yet another doctor. He tried to talk to her about the nature of her care: palliative only, and so forth. She waved that away and asked him about the news. 'No TV before meds,' he said sternly, as he began to treat her.

Only after he'd gone was Frank Wood allowed in, who looked like he'd been sleeping in his suit. Then, at last, they turned on the TV.

The whole caldera was opened up now. The towering cloud it produced was tall enough to be seen from as far away as Denver or Salt Lake City, as evidenced by shaky handheld camera footage from those places. But the images were strange, a yellow-brown light, a shrunken sun. Like daylight on Mars, Frank Wood suggested.

By now that cloud of ash and gas and lumps of pumice was spreading fast and far through the high air. Cars wouldn't drive far before their filters clogged, and so there were eerie shots of freeways full of shuffling people, their faces and eyes swathed in cloth, tramping through the grey snow-like fall like starving Russian peasants, all heading away from Yellowstone.

But of course most people, whoever could, were heeding the systematic calls to step away. And shots from the air, taken from Earth West and East 1, 2, 3, showed the new communities in the footprints of the threatened Datum cities being swamped by a mass of people stepping over, people unconsciously forming up in blocks and streets, in the forms of the schools and hospitals and shopping malls and churches from which they had come, a human map of the doomed communities just a step or two away.

All this was horribly familiar to Jansson. She murmured, clutching Frank's strong hand, 'I remember trying to persuade my chief.'

'Who, dear?'

'Old Jack Clichy . . .'

'We have to get people to step, sir. Anywhere, East or West, just away from Madison Zero.'

'You know as well as I do that not everybody can step. Aside from the phobics there are the old, kids, bedridden, hospital patients—'

'So people help each other. If you can step, do it. But take someone with you, someone who can't step . . .'

Frank just held her hand.

She heard the Sisters talking of Joshua Valienté, Sally

498

Linsay, others, rushing to the Datum to help with the relief effort. The names snagged her attention, before she sank back into deeper sleep.

When she woke again, Sister John was quietly weeping.

'They're saying it's our fault. Humanity's. The scientists. All the local versions of Yellowstone have been unstable recently, but it's only on the Datum that this has happened. Humans disturbing the Earth, like we did the climate. Others are saying it's a punishment from God. Well, it's not that,' she said fiercely. 'Not *my* God. But, how will we cope with this? . . .'

By now Jansson was too feeble to get up. Damn morphine, she thought. Sister John had to help her with the bedpans. She was peripherally aware of a nurse in the background, from the convalescent home; Jansson didn't know his name. But he let Sister John take the lead. That struck her as polite.

And when she woke with a little more clarity, here was Frank Wood, still sitting at her side.

'Hey,' she said.

'Hey.'

'What time is it?'

'The time?' He checked his watch, a big astronaut-type Rolex, then did a double take. 'Three days since the first eruption started. It's morning, Monica.'

'You need a clean shirt.'

He grinned and rubbed his chin. 'This is an all-female establishment, as far as adults are concerned. Don't ask me what I used to shave today.'

Of course there was a TV on, the sound soft, in a corner of the room. The projections were fast changing.

As the tremendous cloud of ash and dust spread across the continental US, even into Canada and Mexico, people were stepping away in their millions, an emigration greater than any in human history, before or after Step Day. Meanwhile the effects of the cloud were already global. Shots of towering sunsets, over London and Tokyo.

It was very strange to watch this, Monica thought, from a world five steps removed, in West 5, where the sun was shining – or not, she realized vaguely: once again it was night. As if she was watching a snow globe, roughly shaken. Or an ash globe.

She felt too weak to move. Only her head. She had an oxygen tube in her nose now. An automated meds dispenser by her bed, like a prop from *E.R.* She drifted helplessly back towards sleep.

'*Carry them in your arms, on your back,*' she'd told Clichy. '*Then go back and step again. And again and again . . .*'

'*You've thought about this, haven't you, Spooky?*'

She murmured, 'It's why you gave me the job all those years ago, Jack . . .'

Frank leaned close. 'What was that, honey?'

But Monica seemed to be sleeping again.

On the seventh day, at last, the eruption finished. No more fresh ash, to global relief.

But it ended with a clash of cymbals, as Frank Wood, sleepless, grimy, watched on the room's wall TV. The caldera, fifty miles wide, emptied of magma, just collapsed. It was as if a chunk of real estate the size of a small *state* had just been dropped a thousand feet.

Some of the younger Sisters, excited, went stepping

over into ash-coated Datum Madison to witness the consequences first hand. After just five minutes the quakes came, a ground-shaking pulse of energy travelling around the planet – though in the ruins of Madison there was only rubble to disturb. Then, after an hour or more, the *sound*, like a tremendous artillery barrage just over the horizon, or like the launch of a space shuttle, Frank Wood thought, digging back into his boyhood memories.

'My God,' Frank said, and he felt for Jansson's hand. 'What is to become of us, Monica? . . . Monica?'

Her hand was very cold.

Acknowledgements

We're very grateful to Jacqueline Simpson, co-author of the invaluable *The Folklore of Discworld*, for advice on kobolds, theology, and other generous and wise contributions. It was Jacqueline who brought to our attention the poem 'Unwelcome' by Mary Elizabeth Coleridge. We're also beholden once again to our good friends Dr Christopher Pagel, owner of the Companion Animal Hospital in Madison, and his wife Juliet Pagel, for their assistance with research, and for another very helpful draft read-through.

All errors and inaccuracies are of course our sole responsibility.

T.P.
S.B.
December 2012, Datum Earth

BOOKS BY TERRY PRATCHETT

The Discworld® series

1. THE COLOUR OF MAGIC

2. THE LIGHT FANTASTIC

3. EQUAL RITES

4. MORT

5. SOURCERY

6. WYRD SISTERS

7. PYRAMIDS

8. GUARDS! GUARDS!

9. ERIC
(illustrated by Josh Kirby)

10. MOVING PICTURES

11. REAPER MAN

12. WITCHES ABROAD

13. SMALL GODS

14. LORDS AND LADIES

15. MEN AT ARMS

16. SOUL MUSIC

17. INTERESTING TIMES

18. MASKERADE

19. FEET OF CLAY

20. HOGFATHER

21. JINGO

22. THE LAST CONTINENT

23. CARPE JUGULUM

24. THE FIFTH ELEPHANT

25. THE TRUTH

26. THIEF OF TIME

27. THE LAST HERO
(illustrated by Paul Kidby)

28. THE AMAZING MAURICE &
HIS EDUCATED RODENTS
(for young adults)

29. NIGHT WATCH

30. THE WEE FREE MEN
(for young adults)

31. MONSTROUS REGIMENT

32. A HAT FULL OF SKY
(for young adults)

33. GOING POSTAL

34. THUD!

35. WINTERSMITH
(for young adults)

36. MAKING MONEY

37. UNSEEN ACADEMICALS

38. I SHALL WEAR MIDNIGHT
(for young adults)

39. SNUFF

40. RAISING STEAM

Other books about Discworld

THE SCIENCE OF DISCWORLD
(with Ian Stewart and Jack Cohen)

THE SCIENCE OF DISCWORLD II: THE GLOBE
(with Ian Stewart and Jack Cohen)

THE SCIENCE OF DISCWORLD III:
DARWIN'S WATCH
(with Ian Stewart and Jack Cohen)

THE SCIENCE OF DISCWORLD IV: JUDGEMENT DAY
(with Ian Stewart and Jack Cohen)

TURTLE RECALL: THE DISCWORLD
COMPANION . . . SO FAR
(with Stephen Briggs)

NANNY OGG'S COOKBOOK
(with Stephen Briggs, Tina Hannan and Paul Kidby)

THE PRATCHETT PORTFOLIO
(with Paul Kidby)

THE DISCWORLD ALMANAK
(with Bernard Pearson)

THE UNSEEN UNIVERSITY CUT-OUT BOOK
(with Alan Batley and Bernard Pearson)

WHERE'S MY COW?
(illustrated by Melvyn Grant)

THE ART OF DISCWORLD
(with Paul Kidby)

THE WIT AND WISDOM OF DISCWORLD
(compiled by Stephen Briggs)

THE FOLKLORE OF DISCWORLD
(with Jacqueline Simpson)

THE WORLD OF POO
(with the Discworld Emporium)

THE COMPLEAT ANKH-MORPORK
(with the Discworld Emporium)

THE STREETS OF ANKH-MORPORK
(with Stephen Briggs, painted by Stephen Player)

THE DISCWORLD MAPP
(with Stephen Briggs, painted by Stephen Player)

A TOURIST GUIDE TO LANCRE –
A DISCWORLD MAPP
(with Stephen Briggs, illustrated by Paul Kidby)

DEATH'S DOMAIN
(with Paul Kidby)

A complete list of Terry Pratchett ebooks and audio books as well
as other books based on the Discworld series – illustrated screen-
plays, graphic novels, comics and plays – can be found on
www.terrypratchett.co.uk

Shorter Writing

A BLINK OF THE SCREEN

Non-Discworld books

THE DARK SIDE OF THE SUN

STRATA

THE UNADULTERATED CAT (illustrated by Gray Jolliffe)

GOOD OMENS (with Neil Gaiman)

With Stephen Baxter
THE LONG EARTH
THE LONG WAR
THE LONG MARS

Non-Discworld novels for young adults

THE CARPET PEOPLE

TRUCKERS

DIGGERS

WINGS

ONLY YOU CAN SAVE MANKIND

JOHNNY AND THE DEAD

JOHNNY AND THE BOMB

NATION

DODGER

JACK DODGER'S GUIDE TO LONDON

BOOKS BY STEPHEN BAXTER

Northland

STONE SPRING

BRONZE SUMMER

IRON WINTER

Flood

FLOOD

ARK

Time's Tapestry

EMPEROR

CONQUEROR

NAVIGATOR

WEAVER

Destiny's Children

COALESCENT

EXULTANT

TRANSCENDENT

RESPLENDENT

A Time Odyssey

TIME'S EYE (with Arthur C. Clarke)

SUNSTORM (with Arthur C. Clarke)

FIRSTBORN (with Arthur C. Clarke)

Manifold

MANIFOLD 1: TIME
MANIFOLD 2: SPACE
MANIFOLD 3: ORIGIN
PHASE SPACE

Mammoth

SILVERHAIR
LONGTUSK
ICEBONES
BEHEMOTH

The NASA Trilogy

VOYAGE
TITAN
MOONSEED

The Xeelee Sequence

RAFT
TIMELIKE INFINITY
FLUX
RING
XEELEE: AN OMNIBUS
VACUUM DIAGRAMS

The Web

THE WEB: GULLIVERZONE
THE WEB: WEBCRASH

–––––––– **The Long Earth** (with Terry Pratchett) ––––––––

THE LONG EARTH

THE LONG WAR

THE LONG MARS

–––––––––––––– **Non-series** ––––––––––––––

ANTI-ICE

THE TIME SHIPS

TRACES

THE LIGHT OF OTHER DAYS (with Arthur C. Clarke)

EVOLUTION

THE H-BOMB GIRL

DR WHO: WHEEL OF ICE

LAST AND FIRST CONTACTS

UNIVERSES

–––––––––––––– **Non-Fiction** ––––––––––––––

DEEP FUTURE

OMEGATROPIC

REVOLUTIONS IN THE EARTH: JAMES HUTTON AND THE
TRUE AGE OF THE WORLD

THE SCIENCE OF AVATAR

More details of Stephen Baxter's works can be found
on **www.stephen-baxter.com**

Coming soon – the dazzling new novel in
the Long Earth sequence . . .

TERRY PRATCHETT & STEPHEN BAXTER
The Long Mars

2040–2045: Datum Earth is in chaos following the cataclysmic Yellowstone eruption. Populations flee from the desolation to the relative safety of the myriad Long Earth worlds.

Sally, Joshua, and Lobsang are all involved in perilous rescue work. Then Sally is contacted by her long-vanished father, Willis Linsay, inventor of the original Stepper device. He invites her to join him on a fantastic voyage – across the Long Mars. But Sally soon learns that he has ulterior motives . . .

Meanwhile U. S. Navy Commander Maggie Kauffman has embarked on an incredible journey of her own, leading an expedition to the outer limits of the far Long Earth.

For Joshua, the crisis is much closer to home. He is persuaded by Lobsang to investigate the plight of the Next: super-bright, possibly post-humans who are beginning to emerge from their 'long childhood' deep in the Long Earth. Provoked by ignorance and fear, 'normal' society seems to be turning against the Next generation . . . and a brutal showdown appears inevitable.

Doubleday